Journals

Kara Ireland
weyheylovato

Chapter 1

So there's this girl.

And whenever I see that face that could've only been sculpted by God himself, I lose my mind. Seriously. Everything goes blank, and she's suddenly the only thing I can see. Everything else just fades away. Too bad I see her every day. Or maybe I should say thank God I see her every day. It's a blessing and a curse. Because I have to harbor and suppress these feelings about a thousand times a day. Because every time she looks at me, I can't breathe. And she looks at me quite a lot.

Her eyes are like this shining emerald abyss, or a lake with a sunset overhead, or galaxies. Yeah, galaxies is about right. Especially when they're grey. I look into her eyes and I see the lumiere of a thousand stars. They lack the pink and purple hues, but they shine all the same.

I look at her, and I see my happiness. I can get through the day, just to pass by her in the hallway. Not even talk to her, seeing her - her presence is a gift itself. Maybe I lost myself somewhere in her soul, but I've found everything I think I need...

Cammie gazed down and reread her work, trying to decide if she was finished or not. Well no, she could never be finished. She could publish a million books about it and would have only accurately covered about one fourth of what she adored about the girl. She decided that she would never *truly* be finished. She *was* finished for now, however, because Diana was impatiently waiting on her in the doorway. She closed her journal and shoved it into her bag before rushing out of the classroom. A goofy smile graced her lips as her mind drifted back to the green-eyed girl that had captured her heart so long ago. Even as she boarded the bus, she struggled to contain it.

1

"Write any more love notes for Lauryn today?" Diana smirked as Cammie took her seat next to her.

"They aren't love notes..." Cammie countered feebly, knowing that she'd never actually give them to her. Therefore, they couldn't count as love notes. Or at least, that was what she constantly told herself.

"Sure. You write that girl about a thousand a day," Diana shook her head.

Cammie discovered that she'd found a solace in writing. Writing helped her to express herself. It never seemed to get old. Regardless of if they were songs, poems, daydreams, stories, or just simple observations, she always found herself scrawling something about her. Although her entries varied in length and content, they were always centered around the same thing - the same person. Lauryn.

She was just about to respond when her breath hitched in her throat. Right as the engine started, the doors opened. Striding towards her was a very beautiful - and very out of breath - Lauryn.

"Hey, Camz. Hey Diana," Lauryn greeted breathlessly as she shuffled down the aisle, eager to take her seat.

"Hey. What's wrong with you? Did you just run a marathon?" Diana quipped at her unathletic arrival.

"Locker... Wouldn't open... Thought I was gonna miss it," Lauryn answered between breaths as she hunched over, resting her elbows on her knees.

"We need to get like Naomi and Allie. They can actually drive," Diana groaned and slumped back against her seat.

"I'm working on it. I should be able to get my license sooner or later..." Cammie interjected, full of optimism.

"Well to do that, you would have to actually pass the test, Cam," Diana laughed as she nudged Cammie in the side.

"I've only failed twice," Cammie side-eyed her best friend.

"At least you can take it," Diana huffed, being the youngest of the trio.

"You'll get it one day," Lauryn added encouragingly. "We all will."

"Yeah. Then you won't have to sprint to catch the bus anymore," Diana laughed again at the opportunity to take another jab at her defense.

Cammie shook her head and removed her bag from her shoulder. She set it on the floor in between her legs, because Diana always called the window seat. Only once had she had the luxury of getting to rest against the window, along with her bag against the wall. She'd given up on trying to convince Diana to do otherwise. Somehow, she always ended up on the outside anyway.

"Did you guys have that current events discussion in literature?" Diana questioned after a moment of comfortable silence between them. She figured she'd given Lauryn enough time to catch her breath. Now was deemed the proper time for an interrogation.

"Yeah," Lauryn answered for the both of them. "It was interesting."

"I thought she talked too much. I went to sleep," Diana responded indifferently.

"What did you guys talk about? I was meeting with the counselor about my schedule," Cammie asked with false interest. Really, she just wanted to indulge on hearing Lauryn's lovely voice.

"I know," Lauryn laughed, then she began to explain detail everything Cammie had missed during their class discussion.

Cammie was trying her best to listen and comprehend what she was saying, she really was. But she got distracted far too easily. The way Lauryn seemed to talk with her hands was captivating to her. Watching her lips and the way they moved instead of focusing on her words was a terrible habit of hers. She was in a trance, watching her speak. She adored how Lauryn seemed to be so knowledgeable about everything. She adored everything.

That brief trance was rudely interrupted from her staring by Diana, who had jabbed her in the ribs.

"Were you even listening?" Lauryn pursed her lips when her detailed recap had gone without any sort of a response.

"Of course she wasn't. She completely zoned out just now. Probably thinking about Harry or something," Diana covered for her, knowing how lost she could get in Lauryn. Those recurring habits didn't go over her head, although Lauryn was oblivious to it all.

"I know, but I'm not repeating it," Lauryn laughed.

The bus came to a stop, and Cammie frowned slightly when she saw Lauryn collecting her things. As she turned around to pick up her book bag and jacket, she took the opportunity to watch her again. She felt creepy, gazing at her so intently this way, but she couldn't help it. Lauryn was so beautiful, she wanted to admire every feature whenever she could.

"Bye guys," Lauryn waved as she made her way towards the door. She bent down to give Cammie a quick hug before she left.

"Bye," Cammie said dejectedly as they parted.

"I'll see you," Diana waved. "Girl, you really need to control that. You're so obvious," she shook her head in amusement as soon as Lauryn had sauntered off of the bus.

"She's so beautiful," Cammie said in awe as she strained to view her from the window.

"For the millionth time, I know," Diana responded monotonously. Cammie sighed and sank down in her seat, not bothering to respond to that. "When are you gonna make your move?" she pressed as the bus pulled off once more.

"Never," Cammie responded immediately. Well, that was a no-brainer. She could never tell her.

"Wrong. The right answer would've been *one day*," she said as she tried to mock Cammie's voice.

"Or... Never. Never works," Cammie countered sardonically.

"I think you have a pretty good shot..." Diana offered some truth after being so playful.

"We can dream," Cammie shrugged and dismissed her words in the same instance.

"I'm serious. You two act like you're dating anyway, always hugging each other and being close for no reason," Diana expressed a valid point to be made. "I'm a little jealous. *I* didn't get a hug."

"It's not like that though. It's different. It only *means* something to me, Diana. You know that," Cammie explained in exasperation.

The two of them had had this conversation multiple times before. Diana believed Cammie had a fair shot, while Cammie believed otherwise. She couldn't be convinced, no matter how hard Diana tried - and boy, did she try. Cammie was stubborn and focused on her negative mindset, only allowing herself to explore the possibilities through her writing.

That kind of writing, she'd never allow anyone to see. She wrote about sappy things like images of her and Lauryn holding hands and sharing kisses, or

3

exchanging *I love You's*, or cuddling late at night - wrapped up with one another, or going on cute little dates and displaying their love for everyone to see – because it would be mutual, or simply being in the position where she could flaunt around that beautiful girl because she would be *her* beautiful girl. Her girlfriend. Yeah.

She was a dreamer, that much was for certain.

"You're doing it again," Diana's voice brought her from her musings.

"Doing what?" Cammie asked nonchalantly.

"You're thinking about her," Diana announced resolutely, already well aware of the denial that would follow.

"I wasn't," Cammie dismissed her, much like she'd predicted.

"Yeah you were, and you still are. That's your Lauryn smile. You only smile like *that* when you're with her or thinking about her," Diana shared fondly. "You've got it so bad."

"I know," Cammie sighed. She didn't even attempt to deny those accusations. With Diana, she might as well have been an open book. Diana sure could read her like one, anyhow.

Diana knew Cammie better than anyone else. She knew a little bit more about her than the rest of her three friends. Naomi, Allie, and Lauryn claimed to know her inside and out, but they didn't, really. Presumably, they knew nothing of the deep feelings Cammie had developed over time. Diana had only found out on accident, by stumbling upon Cammie's journal one day. She only told her because she had no other choice when all of the evidence was there on paper. Ever since then, she'd been more careful. And *much* more secretive.

"Come on. It's time to go, though," Diana said as she slapped Cammie's thigh, prompting her to leave.

She begrudgingly clambered off of the bus and hugged the taller girl before heading home. Cammie trudged down the street and clutched the straps of her book bag. On the way there, she reflected on Diana's words. She wondered why if she was apparently so obvious, how come Lauryn never picked up on it. Then her cynical mind came up with the rationale that Lauryn *did* notice, she just didn't want to act on it. Because she didn't like her. And because she would *never* like her, because that would be weird.

With a sigh, the banished those thoughts from her head. She didn't need to be thinking that way. She didn't need to be thinking about that at all. She figured she should just focus on being friends with her, the way she was with the three other girls. Hopefully, this would all die down if she didn't dwell on it.

When she made it home, she immediately went up to her room. She closed the door behind her and retrieved her journal from her book bag before slinging it to the side of the room. She plopped down in front of her desk and resumed her writing from earlier. Letting it die down and not dwelling on it could wait, for now.

And her lips, her lips are a fucking work of art. She is art. But her lips, God... Her lips are everything. They're perfectly shaped, and perfectly pink. They're a little chapped sometimes, but that's okay because I would still kiss them senseless. I can't help myself when she's talking to me. I always watch her lips instead of listening to her. I mean, I hear her... But I'm not listening. I'm too busy thinking about kissing her to understand what she's saying.

4

She does this thing with her hands when she talks... It's like she can't keep them still. They help her express herself. Her words don't need any help though. She says great, intelligent things...

I look at her, and I see my happiness. I can get through the day, just to pass by her in the hallway. I don't even have to talk to her. Just seeing her - her presence is a gift itself. Maybe I lost myself somewhere in her soul, but I've found everything I think I need.

Cammie concluded her entry as she laid her pen down. She closed her journal with a contented smile and put it away for the day. Following her enamored admission, she rummaged through her book bag, trying to decide which class' homework she would do first.

»»»»

The next day, Cammie sat in class alongside Naomi and Allie. In their history class, they'd been assigned a project. The trio was on their way to the library to begin their research.

"I'm glad we can work in groups," Naomi sighed as she set her stuff down on the table. "Because I was *not* about to do all that by myself."

"Same," Cammie agreed somewhat indifferently.

"Where do we go for research?" Allie asked, eager to begin.

"Why don't you ask the library mouse over here?" Naomi quipped and pointed to Cammie.

"I'm not a library mouse. What even is that?" Cammie retorted with a playful grimace.

"C'mon Cam, you know you basically live in here," Allie laughed.

"Whatever," she waved them off halfheartedly. "They're over here, though..."

They each picked out a book they thought would aid their research. After only about five minutes of "researching", the girls began to get restless.

"That's enough. Let's go to the vending machine," Naomi suggested and went so far as closing the resource book she'd just ventured into.

"We literally just started, Naomi," Allie said in exasperation.

"I know, but I'm hungry. Let's go somewhere," Naomi made up her mind and slid her book to the side for emphasis.

Allie easily gave in. Clearly, Cammie was the only one taking this seriously today. She bit her lip, knowing they should really take advantage of the time they had to work on it in class. Despite the fact, she *was* craving some Skittles. Perhaps a banana. She thought maybe she could take a detour to the cafeteria and see if they had any. Plus, their teacher wasn't in here and the librarians weren't paying attention. Hesitantly, she got up to follow the other two girls.

"Yay!" Naomi exclaimed as she grabbed her arm, checking to see if the coast was clear before slinking out of the library.

Cammie, being the more rational one out of the three, was so cautious as they went down the hallway. She actually started tiptoeing, as if that would do

5

anything to help her if they had gotten caught skipping. Allie and Naomi only laughed at their friend, who obviously didn't do these things very often.

"Relax Cam, we'll be back in a minute," Allie giggled at her antics.

"I just don't want to get in trouble," Cammie mumbled and cautiously looked over her shoulder. She could've sworn she heard something.

"We're going to the vending machine, not the mall," Naomi countered pointedly.

"Yeah. And look, now we're here," Allie added as they rounded the corner and the vending machine came into view.

They quickly deposited their dollars in exchange for their snacks. Cammie didn't see anything in there for her taste. "Can we go to the cafeteria really quick?" she asked just as the other two girls were heading back to class.

"Why?" Naomi asked.

"I want to see if they have any bananas," Cammie answered, gesturing towards the vending machine. "I didn't want anything in there."

"Dang, I wish you would've said that before I bought this," Allie complained as she waved her fruit snacks around.

"Why?" Naomi turned around and asked Allie.

"The snacks in the vending machine in the cafeteria are better than this one," she offered a simple elaboration.

Naomi shook her head in amusement and continued on her way to the cafeteria. They arrived there shortly, and to Cammie's surprise, the lines were already open. She sheepishly walked over there, leaving her friends at the door. The lunch lady greeted her with a warm smile. She had grown to like Cammie over the past three years and often gave her more portions than other students. Even though she didn't know her name. Cammie had that effect on people.

"Hey there, how are you today? You're here a bit early," she noted.

"I'm good," Cammie smiled and looked around for any bananas. "And I know. I was actually wondering if you had any bananas...?" she trailed hopefully.

"We do, in the back. Hang on, I'll go get you one," she smiled and disappeared into the back.

Cammie turned around and gave her friends a thumbs-up. It went unnoticed. They were engaged in conversation as they leaned against the wall. Cammie shrugged and turned back around, happily waiting for her banana. The lunch lady presented her with one and waved her off until later.

As they were walking back to class, Cammie looked at the clocks in the hallway, realizing that they'd wasted nearly *fifteen* minutes. By the time they got back, it would be time to go. She was right. The bell sounded and their leisure walking turned into a jog to get back to class. She quickly collected her things and scrambled off to her next class, not wanting to be late.

»»»

Lauryn had history the period right after Cammie, Naomi, and Allie. She had this class alone, unaccompanied by either of her friends. She took it in stride and made a higher grade without them in there, so it wasn't that much of a loss. When she got the memo of having to do a project, she sighed. She'd have to do it alone, unless someone offered to be her partner. She didn't see that happening, so she picked out a spot near the back.

It happened to be the same area her friends had previously occupied, but that information was unknown to her. When she pulled out the chair, she found a small journal perched in the middle. She picked it up and flipped through it, trying to decipher whose it was. What she saw inside was the furthest from what she was expecting.

»»»»

Math came easily to Cammie. She enjoyed this class the most, mainly because she was able to grasp most concepts quickly. She had a habit of doing her work and writing about Lauryn afterwards to kill time. However, when she finished her class work, her journal wasn't in her stack of binders. She didn't panic, she figured it was just on the floor. When it wasn't there either, *that's* when the panic set in.

While attempting to remain calm, she was mentally retracing her steps. There were only so many places it could've been between the library and this class. She thought it was most likely in the library, where she'd accidentally left it behind. She didn't want to overthink the situation. Even though it posed a very big threat, exposing her biggest secret and all, she wasn't going to worry. She'd just go get it and everything would be fine. No one would know. Simple, right?

Once she composed herself, Cammie raised her hand and patiently waited to be called on.

"Yes, Cammie?" Mrs. Miller questioned.

"Um, can I go to the library really quick? I left something important in there," she asked and shifted uncomfortably, now that all eyes were on her.

"I'm in the middle of a lesson. After class," she said stubbornly.

Cammie nodded obediently, but cursed her under her breath. She slumped back in her seat and picked at her jeans until it was time to go. The minutes felt like hours as she had to wait. Waiting wasn't good for Cammie. It gave her too much time to think, too much time to worry herself, too much time to think of everything under the sun that could possibly go wrong. Little did she know, her worst fear was about to come to life.

Finally, after what seemed like an eternity, the dismissal bell sounded. Cammie shot up and bounded out of the door and down the hallway. She had to go against oncoming traffic and couldn't get there as quickly as she'd hoped. Now she was cutting it close to being late for her next class.

Cammie jogged into the library, slightly out of breath. She briefly wondered why she didn't work out more. A simple sprint down the hallway shouldn't have left her this winded. But whatever. *Journal.* She needed to get her journal. She scoped out her table and walked towards it, expecting to find her journal on the floor or under the table or something. It had to be, *right*?

When she made her way over to her area, she quickly looked for it. It wasn't on the table. She pulled out the chair and looked, but it wasn't in the chair either. She dropped to her knees and peered under the table as well. Her journal was not there. Okay. No worries. Someone probably turned it into the front. The late bell sounded, but it was easily disregarded. She had bigger problems.

She approached the front desk in the library and timidly asked if anyone had turned in a journal. They hadn't. With her eyes wide and eyebrows furrowed in confusion, she went back to get her stuff - *all* of her stuff. She milled down the hallway, keeping an eye out for it just in case she'd dropped it on her way to class. She didn't. An odd feeling formed in her stomach at that realization. It was a sickening mixture of apprehension and dread.

It started in her stomach and spread throughout her whole body. She thought she was going to throw up. She didn't bother speed-walking to class, for now she was late anyway. With no better destination in mind, she made a left and found herself in the infirmary. There was no way she could possibly go to class feeling like this. She wouldn't be able to focus. Instead, she just sat there on the little bed, wondering where the hell her journal went.

Chapter 2

Cammie must've spent about two whole class periods in the infirmary. It wasn't even like she was in there to waste time. She *literally* felt sick to her stomach with the thought of her biggest secret being exposed. If anyone found out about her feelings about Lauryn, she was a dead man walking. Well, not really, but it sure did feel that way. No one knew of her sexuality. Cammie herself didn't even know. All she knew was that Lauryn elicited feelings within her that she'd never felt. Quite often, at that.

She hunched over on the bed and brought her knees to her chest. The feeling washed over her again and she buried her face into her arms. She was actually shaking. Why did she have to write down her stupid feelings? Why did she even have those feelings? Why couldn't she just have a normal friendship like she did with the other girls? Why did she have to use Lauryn's name? Why couldn't she just keep it anonymous?

Cammie's head shot up from her knees. Wait. She *was* anonymous. She'd never once signed her name, simply because she wasn't very fond of her signature. She suddenly felt thankful for her messy script. With that in mind, she relaxed a little. She had horrible handwriting. No one would be able to read it. Well, they *could*... But they would just have to try really hard. But it's not like anyone would want to read all of her ramblings about Lauryn anyway, right? She sure hoped so.

After thinking it over and realizing that the worst of her problems was that she'd simply lost her journal, she returned to normal. She'd somehow convinced herself that no one would read it, that it had just vanished. And she was alright with that. As long as no one knew, she was alright with it. Her headache dissipated and so did the feeling in her stomach. She even felt well enough to go ahead to lunch.

Lunch was Cammie's favorite time of the day. Partially because of the food, partially because all of her friends met there, but mostly because of Lauryn. She got to sit next to her and look at her when she wasn't paying attention. It was her favorite thing to do. She'd accepted how creepy she was a long time ago, so she stole her glances in stride.

When Cammie entered the cafeteria, Lauryn was the first to spot her. She smiled at Cammie and urged her to come over. It was the cheeky smile where she tilted her head and made her eyes all squinty, Cammie's personal favorite. A smile took over Cammie's features as she made her way over. All thoughts of her missing journal immediately faded away. It was impossible to be sad when Lauryn was near.

"Hey Cam," Allie greeted her warmly. "Where were you in class? Did you skip?" she assumed, which caused the other three girls to burst into laughter. Cammie skipping was a joke.

"I was in the nurse's office," Cammie answered, happy to have been missed.

"We have a nurse?" Diana questioned incredulously, her eyebrows furrowing in shock.

"No. Not really," Naomi answered. "It's just a room in the back of the office with a few beds and band-aids and stuff. We don't have an actual nurse."

"Yeah. But the beds are really comfortable. I go in there when I get cramps," Lauryn contributed with her own two cents.

"Me too," Allie nodded in agreement and manipulated the few pieces of food still left on her plate.

"Why am I just now hearing about this? Shoot, I could've been skipping all this time," Diana laughed. "I mean – *being sick* all this time…"

"I don't see how you didn't know," Allie jested in the process of biting into a bitter celery stick.

"Same," Lauryn laughed, then she turned to Cammie. "Oh yeah, Camz. I forgot to tell you. We were just talking about something weird that I found."

Cammie froze for a second. She wondered what Lauryn had found, desperately hoping that it was just a lucky penny or something. She suppressed her apprehension about what she was going to disclose and just waited for her to continue.

"I found this cute little journal in the library," Lauryn started. She retrieved it from her bag and Cammie froze again.

Holy shit.

"Yeah. It's like this journal slash diary thing from someone that's like completely in love with her," Naomi added, hoping to help fill in the blanks of Lauryn's vague statement.

All color drained from her face and her scalp prickled. Panic seized her, but she willed herself to remain calm. There was a tornado in her mind. She tried her best not to seem antsy or fidgety, but how could she not? Lauryn had her journal!

Her breathing became shorter, but she attempted to hide that too. No, really, she thought she was suffocating. Although her face betrayed everything she felt inside, her heart was hammering in her chest. She was pretty sure her heart was in her throat rather than her chest, because her pulse was going crazy. She could *hear* her heartbeat. Her palms became sweaty and she instantly felt nauseous.

Was this what dying felt like? Cammie was sure. She was almost certain her heart would give out on her at any moment now. Maybe if she just passed out on the floor and died, she could avoid the confrontation that was sure to follow. She seriously contemplated it for a second. But the floor was kind of dirty, so she decided against it.

"Yeah, so who do you think it is? Do you know which guys like her?" Allie asked Cammie, wanting to get her input as well.

"I don't know," Cammie managed to say.

"It could be a girl, Allie. I've heard a lot of girls saying they'd go gay for you," Naomi laughed, and Cammie shot her a death glare from across the table.

Cammie wished Naomi would shut up. She didn't want her to allude anything to the idea that it could be a *girl* writing those things about Lauryn. She was awfully intuitive and could easily put the pieces together.

"Well, I know... But it's obviously a boy. Look at the handwriting," Diana laughed passively without hinting anything.

Cammie wanted to agree, but she didn't trust herself enough to speak in this moment. Her heart hadn't calmed down yet. It was slowly returning to normal when she realized that they had no idea it was hers. Oh, God. Diana was the only one that knew, and that meant her secret was in her hands.

"It's so cute. What if it's like Cinderella or something?" Lauryn mused aloud.

"What are you talking about?" Diana questioned with an unmistakable groan of exasperation.

"Like, they left this behind. And I have to search to see whose it is. That's really romantic. What if he did it on purpose?" Lauryn said with a wide smile.

No. *God*, no. Don't do that at all, why would she do that? Cammie nervously glanced at Lauryn, who seemed to have her mind made up.

"That's so cute," Allie grinned at the endearing idea.

"We're gonna help you find your little Prince Charming," Naomi smiled with a nod of determination.

"You guys would? Really?" Lauryn's smile grew even wider.

No! Cammie buried her face into her hands and took a deep breath. She was about to go insane. Why were they actually feeding into this?

"What about you, Diana?" Lauryn asked hopefully.

"I mean, I guess..." Diana shrugged unenthusiastically. When her eyes met with Cammie's she shrugged again, mouthing "*Relax*".

"Great. Camz?" Lauryn turned to face her.

"I don't know... I don't think it's that big of a deal. I think you should just leave it... Or throw it away or something..." Cammie mumbled and tried not to out herself.

"*Throw it away?*" Lauryn repeated incredulously. "Camz, you haven't seen it. The stuff in here is amazing and sweet and crazy beautiful. It actually makes me feel really special. Like holy shit, you should see it. I really want to know who wrote all of this because I actually think that I would marry them."

Oh, she's seen it, alright. But Cammie really tried to ignore the way her heart seemed to swell at Lauryn's words. At least she liked it. Under normal circumstances, she would've written about this moment. But she couldn't. Not anymore, anyway.

"How do you know it's you? There are a lot of Lauryns at this school..." Cammie brought up pathetically.

"Yeah, but not spelled like mine. I'm the only Lauryn Michelle here," she emphasized as she opened the journal. Right there on the page was Lauryn's name in hearts. Actual fucking hearts. Cammie cringed inwardly, cursing herself again. Once for the hearts, and again for writing her full name - like an idiot.

"So?" Cammie shrugged.

"Really Cam?" Naomi sighed in annoyance. She couldn't see why Cammie was being so difficult.

"Camz, please? They're all helping me, and I probably need your help. You read people better than anyone I know. Please?" Lauryn pouted and latched onto Cammie's shoulder.

God, and now she was looking at her so pleadingly with those gorgeous eyes. That puppy dog face that could leave anyone at her mercy. Cammie knew that if she looked at her, there was no going back. She would agree and then her secret would be out. She was sure. But there was an intangible pull between the two of them. It was demanding Cammie's attention and she couldn't resist.

When she finally met her eyes, she melted. Lauryn was looking into her soul. Like, her actual soul. She didn't know how she was able to do that. She always did it. And now in their close proximity, there was no way she could deny her while she was looking at her like that. As she looked down at the green-eyed girl attached to her shoulder, her heart twinged.

She tore her gaze away and turned her head. She was going to regret this. She was going to regret this a lot. "...Fine. Okay," Cammie finally relented.

Lauryn squealed and threw her arms around her, hugging her impossibly tight. She nuzzled her face into the crook of her neck like she always did. Her scent intoxicated her. Cammie knew there was no hope or even any remote possibility of containing her feelings. She loved Lauryn. It was going to show eventually. But for now, she just held on as Lauryn cuddled into her.

»»»»

"Diana, you know that was my journal, right? Lauryn found my journal. *The* journal," Cammie expressed to Diana on their way to their lockers.

She'd waited all day to inform her best friend about it. Previously, they'd all been with one of the other three girls, and she didn't have the chance to talk about it. Now that they were alone, she seized the opportunity.

"Of course I know," Diana rolled her eyes, a bit offended that Cammie assumed she didn't.

"You were acting like you didn't," Cammie said in confusion.

"Well no shit, what did you expect me to do? Say '*Oh, that's Cammie's. By the way, she's in love with you*'?" Diana asked incredulously.

"Shut up," Cammie groaned. Diana laughed, but she tuned that out. Her mind was running rampant. As they were walking, it gave her time to contemplate ways to getting out of it. Faking her own death briefly crossed her mind, but she thought that would be far too difficult. She rolled her eyes at herself. She shouldn't even *have* to get out of it. She shouldn't have agreed at all. None of them should have.

Cammie slapped Diana's arm forcefully. "And why would you agree to helping her find out who it is when you know it's *me*?" she took her frustration out on the younger girl.

"I couldn't say no, then she would've thought I was being a bitch. There was literally no reason to say no, you better chill out," Diana threatened as she rubbed where Cammie had hit her.

"There was *every* reason to say no! Diana, if she finds out... I'll die," Cammie over exaggerated.

"And just because I *said* I would, doesn't mean I actually have to," Diana rolled her eyes. "I covered for your ass earlier. I'm the one who got them thinking it was some boy. Lauryn recognized your handwriting. So you're welcome."

"She *wha*t?" Cammie shrieked with wide eyes. That same feeling surged through her at once, leaving her riled up and flustered all over again.

"Yeah. But I told her you didn't write that badly," Diana added. "And when you came back, Naomi thought it was a great idea to bring up that it could've been a girl. Again. So I made them think it was some dude. Again. So *again,* you're welcome."

"Oh my god," Cammie groaned. This had to be her mid-life crisis, striking at the tender age of seventeen.

"No thank you? Not even one? Okay," Diana said as she playfully pushed Cammie to the side. Cammie, being the clumsy person that she was, stumbled into the lockers. She glared at Diana when she regained her bearings.

"No," she said defiantly as they reached their lockers. She put in her combination and began exchanging things in and out of her locker.

"Seriously though, you have nothing to worry about. You're the one that wrote it. And she's clearly not gonna find you if you're helping her. You're like the last person she expects now," Diana reasoned as she slung her book bag over her shoulder.

Cammie took a moment to reflect on her words. Well, that actually made a bit of sense. She wasn't even an option, right? Lauryn didn't even consider her, which was fantastic.

But a part of Cammie wanted her to know that it was her. The delusional, deranged, completely insane part of her actually wanted that. She wanted it badly. Ah, she could see it now. She'd walk up to Lauryn with her new journal in hand, one that was filled with even more stupid ramblings. Lauryn would read it and fall in love with her. It was as simple as that.

Yeah, that part of her was definitely deranged.

"Stop thinking about Lauryn and listen to me," Diana grumbled.

Cammie felt busted. She couldn't excuse that one, or her stupid smile. She was head over heels.

"Are you listening?" Diana questioned, and Cammie nodded quickly. "I said and even if she did find out, what's the worst that could happen? I really don't think anything would change."

"Yeah, Diana. Nothing would change. Nothing at all," Cammie responded sarcastically. "Nothing would change except the fact that we'd probably drift apart because my stupid feelings would've weirded her out. And she's not even like, gay or anything... She would hate me."

"She wouldn't be weirded out, Cam. Didn't you hear her at lunch? She loved it. And she loves you now, she would love you even more if she knew," Diana countered.

"She loves me like I love you. Not the *wow I really wanna hold you and kiss you all the time* type of love. It's different..." Cammie sighed, and she felt like she'd said those words a thousand times. It was always different. Couldn't she see that?

"Maybe one day you'll see it," Diana shrugged, dropping the subject and heading towards the bus.

13

When she got off of the bus, Lauryn eagerly made her way home. She clutched the journal in her hands on the way there and flipped through the pages. Boy, was this journal dense. Whoever her secret admirer was, it clearly didn't happen overnight. This had to have been *months* of writing.

It boosted her confidence a little to read all of these lovely things about her. What she loved about it most was that they didn't just talk about her physical attributes. These pages went much deeper than what she looked like. The first few pages identified with Lauryn's mind and soul. Whoever it was paid really close attention. Lauryn desperately wished she could recall more conversations she'd had with people, maybe it could shed some light on who this could be. This nameless person adored everything. They even said so. They mentioned everything Lauryn hated about herself and glorified it. This person definitely had her on a pedestal. She really wasn't that great.

A sense of determination overcame her as she entered her house. She was going to solve this mystery. When she got up to her room, she sat down at her desk and sifted through bunches of notebooks and papers for a blank sheet. Then she rummaged through the small drawer for a functional pen. She mentally listed everyone that she'd ever been able to have a deep, philosophical conversation with. Well, that was a short list.

1. Cammie
2. Allie

She couldn't even think of any boys that could make that list, so she tossed it. Then she started listing people that could possibly have a crush on her. She considered everyone, girls included. She made a mental note to watch people's behavior around her. Because when *she* liked someone, there were always telltale signs.

Lauryn knew she was pretty... In a way. People seemed to see something way more impressive than what she saw in the mirror. She didn't know what it was, but she attracted people. They were never people she was particularly interested in, but they were people nonetheless. *That* list was too exasperating to try and write right now. So she made another. Then another. And another.

She listed poetic people, people that she'd been open with, seemingly deep and intuitive people, and just people that were in her classes. She narrowed it down pretty well, crossing out people that seemed to contradict the other lists - like Keith. She had somewhat of a connection with him, but he wasn't anything close to a poet. Jacob seemed to be the artsy type, but she'd never really talked to him before. He wouldn't know that much about her. Harry appeared a few times, but he was just in her class, a face in the hallway, someone she said hi and bye to, or even texted sometimes. He didn't fit most of the criteria, so she scratched him too.

As she further assessed the names, she briefly wondered why Cammie seemed to appear on every list. She dismissed that factor and crossed out her name. It wasn't Camz. She laughed at even considering her. That was weird.

That task was more time consuming than she had planned. By the time she was finished analyzing all of the names and lists, it was time for dinner. She sat down with her family and made small talk, but her mind was elsewhere. She was so distracted.

Dinner in Cammie's household was similar. Cammie barely talked to her family, too busy stressing about her newfound problem. She couldn't let Lauryn find out. But what if she did? What if it turned into something more? What if it destroyed everything? Cammie was at war with herself. Her mind was so contradictory. She couldn't keep one mindset. She tried to be optimistic, but the pessimist in her found a counter to everything she proposed. It was exhausting.

It was still on her mind when she went to bed. Lauryn had the same restless demeanor. They both attempted to sleep, but all of the possibilities kept them awake.

Chapter 3

The following day at lunch, Lauryn was the first to sit down. She patiently waited for her friends to gather around her. Today, she'd brought her numerous lists and was prepared to analyze them with her friends. Their input was necessary, just in case her results were biased. She didn't think she was. She didn't think she'd been shallow or anything, only considering good-looking people. Someone who had a mind like that was downright amazing. No matter what.

The line seemed be moving extra slowly today. As she watched them from their table, she saw that they were in no rush either. They were so busy talking, they didn't even notice when other people moved in front of them. She groaned and strode over to them as she grew impatient.

"Hey," Naomi said with a smile, pulling her into a quick side-hug.

"Hey Lo, what's up?" Diana greeted her.

"Hi," Allie said enthusiastically.

Cammie simply waved. She was always awkward whenever Lauryn first came around. It took a few moments to calm the butterflies. She thought it would've gotten better with time, but apparently that wasn't the case. The butterflies she had right now were relentless. That was probably because Lauryn's form of greeting Cammie was with a warm hug. It always lasted a few seconds, just long enough to make her heartbeat spike. When Lauryn pulled away, Cammie wore a contented smile. Lunch was definitely her favorite part of the day.

"Can you guys hurry up? I have something I really want to show you," Lauryn stated tentatively.

"Don't rush me," Diana said as she jokingly flipped her hair.

"Yeah, we can only go as fast as the line is going," Naomi laughed.

"Not true. You could pay attention and realize when people are skipping you. Like he just did," Lauryn said as she pointed to the boy who had stealthily slid in front of the girls.

"What's the rush? What do you need to show us?" Allie questioned and dismissed his act.

"I made a list. I was serious about finding out who it was," Lauryn informed them.

"What kind of list?" Naomi asked interestedly as she attempted to grab it from Lauryn.

Lauryn pulled back and figured out how to get them to come to the table. Bribery seemed like her best bet. "I'll show you whenever you guys decide to come sit down," she smirked and walked back towards their table.

Well, Cammie was dreading this lunch period. Perhaps it wasn't her favorite after all. Maybe she should replace it with math. She liked math second-best. Chemistry would definitely be at the bottom, because why?

Cammie frowned and crossed her arms over her chest. She really was not looking forward to this conversation at all. There wasn't any chance of Lauryn putting her on that list. She didn't see her that way. Cammie wanted her to, though. Once again, she went in circles with herself. She really needed to consider sorting out the pros and cons of all of her wants and needs. Being immersed in a world of contradictions wasn't very fun.

Soon enough, Cammie found herself perched at the table along with her other friends. Lauryn was finally sated. She barely let Diana take her seat before she divulged her theories.

Lauryn presented her lists on the table and spread them out. She pointed to each of them and gave a brief description of what they entailed. It wasn't necessary. All of the girls could read, and the lists were all clearly labeled. Cammie took a special interest in gazing at all of the names. She thought of it as her competition. Lauryn thought of it as possibilities. Except for one. One of those names was a mistake. Several mistakes.

Cammie shared that mindset too. When she saw her name written in Lauryn's perfect print, she couldn't believe it. Her heart swelled and dropped within the same instance. Her name was there, yet it was crossed out. Of all of the names on the list, hers was the only one that was crossed out. The *only* one. That information didn't exactly sit well with her.

Lauryn took notice and placed her hand on her thigh in reassurance. She saw the way her face fell, but she didn't know why. Was she actually disappointed that she crossed her name out? Lauryn didn't know. Cammie's strange reaction confused her. Lauryn's action of even writing her name down in the first place confused Cammie as well. Naomi offered a solution to this confusion.

"Well, I only see like, three guys that would actually do something like that," Naomi began. "Louis, Patrick, and Brandon seem good."

Lauryn smiled to herself. Those had been her choices too. She wanted to see what the other girls would say.

"I think Cammie is the real winner," Diana smirked. Cammie perked up at the mention of her name, but sighed again when she registered what she'd said.

"I'm serious, Diana," Lauryn rolled her eyes.

"I'm pretty sure Cam has a shot," Allie chimed in, taking part in what she'd assumed to be a joke.

17

"Guys," Lauryn groaned, wanting to return to a more serious manner.

Cammie felt awfully uncomfortable being the butt of their jokes. The joke itself hit a little too close to home. She didn't want being an option for Lauryn to be a joke. She wanted to be her only option. She figured that she could just end this all now. She could speak up and admit that the journal was hers and confess her deepest feelings. At this point, she thought that she would be prepared to deal with the backlash of whatever the outcome might be.

That could've worked. If she wasn't a coward.

However, she was. So she sat there impassively as she wished the minutes would go by faster. Lauryn noticed her lack of conversation, but decided not to put her on the spot. She knew Cammie didn't like to be cornered or pressured into talking about her feelings. But then again, no one did. She made a mental note to come to her about it later on.

The rest of them committed to helping Lauryn list qualities of every boy on the list until their lunch period was over. As soon as the bell rung, Cammie was the first to flee. She didn't wait on Allie, who shared her next class, like she usually would. The other girls didn't know why she was in such a rush to get away, but they did notice how odd she was acting. While Lauryn and Naomi were approaching the trashcans to dump their trays, they started to talk about it.

"Do you think Cammie was being weird today?" Naomi questioned as she looked in the direction the younger girl had gone.

"Yeah. She seemed out of it," Lauryn assumed. "She's probably tired."

"She was fine earlier. It was just when you started talking about those lists..." Naomi recalled conveniently.

Diana heard their conversation from behind and decided to pitch in. Lauryn was bright, and Cammie was painfully obvious. She didn't want to accidentally out her, but she didn't want them to speculate about what was wrong with her. Together, there was no doubt that they'd figure it out.

"Nah, I don't think so. I think she's on her period," Diana lied in an attempt to steer the conversation in another direction.

"Maybe. She's just being weird," Naomi reiterated.

"Yeah, but did you do the homework for Mr. Bryant?" Diana stealthily redirected the topic.

Diana asked, but she didn't really care. Lauryn picked up on that. Since when has Diana cared enough about homework to actually talk about it? She side-eyed Diana suspiciously. She didn't know what was going on with everyone today.

Meanwhile, Cammie had found her escape. She sat in the middle of the stairwell. This section of the school was mostly deserted. Ever since students had been allowed to use the elevators, she assumed they'd forgotten all about the stairs. There were a few odd stragglers here and there, but no one of importance to Cammie.

She was brooding about Lauryn and her stupid lists. Why was her heart so set on finding out who wrote the journal? Cammie suddenly wished she had never even bought it. She'd only bought it because of the sunset on the cover. Sunsets reminded her of Lauryn. They had the same type of beauty. That's when it all started. She started talking about how Lauryn was like a sunset. It was a stupid comparison anyway.

She huffed and sat with her chin in the palm of her hands. She pulled out her phone to check how much time she had to be alone before she had to head back to class. She had roughly five minutes left. Right when she was starting to push the journal and Lauryn from her mind, they both entered the stairwell.

Lauryn entered through the door with Cammie's journal in her hands. They both startled each other. Neither had been expecting to have any company. Cammie just couldn't get a break, could she? No, apparently not. Nonetheless, she smiled at Lauryn as she came closer.

"Hey... I wasn't expecting you to be in here. Or... Anyone, actually," Lauryn laughed and took a seat next to her best friend.

"Same," Cammie shrugged. She was avoiding eye contact. If she looked at her, she would start stuttering and making a fool out of herself. The tactic never failed.

"Why are you in here?" Lauryn asked timidly.

"I come in here to think," she answered. And to write stupid, sappy things about Lauryn. But she couldn't admit that out loud.

"That makes two of us. I thought this was my secret spot... But I guess it's ours now," Lauryn laughed. She was willing to share this spot, only because it was Cammie. If anyone else intruded, she didn't think she'd be so accepting.

"Yeah," Cammie smiled sheepishly.

"Camz, I'm obsessed with this journal. Look at this," Lauryn said as she flipped open a random page. Oh God, it was one of her stupid poems - if it could even be called that.

I think I saw you in my sleep
Our lips were touching
So I know it was a dream.

Cammie read it and rolled her eyes. That one was stupid. It didn't even rhyme. What did that even mean? She didn't know. At the time, she was just letting her pen take over. Despite what it was or what it wasn't, it had come directly from the heart.

But as she looked at Lauryn, who was smiling dumbly down at the pages, it seemed alright that it didn't make sense. As long as Lauryn liked it, Cammie guessed it didn't have to rhyme. Then she went into thoughts about how nice it would be to say those things to Lauryn in person while they were cuddling or something. Lauryn would be in her arms and Cammie would be lovingly trailing her fingers along her body, telling her everything she admired about her. A subconscious smile spread across her face at the mental image.

It felt good to know that she was the reason behind Lauryn's smile. But it felt terrible knowing that she had no idea. Her shoulders involuntarily slumped at that realization.

"Are you okay?" Lauryn asked intuitively.

"Yeah? Why?" Cammie questioned. It wasn't like Lauryn had her journal or anything.

"I don't know..." Lauryn mumbled. Cammie's whole aura was peculiar. She seemed tense, sad, and distant. This version of the brown-eyed girl was foreign to her. Lauryn didn't like that. This whole time, she'd imagined solving the mystery with Cammie by her side; her partner in crime. So far, Cammie was annoyingly uninterested in the whole situation.

"I like it. Even though it doesn't rhyme," Cammie attempted to lighten the mood. She was under the impression that Lauryn had questioned her because she hadn't responded to the poem. Contrary to her beliefs, Lauryn was catching on to her forced behavior.

"No, like... I don't know, you seemed a little- Um, *off*... Earlier..." Lauryn trailed tentatively, not wanting to offend her. She was putting it nicely. To be frank, Cammie had been offbeat ever since the journal showed up. She idly wondered why that was and if the two had any correlation.

Cammie bit her lip and contemplated how bad it could be if she just told her now. They were alone. It would be much more terrifying if the other girls were here, but they were not. She was pretty sure Lauryn would be receptive. Her feelings may not be reciprocated, but they would be acknowledged and hopefully accepted. It really wouldn't be that shocking to Lauryn if she took in her recent behavior into account. It would be like ripping off a band-aid, she just had to get it over with quickly. She would just say it. Okay. This was it. She took a deep breath and prepared herself for the worst.

"Lauryn-" she began, but was interrupted by the late bell. God. Perfect timing. That must be a sign.

"Shit, we're late," Lauryn rolled her eyes and got up from her position on the stairs.

Cammie stood up awkwardly and suddenly felt stupid. Had she really been about to tell Lauryn? Was she serious? She was thankful for that bell. It saved her from making an ass of herself. She was *literally* saved by the bell. Cammie cracked a smile after making that terrible joke in her head.

"But what were you going to say?" Lauryn asked as she walked towards the door, holding it open for Cammie.

"Nothing," Cammie dismissed it quickly.

"Are you sure?" Lauryn questioned as her eyes softened.

"Yeah... It was stupid..." Cammie mumbled as she brushed past Lauryn.

Lauryn was perplexed. What was she going to say? She stood in the doorway and watched Cammie walk away. Naomi was right. She *was* being weird. Surely she couldn't pressure her to talk about something she clearly didn't want to discuss. Lauryn had never been presented with this problem before. Whenever she and Cammie had run into problems in the past, they always attacked it head on. She wasn't used to this newly timid version of Cammie. She missed the normal version of her that could address the problem directly and sort it out. It was clearly a problem regarding Lauryn.

Lauryn trudged down the hallway and spent more time thinking about it. Was Cammie mad at her? Maybe, but she couldn't recall a time where she been in the past. Sure, they'd been annoyed at each other before... But not mad. Cammie wasn't usually a very temperamental person. She doubted anger was the source.

As she slipped into the classroom and took her seat at her desk, she was still wondering about it. It was really recent. That distant behavior only seemed to surface whenever she talked about the journal. Lauryn frowned at that information. Now that she thought about it, Cammie got upset whenever she talked about boys in general. Following that, the strangest plausibility popped into her mind. Could she really have been jealous? Lauryn shrugged and brushed it off. It was time to execute her plan.

She tuned into what her teacher was saying and caught the last part. Someone needed to pass out papers. Perfect opportunity. Lauryn raised her hand and offered to help. When she approached Louis' desk, she wondered how to broach the subject. Just come out and ask him? No, he might feel awkward. She figured she should just ease into it. She put on a smile as she came to a stop in front of his desk.

"Hey, Louis? Can I ask you something?" Lauryn asked sweetly.

"Yeah, sure. What's up?" Louis smiled.

"Do you ever write?" she asked casually as she sifted through the papers.

"Write what?" he asked as he looked up at her.

"Anything. Like, writing about your feelings and stuff?" she listed.

"What? No, I don't write. That's gay," he laughed.

Well, he was off of the list. It definitely wasn't Louis. Lauryn rolled her eyes at that typical response. She saw then just how trying this task would be. Despite the revelation, she was determined to get through it. She figured that most boys shared Louis' mindset, so she braced herself for the next few encounters. Four boys from her lists were in this class.

They all went the same way. She wasn't off to a very pleasant start. She felt a bit juvenile, going about the situation this way. Writing lists and actually going out to interview these boys was very middle school of her... But it was the only way she could think of. Even though it wasn't working.

»»»»

Diana and Naomi were sitting together in the back of their anatomy classroom. This was the only time they didn't accompany Cammie. They weren't particularly fond of sitting in the front row. They often made fun of her as they watched from behind. It was all in good fun, and Cammie knew that, so she was rarely bothered by their incessant giggling. She was so diligent about getting her work completed, she rarely got off track. Her work ethic made Naomi and Diana laugh. She was always hunched over and scribbling wildly, which was amusing to them. But they weren't laughing at her today.

Today, Cammie wasn't writing like a maniac. She wasn't engrossed in the lesson or even remotely paying attention. She was laying her head down on the table, not even attempting to begin her assignment. Something was wrong. Something was very wrong, and Diana and Naomi both knew it.

"Is she sick? Or is she like, upset or something?" Naomi asked with concern.

"I don't know..." Diana said honestly. She didn't know what exactly was wrong with Cammie. She knew it was something pertaining to Lauryn, but she didn't know what had happened. What could've happened since lunch? Or was it the same thing? Diana didn't know. She wished she could discuss it with Naomi, but she wouldn't betray Cammie's trust like that.

"I wish she would talk to us," Naomi sighed. She, for one, was completely confused. She had no idea what was happening between her friends. She felt like Diana knew something she didn't, or that something was being hidden. But she couldn't even begin to think of what. She took it upon herself to find out.

Naomi got out of her seat and approached Cammie, who was still folded over. When she saw Cammie's expression, her face fell completely. She looked so troubled. Her eyebrows were furrowed and she had a blank stare. She'd rarely seen her look this way. Cammie was usually bright and lively, but this was a parody of

21

that girl. Naomi didn't know how to announce her presence. So she settled on placing a comforting hand on her shoulder. She hoped their teacher wouldn't tell her to sit down. That would be embarrassing.

Cammie turned to face her for a second, then returned to her previous position. She didn't want to talk to Naomi. It was nothing personal, though. Cammie didn't want to talk to anyone. She just wanted to be left alone. She didn't have the guts to skip class and go back to sit in the infirmary. She wasn't a very good liar. Of course she'd contemplated the idea, but she didn't have the energy to go through with it. She just wanted to sit here and be sad for now, because everything regarding Lauryn just upset her today. And Lauryn was all she ever thought about.

"Cam..." Naomi trailed. She wanted to make her feel better at least, even if she couldn't get to the root problem.

"I'm fine," Cammie dismissed her.

Naomi sighed again and retracted her hand, padding back over to her seat. Diana gave her a look, silently asking what Cammie had said. Naomi shrugged, and Diana shook her head.

"Whatever though. She'll be okay," Diana brushed it off. "But did you talk to any of the guys on Lauryn's list?" she asked, curious about how their little case was going. She wasn't participating in the search. Why would she? She knew whose it was all along.

"We talked to Trent and Jamie... But it's not them," Naomi answered. "I mean, I just don't see the point. No guy is just gonna admit to something like that, even if it was him."

"True. I don't know what Lo is expecting," Diana laughed.

"Me neither," Naomi joined in her laughter. The conversation tapered off there. They began to answer a few questions on their papers. They were actually getting their work done for once. The whole atmosphere was off, which was Cammie's fault. "Oh, yeah! These guys told us about this other guy that might have written all those things about Lauryn," Naomi recalled from their conversation earlier.

She and Allie had approached Trent and Jamie last period. Really, they had approached every boy they considered, not knowing who half of the people on the list even were. Jamie and Trent were the most interesting to talk to. They sat and talked with them for most of the class period, enjoying their company more than they thought they would.

"What happened?" Diana questioned, suddenly amused. If anyone was going to take credit for what Cammie had done, they were a certified piece of shit in her eyes.

"This boy named Brandon," she answered. "They said he's liked Lauryn all year. Do you know him?"

"Yeah, he's cute," Diana nodded.

"I don't know him. Do you think he could've?" Naomi asked.

"Nah," Diana responded immediately. She wanted to shut down any rumors or possibilities that might arise. She couldn't bear to see how it would all unfold if he actually got Lauryn to believe he was the author.

"Oh, well I don't know then," Naomi shrugged again, dropping the subject and picking up her pencil. She was halfway done with her work, and she wanted to finish for once. Diana let her and followed her lead.

Chapter 4

"So his name is Brandon?" Lauryn asked with a smile. She was sitting on the edge of her bed. They were all huddled up in her room, like they were on most Fridays. Allie was sprawled out across the bed and Diana was spinning in her chair. Naomi was sitting on the floor next to Cammie, who was laying down on the floor with her head in Naomi's lap.

"Yeah," Allie nodded enthusiastically, honestly believing that their search was over. Their mystery was far from being resolved.

"Well, what did they say? I've talked to Brandon a few times before," Lauryn recalled.

"They were just making fun of him and talking about how much he liked you. They didn't really say a whole lot. But I know him. He's really nice and seems like he would do that type of thing," Allie suggested.

Cammie wasn't hearing this. She just was not hearing this. They had to be joking. Were they seriously trying to discover who it was? Still? Nothing else had diverted their attention away from the mystery? It had been a whole day already. She didn't know what she would do if someone stole Lauryn from her through their stupid lies, even though she didn't necessarily have her in the first place. But whatever. She closed her eyes and tried to just go to sleep, which clearly wasn't going to happen when there were so many voices around her.

"Well, he is really cute..." Lauryn mumbled as her smile grew exponentially. In her mind, he was getting more attractive by the second. If he had looks like those *and* an intellectual mind, Lauryn might just fall in love.

"Yeah, he is," Naomi agreed enthusiastically. "Let me see it," she requested as she held out her hand for the journal.

Lauryn's eyes seemed glued to the pages. It was endearing to Cammie to see that she was so enamored with her writing, but her spirits dropped yet again when she remembered that she didn't know she was the source. And at this rate, it seemed that she'd never know.

When Naomi got a hold of the journal, she scanned a few pages. She flipped some more and skimmed, repeating the process. She found a good page and cleared her throat theatrically, preparing to read one of the entries aloud. Cammie dreaded this. Her eyes wandered over to the pages and tried to see how bad this one was.

People write poems about smiles like yours. It's been my favorite thing about you since the day we met. That was the day our two worlds collided, then molded. When you smiled at me that day so many years ago, I was yours. Even then, I knew it. I was wrapped around your finger. I always have been. Because until then, I'd never met anyone whose smile could surpass even the most beautiful sunset. And I'd never met anyone whose grin could light up the darkest parts of me. I had never - in my entire life - met someone whose smile became a necessary part of my happiness. But then I met you, and you did all of that. Because you're just that beautiful inside and out. And oh my god, your laugh. If I could only hear one sound before I take my last breath, I'm pretty sure that would be it. It's my favorite sound on the entire planet. You're so goddam beautiful. The way you -

Naomi continued to read aloud, but Cammie had slapped the journal out of her hands in the midst of it. She was fed up. Before then, Naomi had been struggling to read the messy print, but was so amused by doing so. After certain observations mentioned, she would thrust her hand over her heart and swoon exaggeratedly. Everyone, with the exception of Cammie, was so tickled by her ridiculous display. Instead of eliciting laughter within the silent girl, she roused rage.

She couldn't take this anymore. The way Naomi was reading it aloud like it was some sort of joke left her livid. She was speaking so theatrically and giggling at her heartfelt admissions the entire time. They were laughing at her feelings. But she knew her anger couldn't be directed at Naomi. She didn't know she was broadcasting *Cammie's* deepest emotions to their friends. Admittedly, she felt a little embarrassed. No one was supposed to read those private things. Those words really weren't even intended for Lauryn's eyes. And they sure as hell weren't supposed to be poking fun at them in front of her.

"Muscle spasm, sorry..." Cammie attempted to excuse that reckless act. She should really work on impulse control. And her temper.

"What's wrong?" Allie questioned, slightly startled by the sudden outburst.

"Nothing... I just- Um, I just have a headache. You're talking really loud, Naomi. I'm sorry," Cammie mumbled an insincere apology.

Naomi simply laughed. She wasn't offended at all, and Cammie was grateful for that. Taking it as a playful act worked in her favor, but Cammie was seriously fed up. She was so mad. It didn't occur to her exactly know why or who she was mad at, but she was. She was so angry.

"Isn't that beautiful?" Lauryn grinned goofily, purposely ignoring what had just happened.

"Yeah, it's really sweet," Allie nodded.

"Let's watch a movie. I'm getting bored," Diana suggested in an attempt to save Cammie from her embarrassment.

"Alright, which one?" Lauryn asked as she retrieved the journal from Cammie's grasp. She set it down on her desk and proceeded to sift through her movie selection.

Cammie huffed and sat up. Her headache had worsened. It was probably from stress. For the first time in her life, she didn't want to stay. She wanted to leave Lauryn's house. She wanted to go far away, or back in time. She wanted to go back to the time where she blissfully wrote to her heart's content in her journal. She wanted to go back to the time when Lauryn didn't even know there *was* a journal filled with paragraphs upon paragraphs about her. She wanted to go back to the time before her friends had turned into the Scooby Doo gang or something. She wanted a lot of things she couldn't have, like Lauryn.

"Cam, come with me to make snacks," Diana said as she tugged on her shoulder, brutally bringing her back to reality.

"I don't feel like it," Cammie mumbled, disregarding her request. She'd much rather sulk there, wallowing in self-pity instead.

"Girl, if you don't..." Diana threatened as she made her way over to Cammie. She stood in front of her and gave her a look that made her scramble up immediately. While they were trudging down the hallway, Diana turned to the shorter girl. "What's wrong with you?" she asked quietly.

"I want her to know," Cammie revealed almost immediately. She'd been wanting to talk to Diana about this, because somehow Diana had become the *only* person she could talk to.

"So tell her," Diana said easily, not really seeing what was holding Cammie back. She should just grow a pair and tell her.

"Can't," she rolled her eyes. She was prepared for that. Diana just didn't get it. "But it's not just that..." Cammie continued. "It's how frustrated I am that I can't tell her. Not just because I don't *want* to tell her... Like, I physically just cannot."

"Why?" Diana asked.

"I almost did... Earlier today, but then the bell rung. So I didn't get the chance," she disclosed. "And even if it didn't ring, I don't think I actually could've said it. I got all weird. It was like I was choked up, except I wasn't crying," she struggled to express herself. Everything felt so conflicted. While words usually came easily to her, she was now having problems with that too.

"I don't know what to tell you..." Diana said honestly. "Why can't you tell Naomi and Allie? I think they could help you..."

"They'll tell Lauryn," Cammie disagreed.

"I don't think so," Diana responded thoughtfully as they entered the kitchen.

"I don't know. But either way, I don't really want anyone to know. I wasn't even planning on telling you," Cammie reminded her.

Diana shrugged and sauntered towards the pantry. Lauryn needed to go to the store. She didn't have anything good in here. A bit disappointed, Diana closed the pantry door and leaned against the counter.

"And then she started making those lists..." Cammie whined. She wasn't concerned about snacks. *That* said a lot. Cammie? Not being concerned about snacks? Blasphemy.

"I think you're just scared of someone else taking her away from you. You're all messed up now 'cause she's looking at other people. Lauryn hasn't seriously dated someone in a long time..." Diana said casually as she peered into Lauryn's refrigerator. She really needed to go shopping.

"Who are you, and what have you done with Diana?" Cammie joked.

"What?" Diana asked as she looked back at Cammie.

"You're actually saying something that makes sense," Cammie teased and Diana nudged her in the shoulder.

"I have my moments," Diana gloated playfully. "But seriously, I think you should just ignore her for a while."

"And... Diana's back," Cammie rolled her eyes. Was she serious? Ignore her?

"Shut up," Diana groaned as she pushed her. "I'm serious. If seeing her talking about those dumb lists makes you so mad or sad or whatever... Just don't."

"I couldn't ignore her even if I tried," Cammie acknowledged. And it was true. She was drawn to her. She always had been. Even if Lauryn was on the other side of the planet, Cammie would find her way back to her eventually.

"Ignore who?" Lauryn questioned as she walked into the kitchen, joining the two. She walked in front of them and leaned against the counter opposite to them. Cammie had the perfect view.

"Some girl that was talking shit," Diana lied easily. Cammie was in awe, wondering how she did it. She should ask for lessons sometime.

"Yeah... She was saying um, some mean things about... Uh- me," Cammie attempted to add on. Attempt failed.

Lauryn gave her a quizzical look and laughed. Cammie couldn't help her smile as the sound filled the room. Her raspy laugh was her favorite. It was very butterfly-inducing.

"Well, yeah. Forget her," Lauryn agreed.

Even if Cammie could forget Lauryn, she probably wouldn't want to. God, she had it bad. "Yeah," she nodded meekly.

"What was up with you earlier?" Lauryn questioned, recalling how they'd never really gotten to talk about it.

"She got a B on her test," Diana answered for her again.

"Aw... Which class?" Lauryn asked sympathetically, jutting out her lip in an exaggerated pout.

"Science," Cammie went along with it.

"She was just worrying about how Sonya would react. You know how she gets," Diana waved it off, referring to her mother. Meanwhile, Cammie was insanely grateful for Diana's quick thinking. It made her second-guess some of the things Diana had told her in private, seeing how effortlessly she could lie.

"It'll be fine, Camz," Lauryn assured her as she closed the distance between the two of them. She wrapped her arms around Cammie's torso tightly. Cammie thought she would pass out. Lauryn hugged with her entire body, and it always threw her off. Cammie was focusing on trying to breathe normally once they'd separated. Diana was watching the whole exchange in amusement.

"Is that what put you in that weird mood earlier?" Lauryn inferred.

"Yeah... I guess," Cammie nodded. And the fact that she had her journal.

"She won't be mad. Most kids can't even get B's," Lauryn continued.

"At me, though," Diana laughed.

"You know I'm not talking about you, Diana," Lauryn laughed along.

"Better not be," she threatened.

"Yeah. But you guys are taking forever to bring snacks," Lauryn suddenly remembered her purpose for coming down here.

"You need to go to the store. We didn't bring anything because there's nothing to bring," Diana countered.

"Maybe I would have some food if you guys didn't rob me every time you came over," Lauryn giggled.

Cammie wasn't participating in their banter. She was eyeing Lauryn. She was so casual in the way she just stood there. She wasn't even doing anything, but she looked so damn beautiful. She made simple tasks seem amazing. She made

26

doing nothing at all seem extraordinary. Her hair just fell over her shoulders so perfectly. She was wearing sweats and a loose shirt. But her pants were hanging off of her waist and showing just a bit of skin. It left too much to the imagination. And Cammie didn't need to be imaging anything of that sort - nothing like grabbing her waist and finally getting to kiss those heavenly lips. Why would she think about that? She really needed to stop. Seriously.

Diana waved her hand in front of Cammie's face and broke her from her trance. She smirked at her and Cammie reluctantly shifted her gaze to the floor. Diana knew exactly what was on her mind, if the way she was biting her lip was any indication. But Lauryn had missed all of that. She always missed it.

"Let's just order pizza," Cammie suggested in an attempt to seem normal. She didn't want her friends wondering what was wrong with her all the time.

"Yeah," Diana nodded enthusiastically, suddenly craving pizza.

"You call? Or me?" Lauryn asked as she pulled out her phone, preparing to dial the number.

"You can," Cammie shrugged.

Lauryn ordered the pizza. Half an hour later when it arrived, the five of them huddled around Lauryn's TV and helped themselves. Cammie was doing a good job of paying attention to the movie instead of glimpsing at Lauryn every five seconds. In the time she had to wait for the pizza, she'd come to terms with reality. Because in reality, someone most likely would take advantage of the opportunity. That someone wasn't going to be her. She didn't have the nerve. So she just tried to let it go.

»»»»

Letting it go turned out to be much harder than anticipated. The rest of Friday night was fine. Saturday was alright. Sunday was bearable. Through phone conversations with Diana, she'd been told time after time to just come out and tell her. Cammie shot down every argument Diana made. Those feeble disagreements were no match for her, though. Diana was persistent as hell, and Cammie eventually relented just to make her phone stop vibrating every five minutes. Diana just didn't let up. She'd nearly been *forced* into agreeing to tell Lauryn.

But Monday morning, when she saw her coming down the hallway, all of Diana's progress vanished. Lauryn's hair literally bounced with every step, even though it was cascading down her back. She loved to make eye contact with people, which was slightly terrifying. And her style made her come off as badass. She was somewhat of a model to Cammie. The confidence she exuberated made her seem intimidating, even though Cammie had known her for years. Although she appeared to be that way, she was a big dork on the inside, which Cammie adored. Despite knowing that, she lost a lot of her nerve as Lauryn spotted her and strode towards her.

"Hey," Lauryn smiled warmly, pulling Cammie into a quick side hug.

"Hi. Lauryn... I need to tell you something," Cammie blurted out nervously, wasting no time. If she waited, even a little bit, her cowardice would return. She knew it.

"Okay... What is it?" Lauryn asked timidly, sensing her urgency.

"It's about um... The journal..." Cammie shared tentatively. She was fidgeting with her fingers and her heart was beating wildly. She shouldn't have been this terrified to tell her.

27

"What about it?" Lauryn questioned softly, wanting to aid Cammie in getting whatever it was off of her chest.

"I don't know how to say this... So I'm just gonna-" Cammie began, but was interrupted by a call from down the hallway.

"Lauryn! Hey, Lauryn!" Brandon called as he quickly shuffled down the hall.

Lauryn turned around upon hearing her name. When she recognized him as Brandon, a smile graced her lips. So far, he was the only one that had yet to be interrogated. Maybe she could get a few questions in. Her grin widened as he came closer.

"Hey, how are you?" Lauryn greeted him.

"I'm good. Hey, Cammie," he waved to the younger girl, acknowledging her presence.

"Hi," she greeted him back mousily, feeling herself already receding into the background of their new interaction. Lauryn wouldn't allow that to happen, though. She'd always been one to stick up for her and defend the lost words others had so easily silenced. This time, it was a habit that Cammie could've done without.

"Oh, wait... Cammie was about to tell me something," Lauryn suddenly remembered when she heard her voice. "Hang on for a second. What was it, Camz?"

"It can wait," Cammie said politely.

"Are you sure?" Lauryn pressed, not wanting her to downplay it if it was actually something serious.

"Yeah, go ahead," Cammie nodded.

Okay, minor setback. But that's okay. She didn't need any distractions while she was going to tell Lauryn. Dropping that bomb on her in the hallway wasn't really in her plans anyway. Thinking it would be more private and somewhat sentimental, she wanted to have that discussion in the staircase. Abiding by that notion, she withdrew. She stepped aside and let her have her conversation with Brandon.

"So, what's up, beautiful?" Brandon resumed their conversation cheesily. Cammie glared at him. She could detect his poor attempt at flirting almost immediately. He better not try anything.

Lauryn played right into his hands and giggled at nothing. Cammie was only wondering what could've been so hilarious about his admission. He was annoying her already. "Um, I just got here. So... Nothing really. What's up with you?"

"Nothing," Brandon shrugged. "But I kinda wanted to ask you something..."

"Okay, go ahead," Lauryn encouraged him.

"Have you found my journal? I think I lost it in the library a few days ago..." he trailed with a shy smile.

Wait. What did he say? Cammie's head snapped up in his direction. Her eyebrows creased and she couldn't help it when her jaw dropped.

"Oh my god. It *is* you! I *knew* it was yours!" Lauryn exclaimed giddily. She eagerly rummaged through her bag for it. When she pulled it out, she presented it to Brandon. "This one, right?"

Cammie felt like she was about to cry. There was no way this was happening in front of her. This was exactly what Diana said *wouldn't* happen. She said there was no way someone could pull it off. But Brandon could, and he was. Right in front of her.

"Yeah!" he nodded vigorously. "I can't believe you found it! That's kind of awkward though..." he laughed nervously. He was playing his role perfectly. Lauryn was actually falling for it.

Brandon had been coached by Trent and Jamie about everything pertaining to the journal. Thanks to Naomi and Allie, the boys knew all about her search. They wanted to help hook up their friend with one of his dream girls. They had Naomi and Allie recite a few lines from Cammie's journal while they feigned genuine interest. Trent and Jamie had written it down and passed it to Brandon, giving him enough material to be believable. This information had gone unknown to any of the girls, purposely. They figured there was nothing wrong with a little deception and manipulation to get Lauryn. Their plan and logic was being executed flawlessly.

"It's not awkward. It's so sweet. You have an amazing way with words," Lauryn praised him. She was absolutely elated. She could barely believe her luck. She'd found him.

Cammie couldn't believe *any* of it. This had to be a joke. She was expecting Ashton Kutcher to come out at any minute now. She had to have been being punk'd.

"Really? You think so?" Brandon asked hopefully. "I never really planned on letting you see it..."

"I'm glad I found it," Lauryn grinned. The butterflies in her stomach were relentless. She felt the connection between the two of them already. There was an undeniable chemistry. Her whole body thrummed in excitement, thinking about the possibilities and what could come of it.

"Well, seeing how this is going so far... I guess I'm kinda glad you found it too," Brandon blushed.

Wow. Cammie thought he deserved an Oscar. Wasn't that the award for phenomenal actors? Or was it an Emmy? She didn't know. All she knew was that if he could cue blush like that and make *her* girl fall for him with his web of lies, he deserved some type of award. He was ruthless. He was lying straight to her face. Cammie didn't know what to do. This had quickly become the worst possible time to tell her. So she put her confession on the backburner.

"Oh my god," Lauryn gushed as she clutched the journal to her chest. "Can I keep it? I really love it and I haven't gotten to finish yet. I mean, unless you want it back..." she trailed, suddenly nervous and unsure of herself.

"No, you can keep it," Brandon grinned. Just then, the bell rung. Brandon looked up to check the time and sighed. "Well, I have to go. My locker is way on the third floor. But I'll see you later," he gave her a dimpled smile and held his arms out for a hug.

Lauryn eagerly complied. She closed the distance between him and wrapped her arms around him tightly. They prolonged their hug and she rested her head on his shoulder briefly. Cammie couldn't bear it. *She* should be the one receiving that hug. That journal was *hers*. *Lauryn* was hers.

When they pulled away, Brandon leaned in and kissed her sweetly on the cheek. The way Lauryn blushed and radiated happiness just about broke her heart. Brandon had won. It was official. Lauryn was putty in his hands now. That knowledge was Cammie's final straw. She abruptly turned from them and walked away, not even bothering to bid Lauryn goodbye.

Cammie would've been thrilled if this had been Diana, Allie, or Naomi. But no part of her could muster any form of happiness or congratulatory feelings right now. She was not happy for Lauryn. Why would she be when she was blatantly being lied to? She had half a mind to end it there, to expose him and his lies. But she knew that that would cause for an explanation, and she just didn't have any fight left in her today. Watching this unfold had drained her.

She didn't have the energy for school, or anything for that matter. She wasn't even bitter about the situation. The way things had played out had just left her completely crestfallen. Tears brimmed her eyes and made her vision blurry. She couldn't handle what she'd just witnessed. When the first one fell, she picked up the pace. She had to get out. She hated crying in front of an audience.

»»»»

"There's no point in telling her anymore, Diana," Cammie sniffled into the phone. She'd just finished recapping the confrontation to her best friend. Diana had called the second she realized Cammie wasn't at school. She seriously feared that her best friend had gotten abducted or something. Cammie had never skipped before. It wasn't even an option. It was never in her nature. When Diana found out that she'd ditched school to go home and cry, she felt compelled to comfort her. Hiding out in the restroom during class was her means of doing so.

Cammie didn't even know where Diana was, or what class she was supposed to be in, but she was grateful. If she had to deal with this alone, she might've had to check herself into a mental institution later.

"Not for you. Think about Lo. If you tell her that Brandon is lying, you'll save her from being all heartbroken and shit later on," Diana suggested taking a different approach. If she wouldn't seek justice for herself, perhaps she would for Lauryn.

"She won't believe me until I tell her how I know he's lying. And I can't. Not anymore. It doesn't matter anymore. You know Lauryn, she'll get so defensive about it... It's not worth it. I'll just let her find out on her own," Cammie shrugged and wiped her nose on her sleeve. Crying was gross. Her entire face was leaking. And now she'd run out of tissues.

"If you don't tell her, then I will. I'm not gonna sit here and watch two of my best friends crash and burn just because you're being stubborn as hell," Diana threatened.

"You can't tell her!" Cammie said, her voice raising a few octaves. She agreed with Diana, but she couldn't tell her *now*. Lauryn was so happy. She didn't want to ruin it for her. Cammie had rarely seen Lauryn that bubbly. Even if Cammie wasn't the one causing it, it made her somewhat happy knowing that Lauryn was happy.

"Now you're just being stupid," Diana scoffed into the phone. She was so annoyed. Cammie had the excuse of being nervous before. Then she had the excuse of waiting until "the right time". Time was running out now. Cammie couldn't just keep waiting. She had the habit of being passive, then wondering why nothing ever went her way. She needed to take action, and the fact that she wasn't was annoying Diana more than it should've been.

Cammie rolled her eyes. She didn't answer Diana's call to be insulted. Her thumb hovered over the end call button just in case Diana said something else out of line. "I'm not being stupid. You should've seen her... She was so happy. If it makes her that happy to think she's found her stupid Prince Charming... I'll let her," she

30

explained. Lauryn's happiness always came before hers, no matter how much it would hurt. It didn't occur to her how damaging that was.

Cammie just assumed she would disclose everything before it spiraled out of control. If only she had taken Diana's advice.

Chapter 5

Ever since Lauryn had confirmed that Brandon was the author, she'd been particularly close with him. In truth, the two had been inseparable. It was repulsing and satisfying to Cammie all at once. She hated the fact that Brandon was constantly lying to her, but she loved seeing how happy he made her.

Lauryn and Brandon had exchanged numbers. While she was texting him, he seemed different. Something about him was off, in comparison to the way he wrote. His vocabulary wasn't nearly as expansive, and he never really talked about the things he'd mentioned in his journal. He was able to keep conversation going, but it wasn't what Lauryn was expecting. She was hoping to have intellectual conversations with him about the world and life, to explore that beautiful mind of his in person – not just through writing. He seemed so complex, but he annoyingly kept the topics pretty neutral.

She was confused. The writing in his journal wasn't *all* about her. It was filled with his opinions on a wide range of topics along with his beliefs about certain things. Lauryn was able to recall some of them and broach them to Brandon so they could discuss it further, but his answers were evasive and gave her little to work with. She brought up the peculiarity to her friends.

"It's so weird. It's like he's one person through writing and a completely different person in real life," Lauryn expressed to them at lunch.

They were all huddled around the table, listening to Lauryn update them on her status with Brandon. That was how their lunch periods had been going recently. They sat down, greeted each other, caught up a little, and listened to Lauryn divulge more details about her and Brandon's budding relationship.

Brandon reminded Cammie of a potato. She didn't like potatoes and she didn't like him, either. He was so boring and not right for Lauryn at all. He was without substance. He just stole everything Cammie said and attempted to mold it into something he could reiterate. Cammie called him a potato in her head. What could be more boring than a potato? Bread was pretty boring. She decided to start calling him Bread instead.

"Maybe he just gets nervous when you ask him about stuff he knows he wrote about," Naomi inferred.

"Yeah. That's like when people ask me to sing. I'm like no. But I be belting out them notes in the shower, though," Diana added with a laugh.

"Not Allie. She does her Shakira impression at the drop of a hat," Cammie said dryly.

"That's because she can sing," Diana countered.

"You can sing too, Diana," Lauryn laughed.

"*Cam* can sing," Diana added as she wiggled her eyebrows.

Cammie side-eyed her. She wished Diana would stop trying to talk her up in front of Lauryn. She knew it wasn't going to do any justice. She knew that she could be painted in the most beautiful light and still be outshined by Bread. *He* had Lauryn's focus. Cammie had been painfully friend-zoned now, even more than she'd previously been. She was almost coming to terms with it.

Diana, on the other hand, was not. She resented how she couldn't tell Lauryn. She hated the way Cammie acted now. She was emotionally drained. Everything concerning Brandon had sucked the life out of the brown-eyed girl. She was merely going through the motions. She missed her old friend.

"I know she can," Lauryn acknowledged. "Oh my god, and Brandon can sing too," she tacked on with a reminiscent smile.

Brandon this. *Brandon* that. She was growing to resent the curly-haired piece of Bread. He took over Lauryn and corrupted her mind. All of her thoughts were now tainted or linked with him in some way. Cammie hated every second of it. Lauryn's voice didn't make her smile anymore. Her presence didn't make her feel like she was on cloud nine now. Now, it just reminded her of what had been taken from her.

"So are y'all dating now or...?" Allie assumed.

"I guess we are. He hasn't asked, so I guess it's not official or anything... But we kiss and stuff so basically," Lauryn answered.

Yeah, twist the knife in Cammie's stomach, why don't you. That hurt more than she let on. Lauryn was supposed to be kissing Cammie. The thought of those perfect lips being pressed against someone else's made her heart hurt.

"Well when y'all do start dating, you're gonna be the power couple of the school," Naomi smiled. She was so happy for Lauryn. Hearing her talk about him every day at lunch wasn't annoying to her at all. She practically *waited* to find out more about the pair.

"Thanks, Naomi," Lauryn smiled and hugged her awkwardly from across the table.

Lunch came and went. The days passed by and Cammie really just didn't feel like doing anything. She lacked any type of motivation. Although she had never been the type of person to let her personal problems interfere with her schoolwork, the lines started to blur. Whenever she got into one of these moods, she found her escape through reading or writing. She couldn't write anymore. Lauryn was her inspiration most of the time, but oddly enough, she wasn't feeling very inspired at all.

Somewhere deep within Cammie, she knew she was happy for Lauryn. However, the circumstances for Lauryn's happiness made it hard for Cammie to accept it. Lauryn hated being lied to, and she felt like she was lying to Lauryn as well. It was lying by omission. Diana was guilty of it too. The desire to tell her lessened every day. Diana feared that Cammie was sinking into a state of depression. She wanted to do whatever she could to help her get back to normal.

Diana and Lauryn had anatomy together. The other girls were taking different science classes, and luckily Diana and Lauryn had been scheduled for the same one. They sat next to each other most of the time. Today, their assignment was a lab. They picked their spot in a corner in the back to begin. Diana picked it so they would have some conversational privacy.

"What are we supposed to do first?" Lauryn asked Diana, who was holding the lab instruction sheet.

"I don't know. What's going on with you and Brandon?" Diana changed the subject.

"We're good... But he's still being so weird. I thought it was just because he was nervous, but we hang out so often now, I know it's not that. There's literally nothing to be nervous about anymore. We're so comfortable with each other but he's just so..." Lauryn trailed off as she struggled to find a way to accurately describe him.

"Boring?" Diana assumed as she set up their materials.

"No, not that. He's pretty funny and stuff. I mean, I can talk to him... But I don't know. I don't know how to explain it. I read more of his journal every night... And I'm almost finished with it, but sometimes he just doesn't seem like the person that wrote all of that stuff," Lauryn admitted hesitantly. The thought had popped into her mind initially, but she'd been keeping it to herself. She didn't want to speak it into existence.

Diana smiled in spite of herself. Lauryn was slowly figuring it out. If she could find a way to pave the road for Cammie, they would be home free. She had to be careful though. She had to drop little, subtle hints. Cammie would kill her if she did anything else. It was risky, but Diana was willing to brave it.

"Did you ever think that maybe the journal wasn't his?" Diana suggested.

"Yeah, I have. If I'm being honest, I think about that all the time. But I'm like, this is *Brandon*. He wouldn't lie to me," Lauryn disclosed. She wanted to have faith in her boyfriend. Was that what he was now? Nothing was official yet. Everything concerning Brandon was starting to give her a headache.

"I don't think so, either... But I mean, have you considered anyone else on the list?" Diana asked quietly as she skimmed over the lab sheet. Yeah, there was no way she was about to do that right now. She put it on the table next to everything else that wasn't about to be completed any time soon.

"No. You guys saw me talking to all of those guys. It wasn't any of them. And the only person I haven't asked was *Cammie*..." Lauryn recalled as she resigned from the lab as well.

Diana raised her eyebrows and gave Lauryn a thoughtful look. "Well... Have you asked her?"

"No? Why would I ask her? It's clearly not hers," Lauryn scoffed.

"You thought it was her handwriting at first," Diana stealthily reminded her.

"What are you trying to say?" Lauryn questioned, but there was no malice to her tone. She was genuinely wondering what Diana was so hesitant to disclose.

"Nothing..." Diana shrugged. "But you wrote her name for a reason, Lo."

Lauryn considered that. She *did* write Cammie's name for a reason. What that reason could possibly have been, she had no idea.

"Oh, I guess so... But let's go ahead and do this," Lauryn said determinedly, suddenly eager to finish their lab. That was her mode of distraction.

She was working quietly and diligently. Diana noticed the way her eyebrows were furrowed, meaning she was deep in thought. She knew Lauryn well enough to know that it wasn't due to concentration. She hoped she was really letting what she'd said marinate a while. Diana had merely planted the seed in Lauryn's head. Now she had to play the waiting game to see if it was worth it.

Lauryn was seriously beginning to consider Cammie as the author of the journal. It made sense, but if she was the one who'd written it, why hadn't she said anything? All of the factors had lined up perfectly, except the confession. If Lauryn was the one who'd written that journal, she would've taken no hesitation to claim it. Especially if she supposedly had deep feelings for whoever she was writing about. That was a big part of why she had trouble seeing Cammie as the author.

Also, that would mean Cammie had feelings for Lauryn. *Deep* feelings. They had professed their love for Lauryn multiple times throughout the journal, and she wasn't even finished reading yet. As dense as it was, it held so many secrets. The potential that those were *Cammie's* secrets made her uneasy. She had no problem with it, she was just doubtful that she could reciprocate.

Lauryn knew she and Cammie shared a special bond, sure. They were practically the closest out of the group of five. She couldn't explain why she felt so drawn to her, she just was. Intimacy was a component of their relationship with no questions asked, and it always had been. She was questioning it now. Furthermore, it wasn't one-sided. Lauryn initiated half of it. *But why?* Their friendship had been very touchy from the get go. Lauryn didn't have an explanation for that.

Multiple questions ran through her mind all day. Cammie infiltrated all of her thoughts. She thought about her behavior with her. She was always so happy, always smiling, always staring. Lauryn was guilty of that too, though. Cammie had undeniable beauty and it was easy to be consumed by it from time to time. Lauryn stole glimpses of her from time to time as well. With a new perspective, she reflected on how Cammie always seemed timid, nervous, and antsy whenever she was around. The handwriting in the journal *did* seem awfully familiar...

Lauryn tried to push Cammie from her mind for a little while. Brandon had formally asked her out on a date. She wasn't expecting anything spectacular, they were only having a little coffee date. On her way there, she desperately tried to get in the right mindset of going on a date. Annoyingly enough, she found that her second-guessing about Cammie took no time off. She saw Brandon push through the door of Starbucks and the butterflies followed soon after. When he sat down, the atmosphere shifted. Her anticipation of her first real date with Brandon quickly overshadowed her doubts about Cammie.

"Hey," Brandon waved sweetly and leaned across the table to kiss her cheek.

"Hi," Lauryn smiled. She felt like a dork. She always smiled at his simple gestures, so enamored with the simple things.

"How are you, love?" he asked casually. He looked down at his receipt and idly wondered when his drink would be ready.

"I'm great," she answered too quickly. She was alright... Decent... Okay, rather. She wasn't great. She was far from great. Her mind was cluttered with far too many things for her to be as great as she'd claimed.

"I was doing okay earlier, but I'm great *now*," he emphasized with a smirk.

"Why now?" Lauryn played along with a goofy grin.

"I'm on a date with the most beautiful girl in the world," Brandon answered.

Well, she'd heard variations of that line about a million times. And that wasn't the way he would've said that if he was writing. He usually stayed away from typical clichés like those. But whatever.

"Aww," Lauryn continued to smile, although she was starting to doubt him again in her head. "I'm so glad I found your journal."

"Yeah... Me too," he stated nervously.

Brandon really did like Lauryn. Over the past three years of spending high school with her, he'd grown to have a very deep affection for her. He'd never had the courage to make a move on her, and when he saw the opportunity like the journal, he took advantage of it. It seemed harmless at the time, but the guilt from it was eating him alive.

Every kiss and hug shared between them made him feel terrible. He was as genuine as he could be whenever he was with her, but he couldn't ignore the fact that their relationship was founded on a lie. He always tried to sway the conversation whenever she started talking about it, but he never could do it successfully. She always seemed a little hurt or offended whenever he abruptly changed the topic.

"I was reading it last night, and the page where you said '*You look so beautiful in this light, silhouette over me. The way it brings out the blue in your eyes is the Tenerife Sea'* was my favorite," Lauryn disclosed.

"Really? You liked it? I was just writing, you know... Because you um- you have really pretty eyes," Brandon stuttered. He had no idea what she was talking about, but he was going with it.

He lied.

There was no such thing in that journal. She'd said that because the song by Ed Sheeran was stuck in her head, that line specifically. It had been a mere test, and he failed.

"That wasn't in the journal..." Lauryn informed him.

"Yeah, I was just thinking that I didn't remember writing that..." he excused his slip with a timid laugh, then avoided eye contact.

"Those are song lyrics," Lauryn added dubiously.

Maybe Diana's accusation held some truth. Perhaps he wasn't legit as he seemed to be. Lauryn glanced at him uncertainly. The two of them ran into awkward moments like those quite often. In fact, it was nearly every time Lauryn brought up something about the journal. But it was terribly cute.

The way Brandon refused to look at her was kind of adorable, in a way. It was like his eyes were glued to the table. The only time he looked up was whenever Lauryn spoke, and even then, it was just a glance. And his cheeks seemed to be permanently flushed. He had the nervous habit of playing with his fingers. Either twiddling them or drumming them on the table, he couldn't sit still.

"Yeah," Brandon shuffled uncomfortably. He looked at his receipt again, then back up at the counter. Thankfully, it was prepared. Starbucks had provided a distraction. He gestured towards the front awkwardly and quickly walked towards to claim his drink.

When Brandon came back, he had his drink in hand along with two straws. Lauryn smiled at the gesture, thinking of how cute he was. The idea of sharing a drink was cute to her. She just hoped she liked it. The color was uninviting. She peeled off the wrapper of her straw and stuck it into the drink nonetheless. It was surprisingly sweet and very tasty, contrasting everything she was expecting.

Brandon stuck his straw in as well, leaning in to take a sip once Lauryn pulled away. The two of them begin to take turns swigging their frappuccino. They were both nervous to go in at the same time, but Lauryn decided to take initiative. Now she was close to him, disregarding all established rules of personal space. But neither of them pulled away. They both stopped sipping, oddly not having the desire to keep drinking - although it was delicious.

Lauryn thought about what poetic things he was thinking as they stared at one another. She'd read various entries about how fond he was of her eyes. A smile graced her lips at the thought of it. He was so sweet. Just then, Brandon mustered up enough confidence to lean in a bit further. He connected their lips gently. When they parted, they just grinned wildly at each other.

"Sorry," Brandon blushed as he resumed his seat.

He apologized. He apologized for kissing her. She thought that just had to be the sweetest thing in the world. Lauryn realized in that moment that she was completely smitten with the boy sitting across from her. It didn't really matter to her if he was sketchy sometimes. That behavior only surfaced whenever she talked about the journal. So she just wouldn't bring it up anymore.

Chapter 6

Lauryn was on cloud nine. She and Brandon were inseparable. Things were going smoothly. In the heat of it all, she'd forgotten to make time for her friends. To make up for it, she invited the girls for a day out at the mall, but the only one available to come was Cammie. She felt bad for partially ignoring her friends ever since Brandon had become a factor in her life. She got so caught up, it was easy to forget to set aside time for her friends. She wanted to correct her mistakes.

Lauryn wanted it to be just them, especially because Brandon had to work on Sundays. That just wasn't how the cookie crumbled. Naomi had dance rehearsals, Diana got stuck babysitting, and Allie was on her own date with Trevor. Cammie wasn't doing anything, much like she *never* did anything. Even if she had been, she would've freed up her time to accompany Lauryn at the mall anyway.

They were casually strolling through the mall. Cammie was in a state of bliss, it kind of felt like she and Lauryn were on their own date. She found herself looking at things that way quite often. She liked to pretend, even if only for a little while. It was all she had left. But Brandon corrupted her imagination too. Lauryn had received a text from him, who had found out he had the day off upon arriving to work.

Lauryn wanted to take advantage of his day off, but she was with Cammie. She felt guilty that she thought of Cammie as a burden in that moment. She frowned and looked over at the smiling girl by her side. Cammie was *not* a burden. It was just rather unfortunate that she was here right now. She wanted to be with him. Surely she couldn't abandon Cammie for Brandon, but maybe she could convince her to let him come.

"Camz?" Lauryn prompted quietly.

"Yes?" Cammie asked. Her heart involuntarily fluttered in her chest at the nickname.

"Um... Do you mind if Brandon comes? He found out last minute that he didn't have to work today... If you don't want him to, I can just hang out with him later, but-" Lauryn rushed her words, but Cammie silenced her by raising a hand.

"No, it's fine. Of course he can come..." Cammie forced a smile. She didn't know why, but she was expecting this. Brandon tagged along everywhere, like a puppy. A puppy that stole people's future girlfriends and journals.

"Are you sure? It was kind of supposed to be just us. Well, the other girls too... But they couldn't, you know. So now it's just us. And if he comes, that would kinda defeat the whole purpose of this... You're really okay with him coming?" Lauryn clarified, even though she had already told him to come to the mall.

Cammie sighed. She would just have to get used to this. Lauryn had a boyfriend. This was her reality, and she was going to have to succumb to it eventually. "Yeah," she nodded.

Cammie had tried to forget about her feelings for Lauryn multiple times in the past. It never worked. Now was no exception. She tried to fool herself into believing that her crush on her had passed, but could it even be called that anymore? Cammie was nearly in love with her. She knew she was. There was no point in denying it to herself. But she found that it started to hurt less whenever Lauryn talked about Bread. Her heart didn't plunge when she had to give her advice or listen to her rambling about him. She didn't feel like crying every time she saw the two of them together. She was actually beginning to accept it, or she was getting really good at ignoring it. Probably the latter.

Now she was just third-wheeling with them. She detached herself from the couple and inserted her headphones in an attempt to ignore *them* the way they were ignoring *her*. They were milling in and out of various stores, searching for nothing in particular. Brandon and Lauryn were basically attached at the hip. Cammie was trailing behind. She found herself simply watching Lauryn. That girl was so interesting to look at. What had always been a favorite pastime hadn't faded. Even from behind, Lauryn was beautiful. Her hair, her walk, her body, her clothes, her ass, her stature, everything was perfect. She was annoyed by how much attention she paid to every little detail of the girl who would never spend time doing the same things, but she could never avert her eyes.

Cammie didn't know what had happened, but when she tuned into her surroundings she saw that Brandon and Lauryn were apart. When she looked up, he was walking out of the store. Had she really been that lost in her admiration? She had absolutely no idea what had just gone down. But Lauryn turned to face her, so she smiled.

"Are you ready to go?" Lauryn questioned, and her smile followed soon after.

"Yeah, I guess," Cammie shrugged.

Lauryn smiled and slipped her hand into Cammie's, once again restoring the intimacy between them. Lauryn paid close attention to how Cammie responded to that action. She saw the way her cheeks flushed. She noticed the small smile that played on her lips. She almost wasn't able to detect it, but it happened. When Lauryn intertwined their fingers, she noticed how Cammie pursed her lips and swallowed harshly.

Cammie was just wondering why Lauryn was holding her hand. She'd just gone from two hours of ignoring her existence to holding her hand. The shift caught her off guard. She figured it was because Lauryn felt guilty for not speaking to her. Lauryn did things that way. She was always overcompensating for something.

"Camz?" Lauryn asked as she started to swing their linked hands.

"Yes?" Cammie answered. She surprised herself by how clearly that came out. In addition to her surprise, she tried to ignore the way her heartbeat spiked upon hearing the familiar nickname, even though it was the second time today.

"You don't really like Brandon, do you?" Lauryn asked intuitively.

What? Why was she asking that? What on earth could've given her *that* impression? Cammie was *extra* nice to Brandon, just to make sure Lauryn wouldn't suspect anything. "Yeah... Sure I do... Why do you ask?" Cammie asked nervously.

"I don't know," Lauryn shrugged. However, she did know. She could see straight through Cammie's facade. Cammie's smile always reflected in her eyes. If her eyes weren't smiling, Cammie was not truly happy. Lauryn could read Cammie like an open book. Or at least, she thought she could. Everyone else would beg to differ.

"Well..." Cammie started out carefully. "It's not that I don't like him... But I guess I just kinda feel like he's taking you away from me..."

Lauryn frowned when she heard that. She'd never intended to be *that* girl, the one that was obsessed with her boyfriend. The thought that she was had never once crossed her mind. An immense sense of guilt washed over her when she thought about it, realizing that she actually was. She was very guilty of what Cammie had accused her of.

"I'm sorry..." she mumbled as she thought some more about it. "Wow... Shit, I'm sorry..."

"It's okay," Cammie acquiesced. She let it go, like she let everything go. To Cammie, Lauryn could do no wrong.

"No... That's such a shitty thing for me to do... And I didn't even know I was doing it..." Lauryn spoke truthfully, genuinely feeling bad about her actions.

"It's fine. I mean, like you said, you didn't even know you were doing it, Laur," Cammie offered in an attempt to ease her guilt.

"I'll be more careful. I won't hang out with him as much anymore," Lauryn said determinedly.

Cammie reluctantly accepted that solution. Lauryn's preferable response would've been *I'll break up with him because he's a piece of shit, and I'll date you instead.* But she knew how farfetched and impossible that was.

Lauryn unexpectedly pulled Cammie into her arms, hugging her unnecessarily close. She pressed her entire frame into Cammie and held on tightly. She felt like if she physically showed her that she was sorry, it would correct all of her wrongdoings. She was certainly right. Cammie melted into the hug and breathed in her scent, daydreaming about cuddling her this way all the time. But it ended all too soon. Lauryn and Cammie were separated once more and reality had slapped her in the face yet again.

"Let's go get ice cream," Lauryn said happily. "Then we can *really* go shopping, I'll even buy you something. I'm gonna make it up to you, Camz," she promised as she took Cammie's hand.

»»»»

"She said I didn't like Brandon," Cammie shared with the three of her friends. Lauryn was out with her family for the night. They were situated at Diana's house, snacking on various foods and candies.

"Why?" Allie asked. "You like him as much as we do," she added, clearly unable to read her friend as well as the others.

"Yeah, well..." Naomi agreed, although she could see where Lauryn was coming from. She assumed how Cammie probably felt towards him, although she would never admit it.

"He seems like a tool to me," Diana said casually as she helped herself to the chips.

"I get that vibe too," Naomi nodded.

"He just seems really generic," Cammie allowed herself to say, figuring that it didn't blatantly show her distaste for the boy.

"Come on y'all, am I the only one that really likes him?" Allie whined.

"No... I mean, I liked him at first... But there's something weird about him," Naomi shrugged, unable to name anything specific.

"They're not right for each other," Diana scoffed. "He's no Trevor," she said to Allie.

"Yeah, y'all are perfect for each other. Brandon and Lauryn are just..." Naomi trailed, scrunching her face in disapproval.

"Wrong," Cammie finished for her. *Disgusting* seemed to suit their relationship better.

"But anyway, Cam, we know you don't like him that much," Naomi redirected the conversation.

"He's okay," Cammie responded. There. She didn't confirm or deny it. It wasn't like she could just admit that she almost hated his guts. She blindly reached to get herself some pretzels, but her hand collided with the empty plate. She sighed and picked it up, leaving the group to go refill it.

As soon as Cammie was out of earshot, Diana leaned in and lowered her voice. "How do y'all know Cam doesn't like Brandon?"

"I wouldn't like the person coming between me and my crush either," Naomi shrugged.

"Oh... Yeah," Allie seconded.

Diana just stared at the two of them, completely dumbfounded. "How long have you guys known?"

"Um, forever?" Allie laughed.

"She's not exactly good at hiding it," Naomi laughed as well. "Cam has liked Lauryn since freshman year, at *least*."

"Well shit," Diana breathed. "I didn't know you guys knew. She's so obvious and she doesn't even know it..."

"Who's obvious?" Cammie asked as she returned with a plate filled with far too many pretzels.

"Nobody," Allie answered quickly.

"Okay," Cammie shrugged. She wasn't really concerned with their gossip.

"How long do you think they'll last?" Allie resumed their previous conversation.

"I don't know. Not too long though, since he's sketchy as hell," Diana scoffed.

"Yeah, like what she told us at lunch... I don't think it's his journal. But I'm not gonna be the one to tell her that," Naomi reasoned.

Diana exchanged a look with Cammie, practically begging her to them it was hers. Cammie quickly avoided her gaze, and Diana sighed.

"Cam..." Diana said just loud enough for her to hear.

"No," Cammie said stubbornly.

"They already know anyway," Diana mumbled under her breath, but Cammie perceived what she'd said.

"They already know the journal is mine?!" Cammie shrieked, completely disregarding her inside voice and their whispering.

"That's not what I was talking about," Diana laughed. "But yeah, they do *now*... Nice."

"Wait," Naomi said as her jaw dropped. "That's *yours*?"

Cammie felt like she was definitely under attack. This had to have been a setup. A ploy. A scheme. They'd constructed this to fool her into disclosing her deepest secret. If that wasn't what they'd already known, what the hell did they know?

"Wait... Diana, what were you talking about..." she asked nervously.

"They already know you love Lauryn," Diana shrugged. Anyone with eyes could tell.

Well, shit. Her secret was out, if it could even be classified as such. Cammie guessed it wasn't that much of a secret anyway, seeing how blatantly she admired her. The whole world could see it, but it didn't matter if Lauryn didn't.

"Oh," Cammie mumbled.

Allie laughed, causing Naomi and Diana to join in. They weren't necessarily laughing *at* Cammie, it was just the fact that she thought they didn't know. Was she being serious? Did she really think she'd kept all of her staring and loving gazes subtle? Or her feelings in general under wraps?

"We just never said anything because we didn't want to make you uncomfortable or something," Allie giggled. "But the journal is yours? I kinda knew it was..."

"Same," Naomi nodded calmly. "We were right. Allie, you owe me five bucks," she reminded her with a smirk.

"You guys aren't surprised...?" Cammie wondered as she looked between her friends, all of which were casually sitting there. Apparently not. They'd made a bet on it. She was expecting them to freak out.

"I mean, I guess I kinda figured it out. You always got so sad or like, annoyed or something whenever she talked about him or the journal... I just kinda put it together," Naomi explained.

"Oh yeah, that makes sense," Allie nodded, just now catching on.

"Yeah, Cam. I told you, you needed to watch all that," Diana laughed, gesturing towards her conflicted friend.

"Oh," Cammie responded dumbly, then fear struck. If her friends had caught on, surely Lauryn had too. "Do you think she knows?" Cammie asked, although the chances were slim.

"I don't know," Diana answered with a shrug. "She hasn't broken up with Bread yet, so probably not," she elaborated, catching onto Cammie's peculiar nickname for the boy.

"True," Cammie breathed. Okay. Good.

"Why haven't you told her yet, though?" Naomi questioned.

"She's so happy," Cammie sighed. "That would hurt so badly, realizing that her boyfriend has been lying to her the whole time... And she really likes him..."

"Wrong again. Lo doesn't like *him*. She likes who she *thinks* he is," Diana countered. "She only likes him so much based off of the journal. If you think about it, *you're* the one she really likes."

42

"Yeah, exactly. Before the journal, she barely even knew who he was," Allie added.

"Oh yeah, you're right..." Naomi realized, then she frowned. "That's so annoying. Who *does* that? I don't like him."

"Same," Allie nodded.

"Same," Diana seconded.

"Same," Cammie added, although it was universally understood.

"So... Are you gonna tell her?" Allie asked, not really understanding why she hadn't yet.

"Nope," Cammie shook her head immediately.

Diana was growing exasperated with this whole situation. She rolled her eyes and diverted her attention to her phone. Anything was more interesting than listening to Cammie explain her disposition for the hundredth time. They just went back and forth. She accepted the fact that Cammie would most likely carry that open secret to her grave.

»»»»

"He's so sweet," Lauryn gushed as she picked at her food. "He's been leaving me little poems in my locker. Every time I go to my locker, there's a new one in there," she smiled.

The fivesome were sitting at yet another lunch period. Although Lauryn had promised to alter her behavior about Brandon, she found that she couldn't help herself. Two of the five were growing increasingly more annoyed as the days passed. The other two were feigning interest, becoming slightly irritated at her incessant talk of her boyfriend. Nonetheless, they all offered supportive comments.

"What do they say?" Allie asked with a smile.

"The one from today was so cute. Hang on, I'll show you," Lauryn smiled as she retrieved a folded piece of paper from her bag. She unfolded it and read it aloud.

Peter Pan once said that if you think of beautiful things, you'll fly. But when I think of you, I fall every time.

Lauryn was smiling down at the note like a lovesick fool, understanding the implication. At first, she'd thought he'd called her ugly. Then, she realized that it meant he was falling for her with every thought, and she was even more endeared with him. While she was distracted, Naomi made eye contact with Cammie from across the table. Naomi subtly raised her eyebrows, silently asking Cammie if she was the culprit. Cammie nodded slightly, confirming Naomi's suspicions. Diana and Allie saw the interaction while Lauryn was still rambling.

"I think you should make him tell you something in person," Diana suggested with a smirk. Her desire to out Brandon was becoming overwhelming.

"He doesn't do that. He said he gets his inspiration whenever he's thinking about me," Lauryn smiled.

Wow, some excuse. Cammie thought that was just pathetic.

"That sounds like bullshit. Why would he have to think about you and write later when he has you standing right in front of him? He could literally just *tell* you..." Diana scoffed.

43

"Yeah... That sounds a little weird..." Naomi agreed.

Lauryn thought about their claims for a second. Well, she *had* thought it was rather strange that he couldn't come up with *anything* on the spot. But she trusted him. She really didn't think he would lie about something their relationship founded on.

"I trust him," she defended her boyfriend.

"He could still tell you in person..." Cammie mumbled. Oh wait, no he couldn't.

"What's you guys' problem?" Lauryn challenged, feeling admittedly defensive for some reason.

"Nothing," Diana shrugged and shoved a spoonful of yogurt in her mouth.

"You guys have a lot against him. You don't even know him," Lauryn scoffed.

"Lo, do *you* even know him? You're getting so involved and I just really feel like something isn't right about him..." Naomi added cautiously.

"People who wholeheartedly believe something they assume of someone they do not know and have never spoken to are so funny to me," Lauryn laughed bitterly and stabbed at her salad.

What the hell were they trying to say? What couldn't seem right about him? Have they even talked to him before? Whatever. She trusted him. She believed in him. And she was going to see him and sort all of this out. Right now.

Lauryn got up from the table and pushed her chair in. She picked up her tray and gave the girls a fake smile before walking away to the trash cans. She dumped her tray and left without a second glance at the table. Brandon had the lunch period right after theirs. Waiting on him for those answers seemed like her best bet. She leaned against the wall with her arms crossed over her chest, waiting for him to round the corner. As soon as he did, she grabbed his jacket and pulled him to the side.

"Brandon? Can I ask you something?" Lauryn asked urgently.

"Yeah, what is it? What's wrong?" Brandon asked as he leaned in for a kiss, but she turned her head and evaded his lips.

"What is your favorite thing about me?" Lauryn asked. That was a simple answer. He'd said it in writing an infinite amount of times.

"Uh... Your eyes?" Brandon stated in confusion.

"Is that all you can ever say to me? Yes, I *know* you like my eyes... But isn't there anything else? What else do you think about me?" Lauryn pressed, giving him another chance to redeem himself.

"You're beautiful..." he trailed off. He was beginning to get nervous. What was she going on about? "What's wrong, babe?"

Physicalities. He could only name fucking physical things about her. Nothing about how appreciative he was of her mind. Nothing about how level headed and strong willed she was. Nothing about how intelligent and knowledgeable she was. Nothing at all. But then again, had he ever? She couldn't recall a time when Brandon had uttered anything more than stupid observations about how pretty she was. It was flattering, but that really wasn't what she was looking for. She wasn't fishing for compliments, she was desperately looking for a reason to keep believing in him.

"Don't you like anything *else*?" Lauryn emphasized as she stepped closer to him.

"Your body is great," he smirked as he gave her the once-over.

44

Lauryn was fed up. Her hand struck his face with more force than she was planning, but she was enraged. "Did you even write that fucking journal? Is that even yours? Grow some goddamn balls and tell me something you would've written!"

Brandon was stunned. Holy shit. He was both confused and aroused all at once. Mad Lauryn was becoming one of his new favorites, but his prevailing emotion was apprehension. He knew his time was running out. He just had no idea how it would all surface.

"I... Uh..." he struggled to come up with anything. "Um... You- Uh..." he stuttered. He was making a fool out of himself. Lauryn had given him an ample amount of time, and now she was done. Diana, Allie, Naomi, and Cammie had all watched it go down from around the corner.

Lauryn ran her hand through her hair and simply walked away from him. Her face was red and her fists were shaking as she made her way down the hall. She clenched them and wiped her angry tears. Fleeing the scene quickly, she just wanted to be alone. She strode towards the only place she knew she would be at this hour.

Chapter 7

Cammie felt her own heart clench as she watched the confrontation. She could see Lauryn breaking by the second. That hurt her more than it had probably hurt Lauryn.

When she saw Lauryn make a break, she was still standing there, completely frozen. Her mouth hung open. Her gaze was fixed on where Lauryn had just exited through the door, clearly crying and obviously upset. Cammie felt like crying too after seeing what had happened. She'd understood how much Lauryn wanted to believe Brandon. And she saw the way her trust just crumbled.

"Go find her. Talk to her. Calm her down. I've got this. His beat down is *long* overdue," Diana said in a low voice that gave Cammie a chill. She pushed her out of the way, and Cammie shuffled down the hall quickly. She took Diana's threat to Brandon very seriously and didn't want to be there to witness the aftermath. Or murder. She didn't want to see that. She wanted to go console Lauryn.

Cammie knew just where to find her. Unless she actually ditched school and went home to cry like Cammie did that one time, she should have a pretty good idea of where she went. Her need to comfort her increased as the seconds ticked on. Her power-walk sped up to a jog. Soon enough, she entered the staircase and easily distinguished the sobs coming from above.

She slowly approached her, not wanting to brave the backlash that would come from the situation. Lauryn was volatile when she was upset. More often than not, Cammie was able to get through her barriers and get her to confide in her about the roots of her problems. She hoped her luck would play out this time, not wanting Lauryn to push her away in the heat of the moment. Cautiously approaching her, she made herself visible before she spoke. Lauryn sensed her presence and slowly looked up at her with puffy eyes. The sight made Cammie want to run over and hug her forever.

"Go ahead," Lauryn said sardonically.

"What?" Cammie questioned. Wait, did she just read her mind?

" *'I told you so'*. Go ahead. Say it," she requested bitterly as she shifted her gaze back down to the floor.

Oh, okay. No mind reading had commenced.

46

Cammie steeled herself as she grasped the railing. "Lauryn... You know I'm not gonna say that..." she countered quietly as she slowly took a seat next to her.

"How could I be so fucking stupid?" Lauryn mumbled to herself rather than Cammie.

If she was being honest, Cammie was wondering that too. Despite the occurrence, she definitely wasn't going to second that while her best friend was crying. As she looked over at her, she saw that Lauryn was hunched over with her knees to her chest. Her face was hidden in her arms, and she was breathing heavily. Cammie felt awkward. Should she hug her? Should she rub her back? Should she just leave her alone? She didn't know, but continuing to idly stand there was not an option.

She slid a bit closer to Lauryn, cautiously putting her arm around her. Lauryn leaned into her slightly, and that was all of the confirmation Cammie needed. She pulled Lauryn into a full-fledged hug, disregarding the tears or snot that were sure to stain her shirt later on. Lauryn sobbed quietly into Cammie's chest, trying not to be too loud or obnoxious.

Lauryn wondered why Cammie was even there. She had literally just blown up on her at the lunch table, yet here she was holding her like none of it had happened. Lauryn had a soft spot for Cammie, and defining moments like these proved why. She took initiative to care for her and make sure she was okay while the other girls went on about their business. Allie did sometimes, but it was mostly Cammie. Cammie was the one there, holding Lauryn in her arms and unknowingly mending her broken pieces.

Moments like those confused Lauryn. She went over her theories about Cammie being the author with a clear, open mind. It was basically anyone's game now, wasn't it? She was simply making comparisons, it didn't have to mean anything. Right? Because she was probably wrong. Right? Presumably so.

As she considered the factors, she figured that the person that wrote those things seemed likely to do *exactly* what Cammie was doing now. They would react the *same* way. And Cammie *did* tell her how fond she was of Lauryn's intellect and intuition – often, at that. Cammie wrote songs too, ones with lyrics that made Lauryn pause and think – much like the writing in the journal did. And Lauryn always used to see her scribbling in a little book sometimes in the back of class. She never saw her doing that anymore. Oh, God. Everything was making way too much sense.

"Camz, was it yours?" Lauryn asked suddenly as she leaned back to look at her.

Cammie's heart started pounding. She wasn't supposed to ask that. What made her think that? Why was she bringing this up to Cammie now, when all of that had just transpired? She'd just endured a rather messy break up, or what Cammie hoped was a break up. If she found the two of them together tomorrow, she just might slap Lauryn the way she slapped Bread. Well, no she wouldn't. She wouldn't dare lay a finger on her. But she would want to.

But could she tell her now? Was it safe? They weren't under the same circumstances now. Lauryn was in tears, and Cammie was terrified that her confession would push her over the edge. What that edge was, specifically, Cammie had no idea. And beyond the initial precautions, she knew she didn't want to cross and boundaries or imaginary friendship lines. Once she confessed, it was going to be out there forever. Lauryn would know. It wouldn't be her little secret that had been less than expertly concealed. This was it. She probably wouldn't get another direct chance like this any time soon.

Just as she opened her mouth to speak, the door opened. Jesus Christ. The universe just did not want her to confess. Every time she was about to, something happened. She was going to disregard the interruption until a deep voice boomed and resonated throughout the small staircase.

"You two, get down here. *Now*," Mr. Roberts demanded. The girls quickly complied, getting to the bottom of the stairs as fast as their feet would allow. "What are you doing in here?" he asked rhetorically. Lauryn was about to answer, but he beat her to it. "*Skipping*."

Shit. They were in trouble. Cammie knew it when she saw him whip out a notepad from his pocket. The words were upside down from her position, but she could make out that they were detention slips. Great.

She exchanged a nervous look with Lauryn, then looked back up at him. He really was huge, and kind of scary. Lauryn sensed Cammie's nerve and slipped her hand into hers. She wanted to protect her. She thought she was helping, but that didn't calm Cammie's racing heart at all. Cammie had never had detention before. She worried what her mother would think as they were being written up. And now Lauryn was holding her hand. There was no way she wouldn't pass out.

"Do we have it today? After school?" Lauryn assumed as she quickly wiped her face with her free hand.

"No. You have it now," he answered as he continued to scribble on the small piece of paper. "What are your names?"

Reluctantly, but obediently, they told him. Albeit, they considered going by a fake name, but figured that would only land them in more trouble. Writing based off of the pronunciation, Mr. Roberts didn't spell either of their names correctly. 0 for 2. Cammie noticed the butchering of their names and nudged Lauryn so she could get a kick out of it, too. They both stifled their laughter for fear of getting in more trouble.

He ripped off the two sheets and handed them to the girls. He then directed them to the detention classroom. Cammie didn't even know detention *was* a class, and she really didn't know it could be held during school. As they approached the classroom, she began to realize that the ISS students and detention students were grouped together. She was basically a delinquent. What would Sonya think now? Her mind started drifting off into the inevitable life of crime ahead of her. Slowly, but surely Lauryn's grasp on her hand started to have its intended purpose. Lauryn calmed her down a little. Lauryn was there. Cammie was being ridiculous, anyway. All she did was skip class, she wasn't a criminal. This was harsh punishment for skipping.

They entered the classroom hand in hand and were surprised to find three other familiar faces. Naomi, Allie, and Diana sat in a row, looking painfully unamused. Naomi was resting her chin in the palm of her hands. She didn't even know they had guests. Allie was sitting still with her hands clasped together in her lap. Diana was tapping her pencil on the desk. Cammie and Lauryn stood before them and smiled at the irony of the situation. Somehow, they'd all found themselves in detention. The fact made Cammie laugh, announcing their presence to the other girls.

"Wow," Allie laughed along. She figured that Mr. Roberts had rounded them up in the same fashion he'd nabbed them in the hallway. They'd lingered a little too long after the bell, and now here they were. The gang's all here.

"We got in trouble," Lauryn stated the obvious with a small laugh.

"You don't say?" Diana asked sarcastically.

"No talking," Mr. Smith reprimanded them.

"Sorry," Cammie mumbled, although she hadn't uttered a word.

"Sit down, no cell phones, no iPods, no talking, and no sleeping," he said monotonously.

Cammie and Lauryn walked over the other girls, their fingers still intertwined. Their hold was tight, but they let go begrudgingly when she had to sit down. Cammie was sitting behind Naomi and Lauryn was sitting behind Diana. Cammie just sat there idly, wondering what to do in detention. She didn't have any work, and she didn't have her journal. She was instantaneously bored. Lauryn brushed her knee to get her attention, mouthing the words *Do you have a paper and pen?* Of course she did. She handed it to her.

"Thank you," Lauryn smiled.

"You're welcome," Cammie grinned back.

"*No talking*," Mr. Smith said again.

"Sorry," Lauryn apologized this time, then she took to writing. She pondered how to restate her question. She'd asked Cammie in the stairwell, but of course they'd been interrupted. Somehow, now they were in detention. Cammie's answer to her question was integral. She wrote out her question, the same way she'd asked it earlier. Taking a deep breath, she folded the paper into four and was about to place it on Cammie's desk.

"What is that?" Cammie asked, quickly forgetting that she wasn't supposed to be talking. Diana turned around at the sound of her voice and saw the folded piece of paper in Lauryn's hand. The disturbance caused Naomi and Allie to turn around too. All of the shuffling got Mr. Smith's attention. Lauryn sighed and crumpled the paper.

"Okay, split up. You, stay there. You, over there. You, in the back. You, in the middle. And you, in the back on the other side," he directed them in annoyance.

The girls reluctantly complied. Three of the five were left wanting to know what the piece of paper contained, one of them was nervous about what it most likely did contain, and the other was anxious to get her answer. But now that they were separating, they couldn't figure it out as easily. They were each about three desks away from each other on all sides. No whispering would be perceivable, so now they had to stick to notes. Cammie and Lauryn were the furthest away from each other. So she waited until the detention supervisor was distracted once more, then she threw the paper across the classroom to Cammie's desk.

It flew with enough force to make it over there. Cammie attempted to catch it, but miscalculated. The paper hit her in the face, proceeding to bounce off and roll onto the floor. Lauryn and Diana giggled at their terribly uncoordinated friend, entertained by the whole scene. Cammie rubbed at where it had hit her, then bent down to pick it up. She shared an uncertain look with Lauryn once she had it in her possession. Well, here goes nothing. Cammie tediously unfolded the paper, prolonging the process to stall what she would have to read. She did it with good reason.

Camz… Was it yours?

When she read Lauryn's print, she nervously glanced over at her. Lauryn's eyes had been trained on her the entire time, carefully watching her demeanor. Cammie looked back at the paper and tried to ignore the way Lauryn's gaze was boring into the side of her head.

She retrieved another pen from her bag and went to work. She figured it would be easiest to tell her this way. Through writing, she always expressed herself better. She wasn't going to be fancy. She wasn't going to use big words. She wasn't even going to ramble on and on about how wonderful she thought Lauryn was. She was just simply going to explain how she felt and why she did what she did. Cammie braced herself and let her pen take over. She hadn't been able to do so in a while. When she was finished, she balled it up again and threw it to Lauryn. Much to her dismay, she overthrew it and it landed on Mr. Smith's desk. Wonderful.

Cammie was horrified. She wanted the world to just open up and swallow her whole. Why did this keep happening to her? Her writing always ended up right in the hands of the wrong people. She buried her face in her hands and waited to be yelled at. But it didn't come. When she peered up, she found him smiling down at the paper he was reading. She felt a little embarrassed that he was even reading it at all, but a smile had to have meant something good, right? To her surprise, yes. He got up and placed the paper on Lauryn's desk, then he slunk back to his desk.

Well, that was a change of plans. Cammie anxiously waited for Lauryn to read it. This was it. It was time. She carefully watched how her expression changed. She saw every subtle eyebrow raise and each time her lips parted in surprise. She saw the way her eyes darted across the paper. And she saw the way tears began to brim in them. If she wasn't mistaken, she was... Crying? Oh god, why was she crying? But as Cammie strained to look closer, she saw the small smile she had as she continued to read. She willed herself to believe that they were happy tears, and she relaxed.

Lauryn was completely enthralled. She was reading the paper so intently. Her script was still messy, but Lauryn had had enough practice deciphering all of it. She read it easily, and she found answers to questions she didn't even know existed. As she read further, her mouth hung open in shock.

Yes. Fine. It is mine. That is my journal, that was my writing, and those are my feelings. Oh, yeah, and I'm the one who left the poems in your locker. I'm not going to go into detail about it because I'm pretty sure you know...

But I bet you're wondering why I didn't tell you. Well, it's because I saw how happy he made you. You deserved happiness like that. For some reason, I was okay with the fact that it wasn't me making you that happy... Because you were happy. That's all I ever cared about, Lauryn. Your happiness directly correlates with mine. Seeing you happy with him made everything alright in my world. And I guess that's selfish, but I hope you can see that I mostly did it for you.

I know you're probably mad at me for not telling you all of that stuff. Not telling you it was my journal, not telling you I had those feelings for you, not telling you that Brandon was lying... All of that makes me a terrible person. The only excuse I had was that it made you happy. And seeing your smile every day at lunch while you were talking about him made me feel something I can't even describe. It was weird how it made me smile and broke my heart all at once. It hurt so bad every day, but I was completely fine with it at the same time.

I don't want to cross any boundaries... Well - actually... I'm pretty sure I've crossed every single one by now...... But I guess I can finally tell you that I love you.

It's not the way you mean, though. I really... actually... truly love you. I am in love with you. I think I've always been. And I always want to tell you... I try to... You say it, and I say it back... But you've never known how true it was. You've never known how much I meant it. You've never understood the weight of those words. I say it all the time, hoping that just maybe, you'll miraculously understand. I hoped you'd see it. And you didn't. And you probably wouldn't have if all this hadn't happened. But it did happen. And I don't know, I guess it kind of feels good to get this off of my chest.

I wrote all of my feelings in that journal because I thought of it as my safe haven. And... When it wasn't that anymore, I got scared! I didn't have the closure I usually had... And then when he claimed it... I guess I kind of lost hope. I've always known there was no real chance of me and you actually becoming a real thing, but it was nice to imagine. And he took you. He took you from me when I didn't even have you. I couldn't voice my opinions in my journal anymore so I guess that's why I've been acting weirder than usual. I've retreated from everyone, but that's not really your fault either.

But anyway, I know you'll probably be weirded out or think it's gross or something, but I can't help the way I feel. Sorry.

That letter was all over the place. Lauryn read it time and time again. By the time she was finished, the words were blurry. She was overcome with emotion. The fact that she'd truly found the author of the journal made her happy. The fact that she'd been being lied to for about a month now infuriated her. The fact that she was right in her suspicions about Cammie made her giddy. The fact that Brandon took advantage of Cammie's situation pissed her off more than she'd expected. The fact that Cammie thought she had to hide her feelings made her sad. And the fact that Cammie had secretly gone through all of that made her feel guilty and stupid for not realizing it sooner.

She felt a tidal wave of emotions. Crying felt like the best way to express it all. She continued to reread it until the last bell of the day rung. The realization hit her hard, but it wasn't necessarily a bad thing.

Cammie was unlikely, but not that unlikely. Part of Lauryn knew all along. She *knew* that was Cammie's handwriting, but she had been convinced otherwise. She noticed her behavior. The connection shared between the two of them wasn't like that of their other friends. She was most intimate with her out of the other three girls because it just felt *right*. Their friendship had been very touchy from the get go. Lauryn didn't have an explanation for that, because she'd never questioned the nature of their friendship.

However, she didn't exactly reciprocate Cammie's deep feelings. She didn't love her, not the way Cammie did. But she'd thought she liked her a few times before. She would be lying if she said that going past friendly intimacy hadn't crossed her mind before. And it would be a bold-faced lie if she said she'd never considered their status as being more than friends. She could easily date Cammie. Kissing her wouldn't be too outlandish to be considered. Even so, she'd repressed any sort of feelings that had budded for Cammie over the years. She didn't want to ruin what they had, just in case their feelings weren't mutual.

Meanwhile, Cammie had taken Lauryn's silence as a form of rejection. She was mentally kicking herself as the silence prolonged between them. Although it wasn't necessarily between *them*, the fact that they had to be quiet in detention had easily slipped her mind. She figured that Lauryn would read it and write something back. But she didn't. She kept it in her possession for the rest of the day, not even looking over at Cammie. She didn't know how to take her reaction and just wanted to get out of there as soon as possible. As soon as the dismissal bell rung, Cammie was gone.

While Cammie fled, Lauryn hesitantly got up. She kept skimming over the note. Its value had become a bit sentimental to her. She thought of it as the first step of a new direction. Lauryn wanted to talk to Cammie about it and discuss it after their detention session was over. When she looked in her area, the seat was empty. Cammie was long gone. She'd immediately vacated the room as soon as the bell rung to avoid it.

Lauryn frowned and figured she would just talk to her about it in the morning. She was willing to regard her friendship with Cammie with an open mind. She definitely wasn't against the idea, and she wasn't mad that she'd kept it from her. For the most part, Lauryn thought it was adorable and rather sweet. Cammie clearly put Lauryn's feelings before her own. How could she possibly have any ill-will towards someone with such selfless motives?

Sure, it would take a little time to get used to the idea. Cammie seeing her that way was perfectly fine, and kind of predictable. But Lauryn didn't know if she could see herself with Cammie that way right now. The idea of being in a relationship with her and going past their small cuddling sessions and hand-holding might've been a little farfetched. She could see sharing kisses with her, but for now, that was about it. Lauryn started to see Cammie in a completely different light.

Chapter 8

Lauryn waited patiently for Cammie to board the bus the next day. Sleep hadn't come easy the night before. She was restless with the idea of Cammie being something more than the best friend she'd regarded her as for all of these years. The possibilities of what could come of her confession excited her. She didn't know what to expect. She desperately wanted to talk it through with her.

Cammie had slipped away from detention yesterday. She'd gotten lost in the crowd before Lauryn could talk to her. Then she missed the bus, but Lauryn was starting to think she'd done it purposely. She knew all about Cammie's habit of avoiding problems by *literally* avoiding them. Lauryn wanted to explain that she wasn't a problem. There was nothing awkward going on and there was no tension. Lauryn wanted to clear up her position before Cammie had the chance to assume anything.

Nameless faces continued to pass by her. When she saw Cammie's flushed cheeks, she grinned. She had her head down, staring down at the floor instead of what was in front of her. Lauryn found the way she gripped her book bag's straps and chewed on her bottom lip awfully cute. Cammie was sort of hoping Lauryn had missed the bus today. She wasn't ready to talk about it. She wasn't in the mood to be shut down and rejected.

"Camz!" Lauryn squealed when Cammie got in earshot. For the first time in her life, it was a voice Cammie dreaded hearing.

Cammie sighed and lifted her head. She offered Lauryn a meek smile as she continued to make her way down the aisle. She was planning on occupying the seat next to Diana, but Lauryn grabbed Cammie's wrist and pulled her to sit right beside her. "Sit by me," Lauryn pleaded.

Although she didn't necessarily want to, she knew she was going to. Cammie would end up doing anything for Lauryn, and it annoyed her. So she slid off her book bag and plopped down next to Lauryn, prepared to get it over with. She was expecting awkwardness and a bit of hostility. Why wasn't she speaking? Cammie turned to face Lauryn and saw her staring back at her with a tender expression. It made her uncomfortable. She was having trouble reading her. She had absolutely no idea what to expect of the face to face confrontation.

"Hi..." Cammie mumbled, sufficiently making things awkward.

"Hey," Lauryn smiled. "Are you okay this morning?"

"I guess..." she shrugged. Was she trying to soften the blow by making small talk first? Maybe that was it, keep the small talk going.

"Okay. Well, I just don't want you to feel weird about what you told me yesterday. I actually wanted to-" Lauryn began, but Cammie interrupted her, sensing where the conversation was headed.

"I don't. But guess what Sophia did this morning," Cammie prompted with a small smile.

Even in the relative darkness of the bus, Cammie's smile was bright enough to make Lauryn pause. Instead of wanting to say what she needed to say, she wanted to hear Cammie's little story. So she went along with it. As long as Cammie wasn't feeling bad about her confession, Lauryn assumed all was well.

"What did she do?" Lauryn asked.

"She put hand soap on her toothbrush... Like instead of toothpaste," Cammie laughed lightly.

Actually, that was what Cammie did this morning. It was a mistake she'd made in her sleepy haze. How she could've gotten those two mixed up, she didn't know. But she felt like it was a more socially acceptable thing for her younger sister to have done than her. Then she wondered why out of all things, she'd decided to share *that* with Lauryn. But whatever, keep the small talk going.

"Wow," Lauryn smiled.

"You should've seen her face," Cammie forced another laugh. It was a dumb thing to be talking about, but it was keeping them preoccupied.

"That's so cute," Lauryn said, smiling to herself at how quirky all of her family members were. She was casually going along with Cammie's story, she didn't want to abruptly bombard her with questions. She was waiting until the right moment.

"Yeah, and then I was like *that's not what toothpaste looks like...*" Cammie continued. Actually, that was what Sophia said to Cammie. But Lauryn didn't need to know those minor details.

Lauryn was patiently waiting for this conversation to taper off so she could bring up what she really wanted to discuss. She wanted to broach the subject politely. She didn't want to make it seem like she didn't care about Sophia's antics from the morning, although she was quickly losing interest.

"Yeah... Soap is a bit different than a tube of toothpaste..." Lauryn agreed with a nod.

As the school came into view, Cammie smiled to herself. She had successfully stalled the conversation. Lauryn groaned to herself and rolled her eyes. She wanted to talk to Cammie about her note from yesterday. But she got stuck talking about fucking soap and toothpaste, of all things. Lauryn was annoyed.

"Camz, I wanted to talk to you about what you said..." Lauryn said tentatively.

"We don't have to," Cammie brushed it off, already collecting her things and putting on her book bag.

"I know we don't *have* to... But I want to. Will you come over later then?" Lauryn suggested.

Cammie thought about it. In the privacy of Lauryn's house, it eliminated the possibility of everyone finding out by eavesdropping. Diana, Naomi, and Allie were sort of notorious for that type of thing. Although they already knew, actually having the talk with Lauryn about it seemed like it should be private. It was kind of a personal thing, and she didn't want them in on her personal drama. She didn't want Lauryn in on it either, but it was happening. She couldn't avoid it any longer.

"Okay," Cammie hesitantly agreed.

»»»»

When lunch rolled around, all of the girls were skeptical about how it would play out. Three of the five were eager to find out details of what exactly had happened in detention yesterday, while the other two were apprehensive. By this hour of the day, Cammie and Lauryn had both psyched themselves out of even having the conversation.

They'd gone through the line quietly, and now they were sitting at the table in silence. No one was even eating, because - well, who would eat *that*? It looked disgusting. All of the girls were engrossed in examining and picking at their food. They were all waiting for someone else to break the silence.

"Why are y'all being so quiet?" Allie asked, making all heads turn at the sound of her voice.

"I don't know," Naomi laughed.

"Awkward..." Diana seconded with a short chuckle.

"I guess I was waiting for them to go on and say what happened yesterday," Naomi disclosed, gesturing to the two girls opposite to her.

"Nothing happened," Cammie responded. That technically wasn't a lie. Nothing did happen, because she'd bailed faster than she ever had before.

Diana waved her off and turned to Lauryn. "What happened?"

"She's right," Lauryn laughed, referring to the brooding girl next to her.

"I mean, *something* happened..." Allie insisted.

"She gave me a note... That's all," Lauryn shrugged, sensing that Cammie wasn't too keen on this conversation.

"You guys are so difficult... Why are you so difficult?" Diana sighed.

Lauryn pursed her lips and shifted her gaze to the table. She didn't know what the girls knew and what they didn't. She didn't know what Cammie would allow her to say and what she wouldn't. She wished there weren't so many secrets between them.

"Can I tell them?" Lauryn asked in Cammie's ear.

"They already know," she mumbled, loud enough for the other girls to hear.

"She told you?" Naomi asked.

"Finally," Allie laughed.

"Three thousand years later," Diana said monotonously. "I guess you finally grew some balls."

"I told her everything," Cammie shrugged. "So, everything's all out there in the open. I think I'm gonna die."

"Camz, don't be ridiculous," Lauryn frowned. It was clear to her then exactly what Cammie was thinking. She felt the need to set her straight, but not in front of the girls.

"Yeah, don't beat yourself up about it, Cam," Naomi said softly as she grabbed her hand across the table.

"It's weird with her knowing - like - she *knows*," Cammie reflected out loud.

"I think we've all known for a while," Allie laughed in an attempt to make light of the situation.

"True," Diana seconded.

"What ended up happening with Brandon?" Naomi brought up, earning her a death glare from Lauryn.

All of the girls had witnessed their confrontation. They were each willing to provide comfort and support for their friend if she needed it. They'd all assumed how hurt she must've been from it at first, but she seemed unfazed sitting before them now. Naomi was asking for clarification, knowing how mercurial Lauryn could sometimes be.

"We're not gonna talk about him," Lauryn scoffed. She'd pushed him far from her mind. She hadn't so much as given him a second glance since yesterday. He'd bombarded her phone with calls and texts of endless apologies. She'd ignored all of them and blocked his number. He'd come up to her multiple times in the hallway. She didn't even acknowledge his presence. She was cutting him off, just like that. There was nothing he needed to say to her. His actions were disgusting and inexcusable.

"Yeah... Let's not," Cammie agreed. She did not want to hear any more about Bread preferably for the rest of her life. She'd heard way too much for her liking. They all had.

"Okay..." Naomi said dejectedly.

An awkward silence settled between them until the bell rung. That was the way Cammie preferred it. They all got up and threw away their trays and vacated the cafeteria. Cammie and Lauryn went their separate ways, leaving Naomi, Allie, and Diana with no more answers than what they'd started with.

»»»»

Lauryn waited impatiently all day for school to be over. She wanted to talk to Cammie about the note and the journal and *everything* so badly. She let Cammie sit by herself on the bus, because she wasn't about to be passive when they reached her house. She had questions, and she was determined to get her answers. When they reached her stop, she motioned for Cammie to go with her.

"We're finally alone," Lauryn began once the bus pulled off. "So... Tell me, why didn't you ever tell me before?" she asked as they made the short walk to her house.

Well, she was wasting no more time today. Cammie lowered her gaze to the ground. She focused on her feet as she was walking down the street. She was quickly running out of ways to avoid this conversation. She'd literally done everything. Maybe she could fake injury. Surely Lauryn wouldn't press her for information if she was lying in a hospital bed. Would she? Probably so. So scratch that.

"Cammie," Lauryn groaned.

Cammie mustered up all of the willpower she had, which wasn't much to begin with. "What was the question again?" she tried to further stall the conversation, but Lauryn wasn't having any of it.

"You heard what I said. Please just answer me..." Lauryn requested in annoyance.

"Okay," Cammie sighed. "I already told you why I didn't tell you... In the note..."

"No, not why you didn't tell me about Brandon... I understand that. I meant why you never told me that you had... Feelings..." Lauryn said, carefully choosing her words.

"Oh, because I didn't know how you would react. And I thought it would get awkward. And I was right," Cammie muttered as she kicked a rock.

"*I'm* not the one making things awkward..." Lauryn countered.

"What do you mean?" Cammie asked as she looked up at Lauryn for the first time since they'd gotten off of the bus.

"You're anticipating all of this stuff happening... And you're reacting based on assumptions. You don't even know what I think," Lauryn shared as she fumbled for the key to her front door.

Cammie stood behind her and waited. It then dawned on her that Lauryn was absolutely right. She should have an open mind about this. Not *too* much of an open mind, or she would end up being as delusional as she was before. She had to approach this with a logical and practical mindset. Cammie followed Lauryn up to her room, determined to sort this out rationally.

When Lauryn pushed through her door, she tossed her bag onto the floor. Cammie entered soon after and her jaw dropped. Now lining the walls were a plethora of Cammie's ramblings. Pages from her journal had been cut out and displayed all across Lauryn's room. Cammie stood in the doorway absolutely dumbfound.

"Oh, I um... Made some changes. Do you like it? Or is that weird? Do you want me to take it down?" Lauryn asked tentatively.

"No... Don't take it down. I'm flattered," Cammie joked, slowly returning back to her usual self. "It's quite the renovation."

"I did it a few days ago... And I kept it up because I thought it was beautiful," Lauryn shared as she sat on the edge of her bed.

"Even when you found out *I* wrote it?" Cammie asked. She was so surprised.

"Even when I found out *you* wrote it," Lauryn nodded with a small smile.

"Wow," Cammie breathed as she sat down next to her. She wasn't too close. She perched herself a good distance away from Lauryn.

"You have a gift," Lauryn praised her with a smile.

"Not really," Cammie disagreed modestly.

"It kind of freaks me out that all of this came from you," Lauryn added, then she realized how that probably sounded. "Not like in a bad way. It's just like, I've known you this whole time and I never knew you were capable of doing *that*."

"It's whatever," Cammie waved her off. She really wasn't that amazing. Lauryn thought so highly of it because all of her writing was centered around *her*.

"Like I knew you were good with words and stuff, Camz... But damn," she laughed. "Have you ever thought about making that a profession?"

"Lauryn, what do you really think?" Cammie asked suddenly, wanting to get to the root of the conversation. She was tired of running from her problems. She was about to try a new tactic. She'd never really addressed things head on. She always drip-fed information. Being forward wasn't necessarily her forte, but she was willing to try.

"What do I think?" Lauryn repeated. "About your writing?"

"No... You know what I mean..." Cammie mumbled, her cowardice returning. She was incredibly uncomfortable with acknowledging her feelings aloud. There was no way she could've come out and said "What do you really think about me being in love with you?" That was non-negotiable.

"I guess I'm a little shocked..." Lauryn answered honestly. "But I'm not surprised. Does that make sense?"

"Yeah," Cammie nodded.

"I could've seen it coming. Diana was right, I *did* write your name for a reason. I just didn't put any thought into it. I counted you out before I considered you," Lauryn admitted.

Cammie nodded. She agreed. But wait, Diana? She should've known Diana wouldn't have held her tongue. "Why do you think you wrote it?"

"I don't know. We do things that normal friends don't..." Lauryn trailed. "But I never considered it as a real thing..."

"Yeah..." Cammie shrugged.

"You know the process I went through when I was making those lists. You fit every description. I thought about it then, and I was just like no. It's not that it being you would've been weird... But I just wasn't expecting it. I guess if I'd actually paid attention, I could've figured it out. This all explains why you weren't that eager to help me look for the person," Lauryn laughed. "I guess I just didn't look at it from an outside perspective. The moment you appeared on those lists, I disregarded you completely. I knew something was different, because why else would you be on them? But like I said, I just didn't see it as something real."

"Yeah, exactly. I guess that's where the lines got blurred for me. You know I've never been in a *real* relationship before. Aiden obviously doesn't count," Cammie laughed. "I knew it wasn't real. But it felt that way. And then I liked to pretend that it was... Because you were the closest thing to one, I guess."

"You think your feelings are on a blurred line?" Lauryn questioned, feeling a bit offended. However, she didn't know why she did. Part of her wanted Cammie's feelings to be real.

"Not anymore..." Cammie shook her head subtly.

"Oh, okay," Lauryn responded. Good.

"Wait, what does that mean though? You knew our friendship was different?" Cammie wondered aloud.

"I think I liked you for a minute too... I just stopped myself because - well, you're a *girl*. That would've made things difficult on *so* many levels. Do you know how awkward that would've been if you didn't feel the same way?"

Cammie did know. She knew all too well. But wait, holy shit. Did she just say...? "What did you say? You thought you liked me too...?" Cammie reiterated incredulously.

"I guess..." Lauryn shrugged, just now realizing what she'd let slip out. But was it really a slip? Part of her wanted Cammie to know how she truly felt, but the other part of her wanted to savor what she currently had with Cammie. Lauryn was scared of change. And that little blip could make a world's difference.

"Why?" Cammie pressed.

"Because you're an amazing, beautiful person. You're crazy passionate about all of the right things... You're sweet, kind, and loving... You're drop dead fucking gorgeous, but you're modest as hell. And you're smart and witty... You're actually funny, Camz. Although it's usually really dumb and lame, you're funny without ever being mean. And I love that. You're so selfless and genuine and caring, it would be hard *not* to like you. And on top of all of that, your little hands are so soft and perfect to hold. And your body is the perfect size for cuddling and hugging..." Lauryn rambled, then she stopped suddenly.

Holy shit. She was going on and on about Cammie, and she had so much more to say. She thought she'd suppressed her feelings to the point where they had diminished, but clearly that was not the case. They were very much so present. It resonated with her that she actually might've still had some feelings *left* for the brown-eyed girl. The said girl was now staring at Lauryn with her mouth agape, incredulous about everything that she'd just said.

Cammie had been expecting a mediocre answer like "You're funny" or "You're nice". But she knew she'd underestimated Lauryn. She'd underestimated her a lot. She could barely form a coherent thought, let alone respond to that admission.

"Sorry," Lauryn mumbled.

Cammie had yet to speak. She felt so drawn to Lauryn. She eliminated most of the distance between them and gently coaxed Lauryn into a hug. That simple gesture made her heart flutter and her cheeks flush. Lauryn was the humming in her veins. No words were exchanged, they just hugged. Cammie rested her chin on Lauryn's shoulder and held on tightly. Lauryn soothingly ran her finger along Cammie's side. It was just instinctual, but she couldn't deny the intimacy felt in that gesture. Friends didn't do that. And if they did, it didn't leave them with butterflies in their stomachs.

Lauryn didn't deny it to herself anymore. She'd suppressed those feelings for so long, and they were resurfacing now. Full-fledged. She surprised herself when she realized her eyes were locked on Cammie's lips. An air of realization settled between them. Now that it was established that they both had *some* type of feelings for each other, Lauryn didn't second-guess her next action. Go big or go home.

She grasped Cammie's face and cupped both cheeks, gently pulling her towards her lips. And God, it was unlike anything she'd ever felt before. Lauryn kissed as if she was scared, her lips were hesitant to move. Cammie felt as if her heart was in her throat rather than her chest, it was beating so erratically. Lauryn felt an incredible sense of peace, yet every fiber of her being was alive. Lauryn had kissed boys before, but she'd never had that groundbreaking moment they rave about in the movies. If boys had lips like Cammie's, maybe she would've kissed them a little more often. She had never once experienced the fireworks or butterflies when kissing *them*. However, kissing Cammie now, she felt it all and then some.

The delicacy felt in this gesture had never been replicated. Cammie's lips were so *soft*. Lauryn mentally kicked herself for not doing it sooner. She kept her lips pressed to Cammie's for a few seconds more, then she hesitantly pulled away. Lauryn didn't want to overwhelm her. Lauryn didn't want to overwhelm herself either. They were both ambivalent about the situation. It wasn't even like they'd made out. No tongue was involved at all. It wasn't even necessary, because her lips were more than enough. Lauryn wanted to kiss her again, but refrained in fear of her own feelings.

Meanwhile, Cammie was damn near a heart attack. Lauryn always roused these feelings within her, but this was borderline dangerous. If her heart beat any faster, she was absolutely certain that she'd be going into cardiac arrest soon. She'd only dreamed of kissing her. But never in a million years could she have prepared herself for *that*.

She was so happy. She wanted to run through fields of flowers and cartwheel in the grass. She wanted to squeal out of sheer happiness and pure joy. She wanted to scale a building and express it from the rooftops. Okay, maybe not that. She would probably fall or something. But she was oh so happy.

In reality, she was frozen. Her mind and body weren't making the connections. She was staring at Lauryn in shock. Lauryn had been trying to gauge Cammie's reaction with no luck. Cammie reached up and touched her lips where she'd just been kissed. She feared she'd just had a scarily vivid daydream. But her lips were still tingling. Her heart was still racing. That was real. Her mind couldn't possibly have fabricated that and left her feeling that way. When she registered that it *was* - in fact - real, a smile graced her features.

"Sorry," Lauryn excused herself meekly. She didn't exactly know what was on the criteria for kissing your best friend. What was supposed to happen next was lost on her.

"Me too," Cammie seconded and cast her eyes elsewhere, now feeling just as awkward as Lauryn did.

"What are you sorry for?" Lauryn laughed and wished she'd look back at her.

"I don't know... What are you sorry for?" Cammie giggled as well and reluctantly glanced back up at her.

"I don't know..." Lauryn laughed even louder.

They both overcame the awkwardness following their kiss with a fit of giggles. Weakened by those incessant giggles, Cammie fell back onto the mattress. Lauryn followed her lead and draped herself over Cammie's legs. They didn't even know why they were so tickled, but they were laughing with no end in sight. Perhaps it was the effect of being so giddy from it all.

Once both girls had settled down a bit, Lauryn's door opened and Tori peeped inside. "It's time to eat... Cam, are you staying for dinner?"

Cammie and Lauryn exchanged a look, then Cammie nodded resolutely. Lauryn picked herself up and Cammie followed suit. With a new wave of determination and confidence, she slipped her hand into Lauryn's on their way out. Lauryn intertwined their fingers and led her downstairs with the feeling that things were about to change.

Chapter 9

Days after their kiss, Cammie was still reliving it. It was only about five seconds, but it was probably the best five seconds of her entire life. No exaggerations there at all. She'd ranked it higher than seeing Demi Lovato in concert, meeting Ed Sheeran, *and* getting Harry Styles to follow her on twitter. It easily surpassed her entire relationship with Aiden. She was even willing to bet that kissing Lauryn was better than bananas. Maybe not. Maybe it was a close second. No, it was definitely better. Who was she kidding? Being kissed by Lauryn was by far her greatest accomplishment.

With a new sense of enlightenment, Lauryn had given her journal back. Cammie had spent hours that night describing their kiss with ridiculous clichés. She'd compared it to things that didn't even make sense. Nearly eight pages were scrawled about the kiss alone. And she wasn't even halfway finished yet.

When Monday rolled back around, she entered the school with a glow. Diana took notice of the way she couldn't stop smiling on the bus. She was usually groggy in the mornings or staring at Lauryn. God, she could be so creepy sometimes. But as she looked over at her, Diana saw that Cammie was doing no such thing. She was smiling dumbly, looking straight ahead. Diana looked over at Lauryn and saw that she was curled up listening to music. Lauryn slept in the morning most times too. Cammie wasn't even looking at Lauryn, yet she was still smiling like an idiot.

Her smile didn't falter the rest of the bus ride. Diana didn't have the energy to ask her about it then, but decided that she would later. It hadn't faded in the slightest, even as they were getting off of the bus. Diana trailed behind Cammie with a smirk, waiting for her to share. But Cammie kept it to herself the entire way to her locker. She sensed Diana's gaze on her and turned around.

"What?" Cammie laughed as she began to put in her locker combination.

"You tell me," Diana responded as she put in hers as well.

"Tell you what?" Cammie played coy, but that smile of hers was awfully telling.

"Girl, please. I know something's up. That dumb smile hasn't left your face since you got on the bus," Diana shared. "Oh my god... You got some didn't you? Oh shit, Cam!" she jested playfully.

"No, Diana... Ew, shut up," she laughed.

"Who was it? Was it Sean? Aiden?" Diana continued.

"I'm gonna slap you," Cammie warned as she got her necessary books.

"Seriously though, why are you so smiley?" she asked as she jabbed Cammie in the ribs.

"You wouldn't believe me even if I told you..." Cammie grinned once more at the thought of what had happened three days ago.

"Try me," Diana challenged.

"I kissed Lauryn," Cammie shared. Then her stomach flipped. It always did that whenever she recalled the event. She was almost getting used to the sensation.

"For real, what?" Diana dismissed her statement.

"I just told you..." Cammie lowered her voice to a whisper. "Lauryn and I... *Kissed*."

"You *did*?" Diana asked incredulously. She was so hesitant to take her seriously. Cammie often mixed up her delusions with reality and spewed her fantasies to Diana all the time. Was now any different? Or was she kidding again?

"Yeah..." Cammie nodded vigorously. Then she rested her head against the locker and squealed involuntarily. It was an inhuman noise that almost startled Diana.

With that, whatever it may have been... Diana believed her. "What the hell did I miss?"

"I have a lot to tell you," Cammie began and laughed from her genuine happiness, then she disclosed all of the details. Every glorious moment was relived and she recapped the confrontation with accuracy. After every couple of sentences, she made Diana endure her fangirling session because she couldn't quite contain herself just yet. The butterflies were relentless today. She still needed a second or two to scream after almost every admission. Diana listened patiently, assuming how hard it was to talk about something she was so excited about.

"Damn, Cam... You pullin'," Diana laughed when she'd been completely filled in.

"Not really," Cammie disagreed once she'd found her composure.

"Really? You don't just kiss people for no reason. Y'all are probably gonna date sooner or later," Diana assumed. "I hope it's sooner, for your sake."

Oh, God. Cammie sure hoped so. She balled up her fists in excitement. Her cheeks were starting to hurt from so much grinning. She figured that after a certain amount of time, she would stop losing her shit about it. Apparently, that time hadn't come yet.

"Do you think so?" Cammie asked.

"Based on what you said, yeah. She said all that stuff about you and then she kissed you. *She* kissed *you*. Not the other way around. I don't know about Lo, but I wouldn't be kissing someone I didn't like like that," Diana shrugged.

"I hope you're right," Cammie sighed. Then she smiled. Again.

"Y'all are so cute. I hope you do," Diana smiled. She wanted the best for her best friend. The prospect that she could've been dating one of her other best friends soon was a little odd, but she would support them nonetheless. After all, they would be adorable together.

»»»»

Cammie resumed her previous routine. She always used to sit in the stairwell between periods and scribble something about Lauryn. She could see why no one ever came in here. The light was out and it was rather dim and dusty. Now she was continuing her earlier entries about their kiss. She had roughly four minutes. Various kids passed in and out of the staircase as an alternative route to get to class. Cammie usually dismissed them all. But when the green-eyed girl entered, somehow she knew. She subconsciously looked up and saw her approaching her. Maybe she had Lauryn radar.

"Hey, Camz," Lauryn waved. "Why did I know you'd be in here?" she laughed. Maybe she had Cammie radar too.

"I don't know," Cammie shrugged goofily. "What are you doing in here?"

"I wanted to see you," she responded. "And here you are," she giggled.

Her laugh was among one of Cammie's favorite sounds. She stopped and looked up at her. If Cammie thought she was beautiful before, she had no idea. Her laugh was easily the most beautiful thing she'd ever heard. It was raspy and warm. The butterflies in her stomach still hadn't calmed down, and she was sure she was looking up at her like she was Jesus or something.

Despite all of that inner turmoil, she answered calmly. "Well, I guess you found me..." Cammie laughed as she closed her journal.

"I guess I did," Lauryn grinned as she sat next to her. "I'm gonna tell you something, okay? Don't freak out."

"Okay," Cammie nodded. She didn't know what to expect.

"In case it wasn't clear from Friday, I guess I've figured out that do still like you. I didn't want you to spend any time wondering or anything. So there you go," Lauryn said easily.

Cammie briefly admired her courage. How the hell could she admit that so effortlessly? That virtually took no obvious mental preparation. If only she could've exhibited that confidence before. And she found it ironic that she'd told her not to freak out. She was having trouble not freaking out just by being in her presence. And then she goes and admits something like that? No way. Cammie tried though.

"Oh," Cammie responded dumbly. She didn't know what to say. The smile that followed made Lauryn smile as well.

"Yeah," Lauryn nodded. She felt that everything was settled for the most part. There wasn't enough time to discuss it further, because it was only class change and they'd be late soon.

"Really?" Cammie asked hesitantly.

"Mhm," Lauryn hummed.

"Oh my god," Cammie breathed. Suddenly, everything was turning out in her favor. All of the stars were lining up. She didn't remember rubbing any lamps, but some genie was granting all of her wishes. She tried to recall everything she'd wished for in her mind, but came up short. She brushed it off right when Lauryn started to speak again.

"I couldn't act like the kiss didn't mean anything to me, Camz. So I thought about it over the weekend and just kind of came to that conclusion..." Lauryn admitted as she slipped her hand into Cammie's. She stood up and tugged on

63

Cammie's hand, motioning for her to stand up too. "I just wanted to tell you. There's something there. But I mean, I don't want to move too fast. Like, I don't wanna rush things. I like you but I don't think I'm ready to like... Date or something, you know?"

"Yeah," Cammie nodded resolutely. There was no way this was happening. She could barely believe her luck. She wanted to take chances. She was usually so passive. Whenever opportunity presented itself, she psyched herself out of it. But she was going to take advantage of this. She had to, she couldn't be a coward her *entire* life. With a spur of confidence, she popped her next question.

"But... Can I kiss you again? That wouldn't be rushing it... Would it?" Cammie asked nervously as her gaze settled on Lauryn's lips.

"Um... Sure," Lauryn agreed hesitantly. Their relatively open location was grounds for caution. If someone were to walk in like Mr. Roberts did the other day, she didn't want them to find her in a compromising position. And she especially didn't want them to find her in a compromising position with a *girl*.

Lauryn removed her hand from her grasp and lifted it to her chin, pulling her into another soft peck. Her lips didn't linger for long, but her heartbeat had increased exponentially. Why did kissing Cammie make her feel this way? She was right. There was *definitely* something there. She recognized it when she pulled away and met her eyes. There was an intangible pull between them, and neither of them were looking away. Subconsciously, she felt herself leaning in again. The moment their lips connected the second time, Lauryn melted into her.

She rested her books on her hip and settled her hand on Cammie's waist. Cammie was too enamored to move. Lauryn couldn't contain herself. She swiped her tongue against Cammie's bottom lip, beginning to deepen their kiss. Cammie was so overwhelmed, she didn't exactly know how to reciprocate. Which was fine, because Lauryn had no problem with taking the lead and guiding her through it. Time caught up with them and the bell rung. Cammie was the first to pull away.

Lauryn sheepishly smiled at Cammie and took her hand once more. They were late, but they didn't care. Lauryn took her time going to class. She'd even taken a detour just to walk Cammie to hers. Then she chivalrously moved her hand from Cammie's grasp to rest around her waist, leaving Cammie's mind spinning. Their relationship had really gone 180 degrees. What Lauryn was doing or thinking now, she had no idea. But she was loving it. If dating Lauryn was going to be this way, she couldn't wait.

Once Lauryn had dropped Cammie off, she reflected on what the hell she had just done. It was so weird. After she kissed Cammie, she'd had the insatiable urge to be affectionate with her. She craved closeness and her touch, but she couldn't place why this was happening so suddenly. Holding her hand had quickly escalated to holding her by her side. And one little peck had escalated into some sort of slow make out session. She was the one who'd stressed taking it slow and not rushing anything, but here she was initiating everything. Her doubts and suspicions plagued her mind for most of the day.

Oddly enough, it was also on Diana's mind. The more she thought about it, the more likely it seemed for the pair to end up together. They acted like a couple for the most part anyway. The only new thing would be the title, and maybe a little kissing. But she didn't know how Lauryn felt about it all. It was still in her thoughts when lunch came around.

When she got her tray and headed towards the table, she smiled to herself at the sight of Lauryn and Cammie next to each other. Cammie was *still* smiling.

Lauryn was grinning rather hard as well. It warmed Diana's heart to see her friends so happy after seeing them feel so low. She wanted them to be happy *together*. In that moment, it surprised her how much she wanted them to work out.

"Hey Diana," Naomi greeted her as she reached the table.

"Hey Naomi," Diana reciprocated. "Hey Allie, hey lovebirds," she addressed Allie, then Cammie and Lauryn as one. It went unnoticed though.

"How's your day going?" Allie asked sweetly.

"Pretty good. How's yours?" she answered.

"It's okay. How's y'all's day?" Allie addressed the other girls.

"Amazing," Cammie gushed as she shyly glanced at Lauryn.

"What made it so amazing?" Diana laughed.

"Lauryn and I-" Cammie started, but was rudely nudged in the side. When she looked at her, Lauryn was frowning. She shook her head no subtly then looked down at the table.

Diana faced the two of them suspiciously. Wait, Cammie and Lauryn what? What was she going to say? That they kissed? Diana assumed so. But why didn't Lauryn want Cammie to tell them? Diana narrowed her eyes at the suspicious girls, but decided to let it go.

"What? What did y'all do?" Allie questioned. They'd all been left hanging.

"We uh... Just... Talked... About um... The thing," Cammie attempted to lie. Really, it didn't make any sense to be that much of a terrible liar. She looked over at the expert, but Diana would be of no use to her right now. Diana was in the dark as well. She hadn't told her that she'd kissed Lauryn again on the stairs. It felt sentimental to her. She didn't have to share everything with Diana.

"We sorted out everything about the journal," Lauryn added.

"You guys are always hiding something," Diana shook her head.

"I'm not hiding anything," Lauryn said rather defensively.

Cammie felt awkward. Why couldn't she tell them about their kisses? She was sure they'd be happy for them. She didn't really understand why Lauryn wanted to hide it.

"There's just always something going on. And y'all always tell us after the fact," Allie explained.

Was she being obvious? Lauryn looked down at the table and hoped the girls would infer that they had their separate problems going on. She really didn't want them to catch on to the situation arising with Cammie. She just wanted to solve everything by herself without it being speculated. Not to suggest that she didn't trust the girls, it had more to do with the fact that she was uncomfortable at this moment. Judgement was also a factor. It would be a precaution to any type of relationship with your best friend - especially when it was one who also happened to be a *girl*. She didn't want to deal with any of that now.

»»»

Lauryn was left brooding about the events of the day many hours after they'd occurred. The direction things were going was starting to worry her. But it excited her at the same time. It was the most terrifying exhilaration. The more she thought about it, the more she could see herself actually being in a relationship with Cammie.

As she looked over at her sitting across from her, she envisioned her being her girlfriend for a second. Cammie was curled up in the seat by herself, listening to music. She was dancing subtly, unaware of the fact that she now had an audience. Her head bobbed to the music and her little feet were tapping. She seemed so in her element. Cammie was in her own little world. And Lauryn could see the two of them dating. She wanted to share that world with Cammie. They were feasible.

Lauryn smiled at the thought of presenting her as her girlfriend to everyone, then kissing her in front of them. The thought alone caused the butterflies to return. The three chaste kisses they'd shared left her feeling something she'd never experienced before. It was only logical to give a relationship a shot. But how does one go about these things? It was well established that their feelings were somewhat mutual. So should she just ask? Or should she wait a little longer? What could possibly prevent them from dating if they'd both recognized their feelings? Lauryn didn't know, but she was determined to find out.

"Camz, can you come over again?" Lauryn asked as she reached across the aisle to get her attention. When Cammie removed her headphones, Lauryn repeated her question.

"No, I have to watch Sophia today. You can come to my house though?" Cammie offered hopefully.

"Okay," Lauryn smiled. She looked out of the window and saw that they were approaching her stop now.

"Come on," Cammie motioned as she began to pick up her belongings.

The bus came to a stop and Cammie shuffled down the aisle with Lauryn right behind her. Once outside, the two girls walked side by side in a comfortable silence. Cammie was clutching her journal to her chest. Her eyes were trained on the ground, watching her feet. Lauryn's eyes were trained on Cammie.

She was assessing every feature and every insignificant detail. She noticed trivial things like how long her eyelashes were. And she saw Cammie's frequent habit of biting her lip. She was chewing on it now, seemingly deep in thought. The little mole on her forehead was so cute, and Lauryn smiled at how cute it was. A few wispy hairs were blowing in the wind, and Lauryn kept grinning at how beautiful she was.

Cammie sensed that she was being watched. She turned to face her, but to her surprise, Lauryn was already staring at her. She quickly averted her gaze and her cheeks flushed. This was the first time Cammie had blatantly caught her staring, but she was conscious of it most times. Lauryn liked to look at Cammie just as much as Cammie liked to look at Lauryn. She didn't think either of them minded the extra attention. If it were anyone else, she would've probably given them a dirty look or scoff at their invasive eyes. But not with Lauryn. Everything was different with her.

"What are you thinking about, Camz?" Lauryn asked intuitively, disregarding the fact that she'd been caught staring.

"Lunch..." Cammie answered.

Shit. Yeah, they'd have to talk about that. Lauryn wasn't exactly proud of her behavior. "What are you thinking of specifically?" Lauryn continued, although she had a pretty good idea.

"Why didn't you want me to tell them about how we kissed?" Cammie asked. It had been bothering her all day. What if Lauryn regretted their kiss? What if she was a bad kisser and Lauryn didn't want to talk about it? What if she was just experimenting? Had she changed her mind? It couldn't be over already, could it? It had just started. Instead of overthinking, Cammie ultimately decided to hear her out.

"I got scared," Lauryn answered. "It was a shitty thing to do... But that's the truth. I wasn't really prepared for what they'd say about it, I guess. I just... Want it to be an *us* thing... For now."

"Oh, okay," Cammie accepted her answer. As long as she wasn't regretting it. She wasn't... Right? Better make sure. "It's not because you regretted it or something, right?"

Lauryn stopped walking and grabbed Cammie's hand to halt her as well. She didn't know why she felt the need to stop, maybe because it was important. "No, Camz... Why would you think that?"

"I don't know," Cammie shrugged. She second-guessed herself quite often. Good things didn't usually happen to her. And if they did, she always messed it up somehow. Or it turned out to be a joke. Neither of those situations were desirable for her, so she usually tried to fend off anything that had the potential to hurt her feelings.

Lauryn knew Cammie was doubting her. She saw it in her subtle responses, in those eyebrow raises and shrugs. She wanted her to believe her. Lauryn was well aware of how insecure Cammie was about nearly *everything*. She didn't want her to have feelings like those towards their budding relationship. Was that what it could be classified as now? She didn't know. But whatever it was, she wanted Cammie to have faith in it.

"I'll put it this way, if I regretted it... I wouldn't have kissed you the second or third time," Lauryn expressed. But she felt like she should prove her claim. She pulled Cammie up to her and quickly looked around to see if they had an audience. They didn't. So she kissed her again, just a short peck to prove her point. "And I wouldn't have kissed you just now. Trust me, I don't regret anything at all. It's not like that."

Cammie didn't fight her on it this time. Lauryn grinned and grabbed her hand again, continuing on their way to Cammie's house. They didn't really talk on their short trip there. That was mostly due to Cammie not trusting herself to speak, and Lauryn not wanting to ruin anything by talking too much. So they just walked in silence until they reached her house.

Chapter 10

"I think my face is going to fall off," Cammie laughed.

The two of them were sitting on Cammie's bed. It was twin sized, which forced them to be closer together. Neither of them minded that at all. Lauryn was leaning against the headboard and Cammie was laying against Lauryn. Lauryn's arms were clasped loosely around Cammie.

Lauryn strained to look at her, quite alarmed at her admission. When she saw her smiling, she relaxed. "Why?"

"I've been smiling all day. And now my face hurts, but I can't stop," Cammie answered through her laughter.

"You're so cute," Lauryn shook her head and resumed her previous position. "Why have you been smiling?" she asked even though she already knew. She just wanted to hear her say it. An ego boost, perhaps.

"You," Cammie answered simply.

"Me?" Lauryn asked coyly as her smile returned.

"Mhm. And it's so weird because you've never noticed until I lost my journal," Cammie noted. "I always used to smile because of you. Literally, all the time."

"I just thought you were happy," Lauryn giggled. "I'm probably the most oblivious person on earth..."

"Not the *most*... But you're definitely in the top three," Cammie teased.

"Shut up," Lauryn responded playfully. "You should be nice to me, because I could easily push you off of the bed."

"Like you would though," Cammie challenged.

"Try me," Lauryn quipped with a smirk.

"I won't," she laughed, because Cammie wasn't exactly sure how to "try her". So she just dropped the conversation there.

She leaned further into Lauryn and much to her delight, Lauryn's grip on her tightened. She was being held securely by the girl of her dreams. Cammie's head fit perfectly between Lauryn's neck and shoulder. She was so close to her now. And Lauryn's scent was heavenly. She was so hesitant to do anything before, but as the time passed, so did her tentativeness. Cammie turned slightly and cuddled into Lauryn's side. Lauryn smiled subconsciously and trailed her fingers along her side. Cammie leaned up and pressed her lips to her neck chastely. She was finally able to act on the impulses she'd always had. Now that she was uninhibited, she barely knew what to do with herself.

Cammie was looking up at Lauryn's side profile, and she struggled to find a flaw. She looked at her few acne spots and completely disregarded it. She saw her bushy eyebrows and thought they were flawless. She thought they suited her. She even looked down at her double chin and smiled, that suited her too. Lauryn was so cute. She knew those were Lauryn's main insecurities, but she couldn't bring herself to find something wrong with any of them – none of her.

"This is perfect," Lauryn sighed as she continued caressing Cammie's side. She'd mindlessly began drawing shapes. She stilled her hand and simply rested it on her thigh.

"Yeah," Cammie nodded. "It feels so natural."

"Right?" Lauryn agreed. She'd cuddled with Cammie before, but never so intimately like this. To her, it had always been platonic. Now, she felt a lot with the simple gesture.

Cammie did too, but she was focusing on keeping her cool. She would definitely have to write about this later. She could lose her shit then. But not now. Now was too perfect to disrupt by her embarrassing fangirling ways. But she couldn't help the way she kept thinking about how their dynamic had drastically changed over the past week.

She'd gone from being basically ignored to having all of her attention. From dreaming, thinking, and wishing about kissing her to *actually* kissing her. Four times, to be exact. She had to hold in the squeal that was threatening to escape. It would probably find its way out involuntarily. She was so fucking happy, that was the only way she knew how to express it.

"I am so happy," Cammie stated the obvious. She had probably never smiled this much in her entire life.

"I am too," Lauryn seconded as she nuzzled her face into Cammie. She kissed her cheek sweetly and went back to the way she was.

Cammie boldly leaned up and stole another kiss from her lips. The smile that followed afterwards made her want to do it again. So she did, this time it lasted longer. She repositioned herself to be comfortable, and Lauryn began deepening the kiss again. Cammie got nervous, not really knowing how to reciprocate a kiss that involved using her tongue. Her kissing experience was awfully limited. How embarrassing was that? She didn't want Lauryn to think she was a bad kisser. So she pulled away before it escalated further.

"I've never really kissed anyone before. Aiden tried... But it felt weird and I didn't want to do it that much. Kissing you has got to be the best thing in the world," Cammie shared. "I could kiss you all day."

"Well, I've kissed *my* fair share of people… And I have to say… Your lips are definitely my favorite," Lauryn agreed.

"You're just saying that," Cammie dismissed her statement.

"No I'm not. I swear, the first time we did, I had this *holy shit* moment. Like I got this weird feeling in my stomach and everything, Camz," Lauryn insisted.

Cammie only smiled in response. She could barely fathom that *Lauryn* was saying this to her. Lauryn took her silence as an opportunity to continue.

"And anyway, boys are so rough. They always go straight to making out... But with you, everything is so slow and soft... I love it," Lauryn admitted shyly. She'd never been this open with her feelings before. Definitely not about kissing, in the simplest form. Any discussion of it was merely a segue into something overtly sexual in nature. Cammie offered a genuine, more pure conversation. It was a concept that was definitely foreign to the both of them.

"Yeah. But that's mostly because I'm too scared to do anything else. I don't want to make you uncomfortable. This is okay, right?" Cammie asked out of insecurity.

"I'm not uncomfortable," Lauryn laughed. Actually, she hadn't been in a mood like this in a while. She was immensely happy laying here with Cammie now. "I just said this was perfect. Guys always want something more. But with you... You just want *me*. In any way… And I can tell. It's so sweet," she continued.

Well, at least she knew. Cammie was glad that Lauryn recognized that she had pure intentions. Not to say that lust wasn't a factor, because it definitely had been... But that wasn't all her desire was based off of. She had deep-rooted feelings and Lauryn was well aware of them. Of course she knew.

"And since you've never really kissed anyone before... Why don't I show you?" Lauryn suggested coyly. She gently pushed Cammie off of her, because her body was going numb under her weight now.

Cammie immediately understood her silent summon and sat upright. "Are you implying that I'm a bad kisser?" she laughed.

"If I say no, do I get to kiss you again?" Lauryn smirked as she sat up as well.

"You get to kiss me regardless," Cammie giggled.

"Then yes," Lauryn joked.

"Interesting," Cammie laughed. Then she wondered if Lauryn was being serious. What if she was, and she was just covering it up with a joke? She had to make sure. "Wait... Tell me the truth, am I? Be honest..." she asked rather insecurely.

"No, you're not a bad kisser at all. But there's nothing wrong with a little practice..." Lauryn trailed as she got closer to Cammie's face.

Cammie was on the far side of the bed, propping herself up on her forearms. She'd interpreted Lauryn's change of position as her being tired of cuddling. But that was far from the case. The more contact they had, the more Lauryn found herself craving it. In an attempt to restore it, she crawled to where she was. She hovered over Cammie with a smirk.

"Practice..." Cammie repeated in the same tone. Their lips were just millimeters away. The slightest movement, and they would be touching.

"Yeah," Lauryn nodded once. "Practice," she laughed. There was barely any distance between them at all, and now Lauryn was nearly straddling her.

Cammie took the initiative to kiss her. As soon as they did, Lauryn eagerly claimed her mouth. She wasted no time in slipping her tongue in her mouth. Cammie was still nervous, but she decided to just go with it. There was no way she could keep avoiding this newfound problem. She would figure out how to do this eventually. With Lauryn as her teacher, she was completely fine with learning the ropes.

The feeling was foreign, but definitely not unpleasant. Lauryn was no Aiden. She felt uncomfortable with him, but Lauryn was so gentle. She'd just started to reciprocate when Lauryn lowered herself on top of her. That was when her mind went blank. Because, holy shit. *Lauryn* was on top of her. Everything had been so innocent up until that point, and it probably still was in Lauryn's mind. But Cammie was in a whole 'nother mindset.

She tried not to think about how she could feel her curves. Or the way her chest was pressed against her own. Or the fact that she was completely invading her mouth in the best way. She couldn't think about any of that. She was supposed to be learning how to kiss. But when Lauryn gripped her waist, she exhaled in a breathy whimper that could've easily been mistaken for a moan. Hands were a no-no. Touching was a no-no. She should probably stop now before she ruined it. She sheepishly turned away, wearing a suggestive smirk.

But Lauryn heard it. She kind of wanted to do something to make her do it again. Lauryn smirked to herself, sensing what was on Cammie's mind. If she thought that going past kissing and cuddling would be weird before, she definitely wasn't thinking that now. In the actual situation, it was actually rather appealing - for lack of a better word. Regardless, she wanted to hear that sound again. Just as she was about to make another move, she heard footsteps coming from the hallway.

Cammie froze and looked at Lauryn expectantly. Lauryn quickly pulled away, waiting to see if the footsteps' destination was Cammie's room. When she heard the doorknob turn, she panicked. Cammie panicked as well and pushed Lauryn off of her, *literally*. Lauryn landed on the floor with a thud right when the door opened.

Sophia, being the blissfully unaware seven year old that she was, didn't notice anything peculiar. Even though they both looked *very* guilty. Their shirts were wrinkled and ruffled and what had commenced was written all over their faces.

"Mami said to come downstairs," Sophia informed her sister sweetly.

"Okay, thank you," Cammie smiled. Then she looked at Lauryn, who was now picking herself up off of the floor casually. She laughed a little and exited to see what Sonya wanted. Sophia fell into step right behind her, leaving Lauryn alone.

With Cammie and Sophia gone, Lauryn ran a hand through her hair and sat down on the bed. Cammie had surprised Lauryn with her grace, she didn't appear to be doing anything inappropriate. Cammie was as casual as ever. She wasn't looking as flustered as they both felt. Lauryn watched her disappear down the hallway with a smile of adoration.

Lauryn really had been getting carried away. She was *not* following her own advice about taking things slow. In that moment, she changed her mind. Fuck going slow. Life was too short to go slow. If Cammie was willing, Lauryn was too. Her sweet kisses were only some of the perks to being in a relationship with her. She figured it would be like their friendship now, except better. As long as there were kisses, she didn't care what their fate was.

When Lauryn kissed her the first time, she hadn't been expecting this. How was she to know that only four days later, she would be making out with her? She'd only briefly pecked her. And now *this* was happening. It was a bit too fast, but she acknowledged how reckless she'd gotten. Rushing Cammie into anything would surely fail them down the line. She thought she should tone it down a bit. She was just coming to that conclusion when Cammie re-entered.

"What did she want?" Lauryn asked as soon as she appeared in the doorway.

"She was just asking how long you were staying," Cammie waved her off as she closed the door once more.

"How long can I stay?" she questioned, not wanting to impose if her mom wanted her to go home.

"I told her whenever you leave," Cammie laughed.

"How specific," Lauryn giggled along.

"Sorry I pushed you," Cammie apologized as she closed the door. A bashful smile was served in Lauryn's direction.

"It's okay," Lauryn laughed.

Cammie crossed the room and sat next to Lauryn. She picked up her hand and played with her fingers. The atmosphere wasn't as lustful now, due to the time Cammie spent downstairs. It was more ludic. They were mellow now. They ended up cuddling again. No more words were exchanged for a while.

Lauryn was still deep in thought about being in a relationship with the girl holding her. She considered the factors that posed a problem. And she considered the factors that benefited both of them. She made some preconceived notions about how certain people would react to the news if it happened. She knew they'd have the support of their best friends. Apparently, they'd known about Cammie's feelings all along. They'd obviously been rooting for them from the beginning. It was only logic that they'd accept them. But what about their families? They didn't even know they were... Wait. They weren't gay, not really. Well, Lauryn wasn't. But Cammie...

"Camz?" Lauryn prompted softly.

"Hm?" Cammie hummed in response, and Lauryn felt the vibration.

"Are you- um, do you like *all* girls?" Lauryn asked, worded quite ignorantly. She grimaced at the way that came out.

"No one likes *all* of anything, Lauryn... What are you asking? My sexuality?" Cammie laughed.

"Yeah," Lauryn nodded with reddened cheeks.

"Well, no. Not really. I guess there are some, but not all... Do you mean like, am I gay?" Cammie inferred.

"I guess," Lauryn nodded again.

"Who knows," Cammie shrugged. "I like who I like..."

"Me too. Why the fuck is sexuality so important to everyone? Who cares who I like or who I don't, or what I like or what I don't, or who I wanna be with or love, like why is everyone so fascinated by something so private and individual! They are my feelings, my wants, your feelings, your wants... Why do we have to label everything and turn it all into a warfare of gender and slander and hate? That's the opposite of love. A person's sexuality should not be and is not as significant as a person's smile, or charisma, or honesty, or pretty soul, or music taste, or - I don't know, important things that make people who they are. Who you love shouldn't describe who you are... And who you love is your choice! Fuck anybody that tells you otherwise, don't let anyone tell you who you're supposed to love," Lauryn concluded with a frustrated sigh.

Cammie was gaping at her, completely awestruck. If Lauryn thought Cammie had a way with words, she clearly hadn't heard *herself* speak. Lauryn was preaching just now. Cammie didn't know what to respond to. More specifically, she didn't know where to start. Lauryn had covered so many topics worth replying to just now, but Cammie was still trying to process everything. She was grateful she'd actually been listening instead of watching her speak this time. If she had missed that little speech, she would've been quite upset.

Lauryn's rant had actually stemmed from some of the things she'd admired about Cammie. Especially the ending. She was a fan of most of Cammie's qualities. Her smile, charisma, honesty, soul, and music taste were just among the first she'd thought of.

"Sorry for rambling. I didn't mean to say all that, I was just-" Lauryn excused herself, but was cut short by Cammie's lips being pressed against hers. Lauryn thought her heart had skipped a beat at the sudden act. Her mind was way ahead of her. By the time her body reacted, Cammie was staring at her.

"This is why I love you," Cammie said a little too candidly, then smiled as she pulled away.

"I love you too," Lauryn reciprocated. Following that impulsive admission, she instantly felt guilty. She knew how deeply Cammie meant what she'd said. And she knew she didn't feel that way, not yet anyway. They both knew. An awkward silence filled the room.

Lauryn didn't exactly know what barrier she had to cross from loving Cammie in a friendly way to loving her in a romantic way. What caused the shift? Were there any telltale signs? She didn't know. But she wanted to figure it out. She felt giddy at the prospect of actually falling in love with the girl cuddling into her. It would take time, but her heart wasn't on a clock. She was just going to go with the flow and be unrestrained. She was going to fall whenever it happened. She wasn't going to over analyze anything. What happens, happens.

»»»»

Being unrestrained and preventing herself from over analyzing things proved to be harder than Lauryn expected. Throughout the following week, she'd been tested. At school, Cammie tried to kiss her in the hallway. But she became too nervous and turned her head to make it seem like they were trying to whisper instead. And they kept walking each other to class, but Lauryn slowly stopped allowing Cammie to hold her hand. She barely let Cammie hug her before dropping her off. She even distanced herself from walking with Cammie one time, just because they'd gotten a weird look from someone in the hallway.

Cammie was learning how to cope with her mercurial behavior. She was perfectly fine with only being affectionate in private. She wasn't really a fan of PDA anyway. It hurt her feelings a little at first, but she understood Lauryn's disposition. They went back to the platonic friendship they had while Lauryn was with Brandon, but later in the day they'd cuddle and share kisses for hours. Lauryn attempted to make up for her offenses by spending time alone with her in the stairwell that had become their spot. Despite the way Cammie was under the impression that Lauryn only wanted to see her in private, she was content. She wanted a relationship with Lauryn any way she could have her. She didn't mind the secrecy much.

Diana began taking notice of their odd behavior. She hadn't really been filled in on their status, simply because she hadn't seen Cammie much. Now that she thought about it, she hadn't seen Lauryn much either. The pair always had an excuse for missing lunch. Their locations varied from day to day, but they would always escape to the stairwell. None of their three friends knew of their real whereabouts.

"Where the hell do Cam and Lauryn keep going every day?" Diana asked out of frustration. She missed her friends.

"Yesterday, she said she was going to the library for something. And Lo had to finish a test," Naomi recalled.

"Yeah... But they haven't eaten with us in four days," Allie added.

"They've got things to do," Naomi dismissed it.

"Like each other," Diana quipped under her breath.

"Diana," Allie warned with a laugh.

"Don't you think that's weird? They both disappear at the *same* time *every* day," she reasoned.

"It is weird. They could take some time off to relax... That's what lunch is for. It's the only time you're allowed to talk," Allie laughed.

"Maybe they're mad at us," Naomi suggested.

"For what? We didn't do anything. Well, *I* didn't..." Diana cleared her name as she eyed Allie and Naomi suspiciously.

"What? I didn't do anything either," Allie raised her hands in defense. Diana and Allie both looked at Naomi with narrowed eyes.

"I didn't do anything, what the hell," Naomi laughed, causing the other girls to giggle as well. "Seriously though, lunch is a normal time to be doing something else... Sometimes I go study for a test or something. What are y'all talking about?" she defended them.

"Yeah, *sometimes*... Not four days in a row," Diana rolled her eyes.

"I guess," Naomi shrugged. She didn't see anything weird. She thought they were overreacting. At first.

»»»»

However, that behavior extended into the next week as well. She hadn't seen them at lunch in nearly a week and a half. Nothing appeared to be off whenever they were in class together. It was just lunch. Naomi had to admit to herself how suspicious that was.

"Cam?" Naomi prompted. Cammie and Allie were surrounding her, occupying the desks in front and beside her. Allie looked over as well.

"Yeah?" Cammie turned around.

"Why don't you and Lauryn eat lunch with us anymore?" she asked quietly.

Oh, boy. Cammie knew they'd noticed. How would they not? They went missing around lunch time every single day. She tried to tell Lauryn not to seem so obvious, but it fell unto deaf ears. In Lauryn's defense, she'd uttered it in the midst of their kissing sessions in the stairwell. It had been easily dismissed.

"We've just been busy," Cammie answered, followed by a grimace. Great choice of words.

"Doing what, though? Do y'all have a project or something?" Allie interjected.

"No..." Cammie trailed. She wondered if she should tell them. She decided against it. That would upset Lauryn. But she didn't want to lie to them either. Because that would upset them. And she didn't want to harbor this as a secret, because that would only upset herself. She was torn. "I'm sorry. I was gonna eat lunch today anyway though."

"What were y'all doing?" Naomi probed, sensing Cammie was holding her tongue about something.

74

"Um..." she trailed in a high pitched voice.

"Quiet," Mr. Bryant warned from his position in the front.

"I'll tell you later," Cammie promised as she turned back around. She was thankful for his interruption. She didn't know how to go about telling the girls about them. What were they now? They were definitely a thing, but were they dating? Was Lauryn her girlfriend? She didn't know. Whatever. Their status wasn't of much concern to her now. She would have to meet Lauryn at her next class to discuss that.

Chapter 11

Cammie hadn't gotten the chance to broach the subject with Lauryn just yet. She told Naomi and Allie she was going to eat lunch with them, but she wanted to be with Lauryn. She didn't want to be the person that put the one they were seeing over their friends. But she did want to talk to her about it. She figured she could just do both. She'd spend half of her lunch break with the girls, and the other half with the Lauryn in the stairwell. Simple.

"Look who decided to show up today," Diana quipped when she saw Cammie heading towards their table.

"Be nice," Naomi laughed.

"Hey," Cammie smiled brightly as she reached her seat.

"Welcome back," Diana greeted her shortly. She wasn't actually mad, she was just kidding.

"Hey Cam," Allie returned her smile.

"What's up?" Naomi smiled as well.

"Nothing. What's up with you guys?" Cammie asked casually.

"Nothing," she shrugged.

"Why do people still ask that? No one ever answers the right way," Cammie laughed.

"I don't know," Naomi laughed.

"Where have you been, loser?" Diana asked, she was more than ready to get answers.

"Oh, you know... Just um, the library," Cammie lied.

"For two weeks?" Diana called her bluff.

"Yeah," she nodded.

"Cut the bullshit, Cam. Where were you?" Diana rolled her eyes.

"The library. And I have to go there again in a few minutes," Cammie said nervously as she glanced up at the clock.

"For what though?" Allie chimed in.

"Um..." Cammie mumbled. She hated being put on the spot. And she hated interrogations even more. "I have to go to the restroom," she excused herself quickly. She scooted her chair back and power-walked out of the cafeteria. She held her crotch just for good measure.

"I don't think so," Diana narrowed her eyes as she watched Cammie make a break. She decided to take matters into her own hands. She was going to investigate.

Cammie went in the direction of the restrooms and checked behind her. She had a feeling someone was following her. She was right. Diana had trailed behind her, but stealthily hid behind a wall when she saw her turn around. When Cammie saw that the coast was clear, she headed towards her true destination. Lauryn was waiting in the staircase for her when she entered. She had been getting worried, Cammie was usually never late. She relaxed when she saw her push through the door, but the expression on her face made her apprehensive.

"What's wrong?" Lauryn asked as Cammie climbed the stairs.

Diana smoothly entered from behind, catching the door when it closed after Cammie. She eased into the stairwell quietly.

"Why can't I tell them? I'm pretty sure they already know and you know they'd accept it and stuff..." Cammie blurted out as she reached Lauryn. They'd always sit at the top stair of the middle floor. It gave them enough time to flee if someone opened the door on either level. It was a foolproof plan most times. But Cammie had run up the stairs and now she was out of breath.

"What? Slow down," Lauryn responded softly as she pulled her into her embrace.

"I was late because I went to lunch... They were getting suspicious about why we were never there, like I *told* you they would. They're not stupid, Laur..." Cammie rushed her words.

"You can... I'm not stopping you... I said that then because I was too scared to accept everything, myself. I'm in a different place now, you can tell them if you want to. I don't want to keep it from them... And they're our best friends. Did you think I was hiding us?" Lauryn asked and held onto both of her hands compassionately.

Diana felt like she was watching some sort of terrible soap opera. Those lines were terrible. And were they *serious*? She wasn't a very big fan of this sappy version of her friends. What the hell? They were *actually* a thing now? When did this happen? The past two weeks, apparently. She instantly felt annoyed. Lauryn claimed she didn't want to hide "them" from Diana, Naomi, and Allie, but that was exactly what she was doing. She didn't think Lauryn's intentions were as innocent as Cammie perceived them to be. She climbed a few more stairs to hear them more clearly.

"Yeah, that's what you were doing..." Cammie said flatly.

"At first..." Lauryn defended herself.

"At first? If that's not what you're doing *now*, then why are we in here? Why aren't we at lunch, in front of the girls, if you're not hiding what's going on?" Cammie challenged.

Diana wanted to give them some privacy. Really, she did. Because after all, she'd figured out where they'd been. That was her sole purpose for following Cammie in here. Now she was just eavesdropping rather rudely, but she couldn't bring herself to leave. The plot was thickening and it was getting way too juicy to stop now. Where was the popcorn?

Lauryn was offended. Did Cammie think she was ashamed of them or something? She frowned and loosened her grip on Cammie. Lauryn had honestly thought nothing of it. This was their spot. This was just where they met every day. She didn't come in here because she was embarrassed... She came in here with Cammie every day because she thought this was just their thing. Apparently, that was quite the misperception.

"That's not what- I wasn't- You're wrong..." Lauryn struggled to voice her thoughts. "I'm not hiding anything. I'll admit, I used to want to... But I'm not now. I came in here because I thought *you* wanted to. We can go to lunch right now, if that's what you want..."

Cammie's brief frustration and anger all dissipated. She found her resolve. She should really stop assuming things about Lauryn without talking to her first. A small smile graced her lips, and the tension faded slightly.

"Okay? Do you want to go?" Lauryn smiled and pulled Cammie closer.

"We can go tomorrow," Cammie shrugged and leaned in.

Diana's mouth dropped wide open. Her jaw was on the floor. She'd just witnessed their relationship confirmation *and* a kiss. She'd officially seen too much. She didn't want to intrude, although she had been the entire time. When did Cammie grow the balls to do *that?* And when did Lauryn start letting her? When did she even begin feeling that way? Part of her used to doubt Cammie's story of their first kiss, but the proof was all there now. Diana smiled at the two above her. Seeing her best friend this happy immediately made up for her two weeks of absence.

Cammie pulled Lauryn into a hug without breaking their kiss. Lauryn tightly wrapped her arms around her. They both realized that they'd kind of just had their first fight. But they'd overcome it just as soon as it'd arisen. Technically, it could be counted as a make-up kiss. With that in mind, Lauryn wanted to make it bigger than they usually exemplified.

Lauryn guided her up one stair to where they had more space. They had yet to separate their lips. Lauryn, being the taller and most likely stronger of the two, tightened her grip around Cammie. With both arms wrapped around her securely, she lifted her. Cammie squealed in surprise and clutched onto her. Lauryn spun her around once and planted a grand kiss on her lips before setting her down again. They continued kissing until lunch was dismissed. They'd gotten good at anticipating the time by now. Hand in hand, they descended down the stairs. Diana couldn't exit soon enough. She got caught right as she'd slipped out of the door.

"Diana?" Cammie called. She quickly held the door that was slowly closing behind her friend.

Diana didn't turn around. She walked faster, as if she didn't hear Cammie's calls. But when she felt Cammie's hand around her wrist, she finally stopped.

"What were you doing in there?" Cammie questioned with furrowed eyebrows.

"I got lost," Diana shrugged.

"Right," Lauryn laughed.

"*I did*," Diana insisted, raising her voice a few octaves.

"You conveniently 'got lost'," Cammie said with air quotations, "and found your way out right when we came down?"

"Yeah, it was crazy," Diana laughed.

"She was clearly stalking us," Lauryn laughed as well.

"Just admit it, we're not even mad..." Cammie stated. She glanced at Lauryn to confirm her statement.

"Okay. I was. And y'all are cute as hell," Diana smirked.

"Wait, how much did you hear?" Lauryn wondered warily.

"I heard and *saw* you eating each other's faces," Diana teased.

"Diana!" Cammie groaned. "You're so creepy..."

"It was cute..." Diana offered in an attempt to deflect that accusation.

"We are cute, Camz," Lauryn smiled brightly.

She didn't know when she'd completely come to terms with all of this. Each day in the staircase, her feelings grew. They intensified with every secret conversation and affectionate moment they shared. She'd been spending time at Cammie's house more than she was at her own. The cuddling, the kisses, the hugs, they all contributed to her acceptance of them. It was a slow process, but after two weeks of this behavior, it was almost becoming natural.

She found that she didn't care what people would think. She was willing to brave the repercussions of being with Cammie. If there were any, they'd be minute in comparison to her. She would disregard every negative opinion. Because Cammie made her happier than she had been in a long time. She didn't want to experience that happiness in private anymore. She wanted it all the time. Going public was the one small step they had to conquer together. They could take baby steps to get to that point, though. Telling Diana would definitely be a baby step.

"We are," Cammie agreed.

Lauryn pulled her into her side and kissed her cheek. Cammie blushed almost immediately afterwards, as if on cue. Lauryn smiled at the rosy tint and simply looked at her in adoration.

"I'm gonna throw up," Diana joked. She was watching it all before her, and she actually felt an incredible sense of happiness. Seeing them interact this way made her giddy, just because she knew Cammie had been wanting this for so long.

The girls were oblivious to Diana's words. They were too focused on each other. Cammie radiated as much love as Lauryn radiated affection. They both felt the urge, and they leaned in simultaneously. Diana made over exaggerated gagging noises as she watched the act. But it made her so happy. She smiled dumbly at them when they pulled away from their quick kiss.

Cammie felt elated. That was the first time Lauryn had kissed her anywhere other than the stairwell or one of their houses. She assumed that she meant what she said about not hiding them any longer. She could barely contain her smile. She knew this was the beginning of something big.

»»»»

The fivesome were all reunited at Naomi's house. They'd called for an impromptu movie night, spur of the moment. Naomi had given Cammie and Lauryn a ride to her house from school. Allie and Diana had some activities to attend after school and came together. Once the gang was all there, the movie night began. They all shuffled up the stairs to her room, each of them being pushed out of the way by Diana. She wanted to get to the best spot first.

"Which one?" Naomi asked as she rummaged through her collection of DVDs.

When Cammie leisurely entered Naomi's bedroom, she stayed in the doorway. Diana was comfortably sprawled out on the floor. Allie was sitting cross-legged on Naomi's bed. Cammie was eyeing Lauryn from across the room. She'd positioned herself at the end of the bed, watching Naomi pick out movies. Her gaze was focused on Naomi, then it settled on Cammie. A smile graced her lips and she gestured for Cammie to come over. She eagerly crossed the room and sat in between her legs. Her arms wrapped around Cammie's waist and she pulled her into her chest. She nuzzled her face into Cammie's neck and she laughed because it kind of tickled.

"Well since nobody's answering me, we're watching *I Am Sasha Fierce* again," Naomi informed us as she popped the movie into the DVD player. She fiddled with the TV for a while before sighing. "How do you even turn this thing on?" she groaned as she turned back to us.

"Let me see the remote," Allie requested as she held out her hand.

"It's not gonna work..." Naomi rolled her eyes, but handed Allie the remote anyway.

"How many idiots does it take to play a movie?" Lauryn joked quietly, so only Cammie could hear.

"Well that's two so far..." Cammie teased. Lauryn laughed and Diana smirked, she'd overheard them.

"I give up," Allie shrugged as she tossed the remote back to Naomi.

"Did you turn it to the right channel?" Diana asked incredulously as she held her hand out for it. After flipping to every channel available, Diana surrendered as well. "This thing is dumb," she scoffed.

"Yeah, I told you," Naomi laughed.

"Jesus," Lauryn sighed as she unwrapped herself from around Cammie. She walked over to the TV and looked behind it. "The DVD player wasn't even plugged in..."

Cammie laughed obnoxiously, then covered her mouth. Allie joined her in her laughter, throwing her head back and clapping her tiny hands. Diana and Naomi rolled their eyes before laughing as well.

Lauryn plugged in the corresponding cords and soon they were all engaged in the movie. Diana kept switching her position every five minutes. Allie was watching the movie adorably with her chin in the palm of her hands. Naomi was sitting on the floor leaning against the end of the bed. Lauryn and Cammie were cuddling on the bed, propped up against the pillows.

Lauryn was playing with Cammie's hair absentmindedly. She twisted several strands around her fingers and stroked through them. Both actions left Cammie feeling peaceful. She leaned further into Lauryn and was placated in a way she'd rarely experienced. But she was hungry. Her stomach rumbled, loud enough for all of the girls to hear.

"Dang Cam, are you hungry?" Diana laughed.

Cammie laughed bashfully, feeling a little embarrassed by her involuntary disruption. She clasped her hand over her stomach to silence it, but had no such luck. It wailed again and she hunched over.

"There's definitely a whale in there," Naomi added playfully.

"I'm kind of hungry too. Camz, get up. I'll go get us something," Lauryn offered as she eased Cammie off of her.

"Thanks," Cammie smiled gratefully as she sat up.

"What do you want?" Lauryn questioned as she stood up and stretched.

"Whatever you bring is okay," Cammie shrugged. She never really had a preference. Food was food.

"Do you guys want anything?" Lauryn addressed the other girls as she sauntered over to the door.

"Chips," Naomi responded without shifting her gaze from the screen. Lauryn expected nothing less, though. Beyoncé always had Naomi transfixed.

"Bring me something to drink?" Allie requested.

"Sure. Diana?" Lauryn prompted, but it fell unto deaf ears. Diana was nearly as bad as Naomi, if not worse. Lauryn shrugged and made her way downstairs.

Cammie immediately felt cold in the absence of Lauryn. She slid down to the floor and latched onto Diana instead. Diana pushed her off at first, then let Cammie lay on her. She was *literally* on her. Cammie was laying on top of Diana like a deadweight. She wrapped herself around Diana to provide the warmth she was missing with Lauryn.

Lauryn was in the kitchen. She searched Naomi's cabinets and refrigerator for something to snack on. She found a can of Pringles, which she knew the girls were going to fight over, and a box of Poptarts. She went to the refrigerator to get Allie a bottle of water and made her way back upstairs with her hands full. When she entered, she frowned.

Cammie and Diana were completely wrapped up with each other. Diana had finally accepted Cammie's odd form of cuddling and wrapped her arms around her. They were both laying on the floor with contented smiles. Cammie had her head resting on Diana's chest, and Lauryn admittedly felt a little jealous. She knew Diana was no threat to them, but she didn't really want her to be holding Cammie that way.

Lauryn cleared her throat to announce her presence. The girls all stood up and claimed the snacks they wanted.

"You didn't bring me anything?" Diana whined when she saw the girls getting up and walking over to Lauryn.

"I asked you and you ignored me, so..." Lauryn scoffed.

Diana took her response as a joke, but she really was annoyed. For what reason, she didn't know. Diana and Cammie didn't even like each other. She was being irrational and immature but she couldn't suppress her jealousy. But she wasn't going to blatantly bitter about it. If Cammie and Diana wanted to cuddle, who was she to stop them? With that mind, she retreated to Naomi's desk and sat in the chair alone. She watched the movie with her arms crossed, trying her best not to look upset.

She failed. Cammie watched her curiously. She'd caught on to her tense behavior, but she didn't know what had provoked it. Cammie laid her head on Diana's shoulder and continued looking at Lauryn. She wanted to know what was on her mind or what had upset her, but she was well aware of how closed off she could be. She figured that Lauryn would come to her about it when she was ready.

Lauryn was just becoming more irritated as the minutes ticked on. Why wasn't Cammie coming back to cuddle with her? What was wrong with her? Lauryn looked longingly at the way Diana had her in her embrace. She wanted Cammie to be in her arms like that. It was really stupid to be jealous of those two, but she couldn't help it. Maybe Cammie would come to cuddle if Lauryn sat somewhere else.

She got up and laid across Naomi's bed. She crossed her legs and brushed Cammie's shoulder. Cammie looked up at Lauryn with a smile. Lauryn pat the spot next to her and motioned for Cammie to come back. Right as Cammie began to move, Diana tightened her hold.

"No, I'm all comfortable now," Diana complained stubbornly.

"Camz..." Lauryn coaxed gently, although her patience with Diana was reaching its limit.

"No," Diana spoke for Cammie before she could protest.

"Diana," Lauryn rolled her eyes.

"Ladies, ladies, there's enough of me to go around," Cammie joked. She could tell that Lauryn was actually bothered, and that was her attempt to make her smile. It worked.

"Fine," Lauryn huffed as she sat back. She stepped down to sit on the floor next to Naomi. When she knew she had Cammie's attention, she leaned into her and rested her head on Naomi's shoulder. Naomi, surprised by Lauryn's sudden act of affection, reluctantly put her arm around her.

This method was silly, but she knew it would work. She thought of it as reverse psychology. If she did what Cammie was doing to her, they would both end up getting what they wanted. She wouldn't have to manipulate her friend for long, because Naomi changed her position frequently. Cuddling with Naomi never lasted for long just because of that reason.

Cammie was aware of that, but she was annoyed. She thought Lauryn was being childish. She understood her motives clearly. Her desire to be with her outweighed her desire to spite her though. She side-eyed Lauryn and turned back to Diana.

"Diana, will you go get me some-" Cammie started, but she was interrupted.

"No," Diana denied her without letting her finish.

"What? You don't even know what I was gonna ask," Cammie laughed.

"I'm not getting up," Diana responded with her attention focused on the movie.

"Fine, I'll go get it myself..." Cammie mumbled as she unraveled herself from around Diana.

She crossed the room to go get the Pringles that were perched on the dresser. She retrieved it and helped herself to a few before sitting on the bed next to Allie. The spot she'd occupied had crumbs in it. She shook her head and sat on the floor instead. She kept inching closer to Lauryn, careful not to seem too obvious to the other girls. Eventually, she was being held by Lauryn again.

"Why'd you do all of that?" Lauryn whispered to Cammie.

"You act like I did that on purpose," Cammie rolled her eyes with the full knowledge that Lauryn couldn't see her. "If anything, you should blame Diana..."

"Well, whatever. You're back now," Lauryn laughed at their antics.

The movie ended, and neither Cammie nor Lauryn knew what had happened towards the ending. They had been having staring contests. They looked one another directly in the eye. Eventually one of them would smile, which ended that round. Lauryn won most times, because Cammie just couldn't stop smiling. She was endeared by it. The rest of the girls were paying them no attention at first.

Then they got reckless. They disregarded their friends and became too enraptured with each other. Cammie was the first to kiss Lauryn. She did so so quietly, they figured the girls wouldn't know. They were watching another movie now anyway. Their plan seemed to be flawless at first, relying on the movie onscreen as a distraction from them. It worked in their favor for a little while, but Naomi saw their shadows meshing from her peripheral vision.

She assumed it was just the distorted silhouette against the wall, but it seemed like they were kissing. How ridiculous was that?

When Naomi turned to look at them fully, her eyes nearly bulged out of her head. Cammie and Lauryn *were* kissing. Like, seriously kissing. Their heads were moving in sync. It was dark in the room, but it wasn't that dark. The TV illuminated them enough for Naomi to see what was happening. She saw Lauryn reach up to cup Cammie's face, then pull her in for another one. She kept her mouth shut about it though. She didn't want to put them on the spot. But that was just confirmation of why they'd been disappearing and acting so odd. Wow.

She diverted her attention back to the screen and tried to ignore the acts happening on the other side of the room. A goofy smile overtook her features at the reality of it. Naomi wasn't bothered by it in the slightest. She was happy for her friends, even though a sight like that would take some getting used to.

Chapter 12

The girls woke up disoriented and groggy the next morning. Allie was laying in an odd position, cuddling a pillow on the floor. Diana was just lying on the floor with her limbs spread out in every direction. Naomi was sleeping normally, curled up into a ball, resting her head on Allie's legs. They had all conked out in different places of Naomi's room, in various positions. All except an infamous two. Cammie and Lauryn were in the spooning position on Naomi's bed.

All of the girls had woken up by now except for those two. They had all gathered around Naomi's bed, staring at them. Naomi and Allie were slightly confused. But when Naomi recalled what she'd seen last night, she accepted it. If they were dating, cuddling would definitely be a factor. Allie just assumed they were Cammie and Lauryn, doing what Cammie and Lauryn always did. Just a little closer. But Diana knew it all.

"Aww," Diana cooed as she pulled out her phone to take a picture.

"I guess they're not fighting anymore," Allie smiled.

Diana snickered to herself, because they had *definitely* not been fighting. Constantly sucking face, sure. But surely not fighting. She decided she would have to squeeze some details out of Cammie later on.

Naomi contemplated if she should let her friends in on what she'd witnessed. Maybe it was just a friendly kiss. But then again, she couldn't recall kissing any of them in a friendly way. Or at all. And they'd been friends for years. Perhaps they were actually dating, but it was so difficult to face. This had all come out of nowhere, from her limited perception. Maybe they just really wanted to keep it under wraps.

Naomi felt like her friends didn't have to hide their relationship. Knowing Allie and Diana, there wasn't much left to the imagination. Now that she had seen it firsthand, she could back up that claim. They didn't get weird seeing them that close together. There were no snide remarks. Well, maybe there would be from Diana... Simply because she's Diana. But even then, it would all be in good fun. And if they were hiding it, they weren't doing a very good job of it. With the assumption that they'd find out eventually, she told them.

"Guys," Naomi prompted, breaking their attention from the two sleeping girls.

"What?" Allie responded.

"I saw them last night," Naomi shared evasively.

"You saw them what?" Diana asked. Her statement wasn't clear at all.

Naomi backed up from the bed and urged her friends to follow. She didn't want Cammie and Lauryn to overhear. What if they weren't sleeping? That would cause all sorts of drama.

"They were kissing last night," she said in a hushed tone.

"*Really*?" Allie asked incredulously. "Naomi, are you serious?"

"Yeah..." Naomi nodded as she cast a glance back at the pair. They were still sleeping, so good.

Diana felt the need to share what little she knew about the situation. Cammie hadn't told her any further details. What she had found out, she had to literally *see* for herself. They clearly weren't being open about this just yet. Although she knew it wasn't her place to out them, she was going to. She didn't like the prospect of keeping things hidden within their friend group. That was how unnecessary drama started, and they didn't need any of that.

Diana backed up even further and yanked Naomi and Allie back with her. "I'm gonna tell y'all something," she started off. Then she just decided to stand in the hallway. Naomi and Allie followed her and Allie closed the door for good measure.

"They both go to that nasty old staircase at the end of the hall every day during lunch or something. That's where they've been all this time. I don't know much about it... And I don't know if they're official or not... But they just started coming back to eat with us because apparently Cam thought she was 'hiding them' or something... So Lo wanted to prove she wasn't. Which she still was, because I mean, they still haven't said anything. Then that day Cam was acting hella sketchy, I followed her in there and saw her talking to Lo about it. And they were kissing and stuff in there too... I was like damn. But then I got caught, and they kissed in front of me, which was hella cute," Diana concluded.

Her story was all over the place, but Naomi and Allie had no trouble following. Diana had merely filled in the blanks to everything they'd been suspicious of.

"Dang," Allie breathed after Diana finished.

"Right? But that's all I know now..." Diana shrugged.

"All *I* know is that they better not have been doin' the nasty in my bed," Naomi said and made a face.

"Don't you think we would've heard that?" Allie laughed.

"I don't think they were, Naomi," Diana laughed. She couldn't imagine them doing *that*. How do two girls do that, anyway? She considered it for a brief second and felt disturbed. She pushed the image far from her mind and redirected the conversation. "But *anyway*... That's what you missed," Diana laughed.

"I can't even believe that. When did they..." Allie trailed off uncertainly. How had this been going on right under her nose?

"I have no idea," Naomi shook her head, still in just as much bewilderment as Allie was. They looked to Diana for a little more information, but was met with a blank expression.

"I don't have anything else, except what I told you. But you didn't hear it from me," Diana waved both of them off as she opened the door again.

Cammie and Lauryn were both still knocked out, still holding each other. They hadn't been disturbed in the slightest. The girls smiled at them when they all re-entered.

"Should we wake them up?" Naomi wondered aloud.

"Leave them. Let's go make breakfast," Allie suggested.

"Can we go brush our teeth first, though?" Diana grimaced at the bitter taste in her mouth.

"Oh, yeah... Good idea," Naomi nodded as she headed to the bathroom, with Diana and Allie trailing behind her. They closed the door on Cammie and Lauryn, and the noise woke them up.

Lauryn opened her eyes slowly. She didn't recognize her surroundings at first, but she definitely recognized that lovely, intoxicating scent. She looked straight ahead at the mess of hair that was sprawled out across the pillows and the smallest smile tugged at her lips. Lauryn extended her hand to smooth it down, but it was no use. It couldn't be tamed by a simple hand. Cammie's bed head was terrible. But it was so cute.

Lauryn's light pawing at her head had woken Cammie up as well. She thought it was Sophia or something at first. But when she saw the pale arms wrapped around her torso, butterflies invaded her stomach. It was a lovely thing to be feeling first thing in the morning. She smiled groggily and trailed her finger along Lauryn's arm.

"Good morning, Camz," Lauryn's husky voice sounded from behind her. God, *that* was the first thing she got to hear in the morning. She didn't know what she'd done to deserve that, but she was grateful for whatever it was.

"Good morning, beautiful," Cammie reciprocated lamely. It sounded a lot better in her head. Oh well.

Lauryn smiled and stroked Cammie's stomach in slow, chaste motions. If only she could wake up to this every morning. She could easily do that. Maybe for once in her life, she would be a morning person. Today, she definitely was. Well, not technically. It was nearly twelve thirty. But time wasn't any of their concern. Time seemed to stand still as long as they were laying together.

"Did you sleep well, babe?" Lauryn questioned softly.

Cammie's heart fluttered at how effortlessly she'd said that. *Babe.* She could get used to hearing it. "Yes. That was the best night's rest I've gotten in a long time."

"Same here," Lauryn agreed. "Naomi's bed is so comfortable."

"It's not even because of her bed," Cammie shook her head. It was because of Lauryn. Everything regarding Lauryn had been perfect lately.

"What is it because of?" Lauryn asked. Under normal circumstances, she would probably catch onto Cammie's underlying meaning. But it was too early to be analytical about her words. She didn't even try to decode them.

"Maybe it's the way you're holding me. Or the fact that I can feel your heartbeat," Cammie mused. "I think it's how close we are. Pretty sure that it's because *you* are here in general."

Lauryn recalled something Cammie had written in her journal along those lines. It made her think of the page where she'd said *I just want intimacy with you. And I'm not even talking about sex.* Was this what she meant? Probably. If it was, Lauryn didn't know she'd been craving intimacy too. Sometimes, Cammie didn't have to use colorful language or beautiful metaphors and similes to convey the art of her writing. Simple things like that were what stuck out to her, just because they were Cammie's raw emotions. They held deeper meaning. Lauryn experienced just how deeply she meant it when they had moments like this.

Their serenity was disturbed by a boisterous Diana barging back into Naomi's room. "Wake *up*," she singsonged as she tossed a pillow at them.

Lauryn successfully fended off the pillow, but its end landed in Cammie's face. Lauryn laughed and pushed it off for her. "We're already up. Thanks, Diana," Lauryn said sarcastically.

"Why do you always end up hitting me with something?" Cammie groaned and buried her face into Naomi's comforter.

"Easy target," Diana shrugged with a smirk. "Come downstairs though, we made breakfast."

Cammie shot up, suddenly alert. Diana didn't have to tell her twice. Lauryn, on the other hand, needed a little more convincing. She didn't really appreciate the way Cammie had torn herself from her grasp. But now that she wasn't holding her anymore, she figured she had no reason to stay in bed. After washing up and making themselves look somewhat presentable, Cammie and Lauryn joined the rest of the girls downstairs.

"How nice of you to join us," Allie quipped when she saw them.

"Morning," Lauryn mumbled unenthusiastically. She dipped into the kitchen to fix herself a plate and returned to the living room with it afterwards.

"Did y'all sleep well?" Naomi asked.

"I slept like a baby," Cammie said on her way to the kitchen. Her sentence was followed by a loud wail of disappointment. She slumped back into the living room looking as dejected as ever.

"What?" Naomi questioned.

"I put the last two pancakes on my plate and I dropped it," Cammie pouted. That must have been devastating.

"Aww, Camz... I'll make you some more," Lauryn offered as she was already on her way to the kitchen. She didn't second-guess it at all. She wondered why she was always so eager to do things for Cammie. That hadn't been a new thing or a perk of their forming relationship. She'd always been that way. She didn't know why, though. Diana unknowingly offered an explanation.

"She's whipped as hell already," Diana smirked as she watched the two of them disappear into the kitchen.

"Right," Naomi laughed.

"She just wants to take care of her *baby*," Allie joined in.

Lauryn heard their laughter from the kitchen and wondered what could've been so funny. As she was getting the necessary ingredients, she cast a glance over at Cammie. She was still pouting. Poor baby. That pancake must've meant a lot to her. Lauryn laughed at the thought and crossed the kitchen to be nearer to Cammie.

"Stop pouting like that, you're so cute," Lauryn giggled as she reached past her for the vegetable oil in the cabinet.

Cammie poked her lip out further and exaggerated her pout out of spite. Lauryn smirked and leaned in to kiss those pouty lips quickly. That made her stop for sure. The grin she was rewarded with afterwards was much cuter than the pout she had been wearing before.

"There we go," Lauryn smiled appreciatively. "Do you know how to make pancakes?"

"I guess," Cammie shrugged. She assumed it would be easy. They might not taste all that great, but she was familiar with the process.

"Can you cook at all?" Lauryn laughed as she looked in Naomi's pantry for pancake mix.

"Somewhat," she shrugged again. Cammie propped herself up on the counter and watched Lauryn. She was so graceful. And her butt looked great in those sweats. Cammie always took the time spent away from her to admire her instead. It never got old.

"Well, get down. I'm gonna teach you how to make pancakes this morning," Lauryn grinned as she held out her hand to help Cammie down.

Cammie wasn't so sure. She was well aware of how clumsy she could be, and she didn't want to have to deal with Naomi's wrath for burning down her house. However, something within her said that she could trust Lauryn. She took her hand and slid off of the counter easily. Lauryn led her over to where she'd set up the ingredients. Cammie only looked at them uncertainly.

"I'll turn the fire on, you start mixing," Lauryn instructed her softly. "Put like... Butter and those two eggs in it. Pour the milk in it last."

Cammie followed her instructions tentatively. She knew for sure she would screw something up. She was just waiting for Lauryn to notice. But the reprimanding never came. Instead, Lauryn was just standing behind her with a grin. Her arms were crossed and she looked so pleased with what Cammie was doing. The look Lauryn was giving her made Cammie feel shy for some reason. She was suddenly bashful stirring the pancake batter.

"I've already sprayed it so... Just pour a little into the pan. Or all of it, if you want a huge pancake," Lauryn directed with a laugh. Cammie probably *would* want a huge pancake. Because she was Cammie.

Cammie nodded and picked up the bowl full of batter. She cautiously lifted and poured it into the pan. Surprisingly, she didn't even spill it. It was all sizzling in the pan.

"Great, okay. Now just wait a minute before flipping it over," Lauryn continued to guide her.

Cammie waited just a few seconds more before moving to flip it. The batter was still relatively liquid, and the spatula barely picked it up. She frowned and set the spatula back on the napkin.

"Just a little while longer, Camz," Lauryn laughed.

"Okay," Cammie huffed.

Lauryn giggled again and closed the distance between them. She hugged her from behind and pressed herself into her. While resting her chin on her shoulder, she clasped her hands over Cammie's waist. Cammie leaned back into her and sighed in contentment. She placed her hands on top of Lauryn's and smiled up at her, earning a sweet kiss on the cheek. When the batter started to settle down, Lauryn guided Cammie's arm to flip it together.

Cammie looked back at her with a huge grin. That was the cutest thing ever. Cooking with Lauryn was quickly becoming her favorite thing. They resumed their position while the pancake was cooking on the other side. The way Lauryn was moulding into her and directing her movements made her fall ten times harder than she already had. Lauryn fell just a little bit harder at that simple morning gesture as well. They both thought it was kind of romantic. Diana did too, she had been hanging in the doorway watching them cook together for the past five minutes.

"Okay, will you two lovebirds come in now?" Diana said after she grew tired of hanging out.

They nodded just as Cammie was putting the oversized pancake on her plate. Neither of them denied her accusation. Cammie was especially grateful that Lauryn didn't. It allowed her to imagine that Lauryn was actually in love with her the way *she* was. Which, of course, she wasn't. Not this early, anyway. But it was nice to pretend.

When Lauryn hooked her arm around Cammie's, she couldn't help her smile. They entered Naomi's living room looking very much like a couple. The rest of the girls smirked to themselves, but didn't show them any extra attention. If they didn't want them to know, they weren't going to hint at it. Naomi and Allie made mental notes not to spill their deep secrets to Diana. She would tell someone eventually.

"What are you guys doing?" Lauryn asked casually as she sat on the couch next to Allie.

"We were watching TV," Naomi shrugged. "But nothing good comes on around this time so we were just talking."

"Nice," Cammie nodded, seconds before she was pulled into Lauryn's lap. The motion took her by surprise, and she landed with a surprised squeal. Lauryn simply pulled her closer. Her hands resumed their position around her waist naturally.

Naomi, Diana, and Allie all exchanged a knowing look. They smirked amongst themselves, but said nothing. There was plenty of room for Cammie to sit *next* to Lauryn, but she'd pulled her into her lap instead. To Lauryn, this gesture just said that Cammie was hers. She didn't say anything verbally, but she'd said it loud and clear. She wasn't being obnoxious about it, but she knew that subtle things like that would tell her friends eventually.

"Can we do something today?" Allie asked to distract from the pair across the room.

"Something like what?" Diana asked.

"I don't know, bowling?" Allie suggested brightly.

"Bowling..." Naomi frowned. "We're not like, eighty..."

"Bowling is fun," Allie mumbled indignantly.

"It's kind of cool... But not right now," Lauryn laughed.

"Well what can we do, then?" Allie reiterated, suddenly having cabin fever.

"We can go to the movies?" Cammie proposed as she began to drown her massive pancake in syrup.

"What's even out right now?" Diana asked.

"I don't know, but I'm sure we could find something," Cammie shrugged as she now forked a large portion of her pancake into her mouth.

"The movies are kind of boring," Naomi made a face.

"Well, we can go to the mall?" Cammie suggested again, with her mouth full.

"That's in the same boat," Lauryn countered.

Cammie rolled her eyes. "We could go to the skating rink?"

"I can't skate," Allie declined.

"Let's go to the freakin' aquarium then, gosh," Cammie huffed sarcastically, seeing how no one liked her serious suggestions. "Or the moon."

"Are they open?" Diana asked, perking up at that idea. Sure, why not?

"I don't know. Look up the times," Lauryn shrugged and gave into the idea.

"See how much it is too," Allie added.

"What the hell," Cammie complained with her mouth still full of pancakes.

"What?" Diana asked.

"You guys *really* want to go to the aquarium..." Cammie said incredulously.

"What's wrong with the aquarium?" Lauryn asked as she pressed her fingers into her side. Her legs were starting to go numb now, but she didn't care.

"Nothing... Just, I was kidding..." Cammie shook her head, still struggling to take her friends seriously.

"Too bad. That was the best thing you suggested," Diana laughed.

"Exactly," Naomi pitched in.

"I hate you guys," Cammie laughed as well.

"No you don't," Lauryn grinned as she pressed her lips to Cammie's cheek. She stroked her side affectionately and pulled her even closer.

She was right. Cammie didn't hate them at all. Especially not Lauryn, when she was being cute like that. Cammie felt her friends staring, then she felt her cheeks heating up. She knew that Diana knew, but what about the others? She hadn't really taken Lauryn's words seriously. She thought she'd revert back to her usual secretive affection, but she wasn't. She was being loving with Cammie quite brazenly in front of the girls. She wondered if they took any notice of it, in that way.

Boy, did they. They were all smiling at the two of them because that was adorable. They got Lauryn's message loud and clear. But part of them wanted confirmation. They were just kind of speculating and gathering bits and pieces of information now. None of the girls wanted to be straightforward with the question, but they were wondering.

»»»

They were still wondering when they got to the aquarium. They had Diana's word to go on, but that didn't mean it was official. If they put together Diana's story, Naomi's observation, and their recent behavior, it would be logic to assume that they were dating. But if they were, why hadn't they told them?

Allie watched Cammie and Lauryn's interactions all day. They'd been holding hands almost the entire time. During the car ride there *plus* touring the aquarium, they never broke contact. Whenever they stopped at displays, they would cuddle. Lauryn and Cammie were nearly attached at the hip. She hadn't seen them separate since she found them in bed that morning.

Naomi saw the same thing. While they were walking, Cammie's hand was firmly in Lauryn's grasp. Whenever they weren't walking, Lauryn had Cammie directly in front of her. She'd slip her fingers into Cammie's belt loops to keep her close. Or she would wrap her arms around her small waist. She also saw a few not-so-subtle cheek and neck kisses. Lauryn was loving Cammie up today.

The girls eventually got split up. Diana and Naomi had ventured off to another exhibit while Cammie and Lauryn went in the opposite direction. Allie stayed in the same place, enthralled by her surroundings. When she looked up to find that she was alone, she took it in stride.

Allie was captivated by all of the marine animals. The colors of the fish were beautiful. The bigger aquatic animals like the whales and dolphins intrigued her. The otters and penguins made her giggle. Although she felt bad that they were stranded here instead of living amongst their true habitats, she was glad she got the chance to see them. She was driven by wanderlust, just milling around the aquarium without any motive. She wandered towards the reef exhibit, looking overhead at the thousands of fish above her. When she looked back down, she caught sight of something peculiar.

Against the wall were two figures embracing each other, engaged in a slow kiss. She thought it was kind of romantic. Allie smiled at the pair and went on her way. She approached them, simply because they were where her next location was. She really wanted to see the rest of the reef. As she passed the two, she instantly recognized them as Lauryn and Cammie.

From far away, they were not as easily distinguishable. But up close, she'd identified them almost immediately. Then she realized she hadn't seen them in a while. They'd lost Cammie and Lauryn way back when they were viewing the dolphin show. She hadn't seen them since, but she assumed it was part of their plan to detach themselves from the rest. She understood that they wanted private time to make room for moments like those.

"There they go," Diana pointed them out from the other end of the reef attraction.

The pair recognized Diana's voice instantly and pulled away. They tried their best to look casual. Lauryn's grip on Cammie's hand didn't falter as Diana and Naomi approached. Lauryn didn't want to be caught kissing her just yet, but she didn't mind seeing them showing fondness in other ways.

"Fuck," Lauryn swore under her breath when she saw Allie standing only a few feet away.

Cammie followed Lauryn's gaze and frowned. Allie was doing something on her phone, paying them no attention at all. "Do you think she saw us?"

"Maybe... I don't know," Lauryn answered honestly as she ran a hand through her hair.

"Where have y'all been?" Naomi asked as soon as they were in earshot.

"Exploring," Cammie shrugged and surprised herself with her own mendacity. "Doing touristy stuff."

"Yeah," Lauryn seconded.

"All of y'all just disappeared. I looked up and y'all were gone," Allie laughed as she joined the group.

"I got bored of watching the sting rays. They don't even do anything," Diana laughed.

"But they're so cute... Did you see their little faces?" Allie smiled.

"Yeah... But staying there for ten minutes is way too long," Naomi giggled.

"Exactly," Lauryn agreed with a chuckle.

"Okay. Y'all are just hating on them. They're so cute," Allie dismissed their remarks.

"Yep, shame on us," Cammie shook her head sarcastically.

"I'm hungry," Naomi whined.

"Same," Cammie seconded, which didn't surprise anyone.

"Let's go to the food court then," Diana suggested.

"It has a *food court*?" Allie said with wide eyes.

"I think so," Lauryn assumed, looking at her map. "If not, then they've obviously got something to eat somewhere..."

"Yeah," Allie nodded. "Let's go find it, I'm kind of hungry too. Do you think they have a Waffle House in here?"

"No, Allie..." Naomi laughed.

With that, they were on their way. They searched for a restaurant within the aquarium. Their search didn't last long. There were food stands in various locations all around the vicinity. They didn't want a snack, they wanted a meal. So they kept walking until they approached a cafeteria-styled restaurant by the whales. They stood in line one after another. Naomi was the first to get her order, then she went to find a table. Allie and Diana followed soon after, while Cammie and Lauryn were being indecisive. They stayed in line for a few extra minutes, letting people go in front of them until they were ready.

"Naomi, I believe you now," Allie disclosed as she sat down. She looked over her shoulder and figured she had enough time to share before Cammie and Lauryn would join them.

"Believe me? What did I say?" Naomi answered before biting into her chicken wing.

"How you saw them kissing last night..." Allie answered quickly.

"Why? What happened?" Diana asked, suddenly a lot more invested in the conversation.

"They were like, against the wall and everything," Allie responded as she picked up her burger.

"Damn," Diana laughed with a suggestive wink.

"No, it was sweet. It wasn't like that," Allie added. "At least I don't think it was... Could've been," she shrugged.

"Well, I guess you see what I meant then," Naomi laughed.

"Yeah," Allie nodded. "I just don't get it, if they're gonna date and show PDA, why can't they just tell us?" she asked rhetorically. All the while, Naomi and Diana had been motioning for her to be quiet, but her gaze was settled down on her plate. They'd been gesturing wildly because Cammie and Lauryn were approaching them fast, and they were pretty sure they'd catch the tail end of what she'd said. Thankfully, they hadn't.

Lauryn pulled out the chair for Cammie to sit down seconds before she sat right beside her. Naomi, Diana, and Allie wondered why they were only eating with one hand. Diana dropped her napkin, and saw their hands intertwined under the table when she was picking it up. She rolled her eyes and sat back upright. They were cute earlier, but it was annoying at this point. They couldn't separate long enough to feed themselves? What the hell. Naomi and Allie caught on as well. The girls didn't feel the need to protect their open secret anymore. They were going to confront them head on, because this was just ridiculous.

"What's with all the hand holding, guys?" Naomi questioned innocently.

"Yeah, are you guys dating or something?" Allie added a little more pointedly.

Lauryn and Cammie exchanged an uncertain look. Well, this would be the moment of truth. Cammie looked down at her lap, preparing to hear the words she dreaded. She knew Lauryn would deny it. But Lauryn looked straight ahead with confidence, elated to finally be questioned. She was determined to prove herself to Cammie one way or another. With a firm squeeze of her hand, they both answered.

"Yes," Lauryn said simultaneously as Cammie said "No."

Chapter 13

What? Everyone's eyes widened. Everyone was uncomfortable. This was suddenly awkward. There was a giant elephant in the room. No one was speaking. Naomi, Allie, and Diana had been stunned into silence. All three of them were staring at Cammie and Lauryn with their mouths agape. Cammie's hands started to get clammy, but Lauryn still didn't release it. That spoke volumes to Cammie, for some reason.

"Uh..." Cammie broke the silence dumbly, looking at Lauryn with furrowed eyebrows. She was probably the most confused out of the five, second only to Lauryn. The only reason she'd said no was to protect Lauryn, because she was certain she would say it first. But... She confirmed it. They hadn't even talked about it themselves. Of course they were together, but neither of them had formally asked. Was it technically still dating? Cammie was horrified at that blunder. She wasn't so sure she wanted to stick around to see how it all panned out.

Lauryn was regarding Cammie with the same expression. What the hell? What more did she have to do? She didn't think she'd have to flat out tell her. She thought it had been implied through her actions. But she saw then that Cammie wasn't going to assume anything. Lauryn would have to be straightforward. So she repeated herself.

"We *are* dating," Lauryn reiterated what she'd thought was obvious. And it was, to everyone except for Cammie.

Cammie's mind was reeling. Were they really? She had never considered it. She just thought they were a thing, without labels or titles. Like, they weren't lesbians, and they weren't girlfriends either. To her, they were just Cammie and Lauryn. Except now they kissed and cuddled a lot more often. Then it dawned on her that that was what people who were dating did. Maybe they were dating after all.

"So..." Diana trailed, still lost. "Are you? Or not...?"

"I guess," Cammie nodded in a daze.

"Yes," Lauryn said, quietly urging Cammie to say the same thing.

93

"Yes," Cammie said more confidently, awestruck by the revelation.

"Aww," Naomi and Allie crooned together.

Lauryn smiled and looked at her lap. Her gaze settled on their intertwined fingers, and she ran her thumb over the back of Cammie's hand. Cammie smiled meekly. An unfamiliar feeling started in her stomach, and she ended up laughing. All of the pent up butterflies found their release in the form of laughter. Nothing was funny at all, she was just so happy. Lauryn laughed too, feeling the same sensation in her own stomach.

"Kiss if it's real," Diana challenged with a smirk.

Lauryn looked up at Cammie. She raised her eyebrows, silently asking for permission. Cammie only grinned wider. Lauryn took that as her answer and leaned in. They were both smiling as they kissed. Naomi, Allie, and Diana started cheering around them, and they sheepishly pulled away.

"Nothing we haven't seen before," Diana laughed.

"*What*?" Lauryn questioned once she'd registered what she said.

"We've seen y'all kiss before," Allie giggled.

"All three of us," Naomi nodded.

Lauryn felt embarrassed. She really thought they were doing a good job of keeping it secret. Cammie somewhat knew that they'd been seen before. Their spontaneous kissing happened quite often. However, she couldn't say that she was embarrassed about it at all.

"Where?" Lauryn laughed.

"My room..." Naomi answered.

"Just now..." Allie seconded.

"The stairs..." Diana pitched in.

"*Okay*," Lauryn giggled even louder. "We're shit at privacy, Camz."

"I already knew that. I just didn't care," Cammie laughed.

"It's cute though. Just don't become one of those couples that don't even come up for air," Naomi teased.

Cammie smiled at Naomi's words. She'd called them a couple. They were a *couple*. Lauryn was her *girlfriend*. She realized these things all at once and bent over in an attempt to hide her face. She was smiling way too hard.

"Dork," Lauryn laughed at her fangirling girlfriend.

"You've proved your point, Lo. Now just eat like a normal person," Diana laughed, referring to the hand that was still clutching Cammie's under the table.

"Oh, yeah..." Lauryn said as she begrudgingly released Cammie's hand from her grasp.

Cammie laughed. *She* was the oblivious one now. It occurred to her then that Lauryn was holding her hand for so long as a display. It was excessive and over the top, but she definitely wasn't complaining. It was insanely adorable. Lauryn was a romantic, in her own way.

"What?" Lauryn smirked.

"Nothing," Cammie shook her head. "It feels weird having my hand to myself now."

"Yeah, it's a little weird," Lauryn agreed.

"Get a room," Naomi teased. "But not mine," she added seriously, still dubious of their actions from the night before.

"Oh my God," Cammie laughed.

"Nothing happened," Lauryn snorted.

"Mhm..." Naomi made a face.

"Naomi," Allie laughed at the exchange.

"They can do it in your bed then, shoot..." Naomi suggested, raising her arms in defense.

"Oh my *God*," Cammie repeated as she looked between her friends. It hadn't even been five minutes of their announcement, and they were already making crude jokes.

"I'm surprised Diana isn't the one saying that shit," Lauryn giggled.

"I'm saving it for later," Diana answered with her mouth full. "Genius doesn't happen overnight. I've gotta think about it. It'll be soon though, don't worry," she smirked.

"Wonderful," Lauryn said sarcastically.

»»»

Lauryn had been a lot more relaxed since they'd told their friends about their relationship. She was noticeably less tense and apprehensive. She wasn't so obsessed with secrecy. Lauryn was carefree, and Cammie was loving it. Although they hadn't told their parents just yet, they were comfortable in their homes too. They just kept the door closed in hopes that it would ward off unwanted spectators. They were together at Lauryn's house now. In their usual cuddling position on her bed, they were idly watching TV.

Well, Cammie was. Lauryn was deep in thought. Even days after their announcement, it still baffled her how Cammie didn't know they were dating. She really did think she was being blatantly obvious. Actions tended to speak louder than words, but maybe not in this case. Maybe Lauryn wasn't doing as much as she thought. She nudged Cammie to get her attention, then addressed what was on her mind.

"How did you not know we were dating? I literally did everything to tell you without actually having to *tell* you..." Lauryn voiced her thoughts.

"I don't know. I just didn't want to assume anything. Because it would've hurt if someone asked and you said no... So I just went along with it. I thought I was gonna have to cover for you. And if I'm being honest, I really didn't think we were," Cammie answered earnestly. "Most people actually ask... And neither one of us did, so..."

"I guess you're right..." she mumbled when she realized that the blame partially fell on her for never popping the question. "Well, we are. Officially. You're mine," Lauryn said as she brought Cammie to her lips. Part of her felt guilty for ever making Cammie believe that they had to be hidden. She didn't want Cammie to feel like she had to lie and cover for them. She wanted to have a normal relationship, even though they were off to a rocky start.

"I've always been yours," Cammie responded quietly. She barely trusted herself to speak. She was smiling so goofily, her speech would probably slur.

Lauryn only smiled at her words. Cammie repositioned herself again laid against Lauryn's chest. Her head was situated right above Lauryn's heart. She pressed her ear against her slightly and remembered the time where she'd written about this exact situation. Her heart swelled when she registered that it was actually happening. She played with the draw string on Lauryn's sweatpants and let out a contented sigh.

"I've never really seen myself having a girlfriend," Lauryn disclosed as she played with Cammie's fingers.

95

"I've never really seen myself having *you* as my girlfriend," Cammie rephrased Lauryn's statement. It all seemed so surreal to her. The past month had been insane. Lauryn was starting it with Bread and ending it with Cammie.

"Here I am," Lauryn said cheekily.

"I just feel like one day I'm going to wake up. Like, it's a dream... You know?" Cammie expressed.

"If this is a dream, I hope I sleep forever," Lauryn responded sweetly. She kissed Cammie's forehead and stroked her baby hairs on the side.

"This is why I don't wanna wake up," Cammie laughed.

"Then close your eyes, babe," Lauryn instructed with a light giggle.

Cammie followed through. With her eyes closed, Lauryn saw her undeniable beauty. Her complexion was nearly flawless. The few blemishes there were easily dismissible. She saw then just how mature her features had gotten. She wasn't her baby-faced Camz anymore. And it wasn't a bad thing. Her face was slim and her cheekbones were more prominent. She was just as adorable, just more mature. And she looked a lot more desirable. Lauryn thought about that without feeling weird, for once.

Cammie had taken Lauryn's instructions literally, and Lauryn found her sleeping within minutes. Her breathing deepened slightly and inadvertently let her know. Lauryn chuckled to herself and stroked Cammie's hair. She smiled down at her sleeping girlfriend and just watched her for a minute or two. She could never tire of admiring her. But she thought of a better, more rewarding way to spend her time. Reaching out slowly, careful not to disturb or wake Cammie, she attempted to get her journal.

She stretched steadily to grab it. It was perched on her bedside table. Only a few more inches, and she would have it. She slid out with a jolt to get it, then quickly checked to see if Cammie was still sleeping. She was. She looked disturbed, her eyebrows were furrowed and she clutched onto Lauryn tighter. Lauryn's heart fluttered at the sight and she cradled Cammie's body with one arm. She flipped through the pages of Cammie's journal until she found where she'd left off.

They'd been switching off for the past month. Cammie kept it for a week, scribbling mad ramblings throughout the remaining pages. Then Lauryn kept it over the weekend, reading everything her girlfriend had written. It was a wonderful system. Cammie's perception of certain things never ceased to amaze her. One page in particular caught her eye and made her think.

A few days ago, I was thinking about some things... And I realized that the saying 'there's always a rainbow after the rain' isn't entirely true. Because that day I was sad, and it was raining... But there was no rainbow afterwards. There was a sunset though. And it was so, so damn beautiful. So, I don't know... I just feel like you should keep in mind that your sunset is coming. Sunsets are inevitable. Rainbows are iffy. But sunsets happen every single day.

And Lauryn, since I know you'll be reading this now... You are my sunset. Even before we were dating. Like, if I think about everything that's happened with the whole Brandon thing... And then I think about how things are right now, this is my sunset. And who knows, maybe it won't last. Maybe an eclipse will happen and everything will spiral out of control and go dark again, but all I know is that now... Right now, this is my sunset. And so are you.

Lauryn reread the entry a few times, trying to grasp the concept of the metaphor. She couldn't fathom the fact that *she* was a sunset. She didn't think she was that great. She understood exactly what Cammie meant, but she didn't understand how it pertained to her. Either way, she leaned down to place a kiss on Cammie's forehead. Her heart was filled to the core, the way it always was whenever she read her journal. She loved it.

She kissed Cammie's forehead again. Overcome with the sudden desire for affection, she kissed her cheek, then her nose. She began kissing all over Cammie's face, purposely evading her lips. She covered as much as she could with kisses, until she was turned at an unnatural angle. Cammie was smiling subconsciously. Lauryn smiled as well.

"It tickles," Cammie mumbled with her eyes still closed. Lauryn continued her playful assault. "*Lauryn*," Cammie whined as she attempted to hide her face further into her chest. Lauryn's kisses were relentless. Cammie feigned as if she were annoyed, but she was loving every second of it.

"Babe?" Lauryn prompted when Cammie's eyes began to flutter.

"Hm?" she mumbled sleepily. She made a high pitched sound as she stretched out and curled back into Lauryn.

"What's with you and sunsets?" Lauryn questioned as she tucked a strand of hair behind her ear.

"Why do you ask?" Cammie asked raspily as she finally opened her eyes.

"Well," Lauryn started off. "Your journal has one on it, and I just read the page where you wrote about one. You compare me to sunsets pretty often," Lauryn chuckled.

"They're two of my favorite things," Cammie shrugged. "You complement each other."

"I don't know how your mind works," Lauryn laughed. "But I love you."

"I love you too," she responded effortlessly. She wasn't going to dwell on the fact that Lauryn didn't mean it the same way she did. Those were petty details. Easily dismissible.

"And guess what," Lauryn hummed excitedly.

Cammie grumbled, not really up for conversation at the moment. "What?"

"No wait, guess who," Lauryn corrected herself.

"What?" Cammie asked as she looked up at Lauryn. "Guess who...?"

"Guess who's taking *you* on a date," Lauryn grinned.

"You're taking me on a date?" Cammie assumed as she sat up a little. She smiled and continued to look at Lauryn.

"You didn't guess," Lauryn ignored her question.

Cammie rolled her eyes, amused by Lauryn's antics. "You?"

"Yes," Lauryn nodded as she leaned down to kiss her.

"Where?" Cammie questioned. She kind of accepted the fact that Lauryn wasn't letting her go back to sleep. Even though her chest was so comfortable, and even though sleep was so inviting. She couldn't. So she repositioned herself. She shifted further down and rested her chin on Lauryn's stomach.

"Well, I haven't really figured it out yet. I can't think of anything that's not cliché," Lauryn shared. None of the typical date ideas seemed worthy of being their first. No movies. No dinners. Nothing of that sort. She wanted something both fun and romantic, something she and Cammie could claim to be their own. Something significant. But nothing was coming to her.

"It doesn't have to be fancy..." Cammie trailed with a smile.

The idea of going on a date with Lauryn at all was making her feel overjoyed. She could see it now. She'd wear some type of fancy dress, curl her hair, maybe even put on a bit of makeup. Well, *she* wouldn't. Diana would probably have to fix her up. She didn't even want to think of how beautiful Lauryn would be if she were to dress up. The idea threatened to give her heart palpitations.

"I want to make it special, Camz," Lauryn whined. She puffed out her cheeks and looked insanely adorable. Cammie propped herself up long enough to kiss the frown away before plopping back down onto her stomach.

"And it will be," Cammie assured her. "Maybe there's some confusion up there," she said as she gestured to Lauryn's head. "But I love you. Everything is special to me. *This* is special, and we're not even doing anything. Don't you get that?"

Cammie took her goofy smile as her answer. She laid her head sideways on her stomach. The sounds she heard in there weren't nearly as pleasurable as listening to her heartbeat. So she climbed back up to lay on Lauryn's chest. She found it odd how comfortable and soft *every* part of Lauryn was. Their bodies meshed perfectly together. Cammie was one with Lauryn whenever they cuddled. She picked up an idle hand and held it tightly. The spaces between her fingers were right where Cammie's fit perfectly. Every part fit that way.

"You are perfect," Cammie praised her as she began to play with her fingers.

"No one is perfect," Lauryn shook her head.

"No one except for you," Cammie revised her answer.

"Nope," Lauryn laughed.

"Okay. Fine. I guess you're right..." Cammie relented. "But you're about as close to perfect as someone can get," she added cheekily.

"Camz..." Lauryn smiled bashfully. She wasn't used to these kinds of compliments. She usually heard something of that sort coming from a tool, who had used it on a dozen girls before her. And she usually ignored comments of that sort. But they were so genuine coming from Cammie. It actually kind of made her blush.

Cammie was seriously trying to find an imperfection on Lauryn. Meanwhile, Lauryn was going over date ideas. Her mind was still considering and overruling places. Maybe she could take her to the museum. She immediately vetoed that option. That would cater to her own wants. She loved art. Granted, most people probably wouldn't want to go to a museum under most circumstances. Yeah, she should definitely veto that one.

"Babe?" Cammie called softly as she waved a hand in front of her face. She was elated when Lauryn responded. She got to call her *babe* now. She still wasn't used to that new perk.

"Yes?" Lauryn asked, focusing all of her attention on the girl on top of her.

"I said what are you thinking about?" Cammie repeated. Her question had fallen unto deaf ears. Lauryn's mind was clearly somewhere else.

"Dates," Lauryn said simply. It was beginning to give her a headache. She was stressing herself out about it. But it was only because she wanted to give Cammie the world.

"You really don't have to put that much effort into it..." Cammie frowned. "Maybe we can pitch ideas together."

"I kind of want to surprise you though," Lauryn mused aloud.

"Well, you can surprise me another time. C'mon, let's plan our first date together," Cammie offered as she sat up, looking around Lauryn's room for something to write with and something to write on.

"Really?" Lauryn questioned.

"Yes," Cammie nodded as her eyes landed on her journal. She picked it up, then stretched to get the pen from Lauryn's bedside table. She positioned herself back on top of Lauryn, sitting upright on her lap.

"What do you have in mind?" Lauryn prompted. She didn't want to flat out ask her what she wanted to do. She was going to let Cammie feed her ideas, then decide amongst those she'd suggested.

"Something fun..." she mused. "We can make a fort," Cammie suggested playfully. "With every blanket and pillow in my whole house." She did that with Sophia all the time. She had more fun doing it than she was willing to admit. Maybe doing it with Lauryn would be even better.

"Okay," Lauryn laughed. She would go along with it. She figured that Cammie wouldn't have said it if some part of her didn't actually want to do it.

"And we could go on a walk at night, so I can kiss you under the light of a thousand stars," Cammie continued. She grinned and bit the end of her pen. This playful mood wasn't wearing off. She was just getting started.

"Did you just quote Ed Sheeran?" Lauryn laughed.

"Maybe. And then we could make some more huge pancakes. We should have pancakes for dinner," Cammie added with a wide grin. Lauryn just listened in amusement. Pancakes for dinner. Alright. Keep it coming.

"Write it down," Lauryn instructed through her laughter. She laughed even louder when Cammie shifted back and used Lauryn's stomach as a table. She wrote down her first three ideas in a list and looked up at the ceiling, as if she were deep in thought.

"And then we could go out and eat sushi. Because you like sushi," Cammie added as she took to writing again.

Lauryn giggled at the absurdity of it all. Cammie probably wouldn't even eat it. Here she was, thinking they could go on a nice, normal, mature date. But no. Not with Cammie. A date with Cammie would include fort building and gigantic pancakes, apparently.

"You don't even like it," Lauryn giggled.

"I would try sushi again for you," Cammie countered, and Lauryn's heart melted. Just a little.

"You're fantastic," Lauryn sighed as she pulled Cammie towards her lips. Cammie crashed down rather clumsily, but kissed her softly nonetheless. She cupped Lauryn's cheek and smiled into it.

"We don't have to go for sushi. Maybe we could just have a little picnic. And afterwards, you can take me into your loving arms," Lauryn smirked, continuing Cammie's use of Ed's lyrics.

"Okay, deal," Cammie nodded affirmatively. "Now it's your turn to plan. Two more things," she instructed as she handed over the journal and pen.

"Camz, I'm not good at this. That's why you started helping me in the first place," Lauryn laughed as she pushed it back. "My mind is drawing a permanent blank."

"It's not permanent, come on. What would you want to do?" Cammie prompted as she drummed her fingers along Lauryn's stomach.

"I don't know," Lauryn admitted. She really could not think of a single thing worth doing with Cammie. Nothing they would both enjoy, that is.

"You like to paint... So we could do that," Cammie recalled.

"You don't, though," Lauryn frowned. She wasn't even sure that could be classified as a date.

"So what," Cammie dismissed that fact. She retrieved the journal and pen again to add that to their list. "What else do you like?"

"You," Lauryn grinned dorkily.

Cammie smiled shyly in response. "You know what I mean... What do you like to do? With or without me?"

"When I'm with you... I like to hear you sing?" Lauryn suggested, then blushed. She wanted to face palm herself. She hadn't meant to say that. But that was all that came to her. Even though it was very true. Only a few times had she caught Cammie in her element, singing and playing her guitar. It made her feel warm and fuzzy inside. She'd love to be serenaded, but she wouldn't seriously suggest that. She knew how shy Cammie got whenever anyone was around to hear her. But to Lauryn's surprise, she agreed.

"Then I'll bring my guitar. It can be like dinner and a show," Cammie grinned. "At the picnic, I'll sing to you. *Thinking Out Loud*, since we're talking about it. What else?"

"I think that's enough. I can't think of anything else. We could just cuddle. That's my favorite thing to do so far," Lauryn gave up and pulled Cammie to lay with her.

"No," Cammie protested.

"What?" Lauryn frowned.

"Let me hold you this time," Cammie negotiated.

Lauryn immediately relented. The only thing better than having Cammie in her arms was being held *by* her. They switched places. Lauryn sat up, wincing at the sound of her bones cracking. Cammie giggled and laid back, propping herself up on the pillows. Lauryn clambered over and gently lowered herself on top of her. Cammie's arms immediately wrapped around her. Lauryn leaned up to peck Cammie's lips just before laying her head on her chest. The many ways their date could possibly work out played in their minds. They didn't really talk for the rest of the night. They fell asleep a few hours later in that same position.

Chapter 14

Cammie and Lauryn finished writing down their date plans as a joke. Or what Cammie thought was a joke. She didn't really have any intentions of doing all of that stuff. It was dumb. She was being silly. But Lauryn was going to make it a reality. She thought it would be cute. After all, they had listed all of those things together. And she knew Cammie well enough to know that some part of her actually wanted to do every single one of those activities.

The following week of school passed by in a blur. Nothing of importance had happened. Lauryn's comfortability with Cammie in public had increased infinitely. Where she used to be too nervous to merely hold her hand, she was now brazenly claiming her girl. They kissed anywhere they felt the urge. In the hallways, in class, at lunch, everywhere. They weren't restricted to their homes. They weren't confined to the stairwell. Cammie and Lauryn did whatever they wanted, wherever they pleased.

On Friday, after the final bell, Naomi, Diana, and Allie were exiting their classes. The trio always seemed to meet at the same intersection. Luckily enough, each of them had lockers in close proximity with each other. There were about two or three people in between each of their lockers, but they were relatively close nonetheless. The girls all entered their combinations, missing the presence of Cammie and Lauryn.

It wasn't hard to guess where they were. And their suspicions were confirmed when they looked over at Lauryn's locker, which was the only one further down the hall. The two were lazily kissing against the lockers, regardless of their surroundings. People around them were trying to go to their lockers and head on home, but Cammie and Lauryn served as their obstacles. Diana thought it was kind of inconsiderate, but she shrugged it off. If Cammie was happy now, then so be it. At least their secretive days were over.

"*Okay,*" Diana called out to them, disrupting their little session. A crumpled up paper ball fell out of her cluttered locker, and she chucked it at them.

Cammie pulled back and frowned in Diana's direction. "Do you mind?" she giggled.

"Do *you* mind?" Diana countered, gesturing to the people standing patiently behind them.

"Hmm, nope. Lauryn, baby, do you mind?" Cammie smirked at the girl that was up against the lockers.

"Camz," Lauryn laughed as she pushed her back gently. "Diana's right. We're being obnoxious..."

"Yeah," Diana seconded, although she didn't recall saying those words.

"Fine," Cammie sighed and let Lauryn push her away. The kids standing behind them quickly shuffled over and were gone in a minute. Lauryn took it upon herself to visit her own locker. When she got her book bag, she intertwined her fingers with Cammie's once more.

Diana rolled her eyes. "Don't be *that* couple."

"What couple?" Lauryn laughed.

"The one that's fucking PDA crazy," Diana scoffed as they walked over to Cammie's locker.

"We're not," Cammie disagreed. She put in her combination incorrectly twice before successfully opening it. Lauryn posed as a distraction, even when she wasn't doing anything.

"Sure," Naomi interjected as she appeared beside them.

"I think it's cute," Allie shrugged.

"Yeah... You guys are just mad you're not getting any action," Cammie smirked before pulling Lauryn into another kiss.

"I get plenty," Diana smirked. "Nick's got me," she smiled to herself.

"Well, I just haven't seen him in a while..." Naomi sighed.

"Yeah, long distance is hard," Lauryn nodded sympathetically.

Cammie subtly rolled her eyes. Lauryn didn't need long distance relationships. She was here with her now. No need to dwell on the past.

Naomi shrugged and waved her off dismissively. "Whatever, though. What are y'all doing today?"

"Well, I was going to her house," Lauryn answered first, gesturing towards her girlfriend.

"Well, I know where I'm *not* going," Diana joked.

"Why? What's wrong with tagging along?" Allie teased.

"You mean third-wheeling," Naomi corrected her. "But what's wrong with that, Diana?"

"Hell no, I'm not about to be a third wheel to these two on purpose," Diana grimaced.

"Who needs ya anyway?" Cammie feigned offense as she latched on to Lauryn.

"I guess we'll find something else to do then," Allie assumed, realizing that they most likely weren't included in Cammie and Lauryn's plans.

"We can hang out tomorrow," Cammie promised as she reached for Allie's hand apologetically.

"It's okay," Allie shook her head. She really didn't want to impose if they wanted some privacy. She saw it as making up for lost time. They were adorable, as long as they were keeping things PG. They very well could've had other reasons for wanting to be alone, but she chose not to think about that.

"I feel bad..." Cammie pouted. She didn't want to exclude her friends from anything. In fact, she enjoyed when they were all together just as much as she enjoyed alone time with Lauryn.

"Don't, Cam," Allie laughed. "Just go on. We'll catch up with you guys later or something."

"Are you sure?" Cammie pressed. Her eyes were soft as they bore into Allie's, desperately trying to detect any hint of anger or betrayal. The last thing that she wanted was to abandon her friends.

Lauryn was watching the entire exchange fondly. Cammie's concern for other people was unwavering. It reminded her of why she liked her so much. She was so compassionate and attentive to other people's feelings, it brought a smile to Lauryn's face. Her girlfriend had one of the biggest hearts out of everyone she knew. It was endearing, and the fact that she got to call her *hers* made her heart swell.

"Yeah, of course," Allie assured her with a smile. She turned to Naomi and Diana for backup, but they'd diverted their attention to their phones. "But I'll see you guys later," she dismissed herself as she slipped away from the group.

Cammie watched her walk away, still feeling a bit dubious about her true feelings. Lauryn saw the worry etched onto her face. She wanted to see her smile. So she pulled her closer and pressed her lips to Cammie's temple. Cammie's bashful nature returned as she whirled around and held onto Lauryn in a tight hug. Lauryn reciprocated her hug and looked past her head at Naomi and Diana, who were still enthralled with their phones. She saw it as a chance to go ahead and bid them goodbye.

"We'll see you guys later," Lauryn said, loud enough to get their attention. Barely. They both were texting their boyfriends, having been reminded of them by Cammie and Lauryn. They waved, but they were distracted. Naomi was busy setting up a FaceTime date with Mason. Diana was snapchatting Nick.

Cammie pulled out of their hug and slipped her hand into Lauryn's instead. They exited the school in haste, momentarily forgetting that they had to catch the bus. They rushed outside, only to see the final busses pulling off. Nice.

"I guess we're walking," Lauryn stated the obvious from her position in the doorway.

Cammie grumbled and trudged down the sidewalk, eager to get home. She easily walked out of Lauryn's hold. She wasn't necessarily a fan of walking long distances. She wasn't a fan of any form of exertion. But if she had to, she was going to get it over with quickly. Lauryn had to jog to catch up with her, she was moving so fast.

"Babe," Lauryn laughed from behind. She reached out to grab Cammie's arm before she rounded the curb.

"Yeah?" Cammie responded. The nickname still caused her stomach to flip. She smiled dumbly and turned to face Lauryn.

"You're walking so fast," Lauryn informed her softly as she came to her side.

"Sorry," Cammie apologized sincerely. She didn't realize she was leaving her behind. She kissed her cheek and linked their arms together. "Sorry," she reiterated.

"It's okay," Lauryn chuckled as she leaned into the shorter girl.

They took their time. Hand in hand, they leisurely walked to Cammie's house. Their trip there was relatively silent. Lauryn was leaning on Cammie's arm, clutching it like a pillow. Cammie was reveling in it all, still trying to process how her life had changed dramatically over the last few weeks. It was inconceivable to her. She couldn't really fathom the information that she was actually dating Lauryn.

It was still plaguing her mind when she turned the key to her house. Lauryn broke the silence when they passed the living room on the way up to Cammie's room.

"So... About this date of yours..." Lauryn hinted as she gestured towards the empty living room. The couches in there were so inviting. Lauryn briefly imagined the room completely destroyed, with nothing but a huge fort to blame. The cushions would be ripped from the seats to serve as their floor, or their walls. And a plethora of blankets and comforters would be draped all along the exterior. It would be magnificent.

"You were serious about that?" Cammie asked as she came to a stop.

"Surprise," Lauryn grinned.

"I thought we were just joking around," Cammie smiled as well. "We can really do it?"

"I don't see why not," Lauryn shrugged.

"Yay!" Cammie exclaimed as she shrugged her book bag off. It landed on the floor with a thud, and Cammie was over by the closet in the same instant. She flung the door open and gathered as many blankets as her arms could carry. Lauryn couldn't even see her face when she came back. She was just a walking mountain of blankets and covers.

She found her way into the living room and dropped the heap onto the floor. She went to retrieve another pile, but turned to pull Lauryn along with her. She would gladly take the lead in their fort building. Cammie was usually under Sophia's control and direction, but she hadn't come home from school yet. She was going to take initiative as long as time would allow.

Together, Lauryn and Cammie lugged all of the blankets and pillows they could find into the living room. The amount of supplies they had was excessive, and they probably wouldn't even put a good seventy percent of it to use. They had more than enough to work with. Cammie crouched down to assess what she would start with first. Should she go for a tall one or a long one? How much space should be inside? Would they actually go in it? Of course they would. Obviously. But what architectural feats would they have to accomplish? How were they to know that the fort wouldn't collapse on top of them the moment they crawled inside? Sophia usually figured out the aesthetics. Cammie just helped her put it up. She felt indignant for not knowing how to begin without the help of the seven year old. Perhaps Lauryn would know.

"What should we do first?" Cammie asked casually.

"Um..." Lauryn hummed as she looked around. She was in the same boat as Cammie. Here they were, presented with all of these pillows and sheets, but they had no earthly idea what to do with them. The spontaneous creativity had escaped their teenage minds. They probably did need Sophia's wisdom. "I guess we should get furniture to tie everything to. Like, it could be the foundation?" Lauryn suggested.

"Yeah," Cammie agreed. She thought that was a wonderful idea. She was just going to throw a blanket over the couch and call it a day. Taking Lauryn's advice, she looked around for anything remotely tall. She considered the lamp over in the corner, but decided not to use it. What if it randomly combusted? That wouldn't be particularly fun. She looked at the abandoned coat rack in the corner and soon brought it over. That was much safer to use. She went to go get more inanimate objects that didn't require electricity, like a mop and broom.

Lauryn toted two chairs from their dining room over to their mess. They worked silently, bringing more furniture into the room and adding to the clutter.

Then they started to actually construct their fort. It was all going smoothly. Until Cammie lost her balance. While trying to reach one end of the blanket to another to tie, she leaned out too far. She landed ungracefully on top of their progress. Thankfully, the pillows broke her fall. But the rest toppled over her, destroying everything they'd spent the past fifteen minutes building.

"Nice one, babe," Lauryn laughed when she returned. She'd gone to get some hair ties. She figured they'd get the job done quicker, rather than tying two ends of the covers together in a knot. But of course, she'd come back only to find her girlfriend laying pathetically in the middle of a disaster.

Lauryn crossed the room and assessed the situation. When Cammie playfully cried out Lauryn's name, she hurried to help her up. She climbed onto the couch, careful not to damage the few things that were still intact. From the couch, she extended her hand to the smaller girl's. She attempted to hoist her up. Her awkward hold on Cammie made it easy for her to succumb to the same fate Cammie had endured. Lauryn landed clumsily on top of Cammie, in the same fashion Cammie had originally fallen. Maybe it was just something about that section of the couch. It doomed all who dared to stand there.

Lauryn quickly looked down for any signs of pain from Cammie's expression. Cammie's face was unreadable. But Lauryn soon heard the familiar laughter that caused her heart to leap. It made her laugh too. Cammie wrapped one arm around Lauryn's body and continued her deep belly laughter. Under most circumstances, she would be embarrassed. But not with Lauryn. She was at ease with being herself, for once in her life. Lauryn hadn't even done anything specific to make her feel comfortable, it was just her presence. It was ironic because that same girl used to intimidate her to no end. Cammie didn't know what caused the change, but she was grateful for it. She was able to be her goofy, dorky, awkward self without fearing the repercussions.

She smiled up at the girl that was still on top of her, then leaned up to connect their lips. Lauryn gladly reciprocated. Her hand came to rest on Cammie's side. Their hips were pressed together, kept in place by Cammie's grip on Lauryn's waist. Cammie, deciding to deepen their kiss, swiped her tongue across Lauryn's bottom lip. The two kissed each other fervently, only separating to breathe.

All the while, Cammie's hand had been inching up Lauryn's shirt. When Lauryn pulled away to catch her breath, her face was completely flushed. Cammie watched in amusement as the corner of her mouth turned up into a smirk. She bit her lip playfully, now sliding both hands to rest under the thin fabric. She was testing her limits, gauging Lauryn's reaction to her suggestive movements. Lauryn wasn't showing any signs of discomfort, so she slid her hands up further. The feeling of her smooth skin was getting Cammie worked up. Just a little bit. Lauryn was amused, wondering how much nerve Cammie had. Surely she wouldn't do much, they were in the middle of the living room. Anyone could walk in at any moment. Going further would be too risky. Cammie seemed to realize that and moved her hands. Instead of removing them from Lauryn's body completely, she slid them down further. Her hands were now cupping Lauryn's butt, and she was still watching her intently.

She was taking advantage of this playful mood. Never before had she been given the opportunity to touch her like that. And if she had been, she didn't think Lauryn would let her. But she was now. The atmosphere was ludic, not lustful in any way. Well, at least it was to Lauryn. Cammie's expression made Lauryn giggle. Lauryn couldn't exactly tell what was on her mind, but she knew it was inappropriate - if that look was any indication. She didn't mind much. They'd both had those thoughts before at some point. Nevertheless, she captured her lips once more.

"What are you doing?" Sophia's voice carried through the room, making both girls scramble off of each other.

"Uh," Cammie stalled as she looked to Lauryn with flushed cheeks. She'd never stood up so fast in her life. That exertion combined with Sophia's sudden presence made her heart beat uncomfortably. She thought she might've also had whiplash.

"We were playing a game," Lauryn excused their actions. Which wasn't technically a lie.

"Can I play?" Sophia asked as she dropped her book bag. Thankfully, she didn't press them for any information. She didn't seem to suspect anything. It wasn't like they were in the middle of making out or anything. Not at all.

"Um... We can play a different game," Cammie said nervously. She fidgeted with her fingers and looked at Lauryn for help. Lauryn looked just as flustered as Cammie, and would obviously be of no assistance.

"Were you guys playing castle?" Sophia assumed, pointing to the mess of blankets and pillows behind them.

Castle was the name Sophia had given their fort building. Her imagination allowed her to see it as being just that, while Cammie saw a poorly constructed tent. But whatever. If it kept Sophia happy, then it was a castle.

"No, of course not. I hope you didn't think I would start this without the help of my very own Butterfly Queen One," Cammie smiled down at her sister.

"Yeah," Lauryn added incredulously.

"We were waiting for our Queen. And now you're here," Cammie grinned as she took Sophia's hand, leading her towards the mass of blankets. "We need your help."

"I know what to do," Sophia said authoritatively. She crossed the room and began setting up the couch cushions accordingly. Cammie and Lauryn let her take over. They stood to the side sheepishly.

That stroke of luck was a blessing. They were grateful it had been Sophia. It could've been Sonya. Or Alexander. Her parents could've walked in just as easily. They both made a mental note not to be so obvious. Their reckless acts were going to get them in trouble eventually. So they toned it down. They played with Sophia, building their castle for the rest of the day. Cammie broke it two more times, but they just rebuilt it happily.

»»»

Sophia had finally gone to bed. Well, she hadn't really. She just passed out in her castle and began snoring, telling the couple cuddling on the couch that she was asleep. Beforehand, they'd been playing castle for hours. Cammie was the princess and Lauryn was her prince. The older girls had just as much fun as the little one.

Sophia's character actively switched between the queen and the dragon that guarded the castle. When she was a dragon, she attacked Lauryn by jumping on her and attempting to prevent her from getting to Cammie. But she always found a way. Once Lauryn passed the dragon and it died, Cammie would crawl out of the castle. At one point, Lauryn slayed the dragon and arrived to the castle theatrically, sweeping her princess off of her feet. She held her in her arms bridal style. Then she kissed her on the mouth, right there in front of Sophia. Lauryn had admittedly forgotten that she was there, but when she registered it, she was relieved to find Sophia smiling at them. She seemed to accept their relationship with no questions asked.

That was an hour ago. But now Sophia was peacefully curled up into a ball, snoring loudly inside her castle. Sophia's foot was the only visible part of her from inside the fort. Cammie and Lauryn were in the spooning position on the couch now.

"She's so cute," Lauryn commented.

"So are you," Cammie countered.

"Aww," Lauryn smiled. She pressed a kiss onto Cammie's shoulder.

"You make a really good prince," Cammie quipped.

"I am honored," Lauryn laughed eloquently. "You're the perfect little princess, Camzi."

"You're the perfect everything," Cammie responded immediately. She stretched out, then Lauryn followed her lead. The two changed positions, now sitting upright.

"Are you ready to continue this date?" Lauryn said mischievously.

"It's late," Cammie declined softly. Her head was laying on Lauryn's shoulder. She was comfortably curled into her girlfriend, whose fingers were stroking her arm affectionately.

"I thought you were going to kiss me under the light of a thousand stars?" Lauryn challenged as she faced her. She was quoting Cammie from the other day, vaguely hoping she would recall it.

"I would... But you're taking me into your loving arms right now. We can't interrupt that," Cammie countered with a smirk.

"Camz, come on," Lauryn pleaded. "It's nice," she added as she looked out of the window. It seemed to be a clear night. The February air might be a little cool, but it wasn't anything they couldn't handle.

"My legs don't work like they used to before," Cammie excused herself with a sly smile.

"Then let me sweep you off of your feet," Lauryn continued as she wrapped her arms tighter around Cammie.

"You're such a dork," Cammie laughed. That was her only response, because she couldn't think of any more Ed Sheeran references to tie into the conversation. Quoting *Thinking Out Loud* had sort of become their thing, ever since Cammie had done it while they were pitching ideas. Perhaps they could use lyrics from his other songs.

"Of course," Lauryn nodded. "You don't want to go out tonight?"

"I do... But I don't," Cammie laughed. She would love to resume their date, if it could even be called that. But she was so comfortable now. She didn't want to move at all, if she could help it. And it was probably cold outside.

"Okay, we'll do that some other time," Lauryn relented, sinking back into the couch. "How about those pancakes for dinner, though?"

"We can do that. Are you hungry?" Cammie questioned.

"A little," Lauryn answered. Her stomach rumbled, further confirming her statement.

"Okay," Cammie sighed as she sat up. "Come on."

Lauryn's grin widened and she hopped up after Cammie, following her into the kitchen. The two gathered the ingredients together. Lauryn got her started again, and Cammie followed the steps with virtually no instruction. It was relatively quiet. Nothing needed to be said. But with silence, both girls were lost in their thoughts. Lauryn wasn't thinking about anything in particular, but Cammie's mind was running rampant. One thought led to another, and now here she was thinking about living with Lauryn.

They could make pancakes every morning. Eh, probably not *every* morning. They'd most likely get sick of them. But they could cook together all the time. And they would share the same bed each night. Her life would be perfect. Her days would begin and end with Lauryn. Endless Lauryn. An abundance of her girlfriend. All the time. God, she was really getting ahead of herself. But she couldn't help it.

Lauryn came behind her and snaked her arms around her waist. She placed a chaste kiss on her neck as her hands gripped her hips. For Cammie, it made her feel something inside that she felt the need to hide. The gesture wasn't exactly igniting the sparks from earlier, it was a completely different vibe. She felt it in her stomach and in her chest. A warm feeling spread throughout her entire body, leaving her smiling like the lovesick fool she knew she was. Simple things like what Lauryn was doing now were what made her fall. She didn't even think it was possible to fall after you already had. But here she was, falling a mile a minute. And Lauryn hadn't said a word.

Lauryn's lips were teasing the same spot. They were just brushing across her skin. Her kisses were so light, Cammie almost couldn't feel them. Lauryn had her in her hold so tightly, Cammie almost couldn't breathe. She felt like she was suffocating. But this would be the best way to die, hands down. Could someone die from being too in love? Cammie was sure she would find out eventually. Lauryn would be the death of her.

"I love you," Cammie said quietly.

Lauryn's lips stilled on her neck, taking a moment to process what she'd said. She smiled to herself, then kissed her neck again.

"I love you too," she reciprocated. As usual, it didn't hold the same weight as Cammie's words. But in that moment, Lauryn didn't think they were so different. She *did* love Cammie.

She could sit there and analyze what love meant specifically, but did it really have a definition? It was a flexible thing. She adored everything about Cammie. Even the things that weren't so admirable. All aspects of the girl she now encompassed made her feel whole. They complimented each other. And of course she loved general things like her appearance and her mind, but it ran a little deeper than that.

It was the little things. Just simple things, like hearing her speak. Cammie's talking voice placated her in a way no one else could. She was so articulate. Listening to her ramble was amongst her favorite pastimes. And when she sang, it made her heart ache in the best way. Little things, like her slow breathing whenever she fell asleep in her arms. Or the calming rise and fall of her chest. Simple things, like the way she smiled whenever Lauryn was around - or her smile in general. It was obvious that Lauryn was special to her. And she was special to Lauryn too. Diana liked to call it her Lauryn smile, and Lauryn could attest to that. It was her favorite thing.

It was trivial things like the way she played with Sophia earlier. Her relationship with her sister was endearing. Or just how friendly she was, how selfless the brown eyed girl always seemed to be. Her reaction to leaving Allie earlier that day was a testament to that observation. If Lauryn were to list how many little things she loved about Cammie, she would've been writing all night. Maybe *that's* what love is. Noticing small, almost minute details.

And there was a certain sense of protection she had whenever they were together. The security she felt whenever she was in her arms had been rarely duplicated by anyone before her. It was the two of them against the world. She knew she would defend her to the end. She would fight for her, if it ever came down to it. Those feelings were mutual. She could do anything if Cammie was by her side, and she would do anything for her. And maybe *that's* what love is. Feeling safe and secure.

With the increased amount of time they'd been spending together, Lauryn found that she always craved her girlfriend's presence. She always had to be holding, touching, or kissing her. And if she couldn't, she was satisfied just by being in the same room as her. If Cammie was in her vicinity, Lauryn was happy. Even when she was angry, she always wanted to be with her. Maybe *that's* what love is. A sense of belonging, regardless of circumstances.

Lauryn understood Cammie and vice versa. Everything concerning the other was just *there*. They were in sync most of the time. Both girls had been told on more than one occasion that they did the same things at the same time without knowing it. And it was always easy to talk to her. Wordless communication worked in mysterious ways. Their connection was one that not many people got to experience. They were in the same mindset, most of the time. She knew what she was thinking and how she was feeling without exchanging a word. Her emotions were easily perceptible to Lauryn, and Lauryn's were easily perceptible to Cammie. Maybe *that's* what love is. A strong mental, emotional, and physical connection.

Those were the very things Cammie had written about in her journal. Those were only a few. And Cammie was supposedly in love with her. If Lauryn could identify with those experiences, she must have been too. She saw then that there was no shift. There was no particular moment. It wouldn't be spelled out to her. Nothing profound would suddenly let her know. Cupid's arrow wouldn't be striking her. There was nothing to wait for. She'd been falling a little harder every day. It was gradual.

"I love you too," she reiterated. She smiled at the confession. Although she knew Cammie would never assume that she finally meant it in that way, she wasn't going to tell her. She'd show her through her actions. Actions speak louder than words anyway.

Chapter 15

To Cammie, Lauryn's admission made no difference. She wasn't conscious of what mental analysis Lauryn had just gone through. She didn't know that Lauryn meant it differently than when she'd uttered those same words thirty seconds ago. She wondered why she'd repeated it, but assumed it was because she hadn't responded.

A peculiar smell wafted through the air, and Cammie immediately ripped herself from Lauryn's embrace. They were burning their damn pancakes. Cammie flipped it over. The underside was burnt, which didn't come as a surprise. At least she didn't set the house on fire. Maybe cooking with Lauryn shouldn't become a norm. They got distracted far too easily.

"It's not too bad..." Lauryn commented wryly.

"Lauryn, it's *black*," Cammie countered with a giggle. She thought that if this were a cartoon, the pancake would've surely crumbled into dust. The poor thing was completely singed.

"Let's start over then," she suggested.

This time, they were attentive to their pancake. Cammie didn't take her eyes off of it. Not even once. Lauryn was having a good time trying to distract her though. Kisses weren't working. Holding her in different positions weren't either. She whispered sweet nothings into her ear, to no avail. All she got was a cute little smile. She didn't have Cammie's attention right now. But that was better than burning the house down, she supposed.

With their uncharred pancakes, the girls filed back into the living room. Cammie had Lauryn in her lap, who was happily devouring her pancakes. Cammie only wanted one right now. Or what would've been the size of one. The pancakes they cooked were often the size of four. Or five. They were gigantic. Because they didn't have the patience to cut it into equal halves, Lauryn was just forking small portions into Cammie's mouth. It was a messy job.

Their playful mood from earlier had returned. Lauryn's method of feeding Cammie soon turned from sort of romantic to very childish. She began teasing Cammie, maneuvering the fork to make it difficult for her girlfriend to bite it. She started making airplane noises and everything. But she was so entertained, Cammie went along with it. She soon ended up sticky. The syrup kept dripping onto her shirt, but she didn't care. And Lauryn's back was sticky too, because she kept leaning into Cammie. She was so tickled by her own antics, she threw her head back in laughter every few seconds.

"You're so dumb," Cammie laughed along.

"You love me," Lauryn countered with a knowing smirk.

"I do," Cammie agreed.

"Mhm," Lauryn kissed her sweetly. Literally, because she tasted like syrup now. "And I love you too."

Cammie didn't respond to that. She just pulled Lauryn closer. She knew she'd regret it later when they'd have to detach themselves. They were so gross. Maybe they could shower. Nope. No images of naked Lauryn. No. She shouldn't think of that now. Not here. Not with Lauryn in her lap. Thankfully, the said girl provided a distraction.

"Valentine's Day is coming up," she hinted. Ever since they'd been official, Lauryn had been racking her brain for some romantic gesture towards Cammie. She wanted to go all out for her, regardless of if she would receive anything in return.

"Yeah, I know," Cammie smiled. She'd secretly been doing the same thing. Her planning skills weren't the best, but she was willing to try.

"Do we have plans?" Lauryn asked slyly.

"Not as of now... But I'm definitely getting something for you," Cammie answered.

"Well, I am too. Maybe then we can go on an actual date?" Lauryn suggested. "You know, where you dress up and look even more beautiful than you usually do? Like at a dinner or something?"

The idea of a dinner date didn't really appeal to either of them. It seemed to be a little boring. But it was traditional. And they would be together, so they'd probably enjoy whatever it was that they were doing.

"Where should we go?" Cammie wondered out loud.

"I want to take you somewhere expensive and fancy," Lauryn smirked and looked back at her.

"No, nothing expensive..." Cammie disagreed.

"Why not?" Lauryn laughed.

"I don't know, I don't have a lot of money. And I don't mind spending money on you at all, but I think it should go towards something more memorable. Like, a present. Or a trip. Or something..." Cammie disclosed.

Lauryn was staring at her lovingly. That logic made perfect sense. And besides, doing a dinner date would be way too mainstream. Dinners were for adults. They'd have their time eventually. No use in making reservations if they wouldn't really be enjoying themselves. Lauryn nodded and kissed her nose lightly.

"Yeah, I agree," Lauryn smiled.

"No, I mean - we can go to a dinner if you want... But that's just what I think," Cammie added, fearing that she'd shut down her plans.

"It's fine, Camz. I didn't really want to, but I thought it would be romantic," Lauryn admitted.

"Are you sure? We can go to eat dinner if-" Cammie rushed, feeling like Lauryn was compromising for her. But she couldn't finish her statement. Lauryn's lips shut her up, letting her words hang in the air. Her kiss was short and soft, just long enough to make her refrain from speaking.

"*Camz,*" Lauryn emphasized. "It's fine. We can just hang out here, if you want. I'm seriously okay with anything you want to do."

"Okay," she nodded goofily. She cupped Lauryn's face and coaxed her back to her mouth. She complied, then turned in her lap to be more comfortable. Lauryn's hands found the nape of Cammie's neck as she closed the distance between them. They kissed lazily, with no concept of time. It could've been mere minutes, or it could've been hours. No matter how much had passed, they were sure their time couldn't have been spent better.

»»»»

Lauryn came early. She missed the bus, because there was no way in hell she was going to be carrying all that stuff. When she got out of her mom's car and entered the school, she lugged a huge teddy bear down the hallway. She then positioned it in front of her girlfriend's locker. It was almost her size. After that, she brought a lighter load. She carried the flowers and chocolate and placed them in the bear's lap. She looked at her work and approved of the presentation. She couldn't wait for Cammie to arrive. This was admittedly the most typical thing to do on Valentine's Day, but she didn't care. She knew Cammie would eat it all up anyway.

Cammie was confused when she got on the bus. She was so prepared to make her grand gesture. She had a simple gift. She wasn't really expecting a gift from Lauryn, and she didn't want to make her feel guilty for not getting her anything, like she probably would. It was a single rose, but it was the brightest one she could find. She'd gotten a heart shaped balloon and tied it to her wrist to make sure it wouldn't float away. It was awkward to ride the bus with a giant balloon. She vowed never to do it again.

All the while, she was wondering where Lauryn was. She hoped she wasn't sick. She was actually beginning to worry herself. She entered the school with fidgety hands and twiddling fingers. Where was her girlfriend? Cammie's confusion was just turning into worry as she made her way to her locker. Usually, if Lauryn was going to be late, she'd tell Cammie beforehand. And she hadn't.

Lauryn saw Cammie approaching from the far end of the hall. She could spot her from a mile away. Her fluffy hair and timid walk was a distinguishing factor. It always made Lauryn smile whenever she saw her coming. And here she was. Lauryn wanted to surprise her, so she ducked down behind the bear. It was big enough to hide her effectively, but she stumbled. She was pretty sure Cammie saw her going to hide anyway, so she just stood up and waited for her to come over.

"Lauryn!" Cammie smiled and sped up to a jog to greet her. "What were you doing?"

"I was gonna hide... But then I tripped... And I figured you already saw me... And... It's just all bad," Lauryn laughed in embarrassment. She pulled Cammie into her arms and buried her face into her neck. Hugs were her favorite.

"What's all that?" Cammie asked when they pulled away. She wouldn't infer that those presents were for her. Someone had probably left them there, just waiting for their unassuming significant other to walk up on it. But they probably shouldn't have left in from of Cammie's locker. That was kind of rude.

112

"Your Valentine's Day gift," Lauryn laughed. "This is all yours."

"Mine...?" Cammie repeated in shock. She looked down at the gigantic fluffy bear that seemed to be holding her other two tokens. She looked between the bear and Lauryn, unable to process that it was actually for her.

"Yes, baby," Lauryn laughed. The new name made her smile. She hadn't really called her that before, but it had fallen from her lips without a second thought. She was enjoying this way too much. She wished she could frame this moment. Cammie was adorable as ever.

Cammie crouched down to retrieve the flowers. It was an actual bouquet. And she'd never gotten flowers before. Or anything, for that matter. And as she looked at the chocolate, she saw that it was Kit Kats. Her favorite. She hadn't told Lauryn that was her favorite, but somehow she just knew. God, she was a keeper for sure.

"Oh my God," Cammie mumbled. She brought her hand to cover her mouth, which was hanging open. Tears brimmed her eyes, but she couldn't stop them. One fell, and Lauryn immediately pulled her into her embrace.

Lauryn really hadn't been expecting her to cry. She didn't think the gesture would mean that much to her. But it did. And she was. Lauryn smiled down at her, completely smitten. She placed a tender kiss on her forehead and simply held her until she pulled herself together.

"I think I just died," Diana commented. She'd arrived a few minutes after Cammie, but had been there long enough to witness Lauryn's act.

Lauryn and Cammie both turned at the sound of her voice. Cammie wiped her face quickly on Lauryn's shirt, then looked up at her apologetically. Gross. But whatever. Lauryn's smile didn't falter at all.

"Good morning, Diana," Lauryn greeted her. She rested her arm around Cammie's waist and traced her hip with her fingertips.

"Good morning," Diana returned. "Dang, Cam. She got you all that... She's a keeper," she smiled, unaware that Cammie had just said the same thing in her head.

"It's nothing much. It's not a big deal," Lauryn countered modestly.

"Are you kidding?" Cammie asked incredulously, shifting to make eye contact. "Lauryn, this is amazing..."

"Really?" Lauryn grinned. She'd admittedly gotten a little carried away. But it was nothing compared to what she *would've* gotten, had her pockets been a little deeper. Those sappy presents cost about fifty dollars total, but she had to save her budget for Cammie's *real* gift. Their first month anniversary was coming up soon. She thought that day deserved something special, not commercial items like teddy bears and chocolates.

"Yes, really. No one has ever gotten me anything before," Cammie disclosed shakily. Her stupid tears were threatening to choke her up again. God, all of these emotions. Get a grip, Cammie.

"*Okay*, even though I gave you some candy last year," Diana scoffed.

"Diana, it was one piece. And you ate half of it..." Cammie recalled. "And then you told me that you only gave it to me because it fell on the floor!"

Diana waved her hand dismissively. "Whatever. I still gave you something. And I made you my valentine in the fourth grade. So that's something," she recalled indignantly.

"Shut up," Cammie laughed. She shoved her lightly in the arm and went to wipe those freaking tears again. Jesus. They just wouldn't stop.

"You're so cute," Lauryn gushed. Cammie wrapped her arms around Lauryn. The balloon attached to her arm floated over and bopped Lauryn lightly on the side of her head. It was then that Lauryn registered the balloon tied to her wrist. "Whose balloon is that?" she asked, slightly mocking Cammie's tone from a few minutes ago.

"Yours..." Cammie giggled. She moved to untie it, but failed. Lauryn had to help, but it still didn't budge. Tying it to herself definitely had its intended purpose. That balloon wasn't going anywhere, unfortunately. With a sigh, Cammie gave up and dropped her arms by her side.

"It's stuck," Lauryn stated the obvious.

"Well, it's supposed to be yours. I just can't get it off," Cammie shrugged. "But I did get you this," she said as she took off her book bag. Laying frailly on top of her books inside was the rose.

She realized in that moment that her idea had backfired. Now *she* was the one that had underperformed. Lauryn had gone all out. Cammie felt a little guilty for not doing more. She always seemed to underestimate her girlfriend. Nevertheless, she presented the rose to the green-eyed beauty.

Lauryn's eyes softened tremendously. She's received flowers from boyfriends in the past, but never a real rose. It was always fake, because boys are cheap. Even though it was only one rose from Cammie, it was special to her. She promised then to perch it on her dresser, long after it was wilted. It held a special place in her heart. Cammie didn't have to go all out for her. Simple gestures spoke volumes sometimes. And Lauryn felt like an ass for trying to win her over with all of those material things.

"I love you," Lauryn declared as she stepped towards Cammie. She kissed her on the lips, completely disregarding the students that were now starting to fill up the hallway. Her hands found Cammie's hips, and she grasped them firmly as she claimed her mouth.

"Still here," Diana interrupted from the side.

Lauryn broke away hesitantly. She contemplated ignoring her, but she decided against it. She didn't want to be rude. When she tuned into her surroundings, she noticed the few onlookers they'd accumulated. And surprisingly, it didn't bother her. Let them stare. Who cared? She brushed them off and turned her attention to Diana. "Sorry."

"No, I'm kidding. I'm just a little jealous right now though," Diana smirked.

"Nick isn't doing anything?" Cammie questioned.

"Yeah... But not until later. You guys are so freaking adorable. And now I think me, Naomi, and Allie aren't the only ones who think so," Diana hinted in reference to the spectators.

Lauryn was hesitant to turn around. She thought she'd see a bunch of judgmental looks. Or a group of scornful, homophobic faces. She thought she would see disgust in response to their public affection. But when she did meet their eyes, they were smiling.

"You guys are so cute," Beatrice smiled in passing.

"Thanks," Cammie said proudly. She hooked her arm around Lauryn's waist and leaned into her side. It seemed like she'd been waiting her entire life to hear those words. Lauryn was officially her girlfriend, and now people were commenting on their status. She was ecstatic.

»»»

Cammie had to deal with that damn balloon all day long. It just stayed there, all throughout her classes. She refused to cut it off or pop it, because it was Lauryn's. She wanted her to have it. She could cut it after school. And when they got to Lauryn's house after school, that's exactly what she did. The string had actually left a deep red mark on her skin. She rubbed it with a frown, but finally handed over the balloon to her girlfriend.

"Now I can *finally* give this to you," Cammie emphasized as she waited for Lauryn to take it.

"You should put some cocoa butter on that," Lauryn offered, noticing how deep and red the imprint was. "There's some in my bathroom, if you want it."

"Sure," Cammie agreed. She got up from Lauryn's bed and disappeared into the bathroom to retrieve it.

Lauryn looked at her balloon. It was so cute. There was a pun on it. *You make me float.* That was a very Cammie thing to do. *Very* Cammie. She turned to the rose that was laying in the middle of her dresser. She hadn't gotten a vase for it just yet. Did people put single flowers in vases? Lauryn wasn't sure, but she was going to. Eventually. Her balloon floated back into her field of vision just as Cammie was coming back.

"This is so cute, Camz," Lauryn commented happily once Cammie walked back towards her bed. "Where'd you find this?"

"I had it custom made," Cammie answered with a shrug. She sat next to Lauryn with a dumb smile. "You like it?"

"Of course I do. But they do that?" Lauryn asked incredulously.

"Apparently," Cammie laughed as she gestured to it.

That was so sweet. Part of her wanted to preserve her balloon until it deflated, but a bigger part of her wanted to suck the helium out of it. It would be so much fun.

"Babe?" Lauryn prompted softly.

"Hm?" Cammie faced her.

"Can we suck the helium out of this? Do you mind?" Lauryn asked nervously. She didn't want to offend her or anything.

"No, I actually really wanted to do it too," Cammie admitted.

"I mean, it's really sweet. I kind of want to keep it... But at the same time, I want to do this," Lauryn giggled.

"It's yours. We can do whatever you want with it," Cammie laughed. She was thinking of that earlier. She almost bought two balloons, just so she could have some helium to herself.

"Yay," Lauryn grinned. She picked up the scissors they used to cut it off of Cammie's wrist, then stabbed a small hole into the side of it. She pinched it closed quickly, then brought it to her lips. Cammie watched in amusement from beside her.

Lauryn took it away and yelled at the top of her lungs. Cammie thought she sounded like a happy squirrel. Or an excited chipmunk. Something of that sort. Whatever it was, it was funny. Cammie laughed loudly and waited for Lauryn to speak some more.

"Camz, I love you. Iloveyou, Iloveyou, Iloveyou," she said quickly as she attacked Cammie with kisses. Her voice was so shrill. It was so funny to Cammie. It was like Alvin was declaring his love for her a thousand times over. Cammie's stomach started to hurt, she was giggling so much.

115

"Give it to me," Cammie requested as she grabbed it from Lauryn. She put her mouth over it and inhaled the helium, just like Lauryn had. She couldn't think of anything to say, so she just made a sound. "Ahh..." she squealed.

Lauryn laughed obnoxiously and took the balloon from her again. They both took turns from that point until it was gone. Cammie was now sprawled out on Lauryn's bed. She thought she should've had an eight pack by now, her muscles were so sore. Lauryn was draped over Cammie's body, suffering from the same tension in her abdomen.

"I love you," Lauryn said for the sixth time today. She kept saying it in hopes that Cammie would see the difference. Repetition was key. She'd allowed herself to accept the fact that she may very well have been in love with her. Without overthinking the circumstances, Lauryn was willing to let herself fall freely. Her meticulous analysis yesterday pushed her to believe that she was. Maybe it wasn't as deep as Cammie was, but she was in love nonetheless. Whatever her status, it had surpassed platonic love by far. Cammie had been enduring these feelings for a much longer time. Therefore, her feelings were more intense. But she made Lauryn feel something special within. She made Lauryn feel love. The butterflies and skipped heartbeats were a testament to that.

There were no definitive parameters to love. But she definitely felt something in contrast to the way she felt about her just a month ago. With every hug and kiss, her feelings intensified. During every moment spent cuddling or sharing private conversations, she fell harder. Cammie had a certain power over her that she was willing to succumb to all too fast. She would undoubtedly do anything for her. The way she felt could hardly be described. Cammie made her feel whole. And she wanted her to know. Cammie was everything, and she loved her.

"I love you too, Lauryn," Cammie reciprocated as she ran her fingers through her hair soothingly. She was wondering why she'd said it so much today. She'd said it six times. Cammie had been counting. Because each time she said it, it made her heart flutter.

"Good," Lauryn responded. She rolled over to kiss her. First on the cheek, then she pressed her lips to hers. Her hand found her waist and she kissed her again.

Cammie loosely wrapped her arm around her. Lauryn's body was at an angle at first, with only her torso on Cammie. But she repositioned herself. She shifted over and lowered her body on top of Cammie completely, all without breaking contact. And that was when Cammie lost it. It always had the same effect whenever Lauryn laid on top of her like that. Her weight didn't bother Cammie at all. What started off as innocent kissing would turn into something entirely different in her mind. But she couldn't help it.

Although she thought she was insanely beautiful, there was no denying that Lauryn definitely had her fair share of sex appeal. Her body was one of many things Cammie admired. Everything was the perfect shape. Even though Lauryn would usually fight her claims with modest rebuttals, Cammie saw her as wholly perfect. Especially her backside, which she was particularly fond of. Her hands were skimming down her back slowly, with it as their destination. She was caressing her side, not too eager to ruin the moment by coming on too strong. Lauryn smirked and sucked on Cammie's bottom lip, just before invading her mouth.

Lauryn slipped her tongue into her mouth gently. She knew kissing this way tended to make Cammie nervous, but she'd gotten better with it in time. Cammie's tongue glided over hers confidently, and her grip on Lauryn tightened a little. Lauryn lifted her hand to settle on the side of Cammie's neck. Her hand grazed the wispy hairs at the base of her neck as she continued to kiss her.

Careful not to be overbearing, Cammie only moved one hand to her butt. The other stayed put on her side. Her fingers teased the exposed skin where Lauryn's shirt had ridden up. But Lauryn soon tired of making out. She wanted to explore new territory. She broke away and began to leave loving kisses along Cammie's jawline instead. Cammie's breath hitched in her throat. That was unexpected. Lauryn's hand dropped down to Cammie's side. Her hand slipped under her shirt and she grazed her nails across her skin lightly. And now her lips were on her neck. But it wasn't chaste like in the many times before. Lauryn's intentions were clear. Cammie exhaled in the same breathy whimper Lauryn had been able to elicit before. There was virtually nothing to stop her from continuing this time.

That sound put Lauryn in another mindset. This wasn't so innocent anymore. She continued kissing her neck. With one deliberate swipe of her tongue, she actually made Cammie moan. She tried to suppress that, but had done so poorly. Lauryn pulled back and smirked down at the girl who was now blushing. Nothing was said. Lauryn laid beside her and just went back to manipulating that same spot on her neck. She left hot, open-mouthed kisses just under her jaw. She began to suck on the spot, making Cammie shift under her. Suddenly, she couldn't tell which was her pulse, her heartbeat, or which was Cammie's.

They should probably stop, because Cammie was getting way too heated in places she wasn't comfortable with. All the while, Lauryn's hand had been making its way up her body. Her warm hand glided across her stomach and had just reached the wiring of her bra. Lauryn cupped her breast gently and began to fondle her over her bra. Oh, God. This was going much further than Cammie was planning for. It excited her, but made her anxious at the same time.

There were probably millions of people having sex right now, just for the fun of it. Just because it was Valentine's Day. Perhaps they would be joining that group, and Cammie was kind of scared. Part of her didn't want it to escalate. Lauryn was her first for everything. And Cammie didn't know how far she'd been - simply because she would've hated to hear about it. But she didn't want their first time together to be bad. She felt a little pressured to make it good, although she was clueless about most of it. She didn't want to force the act, and she didn't want Lauryn to feel obligated to follow through just because they'd started. It was a special enough moment for their first time - it was *Valentine's Day*. That's romantic, right? Isn't that special? Sure it was, but Cammie was so nervous. Her mind was reeling as Lauryn began inching her shirt up.

Cammie wasn't all that comfortable with her body, but she trusted herself with Lauryn. She hadn't detached her lips from her skin yet. There was a certain tenderness to her gesture that made Cammie feel safe. Nevertheless, there was still a great deal of apprehension that suddenly made her timid. Lauryn sensed the change in her demeanor. Her hand was still massaging her breast when she finally made eye contact again. She wanted to make sure they were on the same page. While she held her gaze, Cammie saw just how blown Lauryn's pupils were. And she made note of how deeply she was breathing now. Could she really be as turned on as Cammie was? Apparently so.

"Are you okay?" Lauryn clarified raspily as she stilled her movements. She hoped she wasn't moving too fast. The last thing she wanted was to make Cammie uncomfortable.

"Yeah," Cammie husked in response. Lauryn had never heard her voice sound like that before. It was... *Hot.* But something in her expression made her hesitant to believe her. She didn't seem so sure.

"Camz, really... Are you okay?" Lauryn asked again as she removed her hand from her shirt completely. "Tell me if you're uncomfortable, and we can stop..."

"I'm not uncomfortable... It's just..." Cammie started to answer, but her sentence tapered off. She didn't want Lauryn to be upset with her for stopping, but something about this was off. It was hot as hell, and they clearly both felt the same way right now, but something was wrong about their timing.

"It's just what?" Lauryn pressed. Her eyes softened and she pursed her lips. She rested her hand on Cammie's hip anxiously.

"I don't know," Cammie said honestly. She didn't know exactly what it was. Maybe it wasn't a thing at all. Lauryn hadn't done anything wrong. She wasn't uncomfortable. She was just awkward. That was probably it. Perhaps the reality of the situation had caught up to her and it just made her feel awkward. Never in a million years had she thought that Lauryn was attracted to her enough to do these things. She easily saw herself pleasuring Lauryn, but now it was Lauryn who was initiating it all. Maybe it was that plot twist that was so off-putting.

"I'm sorry," Lauryn apologized and stopped touching Cammie altogether.

"No, don't... You didn't do anything. I'm just..." Cammie said quickly, but that sentence faded out as well.

"Shit, I knew I was getting carried away... I'm sorry," Lauryn muttered to herself, disregarding Cammie's words.

"Lauryn, you didn't do anything..." Cammie reiterated. "I'm just... Weird, I guess. It's not you."

"Why didn't you say anything?" Lauryn frowned. She was beginning to beat herself up about it. She felt like she'd just taken advantage of Cammie - like she'd robbed her of her innocence or something. She felt guilty.

"There's nothing to say... I wasn't uncomfortable or anything... I liked it," Cammie said. Her cheeks heated up at the insinuation. This was becoming unbearably awkward.

"Well, I did too..." Lauryn laughed. "But maybe we're just not ready for *that* yet," she offered with an apologetic smile. And she was perfectly fine with the prospect of waiting. They weren't ready. They had been rushing things. Just because it was Valentine's Day didn't mean they had to have sex. Not at all. They were both a little guilty of thinking that though.

"Yeah... I don't think we are," Cammie agreed sheepishly and pulled her shirt back down.

"God," Lauryn giggled and shook her head. "We're a mess."

"I like our mess," Cammie smiled shyly.

Lauryn nodded. She wrapped her arm around Cammie and gently pulled her into her arms. "This is what we do now. We cuddle. Nothing more... Nothing less."

Cammie nodded against her shoulder and nuzzled her face in the crook of Lauryn's neck. She was so embarrassed. Although Lauryn claimed she had nothing to worry about, she couldn't help it. They'd done all of that, only to have Cammie ruin it all. It was wonderful until she started to dwell on it. She made a mental note not to think about any circumstances the next time - if there even *was* a next time. God, there probably wouldn't be. Lauryn would probably play it safe and never start

118

anything ever again. Well, that was a long shot. But it could happen. What if Cammie had to initiate it next time? Could she really take that step by herself? Probably not. Damn it. They were never going to have sex. Because she ruined it.

"Sorry," Cammie mumbled against Lauryn's skin.

"For what, babe?" Lauryn questioned softly. A few minutes had passed. They were silently cuddling, both deeply in thought about what had just occurred.

"I ruined it," Cammie answered simply.

"You didn't ruin anything. You saved us from being in an awkward position later on, actually," Lauryn countered with a light chuckle.

"What do you mean?" Cammie asked.

"I would've preferred to have that realization when we did, rather than when my hand was in your pants," she elaborated with a suggestive smirk.

"Oh..." Cammie blushed. "Yeah..." she nodded subtly. She was grateful that Lauryn couldn't see her. She probably looked like a tomato right now. Her face was burning with embarrassment, regardless of what Lauryn had just said. Nothing could sway her thought that she'd ruined it. Because she definitely had. No matter what Lauryn would say to make her think otherwise.

"So, with that said... You didn't ruin anything," Lauryn reiterated. She knew exactly what Cammie was thinking. And she wanted to get her out of that mindset. But she also knew that Cammie was stubborn. She would think whatever she was thinking until another thought came along to replace it. Lauryn really didn't want her to blame herself. It was inevitable. They really just weren't ready for that step, and Lauryn didn't know what she had been thinking. It was mostly Lauryn's fault. Not Cammie's. Distraction was her best bet to get Cammie's mind off of it.

"And I love you," she added as she pressed a tender kiss on her girlfriend's forehead.

Seven times. This was the seventh time Lauryn had said those words to Cammie today. Maybe she was trying to tell her something. But it couldn't be. Cammie feared she was a victim of wishful thinking. Would Lauryn keep saying it in a friendly way, knowing how deeply Cammie felt? Surely not, she wasn't cold-hearted. And before, she tried to stay away from saying it - just to avoid making things awkward. But she'd said it seven times today. Seven times. In one day.

"Do you?" Cammie asked. That was a loaded question. It was a variation of the question *Are you in love with me?* without being direct about it. But Lauryn understood fully.

"Yes," Lauryn said confidently.

Cammie only smiled. She didn't refute her statement. Somehow, she was able to grasp the different meaning. Lauryn could never mean it the same way Cammie did. But that was fine. If Lauryn loved her in any way other than just as a friend, she would accept it. "I love you too."

Chapter 16

Those eyes
They tell a thousand stories
Can't say I'm surprised
She's poetry.

Cammie bit down on the end of the pen, wondering what should come next. She tapped it against the paper as she racked her brain, trying to come up with the next line. Metaphors were failing her at this particular moment. No clever one-liners came. Nothing poetic blossomed onto the paper, as it usually would. She looked down at her girlfriend, who was staring keenly back up at her.

Lauryn's head was in Cammie's lap. They were on the couch. Cammie was positioned on the far end, scrawling in her journal on the armrest. Lauryn's body was stretched out, taking up the rest of the small couch. And she kept staring at Cammie. She'd been looking up at her, which inspired her to write. Cammie could write about Lauryn's eyes forever. They resembled so many things and depicted so many emotions, it was easy. Most of the time. But now, she couldn't think of anything to follow up those four lines. She pushed Lauryn's hair from her forehead gently, watching as the silky strands fell onto her shoulder.

"You are so beautiful," she praised her quietly. Cammie was grateful that she could finally admire her up close. This was intimate. She recalled once upon a time when she used to have to steal glances from across the classroom. Or across the table at lunch. Those days were over. That thought prompted her next line.

I used to watch her from afar
Can't help it
She's art.

120

She didn't know if it was the makings of a song or just another rambling poem. But she liked it. She picked it up and read it out loud to Lauryn. She watched as her girlfriend's face formed a wide grin.

"*You're* art, Camz," Lauryn said sweetly.

"No," Cammie disagreed modestly.

"I'm pretty sure you belong in a museum," Lauryn continued with a dorky smile.

"You do. You should take the place of Mona Lisa," Cammie grinned.

"Van Gogh couldn't even attempt to paint something as beautiful as you," Lauryn countered.

Cammie laughed. She didn't have any more art compliments. She didn't know much. Lauryn could run circles around her in that department, but she was flattered.

"I love you," Cammie expressed as she leaned down to place a kiss on her forehead.

"I love you too," Lauryn reciprocated.

The exchange came between them easily now. The two of them had been inseparable since their attempted intercourse. In some ways, it brought them closer. What started off as an awkward encounter turned out to have a surprise ending. Lauryn loved her. Now she enjoyed another perk. They got to exchange *I love you's*. And the best part about it was that it was all requited, to some degree. Everything was reciprocated. Their feelings were mutual, for the first time in Cammie's life. She felt the need to share that.

"This is the first time someone has ever felt the same way about me," Cammie said in a daze.

"But you dated Aiden, didn't you?" Lauryn recalled. Cammie wasn't too open about that relationship. Lauryn didn't know much at all about the two of them, other than the fact that they dated for a month or two.

"I didn't *really* like him though..." Cammie made a face. "He was pretty stupid. You two are polar opposites."

"I can tell," Lauryn laughed. "I was wondering why you went for him... But I figured he must've been alright if he had you," she shrugged.

Cammie shook her head. She disagreed with that a lot. "He was nice to me, so I dated him. I guess I liked him a little, but nothing serious. I barely knew him."

"That's the way it was with Brandon," Lauryn rolled her eyes. "I was so stupid. How the hell did you put up with me?"

"I don't know," Cammie laughed.

"I'm still really sorry about that. I can't even believe I did that shit," she shook her head.

"Well, whatever. It's over," Cammie shrugged. She would happily dismiss that part of their past. She'd allow it to escape her memory without a second thought. She didn't want to remember that much anyway.

"It's a sunset," Lauryn smiled up at her.

Cammie regarded her with a smile of her own. Lauryn mentioned the sunset theory. "Yes, yes it is."

"Explain that to me some more," she requested as she clasped her hands over her stomach.

"Well, I say you're a sunset because-" Cammie began, but Lauryn shook her head furiously.

"No, not pertaining to *me*... I mean in general. It was nice. And I kind of understood it, but I want to know more of what you think," she explained.

"Oh. Like, about bad days and stuff? With the whole sunset versus eclipse thing?" Cammie inferred.

"Yeah, like why a sunset and not a sunrise?" Lauryn nodded.

"Oh... I thought that was dumb. But I think of a sunset because it's the end. It's the end of the day, and metaphorically it would be the end of a certain chapter. I guess I could use a sunrise, but it's not as symbolic to me. Sunsets seem more to me like endings. Sunrises are beginnings. I guess it's all one big cycle of a metaphor because there's darkness between both of them... Good days and bad days are inevitable, obviously. I saw this thing that was like, *always believe that something wonderful is about to happen* somewhere, and I guess it ties into that. I'm confusing myself. But I don't know, I like sunsets better. Because you don't have to wake up early to see those," Cammie concluded with a giggle.

Lauryn was listening to her with her eyes closed. Her talking voice was so soothing. Cammie had been playing with her hair while she was speaking. She was so pacified, she almost wanted to go to sleep. She was thinking about Cammie's stance on that theory. She adored the way her mind worked. It was beautiful. She was beautiful. All of her.

"That's beautiful, Camz," Lauryn commented once she'd finished speaking.

"So are you," she countered easily. "Another reason why you're a sunset," Cammie added cheekily.

"Well," Lauryn exhaled. "Then you're my moon."

"Why?" Cammie laughed.

"Because you are," Lauryn shrugged. She couldn't think of some deep metaphor to relate it to Cammie. But she liked the idea of it. If she was the sun, Cammie was her moon. That wasn't a deep enough analysis to speak on, so she kept it to herself.

"Okay," Cammie laughed. "What does it mean, Laur?"

"Because if I'm your sunset, I must be the sun. The sun and moon go together," Lauryn disclosed. She'd initially decided to keep it to herself, but that was before Cammie had pressed her for information. Right after she'd said it, she wished she hadn't. That was a dumb logic.

Moons had a bad connotation in Cammie's mind. Moons usually symbolized darkness. Or bad things, like werewolves and vampires or something. According to most books and TV shows she'd seen, those creatures of the night went insane on a full moon. Why would a moon remind Lauryn of her? She frowned slightly, although she knew Lauryn had good intentions. She didn't want to be a moon. She was better off being a cloud or something.

"It's like, you're the one source of light in all of my darkness," Lauryn revised her answer. It was like she'd read Cammie's mind. They were both much more pleased with that answer in comparison to the other two.

Cammie's heart fluttered. Well, that was a much better answer. It made her smile. "And you said *I* have a way with words..."

"You do," Lauryn insisted as she reached back to grab Cammie's journal. She cleared her throat and prepared to read another entry out loud.

They say too much exposure to something makes you resent it later on. But I could never get my fix of you. It's like you're a drug. And I'm an addict. You give me

122

what I need, yet I'm insatiable. Every day I see you. And every moment I'm not with you, I miss you. I think about you as often as I breathe. You're taking over. God damn it.

Lauryn finished reciting the entry with a giggle. The 'damn it' part was what made her laugh. It was funny to see Cammie swear through writing, for some reason.

"That's not a way with words... That's just me writing dumb stuff about you," Cammie disagreed.

"You just don't see what I see in you," Lauryn responded dejectedly. She knew Cammie downplayed everything as a defense mechanism, but she wished she would accept her compliments. They were always genuine. All of her praises were actually stemming from how she felt about the brown eyed girl. It bothered her when she just dismissed everything that way.

"I guess not," Cammie shrugged. Her writing really was nothing special. Everything Lauryn commented was just a form of flattery. It was so good to her because it was about her. Of course she would think that way.

"You're amazing, babe," Lauryn tried again. All she wanted was for Cammie to accept it. But as usual, she didn't.

"Not really..." Cammie responded.

"Well *I* think you are," Lauryn emphasized. All she had to say was okay.

"I don't," Cammie mumbled.

"You're so... *Ugh*," Lauryn groaned. She lifted from her position on Cammie's lap, then sat up straight.

"What?" Cammie frowned.

Whenever they had an argument, it was over small things. Her modest ways annoyed the hell out of Lauryn. A simple "thank you" shouldn't have been so hard to say. Her self-depreciating ways tainted every good comment that came her way. She fended them all off with jokes and denial. Lauryn just wanted her to see her through her eyes, for once. But she never did, and it was so frustrating.

"What's wrong with you?" Cammie reiterated when Lauryn ignored her question.

"Nothing," she mumbled as she laid down towards the opposite direction.

"Lauryn," Cammie prompted patiently. With a sigh, she closed her journal. She called her name again. When she got no response, she got up.

Aimlessly, she milled into their kitchen. She wasn't hungry, though. She just thought it was best to leave Lauryn alone at the moment. Whatever it was that had annoyed her would probably pass soon. She thought about what she could've possibly have done, but came up short. Lauryn was so mercurial.

She looked over at their refrigerator and admired how adorable Lauryn was as a baby. She'd seen her baby pictures a number of times before, and they always had the same effect on her. Smiling like an idiot never failed. She wanted to hug her and hold her and pinch her cheeks. She was so freaking cute. And she was *still* quite the cutie. Even better, she was her girlfriend now. So she actually could do those things.

She happily strolled back into the living room. When she saw Lauryn laying on the couch, she remembered why she'd left. Oh, yeah. She was mad at her. In the two minutes she'd been gone, she'd actually forgotten that Lauryn was upset with her. It didn't lessen Cammie's desire to be affectionate. She approached her silently, so silently that her presence almost couldn't be detected. Her footsteps made no sound on the carpet. She didn't voluntarily do anything to make herself seen or heard. So she was surprised when Lauryn addressed her.

"You know what?" Lauryn asked rhetorically from her position on the couch. Cammie hadn't walked into view yet, but she knew she was in there. Her Cammie radar was going off.

"What?" Cammie responded as she rounded the couch and stood in front of Lauryn.

"Tell me ten things you love about yourself," Lauryn requested.

"Why..." Cammie trailed. That was weird. Why would she want her to do that? She didn't even think she could come up with ten. Maybe three.

"Just do it," Lauryn responded evasively.

"For what?" Cammie furrowed her eyebrows. Lauryn ignored her question and just stared at her expectantly. "I don't know," she answered when Lauryn wouldn't avert her gaze.

"I know you don't. And that bothers me," Lauryn admitted as she sat up.

Oh. Cammie figured out why she was upset then. She knew Lauryn hated when she self-depreciated. So she stopped doing it. Or at least she thought she had. She didn't know that deflecting compliments also counted as self-depreciation in Lauryn's eyes.

"What did I do this time?" Cammie questioned.

"It's like you refuse to take my compliments. Or anyone's. I've never seen you say thank you to anyone. Don't you believe them? All you do is brush it off or give them a compliment in return. Why don't you see anything special within yourself? I think you're fantastic," she ranted.

"Well, I'm sorry..." Cammie mumbled. She didn't want Lauryn to be mad at her. She thought it was dumb that she was angry over this anyway, because it really wasn't a big deal. She stealthily picked up her journal and scribbled something, hoping Lauryn wouldn't choose to make eye contact with her in that moment.

Because there are fucking galaxies in your eyes and I can't find a single star in mine.

Cammie closed her journal and slid it over to the floor, hoping she was being as secretive as she was striving for. She wasn't. Lauryn was reading every word she wrote from the side of her eye. Just because she didn't turn her head didn't mean she couldn't see it. The fact that she'd witnessed it made her even more upset than she had been.

Lauryn made a promise to herself to help boost Cammie's self-confidence. It was obvious that simple compliments wouldn't help. Her behavior wouldn't change. She was so set in her ways, it would probably take a miracle for her to see herself through Lauryn's eyes. Lauryn thought she was pretty fucking amazing. She would kiss every inch of her skin if it would help her accept herself a little more. She'd whisper praises into her ear every second of every day if it meant she would believe at least *one* of them.

"Don't apologize... Just love yourself," Lauryn suggested long after Cammie had apologized. It was a simple piece of advice. Or at least she thought it was.

124

Cammie didn't respond to that. She just walked around the table to sit next to Lauryn. She did so solemnly, feeling timid next to her now. All she wanted to do was cuddle again. But she didn't even know if she should touch her now.

"Cammie, I'm not mad at you," Lauryn clarified when she didn't come back to her. She sensed her caution and slid over to her, taking her into her arms.

"Oh," Cammie mumbled. She picked up the hand that wasn't around her shoulder and played with Lauryn's fingers.

"I just wish you'd take all of the love you have for me and save some for yourself," Lauryn expressed quietly as she stroked Cammie's side.

That made sense. It was just hard. Lauryn was so perfect in her eyes, it made it hard not to love her. It was much harder to love herself that way when she was so ordinary. Cammie thought about her words as she was leaning into her. She was a little tense though. Little fights and arguments like those always left her feeling awkward. Lauryn got upset over the strangest things. She couldn't really wrap her mind around it. She couldn't really grasp why it mattered to Lauryn so much. A lot of people were insecure. Why was it such a big deal to her?

"Thank you," she mumbled into Lauryn's shirt. It was a simple step to easing the tension between them. All Lauryn wanted her to do was accept her comments. So she would, or at least she would start trying to. Even if she didn't agree with half of the things she said.

"For what?" Lauryn questioned as she looked at her girlfriend's flawless side profile.

"Everything," Cammie answered evasively. Literally for everything. Saying she's pretty, praising her writing skills and her mind, telling her how amazing she was, caring enough about her to want to force her to accept compliments... All of that. She was grateful Lauryn was a factor in her life.

"Oh... Okay. You're welcome?" Lauryn responded in confusion.

"I love you," Cammie said as she wrapped her arm around Lauryn's torso. "I love you a lot," she said definitively.

Lauryn was staring back at her. That smile she'd grown so fond of over the past few years never failed to make her stomach flip. She leaned in and kissed her smiling lips, then rested against the couch in satisfaction.

"You will never know just how beautiful you are to me," Lauryn said soothingly.

"Thank you," Cammie said resolutely. At first, she was going to say some Ed lyrics back to her. Then she figured that Lauryn would like to hear her accept that compliment a little more. That notion couldn't have been more correct.

Lauryn's smile was so bright, it made Cammie's heart ache. That was her favorite type of smile. Her eyes squinted and her cheeks puffed out in the most adorable way. Cammie grasped her face and pressed her lips against hers passionately. Both of their eyes closed immediately as their lips moved in sync. Cammie's hand slid down to rest on her neck as she instinctually swiped her tongue across Lauryn's bottom lip. She took it into her mouth gently and sucked on it before invading her mouth completely.

Lauryn was in a trance. Whenever Cammie kissed her so sensually this way, she had a hard time controlling her urges. When Cammie shifted over to straddle her lap, she clutched her. Lauryn's hands rested on Cammie's ass firmly as she continued to kiss her. Her knees were on either side of Lauryn's hips, and she scooted closer up on her to close the distance. This was one of Lauryn's favorite ways to kiss. It was hot without being too overwhelming. Both girls were comfortable with it. It was a slow pace. Cammie broke their kiss and looked Lauryn directly in the eye.

"I love you," she said, almost inaudibly.

"I love you too," Lauryn reciprocated. Then she rested her forehead against Cammie's. She could feel Cammie's warm breath on her lips as they had another one of their staring contests. Lauryn mentally kicked herself for not realizing or acting on her feelings sooner. They could've been doing this way before, if she wasn't a coward. But that didn't even matter because Cammie was here in her arms. Just as Lauryn was about to resume kissing her, the front door jingled.

With a sigh, Cammie crawled off of Lauryn's lap. She wished they were out to everyone. She was tired of having to hide in front of their families. But she knew it was probably for the best. Neither of their families were homophobic, but they also wouldn't be too inviting to their relationship. They wouldn't go as far as disowning them or anything, but they definitely wouldn't accept them with open arms. It would undoubtedly come as a shock. They weren't ready to endure that awkwardness if they could help it. So they just dealt with their subtle hand holding and kissing behind closed doors for a little while longer.

»»»

The following Monday, Allie had offered to give Cammie and Lauryn a ride to school. She offered because it was particularly cold this morning. She didn't want her friends to be standing out there waiting for the bus. Riding the bus for two years prior, she knew how unpunctual their bus driver could be. She'd agreed to go get them while Naomi picked up Diana. It was a nice system.

"Y'all could come up for air sometimes," Allie said sarcastically from the front. Every time she looked into the rear view mirror, she caught glimpses of the two engaged in a kiss.

Lauryn had originally been in the front seat. Allie picked her up first. But when Cammie joined the two and sat in the back seat, Lauryn found herself climbing back there as well. She felt a little guilty for abandoning Allie in the front, but she brushed it off. Allie usually made this trip alone in the mornings. No biggie.

"Yeah, *Camz*," Lauryn teased pointedly. She was placing the blame on her, when she'd really been just as guilty.

"Sure, blame it all on me," Cammie laughed and finally sat back in her seat. The tension in her shoulder had subsided. She'd been straining against the seatbelt almost the entire time. But she disregarded the discomfort because Lauryn's lips were always a better excuse.

"Control yourself, babe," Lauryn admonished with a wicked grin.

"Uh uh, I saw you leaning in back there too, Lauryn," Allie laughed.

"Oh," Lauryn laughed. She felt busted. Because she was.

Allie smirked at her from the mirror and turned into the school parking lot. When they all clambered out of the car, they all bundled up immediately. It was only about forty degrees, but they were nearly freezing. Neither of the Miami natives were used to this unusual cold front. Allie wasn't either, so she shuffled into the building quickly. Cammie and Lauryn entered together, using each other's hands to hopefully transfer the warmth.

Lauryn's thumb ran over the back of Cammie's hand instinctively as they approached her locker. They still hadn't let go. They went to Cammie's locker first and Lauryn stood out of the way long enough for her to put her combination in.

When Cammie had all of her books and binders situated, she closed her locker. They were about to go ahead to Lauryn's locker until they nearly bumped into someone.

"Sorry," Lauryn said immediately when she brushed their shoulder. When she looked up at the person, she was instantly annoyed.

"Hey..." Brandon greeted her cautiously.

"Excuse me," Lauryn said as she made a move to pass him. She was being nice. Her mind wanted to say "*Get the fuck out of the way,*" but she decided against it. She tugged on Cammie's hand in an attempt to leave. Cammie followed tentatively, but they didn't get very far before Brandon addressed them again.

"Why won't you talk to me?" Brandon questioned solemnly.

Lauryn paused. Was he serious? She thought he would've had enough sense to answer his own question, but apparently not. The boy just could not take a hint. All of his ignored advances didn't faze him at all. Did he really see nothing wrong with what he'd done? Lauryn contemplated responding to him, but she shook her head. She didn't have time for this.

"*Lauryn?*" Brandon called when she started walking again.

"Shut up," Cammie rolled her eyes as she took initiative to walk to her locker. It wasn't that far away, but she hoped that walking away would give Bread a hint. It didn't.

He followed them silently over to their destination. He didn't exactly get the memo that he wasn't invited. All he wanted to do was clear his name. He wanted to formally apologize. A month later. Brandon figured that he'd given her enough time to cool off from his initial mistake. Maybe they could give it a go for real this time, if all went well. Unfortunately, that was way too much wishful thinking on his part.

"What do you want?" Lauryn grimaced.

"I want to talk to you," he stated quietly.

"There's nothing you need to say to me, Brandon..." Lauryn rolled her eyes. Her hold on Cammie's hand was still strong. She hoped Brandon would see it and realize his mistake. Or their blessing. Whichever way one chose to see it.

"No, I have to explain," Brandon insisted.

"Explain what? That you fucking lied to me? I already know," Lauryn countered angrily. She was trying not to completely lose her temper. It was a tedious internal battle.

"It's not like that," he frowned. He didn't want to be portrayed as a liar. That was exactly what he wanted to clear up. If all else failed, he at least wanted to remain friends. He didn't want Lauryn to possess any ill-will towards him forever.

"Please leave me alone," Lauryn requested calmly. She was showing a lot of self-restraint at the moment. If he stuck around much longer, she couldn't guarantee that she'd be as passive. She'd been ignoring him for that very reason. The thought of him at all infuriated her. Whenever she thought about what he did and how she'd been manipulated, she wanted to hurt him. Badly.

"Please?" Brandon pleaded as he stood in front of her. He did so rather rudely. He kind of placed himself in front of Cammie. She scoffed and moved out of the way and closer to Lauryn. Simply because she didn't want to be beside him.

Lauryn ignored him for a second. She didn't even look at him. She focused on her locker, but she couldn't seem to get the damned thing open. Part of her wanted to know why Brandon would do such a thing. And why *her*? It was humiliating. Every time she thought back on it, it nearly moved her to tears how ignorant and unassuming she'd been. She actually used to defend him. Everything about him and that fucking situation hurt. Although she did a good job of acting like she didn't care, she still carried that burden. Eager to get some type of closure for it, she relented.

"You have sixty seconds," Lauryn compromised as her eyes flashed up to Brandon's apologetic ones.

"Okay," he took a deep breath. Then his gaze settled on Cammie. "Could you go...?" he asked her as he motioned in the opposite direction.

"Fuck you," Cammie countered. Did he really just say that? She wasn't going anywhere. Whatever he needed to say, he would be saying in front of both of them. Or not at all. Cammie was kind of annoyed with Lauryn for even agreeing to hear him out.

Lauryn was surprised to hear her say that, but she smirked. She agreed. Fuck Brandon. "Forty seconds," she reminded him in annoyance.

"Okay," he said again. "I swear I didn't mean to lie to you like that. I saw a chance and I took it. But I would take it all back if I could just have another chance with you. I'm so sorry, Lauryn. I never meant to hurt you. And I never exactly wanted you to find out. I was going to tell you sooner or later, but I never got around to it. And it wasn't a joke. I really did like you..." Brandon rambled, then he had to catch his breath. "I mean, I still like you. I really, really do like you, Lauryn. A lot. All I want is another chance. If not, I understand. But I couldn't deal with knowing that you probably hated me. I've tried everything, but you still ignore me. You've ignored all of my calls and texts and I've kept trying to talk to you at school, but you never give me the opportunity. I just want another chance," he concluded.

Well, that was way more than forty seconds. His confessions left Lauryn feeling incredibly confused. She wanted to be mad at him, but he seemed so genuine in his apology. It was almost kind of sweet. She could tell he was serious, but she wasn't so sure she could just forgive him. She *would* like another shot at it, but she was hesitant to believe him.

It was then that she remembered whose hand she was holding. Cammie. Her girlfriend. Wait, what the fuck? What was she just thinking? Another wave of anger washed over her. His damn confession made her momentarily forget. How could she forget? She was now mad at herself. And her anger towards Brandon only intensified. He was nothing in comparison to Cammie. And he wasn't good enough to overshadow her. Lauryn was disappointed in herself at the realization that he'd managed to distract her. Even if only for a second.

Cammie was terrified. She felt like she was reliving him claiming her journal all over again. She nervously looked at Lauryn, desperately trying to gauge her reaction. She couldn't tell what Lauryn was thinking at all. But she saw the way her eyes suddenly glossed over. Crying couldn't have been a good sign. She feared the worst. Cammie figured that Lauryn would have to choose between her and Brandon. She was faced with two options. Lauryn would either fall for Brandon's sob story or stand by Cammie. Cammie prayed for the latter as she anxiously waited for Lauryn to speak.

"No," Lauryn responded after what felt like an eternity to all three of them. "No, Brandon. You fucked up."

"I know. And I'm sorry. But-" he began to defend himself again, but Lauryn raised a hand to silence him.

"*No*," Lauryn groaned. "Stop talking. There are no second chances with this. What you did was so fucked up... And I guess I'll forgive you, but you don't get another chance. You will *never* have me," she added.

"Okay," Brandon nodded. His expression fell. His hopes of getting Lauryn back crumbled. But she wasn't finished yet.

"Because you lied to me," Lauryn continued. Then she faced Cammie with a small grin. She squeezed her hand lightly and looked back at Brandon with a proud smile. "But mostly because I have an amazing girlfriend. I don't need to deal with your bullshit. I love her," Lauryn stated easily.

Cammie was the one with glossy eyes now. She hadn't been expecting her to say that at all. Her words made her heart swell. She turned into Lauryn and gave her the tightest hug she could muster. Lauryn surprised her further by grasping her chin and pulling her into a tender kiss. Right in front of him.

Brandon felt sick. He felt like he had the right to be kissing her, not fucking Cammie. When did *that* happen? When did Lauryn decide to go lesbian? Had he really messed her up that badly? After a few seconds of watching them kiss, he stormed off. He made his way down the hallway and rounded the corner in haste. The two girls didn't even notice him leaving. Diana did, though.

"Hoii," Diana smirked.

Upon hearing her voice, they broke their kiss. What the hell? When did Diana get there? She always seemed to pop up whenever they had a moment. Maybe she had an advanced gaydar.

"Where do you even come from?" Cammie laughed in greeting. Diana's presence had replaced Brandon's. And for that, she was grateful.

"Places. I'm just around," Diana shrugged. "And good job, Lo. Show that no-lip dumbass exactly what he's missing out on," she laughed.

"He's so..." Lauryn trailed. She didn't even have a word. She just rolled her eyes. Pathetic. That's what he was. And he was delusional if he thought he could just pick up where they left off.

"We tried to tell you," Diana laughed. She recalled the brief time they'd dated and was so relieved to see her with Cammie. She'd finally come to her senses.

"I know. I was so stupid," Lauryn laughed.

"We know," Diana spoke for herself and Cammie, knowing Cammie wouldn't agree out loud.

Lauryn just waved her off and pulled Cammie into her. Cammie immediately clutched Lauryn. She held her body so close, as if she was scared to let go. As if she let go, she would disappear. Cammie felt like she'd just been about to lose her. She never wanted to experience that again.

"I'm glad you chose me," Cammie said quietly against Lauryn's neck. The insecurity she felt for their relationship gave her a headache. She didn't want to feel like she was having to compete against someone for her girl. She wanted Lauryn to be hers. Wholly and completely, without question.

"I didn't have to choose," Lauryn remarked as she ran her fingers through Cammie's hair. She was willing to keep her brief internal consideration of reconciling what she had with Brandon to herself.

"It didn't seem that way. You scared the hell out of me," Cammie admitted.

"I'm sorry. You're always my first choice," Lauryn said in an attempt to sway her. "You're my only choice."

Cammie leaned up to connect their lips again. She felt impossibly drawn to Lauryn right now. With her heavenly lips pressed against her own, everything else faded out. The hustle and bustle of the hallway disappeared. The lockers, the hallway, the students, they all disappeared. It was just her and Lauryn in a state of bliss. Until the warning bell disrupted their peace.

"Wait, don't you still have to go to your locker?" Lauryn remembered as she begrudgingly pulled away from Cammie.

"Yeah, but I think I should just go to class. I can't be late to first period anymore," Cammie said apologetically as she began inching away from her girlfriend.

"Okay. I love you, Camz," Lauryn proclaimed happily.

"I love you too," Cammie smiled as she pulled Lauryn into another quick kiss. It was just one short goodbye peck, then she walked away.

Lauryn watched her go down the hallway in adoration. She was so lucky. She was so fortunate. Cammie was everything. And she was all hers. She rested her back against the lockers and sighed deeply. In that moment, she realized just how enamored with Cammie she actually was.

Chapter 17

Two days. In just two days, they would have been together for a month. Although Lauryn wasn't usually one to be particular about those sorts of occasions, this milestone with Cammie felt immensely sentimental. She was proud of them, for whatever reason. For once, it was special to her. She'd never made a big deal out of it in the past. But one month with Cammie was significant to her. It was all she thought about when she woke up.

All throughout the silent bus ride and chaotic class changes, it was on her mind. She wore a dumb smile virtually all day. All of the girls saw it. Cammie was exhibiting the same behavior. They could not stop smiling. The couple hadn't been so open about their relationship, so what they were so smiley about was left to their friends' imagination.

Naomi nudged Diana when Lauryn shuffled into the classroom. She made it in right as the bell rung. Walking to Cammie to class every day had become their norm, and nearly being late every day had also become Lauryn's norm. But there was an extra pep to her step when she walked over to her seat. Diana and Naomi shared a knowing smirk right as she sat down.

"What's up, Lo?" Naomi greeted her with a friendly wave.

"Hey," Lauryn smiled.

"Okay, you and Cam have been smiling nonstop all day," Naomi started. "What happened?"

"Did you finally get some?" Diana inferred. That was her favorite way to tease the two of them, knowing how unlikely that was. She was always rewarded with some type of shy smile or blushing. It never failed.

"No. Jesus, Diana..." Lauryn giggled. Their friends knew nothing of their attempt. And if they did, they'd never let them live it down. She decided then that if they ever got around to it, they'd have to keep it to themselves. "That's not the only reason people smile, you know."

"I know. I'm just kidding. But are you gonna tell us? Or do I just have to steal Cam's journal?" Diana quipped.

"That would probably be the best way to find out," Naomi nodded as she played along.

"No, no robbery," Lauryn declined. "Guess what's in two days?"

"I don't know," Naomi laughed.

"Your birthday," Diana guessed.

"It's February..." Lauryn deadpanned. "My birthday is in June. I thought you knew that?" she pouted as she feigned offense.

"I know your birthday," Diana assured her. And she would know. She'd just have to ask Cammie later. But she knew. "What's in two days?"

"Our one month," Lauryn said as she broke out into another smile.

"Should've known it had something to do with Cam," Naomi rolled her eyes playfully. "That's cute though. Are you gonna do anything for her?"

"I know what she's doing for you," Diana smirked. She'd annoyed the details out of Cammie earlier. The fact that their anniversary was coming up had completely slipped her mind. But she remembered it all now. And it was taking a lot of self-control not to spill the details to Lauryn.

"Really?" Lauryn asked as Mrs. Taylor started speaking. She lowered her voice to a whisper. "What is she doing?"

"She told me not to tell you," Diana smirked. She knew just about everything regarding Cammie's plans. It made her happy to learn just how meticulous each detail was. The only way she'd gotten to her to disclose those things was by swearing not to tell Lauryn. And she wouldn't. She didn't want to betray her trust and miss out on getting insiders in the future. She had to stay on top of their status somehow.

"*Diana*," Lauryn groaned.

"Sorry, Lo. I promised," Diana shrugged.

"Well just give me an idea," Lauryn suggested.

"No," Diana responded. She wasn't about to do anything to jeopardize the likelihood of getting information next time.

"Just like overall," Lauryn elaborated.

"Can't," Diana mumbled as she caught Mrs. Taylor's eye. She looked down and picked up her pencil to mime writing.

"Diana, please?" Lauryn begged as she leaned on her shoulder. All she wanted was one detail. It would help her plan accordingly. She wasn't looking for a spoiler. But she sure wouldn't object to one right about now.

"No, get off of me," Diana laughed as she attempted to shake her off.

"I'll tell you what I'm doing if you'll tell me what Camz is doing," Lauryn compromised. She looked at Diana expectantly, just waiting for her to accept her offer.

"You have to tell me first," Diana negotiated.

Lauryn rolled her eyes. "Fine. But you have to tell me *right* after I tell you..." she warned.

"I will, I will," Diana encouraged her with hand motions.

"Okay... Well... I'm getting her a necklace..." Lauryn disclosed cautiously. She figured she should stop there, knowing all about Diana's big mouth.

"She's getting you a charm bracelet," Diana returned immediately. A smile followed her statement. She felt a little excited for their anniversary gift exchange. She began plotting a miraculous way to show up.

"Really?" Lauryn's eyes widened.

Well, at least they were both planning on going with jewelry. Lauryn didn't usually wear bracelets and such, but she definitely would if Cammie gave one to her. She would wear it every day, without fail.

"Yeah," Diana whispered, acknowledging the glare they were getting from Mrs. Taylor. She picked up her pencil again and wrote her name down on the paper. There. That was a start.

"Do you know if she's planning a date or something?" Lauryn pressed. She also mimed writing, but her mind was too focused on Cammie to think about doing her work right now.

"No..." Diana said evasively. It was clear that she had more details than she was sharing.

"I'll give you a dollar if you tell me. I won't tell Camz that I know, I promise," Lauryn attempted to bribe her.

"I know you won't. 'Cause I'm not telling you," the taller girl laughed.

"You suck," Lauryn huffed as she slumped down in her seat.

"I'm amazing," Diana defended herself with a smirk.

"Well do you think she'll like the necklace?" Lauryn questioned as she began doubting herself. "Or should I get her something else?"

"Probably. What is it? Like a heart necklace with some sappy stuff on it?" Diana inferred quietly.

"No..." Lauryn shook her head. That was far from the pendant that was on it. "It's-" she started to say, then she stopped. "Shut up. I know what you're doing," she rolled her eyes in realization.

"You almost said it," Diana shrugged.

"I just don't know if she'll like it. I think it's sweet but at the same time I think it's kind of dumb what I'm doing..." Lauryn reflected out loud. She wasn't talking to anyone in particular.

Naomi heard her. She'd bowed out of the conversation for a minute or two to complete the few problems from the board. She'd gone through four and figured she'd done enough to start talking again. She faced Lauryn and got her attention subtly.

"What are you freaking out about? Cam will love anything you do," Naomi offered.

"I don't know, Naomi. I'm just scared it's not enough... Or that she'll think it's stupid or something, I don't know," Lauryn reiterated.

"Tell me what it is," Naomi requested. "I won't tell Cam. You can trust me, unlike big mouth over there," she added as she gestured to Diana. She wasn't listening. She'd finally decided to start her assignment.

"Okay," Lauryn agreed. She needed to talk to someone about it before she drove herself insane. "Well, did you hear what I said to Diana?"

"Not really. Something about a necklace though, I think," Naomi tried to recall.

"Yeah. I'm getting Cammie a necklace, but it feels too simple," Lauryn frowned.

"What? That's probably expensive," Naomi commenter.

"I wouldn't say that... I mean, I had to save up for it... But it's not the price that matters to her," Lauryn acknowledged. "While she's probably doing something deep and meaningful and shit, I'm just getting her this dumb necklace."

"What does it look like?" Naomi asked.

"It's like a sun and moon," Lauryn answered. She had it in her bag. She felt like if she left it at home or in her locker or something, it would be misplaced. So she carried it around with her. She had been ever since she'd purchased it.

"Do you have a picture of it?" Naomi asked.

"I have it in here," Lauryn responded as she dug through her bag for it. She presented it to Naomi and watched her reaction carefully. When she smiled, Lauryn felt a little relieved. But she still felt the need to voice her apprehension. "I don't think she'll like it..."

"You're kidding, right?" Naomi said as her expression dropped.

"What?" Lauryn frowned

"It's beautiful. I like it a lot. If Cam doesn't like it, I'll take it," Naomi laughed. "Why'd you pick that design?"

"Because Camz loves sunsets. And she loves me, and I love her. And a few days ago, she was telling me how I was one to her - she has this theory with sunsets that's really cute - and I told her that if I was her sun, then she was my moon. Because they go together, you know? And I don't know, when I saw this online, I just thought about her. I feel like it represents the both of us as one. Look at the way the moon is kind of wrapped around the sun. That's us. It's like our little secret," Lauryn explained as she pointed to the intricate design on it.

Naomi just barely grasped the concept of what she was talking about. She didn't know anything about Cammie's apparent obsession with them, but Lauryn's logic was enough to convince her that Cammie would adore the present. "Lo, if you tell her that, there's no way she won't like it. You have a real reason for picking it out. And it's one that relates to Cam directly. How can you think she wouldn't like it?" Naomi asked incredulously.

"I don't know. I'm psyching myself out of it. I always do that," Lauryn shook her head. "I have this one that's a necklace as a whole. But I bought another one that's magnetic. I'd keep one and Camz would keep the other. I'm thinking about just giving her one half and keeping one. It'll be symbolic, I think. Or I might just give her this one..."

"You should," Naomi smiled encouragingly. She didn't know why Lauryn felt the need to buy three separate necklaces, but she thought it was cute how much effort she was putting into it.

"No... It's dumb," Lauryn recoiled. She put the necklace back into her bag. She sighed and rested her chin in the palm of her hand.

"You're really overthinking it," Naomi reprimanded gently. "Just give it to her. She'll love it no matter what."

"Alright," Lauryn nodded. "I'll just give it to her."

>>>>>

"This has been like, the fastest month in my entire life," Cammie stated. She was wrapped up in Lauryn's arms on her bed. Lauryn had been pressing soft kisses all over her cheek. Had she been wearing lipstick, Cammie would've been completely colored.

"Me too," Lauryn nodded.

"But it's been the best month too," she added.

"Yeah. I wish you'd lost your journal a long time ago," Lauryn laughed.

"I kind of wish I had too," Cammie agreed. "I had no idea it would end up like *this*."

"Me neither," Lauryn reflected as she tightened her hold on her girlfriend. "I can't believe it's *tomorrow*..."

"Same," Cammie seconded.

In truth, it had all passed by in a blur for the both of them. It seemed like just yesterday they were sharing secret kisses in the stairwell. Or like only a week ago had Lauryn discovered Cammie was the author. But at the same time, it seemed like it had been so much longer. Time stopped whenever their lips were connected. Everything was frozen when Cammie was in Lauryn's arms and vice versa.

She'd written about this way too many times to count. What used to be hopeful ramblings in her journal were now vivid actions. The daydreams she used to have about being Lauryn's girlfriend were no more, because she was reveling in her reality. She barely had time for all of the verbose songs, poems, and stories that used to consume most of her days because she was spending nearly every waking moment with her. Her imagination was incapable of projecting just how enchanting it was. The tangibility of it was far more than she could comprehend, even when she was living it. Her relationship with Lauryn was palpable. So real, that she was brought from her musings by the sound of her voice.

"What are we doing tomorrow?" Lauryn questioned. If Cammie had no prepared plans, she would start pulling strings to do something now.

"Well I didn't have anything in particular," Cammie shrugged. "I just wanted to be with you. Were you planning on something?"

"Kind of. I want to do something special for you, Camz. You didn't let me on Valentine's Day," Lauryn laughed.

"Why don't we just finish our date? We never got to finish it," Cammie proposed.

"Good idea," Lauryn nodded. That was simple enough. And it didn't require transportation. It was quite embarrassing that neither of them could drive yet.

"Where's my journal? I wrote it in there," Cammie said as she looked around.

"It's over there," Lauryn pointed out. She hoped Cammie would deem it too far away to go and get. She didn't want her to move. Their current placement was quite comfortable. Much to her dismay, Cammie leaned up and out of her grasp. She returned shortly with her journal in hand. Lauryn begrudgingly resumed their previous position. Her arm found their way back around Cammie's waist as she leaned back into her.

"Okay, so we've already done fort building and the pancakes," she mentally checked off as she skimmed the list. "So we can go with going on that walk, or painting, or the *serenade*," Cammie read out loud as she wiggled her eyebrows.

"Sure, what do you want to do most?" Lauryn asked.

"I think going on a walk with you would be lovely," Cammie answered without hesitation.

"I do, too," Lauryn agreed.

"But why do we always have to plan things? I'd like something to happen spontaneously, you know?" Cammie expressed as she looked up at her girlfriend.

"Okay, then forget that entire list," Lauryn relented. She gently pushed the journal from Cammie's hands and closed it.

Going with the flow wasn't necessarily her forte. She liked being in control of what she was doing and pretty much following a schedule. But apparently,

Cammie didn't. And relationships needed compromises, right? Lauryn could easily meet in the middle with this.

»»»»

"I've never really liked Thursdays before," Cammie laughed.

"It's a day... How do you not like it?" Lauryn laughed as she swung Cammie's hand back and forth.

"I don't know. It's just an ugly day," Cammie shrugged.

"You're insane," Lauryn giggled. "And where are we going?"

The two had been walking around their school aimlessly. They were careful to stay out of view from teachers and administrators. Lauryn was following Cammie, wherever she was headed. Cammie was headed to the most secret place she could think of. Earlier that morning, she'd convinced her mom to drive her to school two hours early. She'd come up with a convincing story about a mandatory National Honors Society meeting that just so happened to be two hours before school started. It was definitely a sketchy story. In addition to that, she convinced Sonya to drop by Lauryn's house to pick her up as well, having warned her beforehand. So for the past ten minutes, she'd been tugging a groggy and kind of delirious Lauryn around. They were almost there.

"You'll see in a minute," Cammie grinned to herself. Spontaneity had struck. She got her inspiration as she was looking up at the dark sky. She decided on taking her to the roof. The actual roof. Freshman and sophomore year, she found her escape up there. No one really challenged the authority of the door that said *Authorized Personnel Only*. But Cammie did. And no adults suspected any students going up there. But Cammie did, or at least she used to. Only recently had she returned to the stairwell. She was a fan of secluded areas.

Lauryn shrugged and kept following her. Cammie's grip on her hand was strong, and she knew she'd probably be following her regardless of their destination. However, when her girlfriend pushed through the door labeled *Roof*, she hesitated. "Camz, wait. Where are we going?"

"Follow me," Cammie prompted, ignoring her question. She began on her way up the ladder and made it halfway to the top when Lauryn tapped her foot.

"Cammie..." Lauryn mumbled warily, looking back at the sign. Were they going to the roof? She must have been crazy.

"Come on," Cammie urged as she paused.

"Camz, we're going to get in so much trouble for this..." Lauryn trailed as she looked up at the ladder dubiously.

"Do you trust me?" Cammie asked with soft eyes. She held out one hand to Lauryn, but quickly reattached it to the bar because she would probably fall. That wouldn't be very pleasant. Better hold on. So clutching the ladder's bar with both hands, she whirled back around to face her girlfriend. She raised a challenging eyebrow as she waited for her answer.

"You're crazy," Lauryn said as an involuntary nervous giggle left her lips. She slowly grabbed onto the ladder and followed Cammie up, both giddy and nervous about their fate.

When they both made it to the top, Cammie slipped her hand back into Lauryn's grasp. The sun was just starting to rise. Lauryn's lips parted as she took in the sight before her. Cammie just stared at her lovingly. This was nothing she hadn't

136

seen before. She could bear to miss this one, but she couldn't miss the way Lauryn looked in that dim light.

The sun was just barely out. Her pale skin was a striking contrast to her dark surroundings. She seemed even more beautiful than before. Her cheeks were flushed. She was adorable, all bundled up in her beanie and scarf. It wasn't particularly hot, but it definitely wasn't cold enough to warrant those garments. Cammie passed it off as a fashion statement rather than as an asset to the weather.

"How do you find out about these places?" Lauryn asked incredulously.

"You find a lot when you wander around by yourself," Cammie shrugged. "And they don't usually lock this door, so..."

"You're mad, baby," Lauryn chuckled as she pulled her into a hug. She kissed her forehead and let her lips linger for a few seconds.

"I brought you up here for a reason, Laur," Cammie mumbled into her shirt, realizing that they only had a limited amount of time. The sun would rise and cast their shadows downward soon enough. People would see them. They couldn't stay up here for long.

"For the sunrise?" Lauryn inferred as she loosened her hold.

"Well, yes. But no," Cammie shook her head. "It's been one month."

"I know," Lauryn said as she broke out into another grin. Her facial muscles were starting to ache.

"And... I got you something," Cammie hinted vaguely. She was unaware that Lauryn already knew about her bracelet. Just like Lauryn was unaware that Cammie knew about her necklace. They really couldn't tell Diana anything and expect it to stay confidential.

Lauryn decided to try her best to act surprised when Cammie pulled it out. She was expecting some type of small bracelet from some store. It probably wouldn't have cost much, because she knew Cammie didn't have much of a budget to work with. Regardless of that, she would love it. She wouldn't have to fake that. Her reaction would be one of endearment, no matter what it was.

"Close your eyes," Cammie instructed with a smirk.

Lauryn complied immediately. She almost extended her hand for Cammie to place the bracelet on, but thankfully remembered not to. While she was expecting cold metal to meet her skin, she was surprised with another sensation. Soft lips were being pressed against hers with such delicacy, she was almost fearful to reciprocate. This had to have been one of the sweetest kisses they'd shared thus far. Lauryn pulled Cammie closer to her by her waist, but Cammie pulled back as soon as they got close.

It was then that she revealed her bracelet. Lauryn's jaw went slack. That wasn't a forced reaction. She didn't know what she was expecting, probably just some dainty little piece of jewelry. This was anything but. *This* was a rather expensive looking charm bracelet. There were five individual charms and as Cammie fastened it around her wrist, she felt how heavy it was. Holy shit.

"Do you like it?" Cammie asked hopefully, but Lauryn was just staring at her with her mouth open. And if she wasn't looking at Cammie, she was looking down at her new charm bracelet. Cammie was enjoying Lauryn's tender expression. At first. But then it lasted too long. And looking without speaking tended to make her nervous, especially if she wasn't clear on what the specific look meant.

"Why are you looking at me like that?" Cammie voiced her thoughts insecurely. Lauryn didn't like it. That was the first thought that ran through her head. Followed by Lauryn hates it. Cammie shifted her gaze to the concrete below to avoid Lauryn's impenetrable eyes.

"God, Cammie..." Lauryn breathed as she lifted her arm to look at it closer. She couldn't fathom it. How? How did Cammie always manage to do these things and leave her absolutely speechless? It wasn't much, but it meant the world to her all at once. In this case, it was definitely the thought that counted most.

"What? I can take it back if you don't like it..... I'm sorry," Cammie frowned as she made a move to remove it from Lauryn's wrist. But the older girl swatted her hand away, clutching her bracelet defensively.

"*Take it back*?" Lauryn asked incredulously. She must've been the most oblivious person on earth. "Camz, this is probably the best gift I've *ever* received... I love it. What's wrong with you?"

Cammie couldn't help the exaggerated sigh of relief she let out upon hearing that. Now maybe her heartbeat could start to come down. She'd been terrified that Lauryn wouldn't like it since she'd picked it up two weeks prior. She finally had an excuse to shower her with gifts and presents. She wasn't letting it go to waste. She was a little too excited, and she surprised herself that she'd managed to keep it a secret for this long.

"You're amazing, what the fuck," Lauryn sighed as she pulled Cammie into her arms. She wanted to express her thanks through her kiss. Cammie eagerly stepped forward as Lauryn grasped both of her cheeks, coaxing her to her inviting lips. Her nose was cold as they touched, but her mouth was warm. Cammie was a contrast to everything about the cool weather.

"Okay. This makes what I got you really shitty in comparison..." Lauryn sighed as she ran a hand through her hair. Or at least when she tried to. Her hand collided with the beanie and her hand just fell to her side.

"I bet it doesn't," Cammie countered sweetly.

"It does... I almost don't even want to give it to you now," Lauryn laughed as she clutched the necklace in her pocket.

"Lauryn, come on," Cammie encouraged her softly. She rested her hand on Lauryn's arm and simply looked at her.

"Turn around," Lauryn instructed after a few moments. When Cammie did, she retrieved the necklace from her pocket. Fuck. It was tangled. She knew she shouldn't have taken it out of its box. For a few seconds, she fumbled with it.

"Can I turn back around yet?" Cammie laughed. She began twiddling her fingers as she waited for what she knew was coming. It came soon enough. Lauryn finally detangled it and stepped behind Cammie, preparing herself to put it around her neck. It was kind of cold, maybe she should warn her. "Brace yourself..." she said as she placed it in front of her, then fastened it around her neck. She heard Cammie gasp, but she hoped it was the good kind.

Cammie's head ducked down to look at the pendant hanging from her neck. Lauryn tentatively stepped around to gauge her reaction. The most easily distinguishable emotion was shock. "It's a sun and moon," Cammie grinned as she picked it up to examine it further.

"Yeah..." Lauryn nodded hurriedly. She took one look at Cammie's expression and felt the need to explain. "It's - It's because of your sunset theory. I got you two, actually. See, I didn't know if you'd want the whole thing or if you'd just wanna like, split it and you keep one half and I keep the other. Because one of the necklaces are magnetic and they break in half..... And if we were to do that, I don't know if you'd want to keep the sun or the moon... Because, well, you like sunsets..... Or maybe I should keep that half because you say *I'm* your sunset... So figuratively, I'd be the sun... And I said you were my moon... So maybe you should keep it. Or maybe if-" Lauryn rushed, but she was silenced by Cammie's urgent kiss.

Her hands settled on her cheeks and she kissed her deeply in hopes of easing her worrisome ways. "You were rambling..." Cammie giggled as she cupped her face.

"Sorry. I'm nervous," Lauryn excused herself with a timid laugh. It was uncharacteristic enough. Cammie captured her lips yet again. She threaded her hands through her hair for a second before she pulled away again.

"Lauryn, I understand it," Cammie laughed when they parted. She understood it perfectly, wondering why *she* hadn't thought of it. "I know exactly what it means, and I love you."

"I love you too," Lauryn reciprocated immediately.

The warning bell blared from below, signaling that they only had about ten minutes before class was supposed to start. In that moment, Lauryn took notice of where they were - on the fucking roof. Her girlfriend was a romantic. Professing their love and exchanging first month anniversary gifts on the rooftop of their school. Nice. Cammie was rare in ways she couldn't even think of. Her surprises were always fun, romantic, and special. She'd definitely never been on rooftops in the past. Cammie offered a new perspective to everything.

"We should probably go," Cammie suggested as the sun hung high overhead. In the sunlight, she saw Lauryn's beauty in all its glory. The sun hit her features perfectly. It made her eyes seem like they were glowing. With skin so radiant under the sunlight, the girl looked godly.

"This is my favorite day with you so far," Lauryn commented. It was completely off topic, but she felt compelled to say it.

"Me too," Cammie smiled broadly. She watched as Lauryn idly played with her new bracelet. She manipulated each charm individually and twisted them in between her fingers. She looked at the small smile Lauryn had and felt her stomach flip.

They started walking back the way they came. Both girls were fascinated by their new possessions. Lauryn kept looking at her bracelet as she walked alongside Cammie. And Cammie kept staring down at her chest, admiring the necklace she now wore. The couple entered the school with goofy smiles. Even when they went their separate ways, their expressions never changed.

Cammie forgot about the letter she had for Lauryn. After she'd kissed her goodbye and been dropped off at class, she remembered. She quickly rummaged through her bag for it and fled from the classroom to catch her before she disappeared amongst the crowd.

"Lauryn!" Cammie called right before her girlfriend turned the corner.

Lauryn turned around so quickly at the sound of Cammie's voice, her neck started to hurt. She stopped walking and rubbed it sorely as Cammie sprinted over to her. There was a folded up piece of paper in her hand.

"I forgot to give you this," Cammie reminded her, completely out of breath. She really should work out more. This just wasn't healthy.

"What is it?" Lauryn questioned as she looked up at the clock. She only had one minute to get to class now, but that wasn't such a pressing matter.

"You'll see. Read it whenever you get the chance, but don't be late," Cammie answered as she started pushing her towards her class.

"Okay," Lauryn laughed as she turned to be on her way. Just as Cammie was heading back to her own class, Lauryn grabbed her waist and made her face her. She kissed Cammie on the mouth, blatantly in the middle of the hallway. Happily, she grinned and went on her way, leaving Cammie smiling behind her.

Chapter 18

Dear Lauryn,

One month with you. Four weeks of endless cuddles and unnecessary closeness. Four weeks of putting your open lips on mine and slowly letting them shut. And four weeks of incorporating Ed's lyrics into dumb conversations.

Thirty one days of endless hand holding, telling everyone that you're mine. Thirty one days of walking with your arm around my waist, proving to everyone that I'm yours. It's been thirty one days, and I'm still not used to saying that.

730 hours of sheer happiness. Regardless of all of those stupid little arguments we have... I'm always happy with you. I don't think there's anything you can do to make me seriously upset. Not anymore. Except for obvious things like breaking up with me... (please don't...) And 730 hours of being comfortable in my own skin. I'm amazed by how easy everything is with you. Initially, I thought I would be awkward and insecure in this relationship, but you don't allow that. You take every opportunity to lift my self-esteem, and although I don't really show it, I appreciate it.

43, 829 minutes of living my biggest dream. Not being a celebrity, but being with you. It's just amazing to have someone always there, unconditionally. Even if we aren't talking, your presence is a solace to me. It's all of the reassurance I ever need. I love you a lot. All of the times we spend talking about everything but nothing at all are the best. It's deep, philosophical discussions and then utter bullshit not even five minutes later. Even our fights are fine with me. Everything is a perk.

2,629,743 seconds of you finally being mine, the way I've been yours all this time. Because even when we aren't together, you're still mine. 2,629,743 seconds and counting.

I don't even have words, for once in my life. All of this, collectively, has left me speechless. I have absolutely no idea what to even say to describe how overjoyed I am. It's been a month, Lauryn. A whole month. I've imagined it way too many times to count. And every time I look back on the way that I used to write about you and dream of actually dating you, I can barely comprehend that this is real. Remember that day I told you I felt like I was just going to wake up one day? Well, I haven't opened my eyes yet. And I don't think I will.

There was once a time where I thought I didn't even want to date you. I used to think that everything had an end. You know, girlfriend. I used to think that if I could just kiss you and hold you the way I do now, I would be satisfied. But there's a certain sense of security that comes with getting to call you my girlfriend. I feel entitled to you. Like you're officially mine. How dumb was I to think that things would be better without labels? Calling you my girlfriend is the greatest thing I've ever achieved. I think.

But at the same time, I know why I was scared of labels. Apparently we're in the honeymoon stage, or whatever it was that Allie called it. But regardless of its name, I know I want this forever. There's something in you that I know I'll never find in anyone else. And I'm not looking. But if there ever comes a day where you're not mine anymore, I'll know that it was you. It was always you. You're the one. And I don't know where this is going. I've been talking (writing?) too much. So I'll shut up now. But I love you. So much.

Lauryn looked down at her note from her girlfriend with misty eyes. Cammie always found a way to leave her speechless. She'd really never been this emotional before. What the hell was Cammie doing to her?

"What is that?" Allie questioned. She noticed how quiet Lauryn had been at the start of class. Her unusual behavior extended throughout most of the period. She'd caught onto the way she kept rereading that paper in her hand, but when she saw the tears in her eyes, she felt the need to address her.

"Cammie's um, note," Lauryn settled on saying, unsure of what to call it.

"Oh," Allie smiled. A little part of her wanted to see it, but she could easily grasp the personal sentiment it held with Lauryn. It was none of her business anyway. "I'm so happy for y'all."

"Thanks, Allie," Lauryn smiled appreciatively. The desk posed as an obstacle, but she leaned over it to pull the older girl into an awkward side hug anyway. Lauryn's bracelet made a lot of noise as she settled back into her seat.

"Did Cam get you that?" Allie inferred, pointing to the shiny metal on her arm.

"Yes," Lauryn nodded goofily. While she was usually cool and collected, Cammie brought out her dorkier side. Another power she had over her.

"It's beautiful," Allie complimented genuinely.

"Thanks," she smiled again. "And I know, right? Jesus, she must've spent a fortune..."

"Yeah, it looks pretty expensive," Allie agreed.

Lauryn took her time to look at each individual charm. They each had different shapes and colors and intricate designs. The charm bracelet was adorned with a book, a sun, a paint brush, a heart, and a beautiful gem. Her fingertips grazed one of them, then she held it between her fingers delicately. The charms varied. There was no clear theme, but Lauryn was sure her girlfriend had some philosophical explanation as to why she'd chosen each one of them.

»»»»

Two days later, all five girls were seated around the lunch table. Cammie and Lauryn had been inseparable. Their gifts were still the topic of conversation. One thing led to another, and they were back to speaking about it now.

"It only cost like ten thousand dollars," Cammie joked.

She was sarcastically speaking about Lauryn's bracelet, surrounded by her four best friends. Lunch could be classified as her favorite time of the day again. It was when they all came together. Lunch had only been knocked from its number one position because for a while, Lauryn used it as her stupid Bread outlet. Now the table was filled with gossip about her own relationship *with Lauryn*. She listened to the other girls ramble about their drama with an open mind. None of their admissions lit the already burning pit of jealousy in her stomach the way Lauryn's used to. She was able to comment and offer honest advice to them without it being forced. Everything was going great.

"Right," Lauryn rolled her eyes jokingly.

"We all know that if Cam even *had* ten grand, you'd be the one person she'd spend it all on," Diana commented as she bit into her celery.

"True," Naomi laughed.

"Probably, but whatever. How much it cost isn't a big deal," Cammie shrugged.

"I love you," Lauryn declared shamelessly as she leaned over to peck Cammie quickly on the lips.

Much to her amusement and their surrounding friends', Cammie's cheeks darkened. She looked down at the table. The same dumb smile she was always able to elicit started to spread. It soon completely took over her features as she returned Lauryn's statement. "I love you too."

"Get a room," Diana quipped with a smirk.

"Leave them alone, they're cute," Allie laughed.

"So what are you gonna do later on? Do y'all have something planned?" Naomi asked as she picked over her salad.

"Kind of," Lauryn responded, giving Cammie a smirk.

"Kind of?" Cammie repeated with a smile. She knew nothing of Lauryn's plans. And Lauryn wanted to keep it that way, knowing she most likely wouldn't agree to it.

"Yes," Lauryn nodded and strove to end that conversation right there. "Kind of."

》》》》

"Okay, *now* will you tell me?" Cammie asked impatiently as soon as Lauryn started to approach her. She was already at her locker, having already been to hers, equipped with her book bag and jacket as she stood in front of her.

"Allie is going to drive us to my house, so we don't have to worry about catching the bus today," Lauryn informed her with information she wasn't looking for.

"*Lauryn*," Cammie groaned. She'd been waiting all day. Lauryn was so good at holding her tongue.

"We're going on a walk tonight," Lauryn finally answered. She laughed and began putting in her combination. She didn't know why she'd been withholding that information. It wasn't a big deal. But it was fun to tease her.

"Oh," Cammie smiled. She rested her back against the lockers, finally sated. She thought it was going to be some big thing. It wasn't. She slapped Lauryn's arm lightly. Lauryn looked down at her arm, then back at Cammie.

143

"Ouch," she tried to frown, but her facial muscles wouldn't let her. It turned into a wider grin than she already had, and that turned into laughter. They were both laughing when Allie came up to them.

"Are y'all ready to go?" she questioned. She cracked a smile, wondering what was so funny as she looked between the both of them.

"Yes," Lauryn nodded. She swung her locker closed and slid on her book bag.

The short car ride to Lauryn's house was relatively quiet. Other than small talk about how everyone's day was, they didn't really speak much. Not that they needed to, the trip was only about five minutes. Allie pulled up to the curb and let them out, bidding them goodbye as they expressed their thanks.

Lauryn immediately took Cammie's hand. "Do you want to go inside or do you just want to go ahead and go now?"

"Let's go inside and put our stuff down first," Cammie suggested.

Lauryn agreed with that. Good idea. She led Cammie inside and up to her room. They both discarded their bags and things, then flopped onto her bed. Cammie noticed the wilting rose that hadn't moved from its position since she'd given it to her. Lauryn was so sentimental about little things, it warmed her heart. She looked over at her lovingly, then leaned over to kiss her cheek and watched as the corners of her mouth tugged into a small smile.

Lauryn laid there deep in thought about what would this specific date would entail. She considered bringing her to a relatively secluded area, to ensure privacy. She sometimes went there alone to clear her head. It would be a nice area to bring Cammie. Very quiet. Very serene.

"Camz, can we go to the park?" Lauryn questioned as she looked over at her.

"Yeah," Cammie nodded. She figured that they were actually going to the park in the first place, because where else do you go for a walk? Highways.

Lauryn kissed Cammie where her eyebrows were still creased in confusion. They just settled down in her room and watched movies until about ten o'clock. Cammie went home around that time to lessen possible suspicions. Their plan wasn't in motion until midnight. When she was sure everyone had retired to their rooms for the night, she slipped on her shoes and jacket. She pulled out her phone to tell Cammie to get ready as she slipped out of her own house.

"Hello?" Cammie answered. There was a bunch of shuffling in the background.

"Hey, it's me," Lauryn greeted her. A smile was present just at the sound of Cammie's voice. "Are you almost ready?"

"Yeah. This will be fun. I feel bad," Cammie said with a devilish tone.

"Why? We're not doing anything bad," Lauryn giggled. She shoved her hands into her pockets as she milled down the street.

"Laur, we're *sneaking out*," Cammie emphasized. The shuffling in the background returned, and Lauryn wondered what on earth Cammie was doing.

"If that's what you want to call it..." Lauryn shrugged. "I'm almost there."

"Okay. I'll probably be outside too by the time you get here," Cammie assumed.

Lauryn kept walking towards her house. The streets were dark, but the streetlights provided enough security for her. She felt safe, and her girlfriend's presence on the phone was more than enough comfort. She was almost there, anyway. Cammie's house came into view, and she saw the light emanating from her window. She looked up at it in amusement, figuring that she'd forgotten to turn off the lights again. But when she came to stand in her yard, she was more than surprised to see her girlfriend's figure in the window.

"Camz, what the hell are you doing?" Lauryn said into the phone as she looked up at Cammie's window.

"I'm coming, just wait a second," Cammie assured her. She seemed to be struggling to get the window open. She tried for a few more seconds before bringing the phone back to her face. "It's just... A little... Stuck..." she grumbled as she strained against the pane. It still wouldn't budge.

"What are you trying to do?" Lauryn asked in amusement.

"Sneak out?" Cammie answered in the same tone as she peered down at the tiny person below.

"Wait..." Lauryn trailed in realization. "Are you trying to climb out of the window..?"

"Yeah. It's just stuck. I'll be down in a second though, just let me..." Cammie's sentence tapered off as she tried her hardest to pry the window open.

"Camz, use the fucking door..." Lauryn deadpanned as she looked up at her girlfriend.

"Oh," Cammie mumbled. "Well I guess I could do that, huh?" she laughed.

"Wow, babe..." Lauryn shook her head. She watched as the blinds closed and Cammie's shadow disappeared. Within a few moments, the front door opened. Cammie appeared meekly, trying her best to be quiet as she closed the door. Lauryn could tell just by her demeanor that she was taking their sneaking out seriously. She'd clearly watched one too many cartoons.

"Hi," Cammie said as she stood in front of Lauryn, still pressing her phone to her ear.

"You're so dumb," Lauryn laughed as she gripped her waist and kissed her sweetly.

"I thought you meant like they did in the movies," Cammie excused herself with a timid laugh.

"Just curious... How were you planning on getting down?" Lauryn kinked a challenging eyebrow.

"I hadn't planned that far ahead," Cammie laughed. "I think I was probably gonna jump or something..."

"No... And knowing you, you'd probably get hurt," Lauryn frowned at her lapse in judgement.

"Probably," Cammie agreed.

"You're an idiot," Lauryn found herself giggling when she realized that she'd made it down unharmed.

"But I'm your idiot," Cammie giggled as well. She leaned in to kiss Lauryn again as she was laughing. It didn't exactly go as planned. They were just bumping mouths.

"God, I love you," Lauryn sighed as she gave up on trying to kiss her girlfriend. It just wasn't going to work out. Their smiles were so incessant, they couldn't even kiss properly.

"I love you too," Cammie reciprocated. She and Lauryn picked up their pace once more, rounding the final stretch until they reached the park. Cammie went in the direction of the main entrance, but Lauryn gently directed her further past it.

"I don't go in through there," Lauryn said softly as she linked her arm with Cammie's. She was leading her through an alternative route. The park was closed and they'd get in serious trouble if someone saw them on that property after hours.

Cammie just followed her, completely enraptured with her presence. This was probably her favorite date so far although they weren't even doing much. Had she known she could have this much fun just by simply walking, maybe she would've done it more often. As she paid close attention to Lauryn and the features she could make out in the moonlight, she felt Lauryn grab her hand. Only then did she tune into her surroundings. She had absolutely no idea where they were. She didn't even know the route in which they came, because she'd been staring at Lauryn instead of their path.

Lauryn regarded Cammie with a warm smile. She'd taken her to her secret place. Her escape. Her getaway. Eager to provide her muscles some relief, she clambered over to the bushes to get the blanket to sit on. There was a little backpack she kept out here. It was equipped with an old fluffy blanket and a spare set of headphones. She kept it hidden in a bush, hopefully to keep it dry when it rained and hidden from public view. Apparently it worked. It didn't appear dingy as she retrieved it. She spread it out over the grass and pulled Cammie with her to sit on top of it.

She sat down with her legs crossed and Cammie followed suit. Lauryn looked through the open hole in the bush, and Cammie did too. It was an outlook on the park. She would usually see the other people through the gap, but now she just saw relative darkness. It might have been creepy, but she enjoyed people watching. She wasn't so sure Cammie would appreciate the subtle scenery, but she sure did. She'd never been here at night before. It was almost eerie how calm and quiet everything was. What was usually filled with screaming kids and squeaky playground equipment was now deadly silent. Nothing was moving. There was no one there. No one was here at all, except for Lauryn and Cammie.

"I read through like twelve pages of your journal here," Lauryn broke the silence with that random fact. "On the first day I found it. I came here and I read it."

"Why here?" Cammie questioned.

"Because my family kept coming into my room. They were annoying. But here, no one disturbs you," Lauryn shrugged.

"I bet it's pretty in the daytime," Cammie said, taking in her environment. It was a nice subtle area. It was peaceful.

"You're pretty in the daytime," Lauryn quipped, taking the opportunity when it presented itself. "And in the night time too. All the time," she added with a smile.

"So are you, Lauryn," Cammie returned her compliment, then remembered how she was supposed to start accepting them now. "I mean, thank you," she revised her response.

"Thanks, Camz," Lauryn laughed. She propped herself up on her arms and smiled over at her girlfriend. It was warm out here now, a vast contrast to that morning. They were comfortable sitting here.

"You're welcome," Cammie smiled back. Lauryn's bracelet jingled, and she suddenly remembered that she'd never told her what the specific charms meant. "Lauryn," she called.

"Yes?" she turned at the sound of her voice.

"I forgot to explain this to you," she frowned, grasping Lauryn's wrist. "Give me your hand," she requested.

146

Lauryn complied and eagerly waited to hear Cammie's reasoning.

"Okay. I think this represents you, but only a few aspects. My favorite ones. This one is because of your love of books and thirst for knowledge. You're smart. You're incredibly intelligent. And I admire the way you don't dumb yourself down for other people," Cammie explained fondly as she clutched the book charm. "Also, it represents my journal. Because without it, we wouldn't be sitting here right now," she laughed nervously.

Lauryn didn't respond. She held her feedback for after she was done. It was clear to her then just how much thought had gone into this gift. It made it even more special in her heart. She vowed to never take it off. Ever. Not even in the shower. It would have to rust and disintegrate to be removed.

Cammie pointed to the paint brush charm and felt her cheeks heat up. "Um, I guess this one is kind of stupid... But this one is just because you love all forms of art. You're an amazing artist too, from what I've seen of your drawings and paintings. And it's also because you're beautiful. You're art," Cammie quoted herself from her journal, vaguely hoping Lauryn would catch her reference. She did. Cammie knew by the way her smile widened.

"This one is just your birth stone, because I'm happy you exist. You're my favorite person on the planet. I chose your birth stone, the Alexandrite. You actually have two... But I thought this one looked prettier than the pearl. I think it's a real one, but it might not be. I hope it is though," Cammie laughed as she grazed the gem with her fingertip.

Holy shit. Lauryn's eyes widened as she looked at it closely. Did Cammie really get her a real birth stone? That must've been expensive as hell. She felt even cheaper than before as she looked at the sun and moon necklace hanging from her neck. In the same instance, she felt an immense surge of love for Cammie, just waiting to be expressed.

"I think this one is obvious," Cammie said as she picked up the sun charm. "I don't think it needs explaining. You know all about that," she shrugged and looked at Lauryn for confirmation. When she nodded, Cammie moved to the last charm. She showed the heart charm to her symbolically. "And this one is simple. It's because I love you, Lauryn," Cammie concluded with a smile.

"I don't even know what to say," Lauryn exhaled. "What the hell," she mumbled as she looked at the jewelry hanging from her wrist. "I just love you. I love you so much. That's it," she shrugged. She slowly came to the realization that if she wasn't in over her head before, she was now. She was falling way too hard, way too fast.

"I love you too," Cammie said simply. She was elated to see that Lauryn was so infatuated with her gift. The green-eyed girl kept looking down at her bracelet. She kept lifting each charm to stare at it, finally grasping its true meaning. Cammie was happy she finally got the chance to explain.

Lauryn only smiled wider at Cammie's admission, then she shifted back to lay down and stared up into the sky. Along with thoughts of how amazing Cammie was, she was thinking about oblivion overhead. She wished she was in the country, with vast open fields and no city lights. Maybe then she would see the stars. She'd never seen a star-speckled sky, due to living relatively close to a city. The suburbs didn't give enough for stars to shine. There were a few, but nothing like the skies she'd seen online.

Cammie felt the same way. Star gazing would be a lot better if there were actual stars to gaze at. There were less than twenty out here tonight, from what she could see. There was barely even one to wish on. They were all dull and not sparkling at all, but she was content. And she had her wish anyway. Her wish was laying right next to her.

"I just wanna do this for the rest of my life," Cammie said in a daze.

"With me," Lauryn grinned.

"No," Cammie lied.

"Yeah," Lauryn said knowingly. "Admit it," she giggled.

"Yeah," Cammie nodded goofily. She rolled over and landed on top of Lauryn. When she thought Lauryn would push her off, she actually settled her arms around her. Her hands clasped loosely over the small of her back. Lauryn just stared at her lovingly. They simultaneously cracked a smile and leaned in for yet another kiss. Cammie certainly wouldn't be kissing her under the light of a *thousand* stars, but they were stars nonetheless. And that was the sole purpose of this particular date. So she kissed her passionately, fervently moving her lips against Lauryn's.

As soon as their lips connected, Cammie relaxed. She placed most of her body weight on her forearms, which were helping her steady herself on either side of Lauryn. Lauryn claimed her mouth relentlessly. Her tongue probed through Cammie's lips skillfully, wasting no time exploring the familiar depths of her mouth. Cammie rested her hand on her waist and felt Lauryn smirk before she rested her hand on her side in response. With a new wave of bravery, Lauryn slid her hands down to her Cammie's backside - one of her favorite assets. She eyed her every few seconds to make sure she was completely okay with their pace as of now.

To Lauryn's surprise, Cammie moved slowly to slip her hand under her shirt. Her fingertips teased the area just above Lauryn's hip bone, which made her squirm. It kind of tickled, but instead of eliciting laughter, she felt the sensation elsewhere. Cammie gently caressed the smooth skin of her stomach without breaking their kiss. Her warm hand coming into contact with her skin made Lauryn draw in a sharp breath. Cammie pulled away from their kiss for a second, wondering what the nature of that sound was. It wasn't exactly a moan, but it was hot. She felt emboldened with the fact that they were completely alone. No intrusive parents or little sisters would barge in on them and ruin the moment - if she could get it there. When she made eye contact and saw Lauryn's newfound flustered state, Cammie bit her lip.

Lauryn knew that was a habit of hers, but it was different. Something in her eyes told Lauryn that it wasn't her usual innocent, flirtatious lip biting. No, this look was way more suggestive. That carnal gaze made her smirk in response. It was the same way she'd looked at her in Lauryn's room that day. This time, she was willing to react to it. Lauryn brought her back to her lips, letting her hands roam Cammie's body. Slowly, though. She didn't want a repeat of what happened last time.

"Cammie," Lauryn paused. She feared that groping would make Cammie uncomfortable. She just had to check on her.

"Yes?" Cammie answered from on top of her. The distraction mildly annoyed her.

"Is this okay? We're not moving too fast or anything, right? Because-" Lauryn began to clarify, but she was cut off by Cammie's eager kiss.

Based on that response, Lauryn assumed they were on the same page. She didn't want to come on too strong, but she gripped the curves below her waist a little more securely anyway. Because she didn't want to be completely on top of Lauryn, Cammie shifted over. It would make it easier to touch her. She settled herself between Lauryn's legs. In doing so, her thigh pressed against Lauryn's center. And she moaned - a sound that completely shocked Cammie. It was more like a pant than a moan, but it caused a reaction within her anyway. And it wasn't intentional, but she did it again and was rewarded with the same sound, just a little quieter.

Eager to provoke it again, she moved Lauryn's hair to the side, exposing her neck. She leaned in and placed light kisses along her jawline. The second her lips made contact with Lauryn's heated skin, she shivered involuntarily. She wasn't used to be this worked up over simple gestures, but Cammie was the first to make her feel a lot of things. Cammie kissed down her jawline to her neck, trailing her tongue along her neck lightly before she started to suck on it. She didn't want to mark her, she just wanted to elicit another response from her. And she did.

"Shit, Camz..." Lauryn mumbled breathily as Cammie continued kissing her neck. It was a weak response. She still wanted to make sure Cammie was okay with where this was headed, but it was *clear* that she was.

"Hmm?" Cammie answered against her skin, leaving light goosebumps in its wake. She simultaneously trailed her hand further up Lauryn's shirt. Her hand came to a rest just below her bra, but she couldn't think too much about it. Because then she would freak out and make a fool of herself, just like last time. So she refrained from excessive forethought and just performed.

There was just one question she needed to ask, because she shared the same fear Lauryn had of coming on too strong. And after that, whatever Lauryn's response should be, she would just act on her impulses. "Do you want me to stop?" she asked as she trailed her fingers along the wiring.

"No..." Lauryn admitted with a smirk. Although she was nervous, a big part of her wanted to take this step in their relationship. That was true for both of them. It wasn't some drunken hookup or one-night-stand. There were feelings involved, deep feelings. They'd both professed their love to each other. It was okay to do this. They were both willing and clearly consenting. And more importantly, it didn't feel forced this time. It was natural. With that in mind, Lauryn took the lead.

"Let's take this off," Lauryn said before lifting her shirt over her head, ever so gently. Cammie straddled her to aid her in removing her shirt. Lauryn was looking up at her godly girlfriend in awe. She was so damn beautiful. Every part of her. The sight of Cammie's exposed skin made the space between her legs pulsate. She stared at her semi-clothed body with parted lips. Emerald eyes skimmed over Cammie's small frame and they burned with desire. She'd never felt this amount of lust towards her, or anyone before. They weren't even really doing anything yet. It was a strange occurrence, but definitely not uninviting.

She ran her hand down Cammie's bare side and leaned up to kiss her lips again. Cammie kissed her back forcefully, immediately slipping her tongue into her mouth again. Lauryn rolled over, gently laying Cammie down on the blanket without breaking their kiss. She came over her and looked down at her, still unable to fathom how beautiful she actually was.

Cammie was only wearing a bra and her pants, and she was erotically beautiful. The fact that she was completely unaware of her own sex appeal only made her more attractive in Lauryn's eyes. And she wanted her. All of her. Deciding to give Cammie the same treatment she gave her, she kissed her neck lightly. Cammie's hands blindly gripped the end of Lauryn's shirt, clumsily tugging it upwards. Lauryn stopped kissing her to discard her own shirt, then resumed. Lauryn's hands wandered up to unclasp and remove her bra, exposing Cammie's torso completely. Lauryn drew in a deep breath to compose herself at the sight. She was definitely a fan of the female anatomy, although she wasn't particularly gay. And Cammie was undoubtedly a sight to marvel over. Lauryn continued her kisses and made her way down to Cammie's chest. Cammie was already highly aroused, but when Lauryn began to kiss her chest, she moaned quietly.

She was looking down at Lauryn in awe. Lauryn descended down her chest, placing light kisses all over her collar bones. Then she tentatively cupped one of her breasts. When Cammie felt Lauryn's lips close over her nipple, she shuddered. Lauryn quickly looked up at her, making sure this was okay – and it certainly was. She ran her tongue over it and watched as her girlfriend's lips parted. Lauryn was pleased by Cammie's expression. She showed her other breast the same attention and enjoyed the girlish cries that escaped.

Cammie suddenly sat up, more than determined to do the same thing. Lauryn pulled back and watched her warily, fearing that she'd done something wrong. But when Cammie eagerly kissed her, she relaxed. Cammie's hands roamed around her back to undo her bra as well, but she couldn't quite get it at first. With Lauryn's help, it soon fell onto the blanket. Cammie's cheeks were burning with embarrassment, but she redeemed herself by taking Lauryn's breast into her mouth. Lauryn shifted backwards, and Cammie followed without detaching her lips. The sensation elicited another moan from Lauryn, and Cammie stared up at her in shock. But she quickly refocused on the task at hand. She palmed the breast she wasn't tending to and toyed with Lauryn's nipple between her fingers. Lauryn moaned again and desire pooled between her legs. She wanted Cammie now.

She was terrified to make the next move, but one of them had to do it. Her hands were threading through her hair, but she instantly realized there were better places they could be. They roamed downwards and Lauryn slowly moved her hand to the waistband of Cammie's jeans. She went back up to kiss her mouth in the same instance. Her hand started to work slow circles, and Cammie moaned into her mouth in response. Lauryn smirked and began to rub the outside of her pants with a little more pressure, and Cammie squirmed from her touch. She wanted to moan her approval again, but Lauryn's mouth restricted the sound. Lauryn teasingly trailed a finger across the top of Cammie's pants. Cammie pulled away and looked down at what Lauryn was doing. When she met her eyes, Lauryn raised an eyebrow - silently asking for permission.

Cammie nodded subtly, giving Lauryn all of the reassurance she needed. Lauryn switched positions with her yet again, settling herself on top of Cammie. She hurriedly unfastened Cammie's pants. Cammie kicked them off and tentatively reached for Lauryn's. Lauryn quickly obliged, lifting off of Cammie long enough to abandon her own. She kind of wished they were in one of their beds, which would've been a lot more comfortable and romantic, but this was what they had to work with. And she wasn't going to ruin it by paying too much attention to their environment.

Cammie took a second to admire Lauryn's body. It was dark, but the moon was bright enough that she could see her clearly. She looked at her face, where her dark features were a perfect contrast to her pale skin. Then she directed her attention to her curvaceous body. And plaguing her body were a bunch of natural imperfections. Birth marks, childhood scars, and a few stretch marks decorated her body in the most compelling way. This was a part of Lauryn she'd never been exposed to before. Especially not in this way. She was grateful that Lauryn wasn't perfect. It made it more real. Lauryn was a real girl, with a real girl's body. She was gorgeous, but she wasn't flawless. Albeit, her flaws didn't matter at all to Cammie, who loved every inch of her - regardless of her imperfections.

Cammie kind of wished she'd worn a different pair of underwear. Had she known *this* was going to happen, she probably would've worn a solid color or something. The flower ones she had on weren't really sexy. They were polar opposite of Lauryn's, who was wearing a simple black pair with lace around the top. It also matched her bra. Cammie rarely matched her underwear. Because it usually didn't matter, she used to have no one to impress. She didn't even own any lingerie. Maybe the next time they did this, she would come better prepared. She hoped Lauryn wouldn't comment on it. Thankfully, she didn't. What she did was much better than a snide remark about her flower panties.

Lauryn unexpectedly cupped Cammie's center, making her gasp. With her lips parted, Lauryn took advantage and slipped her tongue back into her mouth. Then she placed a delicate kiss on her lips and gave her body the same treatment as before. Soft kisses littered her neck and chest. Lauryn's lips brushed over her smooth skin and Cammie writhed slightly. All the while, Lauryn's fingers had been teasing her through her underwear. Cammie was breathing heavily by the time Lauryn sensually kissed her stomach.

"Oh my God," Cammie sighed breathlessly.

That only spurred Lauryn on, and she continued to kiss all over the taut muscles of her abdomen. She slowly descended towards the waistband of her underwear. Going down a little further, Lauryn began to kiss her inner thighs. She stopped at her center. She looked up at her girlfriend, but her eyes were closed tightly in anticipation. Lauryn smirked to herself and once again rubbed her center, with only the thin fabric of her underwear between them. The more she teased, the damper the space became. Cammie was moaning louder than she was before, and Lauryn decided to slide her hand inside of her underwear. It was unsurprisingly slick as she continued to explore the area between her legs. When she slipped her finger in, she felt Cammie tense up.

"Are you okay?" she asked cautiously. She wasn't really well informed on this activity just yet. She didn't want to accidentally hurt her, so she tried to make sure she wasn't. "Does it hurt?"

"No... Just... Keep going," Cammie said shakily. It wasn't a lie. The feeling was definitely foreign, but the way pleasure rippled through her body at the intrusion made her want more of it.

Lauryn removed the final offending garment with shaking hands, tossing it in the same direction of her pants. She resumed what she was doing. Without a word, Cammie brought her hand to Lauryn's wet center. She timidly began rubbing and soon developed a steady pace. She had no idea what she was doing, but was mirroring what Lauryn had just done to her. Cammie helped Lauryn out of her underwear and began pleasuring her simultaneously. Her middle finger disappeared into Lauryn's core, and Lauryn let out a whimper. Cammie nearly lost it when she felt Lauryn grinding into her hand. Her center throbbed at the sudden awareness that she was actually doing this to *her*. She was making her moan and pleasuring her in ways she'd only fantasized about. That information encouraged her release.

Cammie's eyes were closed tightly in concentration, both on finding her release and helping Lauryn approach hers. Lauryn wore the same expression. Cammie applied more pressure to her sensitive spots. When the moaning got louder, they both picked up their pace. Not long after she began, Lauryn felt Cammie tensing up again, yet in an entirely different way. She arched her back, trembling under her touch.

"*Lauryn*," Cammie whined. Her name fell from her lips, and Lauryn became wetter at Cammie's sultry tone. Her pace increased, and her fingers rocked into her faster than before.

"*Cammie*," Lauryn moaned in response. Cammie's eyes flew open. She'd moaned her name. Oh man, that was going to be her undoing.

"Lauryn, I'm gonna..." Cammie husked, but her sentence was replaced by a throaty moan. Lauryn's thumb began working on her clit. When her fingers curled inside of her, it sent white heat throughout her entire body. Lauryn felt her clench around her finger. And that, along with Cammie's help, pushed her over the edge at the same time. Cammie's hips jerked slightly as Lauryn's body went rigid on top of her. Lauryn moaned a string of profanity as she finally came, dousing Cammie's hand in her arousal. Lauryn collapsed on top of her and withdrew her fingers. Both of their chests were heaving as they tried to catch their breath.

Cammie's arms immediately enveloped Lauryn as they both came down from their high. Lauryn was hot now, although it wasn't hot outside. She'd actually worked up a thin layer of sweat. Pleased with herself and the ending result, she laid next to her girlfriend. Cammie blindly reached for her hand and intertwined their fingers. She was still trying to recuperate and her breathing was still labored. Once she caught her breath, she turned to smirk at Lauryn.

"Fuck," Cammie exhaled.

"Holy shit," Lauryn seconded.

"That was... *Fuck*," she reiterated. She was barely able to form a coherent thought, let alone a full sentence. She was still trying to wrap her mind around what had just happened. And she was trying to calm down.

"Yeah," Lauryn agreed, although Cammie hadn't really said much of anything.

They both laid there, silently coming to terms with what had just commenced. Their bodies cooled off and the aftershocks faded. Lauryn was breathing evenly now. She was so sated, as was Cammie. The breeze drafted over her bare body and she shivered. She sheepishly clambered over to retrieve her clothes and put them back on silently. Lauryn followed suit and came back to cuddle with her. Her head rested on her stomach and they looked back up at the stars. No words were exchanged for a few minutes. They just laid and looked.

"Camz?" Lauryn prompted raspily.

"Yeah?" Cammie answered.

"I think I know the *real* significance of the moon now," Lauryn smirked suggestively, pointing overhead.

"I think I do too," Cammie laughed.

Chapter 19

Following the events of last night, Lauryn and Cammie ended up at Lauryn's house. The two snuck back inside at around one in the morning, because Lauryn didn't trust that Cammie would get home unnoticed. Proposing that she spend the night at her house seemed like the best solution.

They'd fallen asleep sharing hazy kisses. Their atmosphere was relaxed. Cammie fell asleep in Lauryn's arms a few minutes after they'd gotten inside. Lauryn just watched her in adoration, but soon succumbed to sleep as well. They were only in underwear, having shed their clothes because they were hot under the blankets. Lauryn's head was on top of Cammie's chest, and her entire body was curled into her girlfriend. She didn't need a blanket when she had the warmth from her girlfriend's body. Cammie was sprawled out underneath her, with her legs intertwined with Lauryn's.

Lauryn's mother knocked timidly at the door. When she got no response, she chuckled to herself and entered Lauryn's room. She was a little shocked to find Cammie in Lauryn's bed. Did she say she was sleeping over? Perhaps it slipped her mind. Either way, she crossed her room to wake the both of them up. When she walked up to the foot of the bed, she was shocked again. Lauryn was completely wrapped up with Cammie. Her daughter's face was buried into Cammie's chest, and Cammie was holding her so tightly. And to top it all, they weren't wearing shirts.

Cara was a little confused, to say the least. She knew Cammie was best friends with her daughter, but she didn't know they were *that* close. It was almost strange to see them so intimate. Now that it was on her mind, their behavior *had* been odd lately. Cammie never used to come over this much. Her visits were always sparing, and she never stayed for long. But she'd been sleeping over a handful of times over the past month. In the past when they used to stay overnight, they were always on separate sides of her bed in the morning. When she approached the pair, she saw that under the covers, they weren't two figures. Their bodies were meshing. Their legs were intertwined. Cara's expression changed slightly. Her suspicions were slowly being confirmed. Instead of rousing them from their sleep, she slipped out of the room and back down to the kitchen.

"Hey..." Cara trailed as she approached her husband.

"What?" Miguel responded.

"I saw something... Interesting," Cara trailed as she sat across from him.

"What?" he repeated, only a tad more interested than two seconds prior.

"Lauryn and Cammie were in bed, *shirtless*," she disclosed.

"It got kind of hot last night," Miguel shrugged.

"They were *on top* of each other," Cara emphasized.

"They're best friends. Girls can get away with that sort of thing," Miguel shook his head.

"Maybe..." Cara relented. She frowned and thought back to the way she found the two of them, but brushed it off. Unconscious cuddling. That's what she was going with.

"Well, do you still think Cammie is gay?" Miguel wondered out loud.

Someone clambered down the stairs with heavy feet, whom they only assumed to be Christian. Their conversation ended with a brisk nod of Cara's head. They were proven right when their son entered the kitchen, yawning and stretching.

"Morning," he grumbled sleepily.

"Good morning," Cara greeted him with a smile, although she was still disturbed by what she saw in Lauryn's room.

Christian fixed his plate and headed to the living room to claim the TV. Cara was pleased to see him leave, only because she wanted to further discuss what she'd witnessed. But Tori replaced his presence as she sauntered into the room and she decided to stay in there to eat. They all sat around the table and made small talk. They were missing the presence of the two suspicious girls, but assumed they'd be joining them later.

Lauryn woke up seconds before Cammie. She noticed their lack of clothing and quickly got out of bed to get tee shirts for the both of them. She desperately hoped no one had come in. When she checked for any signs of intrusion, she saw that the door was closed. A closed door must've meant no disruptions.

"Camz," Lauryn shook Cammie's shoulder softly.

Cammie grumbled into the pillow and turned away from Lauryn. Lauryn laughed and shook her again. "Get up," she coaxed her gently.

Cammie only grumbled again, trying her best to ignore her. She pulled the covers over her head in an attempt to make her voice disappear. And it did, for a second. But then she felt Lauryn sitting on top of her, shaking her more forcefully. "Camz..."

"You're so annoying," Cammie complained as she finally opened her eyes. She was pleased to find Lauryn perched on top of her, smiling down at her dumbly. Her hair was unruly and she'd clearly just woken up, but Cammie found her to be beautiful anyway.

"Good morning to you too," Lauryn quipped.

"Good morning," Cammie grinned.

"You have to put this on," Lauryn said as she picked up the shirt that was hanging off of the comforter.

"Yay," Cammie smiled and finally rolled herself out of bed. Wearing Lauryn's clothes was a perk she'd been looking forward to and now she could. She slipped it on eagerly. A contented sigh left her lips as Lauryn's scent surrounded her completely. It was hanging off of her a bit, but it fit nonetheless.

154

"You're so cute," Lauryn giggled at the way Cammie was so smitten with the shirt. "You can have it, if you want?" she offered.

"I do," Cammie nodded immediately. She crossed the room and cupped Lauryn's face, pulling her into a kiss.

"*Okay*," Lauryn recoiled. "We need to brush our teeth," she made a face and wiped her mouth playfully. Cammie narrowed her eyes at her, but agreed.

After they'd washed up, Lauryn and Cammie made their way down the stairs with their fingers intertwined. They released their hold just before they were in sight, a poor attempt at concealing their secret. However, their execution was flawed. From Cara's position, she could see them before they saw her. And she saw them let go. Lauryn's mother had slowly been catching onto them. With that serving as another form of confirmation, she had just about figured it out. She just didn't want to accept it.

"Good morning," Cammie greeted Lauryn's parents cheerfully.

"Hey," Lauryn waved.

"Good morning, ladies," Miguel returned with a smile.

"Good morning," Cara nodded in their direction. Tori waved back at her sister and smiled at Cammie.

Lauryn walked over to the countertops, where a lovely breakfast selection was situated. She helped herself and made Cammie's plate as well, then she dismissed her parents and retired to the living room. Once out of view, Cammie thanked her for the favor with a quick peck on the cheek as she took her plate. When they joined Christian and occupied the couch to eat, she was just focusing on not making a mess. Lauryn was eating quietly right beside her. Christian thought she could've been a little more over, offered Cammie a little more personal space. There was more than enough room, but she wanted to be close to her girlfriend. Mutually, they felt more connected after last night. They craved more closeness than usual.

Both of them finished their food with only the sounds of the TV filling the room. Lauryn offered to take Cammie's plate back into the kitchen, so she gave it to her. Christian grinned at her, and she returned his smile sheepishly. He knew nothing of their relationship. None of her family did. The only people outside of their friend group that knew were the people that had decided to pay them attention in the hallway, Brandon and Sophia. They didn't feel like it was anyone else's business, and they didn't feel the need to flaunt it around either. Their public displays of affection were for their own selfish wants, not for other people's eyes. For the most part. Cammie was guilty of wanting to show Lauryn off, but she refrained from doing so most times.

Lauryn placed their plates in the sink. She was going to leave it, but she decided to go ahead and wash them off. With Lauryn's extended absence, Cammie started to miss her. She had it bad. It had only been about three minutes at most. So she wandered back into the kitchen, pleased to find her girlfriend at the sink. Lauryn was diligently cleaning their plates off, and she'd just finished when Cammie appeared by her side.

"Hey," Lauryn grinned.

"Hi," Cammie smiled back. Lauryn wanted to kiss her then. Each time she smiled, she had the desire to kiss her. And Cammie smiled a lot. But of course, she couldn't. Not in the presence of her parents, but she could in her room.

"Come on," Lauryn gestured upstairs as she set the plates on the dish rack and wiped her hands on the towel. Cammie eagerly followed her out, and once they were out of the kitchen, she slipped her hand back into her grasp. They shuffled up the stairs together and hurriedly made it to Lauryn's room.

"Did you see how close they were?" Cara commented to Miguel when she heard Lauryn's door close upstairs.

"Sure," Miguel shrugged.

"And I'm pretty sure that was Lauryn's shirt..." Cara noticed skeptically.

"Oh," Miguel shrugged.

"No red flags? At all?" Cara asked incredulously, unwilling to believe that her husband hadn't noticed anything peculiar.

Miguel didn't really respond, he just offered a dismissive grunt in response. He had noticed, but he didn't feel like it was his place to speculate. Whatever his daughter was doing with Cammie was fine with him. He liked Cammie. She was a nice, sweet, respectable girl. He wouldn't object to it if they actually did have something going on. And he trusted that if they did, Lauryn would come to them about it eventually.

»»»»

"Last night was fun," Cammie smirked. She lovingly ran her fingers through Lauryn's hair. Lauryn's chin was resting on her stomach, and she was looking back at Cammie with bright eyes.

"Oh yeah," Lauryn seconded. "Was it good, though?"

"Yes," Cammie nodded immediately. She didn't know why she'd never considered it before. Sex was never really a tangible factor in her life. She'd thought about Lauryn before, but had never gone as far as touching herself. She thought it was weird. So last night was her first sexual experience, ever. "It was amazing."

"Okay, good," Lauryn sighed.

"Did you think it was?" Cammie asked insecurely. She wasn't aware of Lauryn's sexual past, but she hoped that her time with her was good. Even if she'd been with someone before, she hoped hers was decent in comparison.

"Yes. That was... Fuck," Lauryn laughed when she couldn't come up with a better word.

"Have you ever..." Cammie started to ask, but her nerves got the best of her. She felt weird asking that question. Now that she had, she wasn't really sure she wanted to know the answer.

Lauryn looked at her expectantly, waiting for her to finish. But she soon caught her drift. She shook her head no quickly. "You were my first, Camz," she laughed lightly.

Well, that was a plot twist. Kind of. She didn't really expect her to *not* be a virgin, but at the same time, she kind of did. Understandably so, when she'd had so many boyfriends in the past. That, along with her good looks, kind of made it almost expected. But she hadn't. Her respect for the green-eyed girl grew exponentially. And her heart surged at the fact that they were each other's first time.

"Really?" Cammie grinned widely.

"Mhm," Lauryn nodded again.

"Whoa," she breathed with a dorky smile. She couldn't keep it off.

"Don't act so surprised," Lauryn quipped playfully. She wasn't offended. Being a virgin as an upper-classman in high school was rare, but she was. Most of her friends outside of that friend group were not, so the inference was understandable.

"No, I mean - I didn't think, like - I wasn't trying to say that you were - I - I wasn't implying that-" Cammie stuttered, quick to defend herself and her train of thought. God, she didn't want Lauryn to think that she thought she was a floozy or something. That was far from the case. Lauryn saved her from making a further fool out of herself by kissing her.

"Camz," Lauryn chuckled. "I was just kidding. I know you don't think that," she giggled again.

"Okay... Good. Because I don't," Cammie assured her again, just before capturing her lips with her own.

"I know," Lauryn giggled at her flustered state. "I mean, I've had some *heated* makeout sessions before... But never that. That was... Something else," she laughed.

"Oh," Cammie mumbled. She didn't want to think about Lauryn having "heated makeout sessions" with anyone else. Her subtle jealousy faded when she realized she'd had her in a way that no one else had. Cammie was Lauryn's first. She smiled as that crossed her mind again.

"What are you smiling at?" Lauryn questioned in amusement.

"Because that just makes it so much more special," Cammie answered.

"Yeah," Lauryn nodded. "Although I wish it would've happened in one of our beds..."

"It was in your secret place, though. That makes it special too," Cammie countered. "Everything about it was perfect."

"Everything about you is perfect," Lauryn complimented her, recalling the way her nude body looked last night. She pushed that thought from her mind immediately, before she acted on it.

"Thanks," Cammie shrugged modestly. She'd been getting more comfortable with the compliments. Lauryn showered her with them endlessly. It was starting to pay off.

Cammie looked around Lauryn's room. Her writing was still on display. Short poems and concise observations lined the walls. They'd been there ever since she'd put them up. And she looked over at the rose that was almost completely withered, noticing that she hadn't moved that either. The bracelet she'd put on three days ago was still perched on her wrist. She smiled subconsciously at the fact that Lauryn carried a small part of Cammie with her. It was evident just how sentimental she was.

"I love you," Cammie sighed happily.

"I love you too," Lauryn reciprocated.

Cammie continued looking around Lauryn's room. She was a relatively clean person. Her floor was a contrast to Cammie's. There were no clothes distributed on the floor. It was bare, while Cammie barely had a path to walk through on hers. She continued to look around and her eyes settled on the guitar in her closet. It was leaning against the wall. It almost wasn't visible, but Cammie could make out a Fender from a mile away. Not really. She still had to wear her glasses sometimes.

"I didn't know you had a guitar?" Cammie voiced her observation as she peered down at Lauryn.

"What?" Lauryn questioned. She looked in the direction Cammie's gaze was settled and raised her eyebrow. "Oh, that? I've had that for a long time," she shrugged.

"I didn't know you played," Cammie smiled, pleased at the new fact.

"That's because I don't," Lauryn countered with a light chuckle.

"Then I'm gonna teach you," Cammie declared.

"Okay," Lauryn agreed. She assumed it would be later on. Another one of their dates, perhaps.

"Right now. Get up," Cammie said with a mischievous glint in her eye.

"Now?" Lauryn squeaked. She wasn't too eager to move. Their current position was incredibly comfortable. Cammie herself was incredibly comfortable. And her body was soft.

"Yep," Cammie nodded as she waited for Lauryn to sit up. Lauryn relented and got up with a pout.

Cammie took no notice of it and walked over to retrieve her instrument from the closet. She picked it up carefully and strummed it as she walked back towards the bed. Man, was it out of tune. Luckily, she had a tuning app on her phone. She always misplaced her actual tuners, so her phone tuner usually came in handy. She sat down on the bed and brought it into her lap, tuning each string carefully. She had to be careful. Popped strings had licked her in the face a few times in the past. She didn't want it to happen in front of Lauryn.

Lauryn was looking at her intently. She was so focused on what she was doing, it was cute. Her forehead creased in concentration as she turned each peg. Clearly, she knew what she was doing. This was her element. Lauryn just sat back and watched until she was called.

"Lauryn," Cammie motioned her over with a smile. "Come here, babe."

"Are you gonna sing?" Lauryn inferred.

"No. I'm gonna teach you how to play," Cammie shook her head.

"But babe, I love it when you sing," Lauryn negotiated. Playing instruments didn't come easy to her. She played a bit of piano, but guitar was kind of hard. In comparison to Cammie's experience, she wasn't necessarily ready to be in that vulnerable position. But she couldn't say no to eyes like those. Cammie was tantamount to a puppy most of the time.

"I'll sing to you next time," Cammie promised and kissed her nose gently, having already had her mind made up about the lesson. "Promise."

"Fine. Well, at least let me hear you play?" Lauryn requested begrudgingly, eager to take whatever she could get.

"That, I can do," Cammie obliged and positioned her fingers.

With slightly shaking hands, Cammie formed the chords. She began playing and strummed for her girlfriend as a mere showcase. Without a song in mind yet, she started plucking the strings and it very well could've been the introduction of a song that had yet to be written. The melodic sounds of her plucking instantly pacified Lauryn. When Cammie felt like she'd presented enough of her talents, she stopped and awkwardly glanced at Lauryn.

"You're really good with your fingers," Lauryn smirked.

"Thanks," she chuckled obnoxiously, immediately catching onto that double meaning. The innuendo made her laugh again.

"I love you," Lauryn sighed.

"I love you, too," Cammie returned and leaned over the guitar to second it with a kiss. "Can I teach you how to play now?"

"Sure," Lauryn agreed and held up to her end of the bargain.

"Wanna learn how to play an Ed song?" Cammie questioned.

"Sure," Lauryn agreed again.

"Okay," Cammie said as she mentally formed the chords again, then she handed it over to Lauryn.

Cammie attempted to show her how to play, staring with the chords. Lauryn had stubborn fingers, and they weren't stretching the way Cammie wanted them to. She showed her a *C chord* first, and played it as example. Lauryn strummed as well, but the sound was frayed and muted.

"No... It's more like this," Cammie said as she came behind Lauryn, wrapping her arms around hers to guide her fingers to the according strings. Cammie took the opportunity to completely wrap herself around her girlfriend, just because she had the privilege. Lauryn felt a particular closeness and intimacy in her gesture that she couldn't quite place. It was nice; being this close to Cammie. She smiled at the younger girl, who reciprocated it gingerly.

"You should just kinda... Arch your fingers... Yeah, like that," she nodded as Lauryn followed her instructions.

Lauryn strummed again, resulting in the same sound she got the first time. She groaned in frustration. "I can't do it," she pouted, and Cammie leaned over to kiss her. It fixed the pout instantly.

"Yes you can. Try again," Cammie encouraged her, giving her shoulder a light squeeze. She was still positioned close behind Lauryn, with her arms still around her arms.

"But it hurts my fingers..." Lauryn complained as she stretched out her hand.

"Yeah, it will at first. But the pain goes away after a while..." Cammie stated.

"Camz, I can't," Lauryn sighed, shaking her head.

Cammie focused on repositioning Lauryn's fingers on the frets. After trying and failing three more times, Lauryn finally produced the desired sound. She attempted to play the whole progression, but failed. Eventually, she did it. Once. And it was painfully slow, but she did it. She grinned widely at Cammie and giggled in delight. Cammie regarded her with adoration and pride. She wrapped her arms around the older girl's torso and nuzzled her face in her neck.

"Good job, baby," Cammie smiled.

"Thanks," Lauryn smiled back brightly. She was proud of herself, and thankful for Cammie's patience. If it were up to Cammie, she would've held Lauryn like that for a million years.

"I'm proud of you," Cammie shared fondly.

Lauryn set her guitar up against the wall, silently resigning from any further lessons. After all of that hard work, she found that she missed the taste of her lips. So she leaned in to kiss Cammie again, but Cammie turned her head. Lauryn looked at her in confusion. Why'd she move? She tried again, but got the same result. Cammie kinked a challenging eyebrow, daring her to try again. Lauryn pursed her lips and cupped her face, directing her to her mouth. But Cammie squirmed and Lauryn ended up kissing her chin.

"*Camz*," Lauryn huffed.

"Yes?" Cammie giggled. She felt playful. If Lauryn wanted to kiss her, she'd have to earn it.

159

"Why do you keep moving?" Lauryn questioned as she tried to go in for another one. This time, Cammie tilted her head down to make Lauryn kiss her nose.

"Cammie!" Lauryn groaned. She gripped her body in an attempt to keep her still. The need to kiss her just increased at every failed endeavor. Cammie's teasing only made her want it more.

"Lauryn!" Cammie mocked her tone of voice. She giggled at her girlfriend's frustration and bit her lip.

"Okay," Lauryn smirked. Challenge accepted.

Cammie was laying back on her bed, looking at her with a devilish grin. She wasn't exactly prepared for Lauryn to jump on her like she did. And she kind of got the wind knocked out of her. But she regained her bearings in just enough time to dodge Lauryn's lips. Lauryn grimaced and tightened her hold on her, finally connecting their lips successfully - for a second. She pinned Cammie down by her arms and straddled her lap, then she kissed her fully on the mouth, to her heart's content. Cammie relented instantly. When they meshed, she reveled in the feeling. Cammie gladly kissed her back, enjoying it just as much as Lauryn.

When she made note of their position, Cammie blushed slightly. Lauryn's aggression mixed with this new dominant side was successful in unintentionally turning her on. Lauryn seemed to experience the shift too, and she attached her lips to Cammie's neck instead. Images of last night returned. It left both of them sated, yet eager for another encounter. And this time, it looked like it would be in the bed.

Lauryn teased the spot, then sucked on it. Because it was their first time, Lauryn refrained from leaving any marks on her last night. Now, the atmosphere was different. Her tongue trailed from the base of her neck to the bottom of her jawline, causing the smaller girl to sigh. Cammie wanted to touch her, but Lauryn's grip on her wrists wouldn't let up. It frustrated her, but in a different way than Lauryn was just a few minutes ago. Lauryn's mouth was unforgiving against her neck, and she didn't lift her lips until a red mark was present.

Cammie wanted to touch where she was sure Lauryn had just given her a hickey, but she was still restricted. Lauryn's grip on her wrists didn't falter at all. She kept her pinned to the bed as she smirked down at her. Lauryn had taken complete advantage of Cammie's playful mood and now she was in control. She contemplated what to do to tease Cammie the way she'd teased her with her lack of kisses, but she came up short. And she missed her mouth anyway. So she took Cammie's bottom lip between her own, without releasing her hold.

Lauryn lowered herself slightly to gain better access to Cammie's lips. Her chest pressed against Cammie's, and the girl shifted under her. Lauryn swiped her tongue across her lip and Cammie eagerly accepted her tongue into her mouth. They moved in sync. Their tongues clashed against each other's and it became increasingly hungrier. Cammie longed to let her hands roam Lauryn's body, but they were still fucking held down. She struggled against her, but Lauryn was definitely stronger.

"Lauryn..." Cammie grumbled, turning away from her kiss until she let her up.

"Cammie..." Lauryn quipped, mocking Cammie's tone, just like she had done to her. This was her form of payback, and she was thriving in it.

"You're evil," Cammie laughed. She accepted her circumstances and just laid there helplessly. She was at Lauryn's mercy, and she knew it.

"Payback," Lauryn smirked.

"You've paid me back already," Cammie rolled her eyes in good nature. She wasn't really annoyed with her, although she wished she had the free will of her limbs back.

"Hmm, have I?" Lauryn teased as she placed a kiss on her jawline. Her lips grazed just over it, barely making contact.

"Yes..." Cammie trailed. All of this "payback" was getting her worked up. And she couldn't do anything about it.

"You're way too easy," Lauryn giggled as she finally released Cammie's wrists.

"Well, of course... Especially when you do *that*," Cammie groaned as she finally was able to touch her. She settled her hands on her hips, looking up at the girl that still sat on top of her.

"What did I do?" Lauryn asked condescendingly.

"This," Cammie laughed as she grazed her forming hickey with her fingertips. "Like I said, you're evil."

"Oh," Lauryn said coyly. "*That's* not evil..."

"I'm pretty sure," Cammie disagreed.

"*This* is evil," Lauryn's smirk only grew as she rolled her hips once against Cammie, earning herself a soft moan.

Okay. That was uncalled for. Cammie looked at her with wide eyes and instantly could tell how much Lauryn was enjoying all of this. But she was enjoying it too. She felt like if Lauryn's little game continued, they'd have a repeat of last night. Cammie was just staring up at Lauryn in awe. She'd seen her do that move a few times before while she was goofing around with Diana. But nothing could've prepared her for Lauryn demonstrating that same move *on top* of her. She hadn't responded yet. Lauryn took her silence as an opportunity to do it again.

"*Okay*," Cammie nearly moaned again. "Okay. You should stop."

"Why?" Lauryn tilted her head.

"Because..." Cammie trailed, too embarrassed to disclose the real reason. She wasn't comfortable with the vulgarity that would come with telling her. She was a bit embarrassed to keep having these reactions within herself, but Lauryn elicited them quite often.

"Oh, right," Lauryn laughed. "You're so cute, Camz."

Cute wasn't necessarily the word Cammie would've used to describe herself right then. There was nothing cute about the state she was in in that moment. And Lauryn just fed into it. She leaned down to kiss her lips softly, still sensually grinding into her. Cammie's hands found the curves below her waist and she grabbed it as Lauryn moved against her. Her eyes closed and she tuned everything out in the moment, like the droning of the TV. Or like the quiet creaking of the bed while Lauryn continued to drive her slowly insane. And like the faint sound of the approaching footsteps in the hallway.

Lauryn's bedroom door had been opened. By the time both girls registered the intrusion, Cara was already standing in the doorway with her mouth agape. Her brow furrowed, along with an unwarranted flash of anger in her eyes. She looked on as her daughter scrambled off of Cammie. She couldn't seem to piece together the situation. The only explanation she came up with couldn't possibly have been the actual case. But as she looked between the two of them, she realized that it was.

The silence stretched out in the room. The atmosphere only grew more uncomfortable as the seconds ticked on. Were they really...? No. Cara must have been seeing things. But their disheveled clothes were a testament to her assumption.

And both girls had guilt written all over their faces. If she needed further confirmation, she looked to the blatant mark on Cammie's neck. How else would that have gotten there, when she'd walked in on them on top of each other? For the second time today, might she add. Only now, she'd caught them in the act. She crossed the room to stand in front of both of them, still unable to process what she'd just witnessed.

"Get out," Cara ordered Cammie, who looked terrified.

"Mom, it's okay..." Lauryn responded tentatively.

"No. Get out," Cara repeated herself. Her chilling tone let both girls know that it was better not to argue.

Cammie immediately followed her instructions. She hurriedly clambered out of Lauryn's bed and rushed over to the door. She stood in the doorway tentatively. Did Cara really want her to leave? If so, leave the house or leave the room? Her heart was hammering as she waited for the answer to her silent question.

"Cammie," Cara addressed her one last time. She was trying her best to keep her cool. Her indication was clear. Cammie backed out of Lauryn's room and headed down the stairs timidly.

"What the fuck?" Lauryn scowled at her mother, who was regarding her with a cold, distant expression.

"I could ask you the same question," Cara quipped. She knew she was right. And that information made her feel sick to her stomach. Her daughter wasn't a lesbian. She couldn't have been. She prayed that what she'd witnessed was the result of a little experimenting.

"You can't just kick her out..." Lauryn grimaced as she eyed her mother harshly. "Camz!" she called out to her girlfriend, but she was gone.

"Don't you bring that lesbian girl back in here," Cara admonished in a voice that made Lauryn glare at her.

Under most circumstances, she wouldn't have tested her mother. But Lauryn was outraged. Any fear or apprehension she had instantly vanished. Her anger towards her mother outweighed all of those types of emotions, but Cammie's wellbeing trumped all of those factors. She needed to be with her. She had no idea how Cammie would deal with this. Cammie needed Lauryn's reassurance. And she was more than willing to give it to her.

"I won't," Lauryn glared at her mother. They'd fought before, but Lauryn had never felt so distant from her mother in her entire life. Who was this woman? She wasn't so sure. And she wasn't about to stay here to talk with her. "Excuse me," she said on her way past Cara.

"You're not going anywhere. What the hell was that, mija?" Cara asked incredulously. She was trying her best to be sensitive to the situation, but she felt so disturbed. She just wanted to understand. She wanted Lauryn to talk with her, openly.

"Nothing," Lauryn brushed past her. Angry tears formed in her eyes. All she wanted to do was be with Cammie. But the likelihood of that was diminishing as well.

"Lauryn," Cara called out to the girl that was halfway down the hall.

"What?" Lauryn muttered as she clutched the stair railing. Her grip on it was so tight, her knuckles turned white.

"*What*?" Cara repeated. "I walk in on you kissing that girl, and you have the nerve to ask me what?" she asked sarcastically.

She knew Cammie's name. She knew it well. The fact that she'd been demoted to "that girl" pissed Lauryn off more than anything. With half a mind to ignore her altogether, she turned abruptly to leave. She nearly ran down the stairs. Cammie was the only important thing to her right now. Her mother's opinions could wait. This conversation could wait. Where was Cammie?

"If you go out of that door, don't bother coming back," Cara proposed halfheartedly as Lauryn grasped the doorknob. That wasn't a serious threat. But she wanted it to come across as though it was, and it did. That was enough to make Lauryn pause.

"What, or you'll kick me out too?" Lauryn rolled her eyes as she faced her mother again.

"Watch your mouth," Cara warned. Perhaps too shocked by the situation to react as she usually would, Cara faltered in her discipline. She saw then that now was not the time to have a heart to heart. So she wanted to keep the confrontation short and sweet. She drew in a deep breath and exhaled with her eyes closed. Keep it simple. "I don't want you seeing that girl anymore."

"*Her name is Cammie,*" Lauryn emphasized. The fact that she refused to even say her name was making her livid. "And why not?" she challenged.

"You just don't need to be around her anymore," Cara said calmly as she walked away, on her way to her own room.

"Okay, I didn't know I was living in a fucking homophobic household," Lauryn called up the stairs bitterly.

Cara planned on ending the conversation there. But she'd just been called homophobic. She couldn't leave with Lauryn thinking that. Part of her was wondering where Lauryn had gotten the nerve to speak to her that way, but she wasn't too surprised by her foul mouth. She'd heard it in passing countless times before.

"You don't. And I'm not, but that..." Cara trailed, trying to come up with an argument valid enough to fend off that accusation. "*That's* just not okay. That doesn't fly here. Now fix your shirt and go and set the table. That's what I came in there to tell you..." Cara informed her as she began walking away, letting Lauryn get away with her vulgarity for once.

Lauryn didn't respond, she just watched her mom descend down the hallway. A wave of resentment washed over her as Cara disappeared around the corner. There was a reason Lauryn had been so secretive in the first few weeks she and Cammie had been a thing. That was every reason why. She knew it would happen this way. Her entire body felt hot as she stood there. She was so angry. Tears were streaming down her face, but she couldn't find the will to move. She steeled herself against the door and turned around to retire back to her room. Fuck setting the table. She had bigger problems.

She landed face-down on her bed, burying her face in her arms. A sob finally left her lips, and she swore under her breath. She'd been controlling that. She hadn't cried on a sad occasion in a long time, but this warranted her tears. She wasn't even sad, she was resentful, humiliated, and she was worried. In that moment, she seized her phone and shakily sent out a text to Cammie. Within seconds of sending it, she just pressed the call button. She needed to hear her voice.

Cammie was almost at her own house by the time the text came in. She ran. She didn't feel the strain of her heart in her chest or the aching of her muscles. She felt adrenaline. Tears blurred her vision and she bent over to catch her breath. She felt sick to her stomach at the thought of what would come of them. The dread she felt when that door opened had yet to subside. Her stomach lurched uncomfortably every few moments as she kept replaying it in her mind. She feared that Lauryn would be taken away from her. When she felt her phone vibrating in her pocket, she ignored it. She couldn't talk to anyone right now.

When Cammie's phone went to voicemail, Lauryn looked at her phone sadly. Cammie didn't answer. She called again, but got the same result. She threw her phone to the end of the bed and resumed her previous position. A muffled scream filled the room as she tried to express her frustration. Cara fucking made her leave, and now she wasn't answering the phone.

Cammie felt bad for not answering the call. When she retrieved it from her pocket, she could make out that she had two missed calls. She wiped her eyes to clear her vision and checked who the caller was. Her heart leaped at the name on the screen. Lauryn had called. Twice. She scrambled to call her back.

"Hello?" Cammie answered hoarsely. Her voice wasn't doing so well. She was still out of breath and trying to recuperate.

"Cammie," Lauryn said shakily. She instantly felt relaxed. Her voice was a solace as long as she wasn't with her. All of this felt so dramatic, but it was the realest thing she'd had to deal with in a while.

"Are you okay?" Cammie questioned.

"Are you?" Lauryn countered, instantly noticing the wavering of her voice.

"I'm okay... Just, scared..." Cammie admitted. "What happened?"

"I don't even know. I don't know what that was. After she made you leave, I was so fucking mad. She was too, I guess, and she didn't say much. She just looked at me and said I couldn't see you anymore," Lauryn recapped.

Cammie's heart dropped. Those were the words she dreaded hearing. Just when she'd composed herself and gotten the tears to stop, they started up again. If she couldn't see Lauryn anymore, what was she here for? It was an exaggerated thought, but her logic was hazy at the moment. "Oh," she managed to choke out. Her responses were monosyllabic, because that was all she could get out.

"No, don't cry... I'm still gonna see you, I don't give a fuck what she said," Lauryn assured her, and she meant it. She wasn't about to let her mother come between the two of them, not when things were going so smoothly. "I'll still spend every moment I have with you. Just like I always do, Camz."

Her claims were kind of just going in one ear and out of the other to Cammie. She wanted to believe her, but something was preventing her from putting all of her faith in her. Her tears were falling more quickly now, but she tried to muster up a response. "Okay," Cammie mumbled.

"Camz..." Lauryn trailed sadly. She could hear Cammie's deep breaths coming through the other line. She could only imagine the state she was in now. It made her feel lower than she already felt.

"I have to go, Lauryn," Cammie said quietly. She felt herself about to break. She didn't want Lauryn to stick around for that. Her emotions were starting to get the best of her.

"Babe," Lauryn objected weakly. It pained her to hear that desolate tone in her girlfriend's voice.

"I'll talk to you later," Cammie insisted. A lump formed in her throat. Cara told Lauryn she couldn't see her anymore. She was taking her away from her. She grimaced as the pit grew in her stomach. Shakespeare was dumb. There was nothing beautiful or romantic about forbidden love. It just hurt. Especially when someone was told to their face that they couldn't see the person they fell in love with anymore. It hurt like hell.

"Okay," Lauryn accepted her claim dejectedly. "I love you?" she reminded her.

"I love you, too," Cammie sniffled and wiped her nose with her shirt. She waited for Lauryn to say something else. When she didn't, Cammie simply ended the call.

Chapter 20

Cammie took Cara's words very seriously. For the rest of that Saturday, she didn't bother texting or calling Lauryn. It wasn't like Lauryn hadn't made an effort, though. She'd texted her a few times just to make sure she was alright, but after several failed endeavors with no responses whatsoever, she gave up. Sunday, no interactions between them occurred at all. Cammie received no texts, calls, or visits from Lauryn - which was rare. Lauryn was always with her in some way, whether she was right beside her or through a phone screen. She was always there, but she wasn't.

It was mostly Cammie's fault. She took Cara too literally. She interpreted it to mean don't talk to Lauryn *at all*, so she didn't. And she couldn't bring herself to respond to anything. Each time she was about to, she was reminded that she wasn't supposed to. Because her mom didn't want her seeing her anymore.

For the most part, the rest of her weekend was spent in her room. She spent hours upon hours just lying there, solemnly reflecting on how they ended up. She found it kind of funny how vastly things had changed. They'd gone from ultimate secrecy to complete recklessness. This weekend had been a whirlwind. Friday night was amazing, followed by a great Saturday morning. Saturday evening was when everything crashed. Right when things were finally starting to go in the preferred direction. And here she was on Sunday, looking back on all of it.

Cammie felt like she'd shed enough tears about the situation. Instead, she figured she'd try her take on being optimistic. If this was the end, then she was grateful that it lasted that long. There were still times she had trouble picturing herself with Lauryn the way she actually was. They were still dating, she assumed. They just weren't exactly on speaking terms right now.

Her parents caught onto the shift. They'd been observing Cammie's recent social behavior. There was once a time she barely left her room, but now she was

166

rarely in the house. Sonya and Alexander weren't exactly informed on what caused the change, but they were grateful that Cammie was finally branching out. Unfortunately now, she'd reverted to her old ways. They were kind of concerned.

"Mija?" Sonya prompted quietly. She knocked on the door softly and peeped her head inside.

Cammie turned at the sound of her voice, but didn't have the energy to speak. She just looked at her mother expectantly, waiting to see what she wanted.

"Are you alright?" Sonya asked as she leaned against the door frame. Cammie shrugged and laid her head back down on the pillow. Sonya sighed and crossed the room, sitting on the edge of Cammie's bed. She soothingly trailed her finger along Cammie's back. She was sensitive to her situation, although she was clueless as to what it was.

Cammie debated on telling her. Not that it would matter anyway. It probably wouldn't change anything. They'd probably have to break up soon. You couldn't exactly date someone you weren't supposed to be seeing. And Sonya's gesture was comforting, but it saddened her at the same time. Lauryn did that same exact thing whenever she was feeling down.

"Lauryn's mom said I couldn't see her anymore," Cammie admitted after a few more seconds.

"Why would she say that?" Sonya asked with a frown.

"Because..." Cammie trailed with little intentions of finishing the sentence.

Sonya wondered if Cammie would admit to dating Lauryn. She'd known all along, and so did Alexander. It wasn't exactly rocket science. Anyone could catch on to the never-ending smiles and clear joy Lauryn elicited. The hand holding and cuddling would've been indication enough, if the few times they'd caught them kissing didn't spell it out for them. And they were fine with it. As long as Cammie was happy, it was fine. Perhaps Cara could learn a few things from those two.

"We um..." Cammie searched for the words, but she couldn't bring herself to do it. "She just said I couldn't see her anymore," she settled on saying. She didn't want to lie, but she really couldn't share that with her. Not right now.

"Things will work themselves out," Sonya said encouragingly. She wasn't going to press Cammie for information, so she just continued to stroke her back. No more words were exchanged. The gesture soothed her in a way that almost made her want to fall asleep. Soon enough, she did. The last thing on her mind was Sonya's words, echoing in the back of her head. She chose to dwell on that statement rather than Cara's.

》》》》》

By Monday morning, Lauryn was done with trying to check on Cammie. She assumed that she was alright. She eagerly waited for her to get on the bus with hopes of mending things. But when Cammie got on, she didn't even look in Lauryn's direction. She just shuffled into the seat and curled up.

Naomi was grounded, and her keys had been taken as punishment. While she couldn't drive to school anymore, she had to resort to riding the bus. She'd only been riding for about a week now, but she'd caught on to Lauryn and Cammie's morning habits. It was almost a ritual. She assumed that that Cammie would clamber into Lauryn's seat, like she always did. She'd grown so accustomed to seeing their figures become one and overhearing all of the sweet nothings they whispered. Whenever Cammie boarded the bus, she immediately went to Lauryn's

167

seat. Naomi didn't even get a hello most of the time. And she didn't today either, but obviously it was different.

"Is everything okay with you guys...?" Naomi asked Lauryn intuitively.

"We're going through something," Lauryn answered as she leaned over to ensure privacy. "She won't talk to me..." she sighed as she peered over in Cammie's direction.

"Why? What did you do?" Naomi frowned. She didn't like the idea of something tearing them apart. Especially when things seemed to be going so well.

"*I* didn't do anything," Lauryn rolled her eyes.

"Then why won't she talk to you?" Naomi wondered.

"I think *she* thinks she can't," Lauryn realized.

"*Why?*" Naomi emphasized. Lauryn was drip-feeding her information. All she wanted to know was what caused the problem, but Lauryn was beating around the bush.

"It's stupid," Lauryn dismissed her, ending the conversation there. She shook her head and retreated back into the corner, pulling out her headphones and tuning out everything else.

Naomi scoffed and sat back in her seat. She was going to find out. She wanted them to be together more than she wanted her own relationship to work out. Unlike most times, she wasn't being nosy. She just wanted to help. She considered going to Cammie about it, but Cammie was isolating herself. The bus ride dragged on in silence, but as soon as they got to school, Naomi tugged on Cammie's arm.

The sun was coming up, and it wasn't so dark anymore. Naomi could just barely make out the mark on her neck that had yet to disappear. It was faint, but Naomi immediately noticed the discoloration. A smirk took over her features, but she saved her snide remarks for later. Cammie was upset. "Cam..." she trailed sympathetically.

"What?" Cammie mumbled. Her eyes were trained on the ground as they entered the school. She wasn't up for conversation, but she couldn't ignore her. Naomi hadn't done anything wrong.

"Are you okay?" she asked.

"Yeah," Cammie gave a rather unconvincing answer. While she was usually lively or wrapped up in Lauryn in the mornings, she was back to her quiet, subtle ways.

"Then why aren't you talking to me?" Naomi nudged her softly. Cammie shrugged her shoulders and hummed in response. "You weren't sitting with Lauryn on the bus..." Naomi hinted, trying to persuade her to vent a little bit. She could tell there was a storm in her mind. An outlet would've been just what she needed. And Naomi wanted to be that for her.

"Because I can't," Cammie sighed, which gave Naomi zero to work with.

"What happened?" she probed.

"We got caught," Cammie admitted vaguely.

Naomi's eyes widened. She pieced together what little details she knew and her jaw dropped in surprise. They'd gotten caught having sex. Obviously. She could barely hide her shock. That was the furthest from what she was expecting. Oh God. If that was her, she'd never be able to look her parents in the eye ever again.

"Oh..." Naomi mumbled. She was almost rendered speechless by her assumption. And she doubted that Cammie would admit to it openly.

"Yeah," Cammie nodded. She approached her locker, forcing them to go their separate ways. "I'll see you later, Naomi."

Holy shit. Naomi just watched her walk away, unable to process that bit of information. That must've been traumatic. She was pretty sure she'd die right there on the spot if she'd been caught like that. Damn. She shook her head and wandered over to her own locker, wondering just what had happened between her favorite couple.

Lauryn was wondering the same thing. She'd told Cammie not to worry about anything, and that she would see her regardless of what Cara said, but it was *Cammie* who was recoiling. She wouldn't approach her at all. She hadn't so much as seen those beautiful brown eyes that'd inadvertently captured her heart about a month ago. And she hadn't heard her voice in three days. Three whole days. That was equivalent to a month in Lauryn's eyes. Since they'd been officially dating, she hadn't had to be without her for long. They spent all of their free time together, and three days felt like a lifetime without her.

It was ludicrous to miss her this much. She didn't want to corner her, but she desperately wanted to see her. When she hung up the phone that Saturday night, she figured she'd have the night to give her some space. But when she didn't return her missed calls or answer her texts, Lauryn sensed a bigger problem. She was forced to give her the weekend, because she was on something like house arrest. Cara wouldn't let her go anywhere, regardless of the reason. She made her go to church, though. She made sure of that. And Lauryn loathed it all. By the time Monday rolled around, Lauryn was sure that Cammie would be running into her arms. But she didn't even look at her.

Cammie and Lauryn only had one class together. Lauryn was banking on that time to hopefully tell Cammie everything she needed to say. She waited impatiently all day. Tapping pencils, doodling on the paper, and sleeping helped to pass the time. A little bit. When she finally got to approach their literature class, she didn't really get her hopes up.

Lauryn was amongst the first in the class. She knew where Cammie sat and occupied the seat next to her. Their seats weren't next to each other, but they were going to be today. She hated alphabetical order for that specific reason. Cammie walked in the class quietly, not even bothering to look in Lauryn's direction. To say she was startled when she saw the green-eyed girl beside her would've been an understatement.

"Lauryn, why are you sitting there?" Cammie mumbled uncomfortably.

"Because I need to talk to you, and this was the only way I could think of before lunch," Lauryn said quickly. She hoped Bri wouldn't be coming in any time soon. All she needed was a few minutes.

"Well... What do you need to talk to me about?" Cammie asked without making eye contact. She was rather embarrassed by now. She'd had more than enough time to think about the situation. And she realized how dumb she was being. Through careful analyzations, she'd come to realize that Cara wouldn't know if Lauryn was seeing her or not. She didn't even have to avoid her the way she had been. Her logic and impulse was dumb. She was avoiding her for a much different reason now.

"Are you kidding?" Lauryn asked incredulously. "Why are you acting like that?"

"I don't know," Cammie admitted. Her gaze was trained on the desk. She really didn't want to look at her. She didn't know what she would see. And she wasn't prepared for any negative reactions.

169

"I know it's about what my mom said, but didn't you hear what *I* said?" Lauryn placed a hand on Cammie's arm tentatively, and she flinched.

"Kind of. I just didn't want you to get in trouble... So I avoided you. I thought that's what both of you would want. But then I realized I was being stupid. And I avoided you again," Cammie said carefully. If Lauryn thought she was mad at her, she was wrong. Way off. Cammie was just an idiot.

"Oh," Lauryn exhaled in relief. "Camz..." she rolled her eyes. She should've known.

"Sorry," Cammie mumbled. Her cheeks were probably red. Maybe her whole face. She wanted to leave again. This was the reason she'd been avoiding her. Letting her reasoning surface was always risky business. And now she sounded even dumber than usual.

"Don't apologize. Just come here," Lauryn prompted softly. She held out her arms expectantly, and Cammie slid out of her seat to hug Lauryn graciously. They both sighed in relief when they were in each other's arms. "I missed you," Lauryn said against Cammie's hair.

"I did too," Cammie agreed, which was stating the obvious.

"And I missed this," Lauryn continued. She cast a quick glance around the classroom and saw that they hadn't really drawn anyone's attention. In the spur of the moment, she placed a quick kiss upon Cammie's lips. Her lips didn't linger for as long as she would've liked, but she'd kissed her nonetheless.

"Me too," Cammie grinned goofily, then felt herself being guided into Lauryn's lap. She looked around at everyone, but they were still ignoring their display. Lauryn finally got to admire that smile up close, instead of merely thinking about it. "Laur..." she trailed, not wanting to be obnoxious.

"What?" Lauryn smiled, placing her arms firmly around her girlfriend. She could bear Cammie's weight. And it wasn't like anyone was watching them. Because they weren't, Lauryn took the liberty of brushing Cammie's cheek with her lips. She kissed her sweetly, then grazed her lips over her skin. Beneath her playful teasing, she felt Cammie's features take on a smile. Her heart surged at the feeling, but it dropped at the next words she heard.

"Can you guys go have your lesbian reunion somewhere else..." Bri scoffed. She stood in front of them with her face wrinkled in disgust. Clearly, she wasn't one of their admirers. Her books rested on her hips impatiently and her stance put them on edge.

"We're not lesbians," Lauryn rolled her eyes as she loosened her hold on her girlfriend.

"Whatever. Just move," Bri instructed them rather rudely, gesturing to her desk with her free hand. "You're in my seat."

"Yeah, sorry..." Cammie mumbled as she pried Lauryn's hands from around her. Choosing to ignore the remark, she sighed. It didn't bother her one way or another, but she awkwardly slid back into her own desk to avoid a problem, leaving Lauryn still sitting in Bri's seat.

"Are you going to get up?" Bri asked incredulously, louder than before.

"Can't you fucking say excuse me?" Lauryn huffed. Out of spite, she took her time in moving to get up.

"You're right," Bri feigned remorse. "Excuse me," she said in a tone that was laced with sarcasm. The way she said it annoyed Lauryn, but she got up anyway.

"Thank you," Lauryn rolled her eyes and got up. She stood in front of Cammie's desk and leaned against it. Cammie had been nervously watching the encounter. She looked up at Lauryn, who was now in front of her. Lauryn offered a small smile, which made Cammie smile in response.

"Dyke," Bri said under her breath as she dropped into her seat.

The smile she was wearing dropped immediately. Her comment pissed Lauryn off. The lesbian thing could be dismissed, but *that* was just derogatory. She didn't like being called a lesbian. Not that she had anything against them, it was just the *way* she'd been called one. Bri hashed out those words like they were insults. And Lauryn didn't like being labeled by someone that knew nothing about her. She wasn't necessarily a fan of assumptions. Everything negative regarding her relationship with Cammie seemed to be surfacing all at once. Her mom was the one that showed obvious disapproval, and now Bri was coming with her fucking comments. Although it bothered her, she didn't want to make it obvious. So she plastered the best smile she could muster across her face. When she was sure she'd caught Bri's eye, she leaned down to be eye-level with Cammie.

"I'll see you after class, baby," Lauryn said to Cammie, loud enough for Bri to hear. She looked over her shoulder and saw Bri's judgmental stare, which only fueled the desire for her next move. She cupped Cammie's face gently and pulled her into a kiss. When they parted, she gave Bri a condescending smile before crossing the room and going over to her own seat. If she was going to be called a lesbian, so be it. She figured she might as well have acted the part, too.

Cammie felt indignant. She instantly caught on to Lauryn's motive. It was almost like she was making a show out of it. She could count on her fingers how many times Lauryn had called her baby before. It felt a little weird to have Lauryn doing that, but she wasn't complaining.

Lauryn sauntered back over to her seat and flashed a smile at Cammie. Despite the odd feeling, she got butterflies at the action. She assumed that with time, she'd get used to seeing it, but clearly that wasn't the case. Cammie earned herself another smile by looking at her goofily. But she saw Bri side-eyeing her from her peripheral vision and shifted her gaze to the desk.

The look itself dampened her mood. She'd never really encountered homophobic people before, and she didn't exactly know what to do. It upset her that people couldn't get over simple prejudices. It wasn't even like they were bothering anyone. She could recall several times where Bri and one of her thousands of boyfriends were making out in inappropriate places and causing people to be uncomfortable. But Cammie and Lauryn weren't doing anything wrong. Her comment plagued her thoughts for the rest of the period and it extended into lunch.

Her mood increased exponentially when she entered the cafeteria. Lauryn spotted her and strode over right as Cammie was entering the line. The line wasn't moving at all, and Lauryn came up behind Cammie, the way she always did. Cammie melted into her and smiled appreciatively. She needed a hug. Today had been a weird day, and Cammie was in a weird mood. But like always, Lauryn made everything better.

"How are you? Are you okay today?" Lauryn questioned. Her face was right beside Cammie's ear, and she could feel her warm breath behind her.

"I'm okay," Cammie answered, which was an honest answer. She was far from good, but she wasn't necessarily bad. Okay was an accurate representation of how she felt.

"Why just okay?" Lauryn probed as the line inched forward.

"I don't know. I think it's because of the weekend. And what Bri said," Cammie shrugged.

"Fuck her," Lauryn scoffed. She'd dismissed Bri's comment as soon as she'd heard it. She didn't care much. Bri wasn't important.

"It's just bothering me a little. And your mom... I don't think I can go to your house anymore," Cammie frowned.

"Well, try to forget what she said, babe. And that's okay. I can just go to yours," Lauryn reasoned. She was determined to fend off any negative thoughts Cammie was having. This version of her girlfriend was much like around the time Lauryn was testing out her lists. Cammie was visibly upset, and Lauryn wondered how the hell she wasn't able to register that before.

"I guess," Cammie sighed. The line seemed to go forward all at once, and she had to scramble to keep her spot in line. Lauryn released her hold on her long enough to get herself a tray. They approached their table side by side.

"Hey guys," Diana greeted the two girls. Cammie waved subtly and took her seat.

"Hey," Lauryn returned.

"How are you?" Naomi questioned with a smile.

"I'm good," Lauryn answered cheerfully while Cammie simply shrugged.

"You okay, Cam?" Allie frowned.

"Yeah," Cammie nodded unenthusiastically.

"Naomi said you were out of it this morning," Allie shrugged. "You still seem a little sad."

"It's just a crappy day. Nothing serious," Cammie dismissed her claim and picked up her fork. She wasn't even hungry.

"Stupid things were bothering her. But I think she's okay," Lauryn added. "Right, Camz?" she asked for clarification.

"Yeah," Cammie offered a small smile.

"Of course Lo would know," Diana teased as she watched the two interact.

"I'm pretty sure she knows everything about her little *Camz*," Allie jested, trying her best to mock Lauryn's voice.

"If you're going to mock me, at least do it right," Lauryn laughed.

"I bet I'd do a good Lauryn impression," Diana proclaimed proudly to the table. By her look, everyone could tell she wanted someone to challenge her to do so.

"I bet you can't," Cammie quipped.

"Can too," Diana countered. "See, watch," she smirked. Then she made direct eye contact with Cammie. The rest of the girls were waiting for her to speak, but she didn't seem like she'd be speaking any time soon. She was just staring at Cammie, then she closed her eyes dramatically. "Done."

"Diana, what the hell," Cammie laughed. That wasn't an impression at all. She hadn't said a word.

"Oh, no. I get it," Naomi laughed. "She's talking about her eyes."

"Oh," Cammie laughed, and Allie joined in, followed by Lauryn. Diana sat there looking pleased with herself for eliciting laughter within the group.

"I can be Cam," Naomi claimed, then she just stared blankly ahead at Lauryn. Her mouth dropped open, and she could've been the perfect depiction of heart eyes.

"That's great," Lauryn laughed, giving Cammie a joking eyebrow raise.

"Nah, girl. You forgot the drool," Diana smirked.

"I don't drool!" Cammie giggled.

"You totally do. But it's okay," Allie pitched in.

"This is Cam, part two," Diana took over as she eyed Lauryn from across the table. Her look changed from a goofy expression to an obvious flustered state. She bit her lip as her eyes focused on Lauryn. Suggestively, her eyes scanned up and down her body. She gave her the once-over and her breathing deepened exaggeratedly.

"Shut up," Cammie objected halfheartedly, but she knew that was an accurate mockery. Both of them were. She had a staring problem.

"You know that one was dead on," Naomi laughed.

"It *so* was," Lauryn nodded, finally able to catch her breath.

"You shut up, too," Cammie huffed at Lauryn. Sometimes, she really couldn't help her staring. It was hard to refrain when Lauryn walked around looking like that. And she still caught herself doing it sometimes, but the best part about her current situation was that she could act on it.

"Okay, I'm done," Lauryn giggled, raising her hands in defense.

"Diana was right, though. Y'all have some major sexual tension going on," Allie agreed. "Like, all the time."

"Looks like they don't have that problem anymore," Diana smirked as she took a sip of her drink. Her gaze landed on the hickey Cammie was still sporting and she raised her eyebrow knowingly.

"Dang," Allie murmured as she caught sight of it as well.

Cammie's hand immediately flew to her neck to cover it. Admittedly, with everything that happened after getting it, she'd forgotten about its presence. Immediately, she felt herself turning several shades darker. Oh God. How could she forget? She hoped her hair had been obscuring it from view for the most part.

"Damn, I must've done a good job then," Lauryn quipped.

"Gross," Diana said immediately, hoping they'd spare her the details.

Naomi was the only one that wasn't surprised by it. She'd seen it earlier. She wondered if it would be appropriate to broach the subject in front of everyone else. Her forehead creased in pensive thought, but the bell decided on her answer for her. While all of the girls moved to get up, she pulled Cammie back and let everyone else go ahead to the trash cans.

"So what did your mom say?" Naomi questioned casually, now that they didn't have an audience anymore.

"About what?" Cammie looked at her quizzically.

"You said you got caught... Didn't you?" Naomi recalled, suddenly fearing that she'd misinterpreted something.

"Yeah..." Cammie nodded, unable to grasp what Naomi truly meant.

"So... Then what happened?"

"Her mom just walked in on us. And I was upset this morning because she said we couldn't see each other anymore," Cammie explained quietly, the mention of it killed her vibe a little bit.

"That's all you got off with?" Naomi asked incredulously.

"Yeah, but it's still pretty bad. Lauryn said she wasn't talking to her mom," Cammie frowned.

"If I got caught having sex, I'd probably get kicked out. And my dad would probably kill him," Naomi giggled at the thought, but nearly bumped into Cammie when she stopped in front of her.

"*What*?" Cammie faced her quickly. "That's not what - We didn't... Where'd you get that from?"

"I thought you meant..." Naomi trailed, but her sentence tapered off.

"No... Not *that*, Naomi. Lauryn's mom walked in on us *kissing*..." Cammie clarified with flushed cheeks. The image of Cara walking in on them doing *that* was just... She couldn't even think of it.

"Oh," Naomi mumbled, suddenly embarrassed that she'd inferred that at all. "Well, that's awkward....." she laughed.

"Just a little..." Cammie agreed with a nervous laugh. "But I have to go," she shook her head. The two of them fell into step as they made their way back to class. She parted ways with Naomi when they reached the intersection, and she bid her goodbye with a hug.

When she reached her classroom, she sat down with a sigh. As she squinted to see the board up front, she opened her binder. After writing down her heading and the prompt, she realized she'd taken the wrong binder. She groaned and closed it, knowing she'd most likely lose it and get a zero if she didn't go switch out her binders now. Leaning over to check the time, she assumed she had enough time to go exchange them. Her locker wasn't too far away, and if she power walked, she could get there and back in time.

She quickly got out of her seat and slipped out of the classroom. When the clock changed, she sped up to a jog. As her locker came into view, a victory smile creeped onto her lips. Perhaps she'd actually pull off this stunt. She hurried to open her locker and switch binders, and right when she was turning around to head back to class, someone called her name. Or at least, the variation she'd learned to answer to over time.

"Cammie," a familiar voice called from down the hallway.

"Hi," she offered her ex-boyfriend a smile when he came to a stop in front of her.

"Hey. How are you?" Aiden grinned back and went in for a hug, but Cammie politely gave him a high five instead. He frowned. "What was that about?"

"Nothing," Cammie shrugged as she glanced up at the clock. Nothing, except Lauryn probably wouldn't like that. She'd expressed her dislike for the boy multiple times in the past, so Cammie kept her distance.

"Okay..." Aiden cleared his throat. "I actually wanted to talk to you about something..."

"What's up?" Cammie played into the conversation as she looked up at the clock once more. She really should be going.

"Brandon said something weird about you..." Aiden trailed.

Cammie leaned against the locker, suddenly interested in the conversation. She clutched her binder to her chest and looked at him. "What did he say?"

"He said you were dating Lauryn..." Aiden laughed, resting his hand on Cammie's shoulder. "Isn't that insane?"

"Well, actually-" Cammie started, but she stopped herself. She was about to confirm his statement, but thought of a better idea. "Actually, what did you say when he said that?"

"I said that you weren't, because that's weird..." Aiden answered.

"I am, though," Cammie smiled proudly.

"Good one," Aiden chuckled. "Anyway, when he said that... It kind of made me think of you. And I think I miss you," he said as his fingers started stroking down her arm softly.

"Didn't you hear what I said?" Cammie reiterated as she shrugged away from his hand.

"Yeah," he laughed it off smugly. "But don't you miss me, too?" Aiden redirected the conversation again. He slowly started closing the distance between them, cornering Cammie against the locker. He wore his signature player smile and settled his hand on her waist.

"Stop it. I wasn't kidding. I'm dating Lauryn," Cammie said more confidently. She pushed against his chest and his ego took a significant knock.

"What do you mean you're dating her?" Aiden asked as he stepped back, furrowing his eyebrows in anger.

"I mean she's my girlfriend, Aiden..." Cammie said again, losing her nerve by the second.

"Since when were you gay..." Aiden scowled. He seemed angry. Maybe even a little bit offended.

Cammie didn't know. This was the second time today that she'd been called a variation of the word. Maybe she was, if that's what dating Lauryn had to mean. She'd never really given it any thought, other than the time Lauryn had asked her if she was. Since then, it hadn't crossed her mind. Those trivial technicalities didn't matter to her much, she just wanted to be with her. Labels didn't appeal to her. It made her feel like she was in a box, when she was almost certain her sexuality would fluctuate from time to time. And she didn't feel like Aiden deserved an answer, so she turned away from him and hurried to class, with only a second or two to get there.

Chapter 21

Gay.

When did that word become an insult? Why was it said so venomously by those that claimed they weren't? Why did there even have to be a claim at all? Why couldn't people just love who they love without all of the labels and slander?

Cammie frowned as she finished jotting down those thoughts in her journal. She closed it and begrudgingly completed her assignment. The things on her mind were making it hard to focus on just her classwork. She finished soon enough, then her mind drifted back to Aiden's expression when he questioned her sexuality. He seemed so disgusted at the fact that it could've been a possibility. What did it matter to him at all? It wasn't any of his business. It wasn't any of anyone's business. It was her business. And it was Lauryn's business. That was it.

Despite her friends' endeavors to boost her mood during lunch, it all diminished as she continued thinking about everything. It just wasn't a good day. Her mood was even sourer than before. She just wanted to go home. Mondays fucking sucked. She only had one more class before then. Once the bell rung and class dismissed, she filed into the hallway immediately.

While she was usually invisible on her journey to class, she felt like everyone was staring at her this time around. An unfamiliar wave of insecurity washed over her. Why was everyone staring? And were they really focused on her? Or was she just being paranoid? Cammie wasn't so sure, but she kept her head down anyway. Her hair fell around her face and partially hid her from public speculation. She kind of felt like it helped make her as invisible as she usually was. But it didn't. Everyone saw her as she headed towards her locker. Everyone was making their new judgements based on what they'd heard.

The mumbling and whispering got louder as she went on her way. It was different than the casual murmuring of the student body. They were whispering. And they hadn't diverted their eyes yet. Cammie was certain she was the center of the hallway's attention now. However, she didn't have the nerve to confront them all. She wished Lauryn was by her side. The looks were starting to get under her skin. But it was nothing compared to the *reason* they were looking at her so harshly.

"There goes that lesbian girl," she heard someone say as she passed them. Were they talking about Cammie? Surely not. Or at least she hoped not. She just kept looking down at her feet and increased her pace. Class seemed like a really good option right about now. It would be her safe haven, for a little while.

When she got into class, she let out a sigh of relief. She placed her things on the desk and laid her head down until class began. The more she began to anticipate going home, the slower the day seemed to go by. Watching the clock didn't do her any justice. It felt like forever. The simple assignment they had to do didn't faze her. She finished it within a few minutes, like she always did. With nothing better to do and no inspiration to write in her journal, she just went to sleep. It was a little nap, and as soon as the final bell sounded, she was out of there.

An overwhelming urge to go home nagged at her. As she weaved through the crowd, she sensed their eyes on her again. Whatever their reasons, she wanted it all to stop. Maybe she could just come back tomorrow and give this whole school thing another shot, because it just wasn't working for today. By the time her last class of the day dismissed, she was more than ready to go. That final bell was long overdue. She reached her locker in record time and hastily exchanged her belongings.

"Hey, these are nice. Don't you think?" a boy asked Cammie as he came up beside her. She didn't know his name, but she recognized him from lunch. She didn't even know what he was talking about, but she was annoyed. What's nice? What the hell? Cammie focused on getting her book bag out of her locker before giving him any attention.

When she turned around, she wished she hadn't. He nearly shoved his phone in her face. The image on the screen was a rather explicit picture of a nude woman clutching at her breasts. The picture caught her off guard. Why was he showing her that? And why did her opinion matter? "Um..." she trailed, not really sure how to respond.

The boy and a group of people behind him burst into laughter. Cammie figured out she was being made fun of when the boy retreated back to his friends. Anger coursed through her system. She wanted to hit him. Or someone. She took her anger out on her locker and slammed it.

It didn't take a genius to figure out what provoked that form of ignorance. Obviously, someone had told everyone she was a lesbian or something. It was then that she realized how ignorant and close-minded her peers were. As she mentally went through the list of people that knew she was dating Lauryn, only a few names came to mind of who would spread a stupid rumor like that – although it wasn't rumor-worthy at all. It had to have been someone that wanted revenge for something. A spiteful person. Those factors led her to believe it was one of two people. Aiden or Brandon.

Aiden was pretty popular, if Cammie had to give him a description. Popularity didn't matter at all to her. While she was dating him, her popularity increased quite a bit. But when they broke up, it plummeted. So did the hype. She figured out immediately what everyone was talking about. All of it was based off of Aiden's word. Or maybe it was Brandon. Perhaps Brandon was angry that he'd fucked up his own chances and wanted to ruin things for Lauryn. But mostly for Cammie. She didn't know if Lauryn was receiving this type of treatment from their class. She didn't even know where she was. Where was she?

She found her answer when she felt familiar arms wrapping around her waist. Lauryn's habit of hugging her from behind never failed. Lauryn nuzzled her face into Cammie's neck before kissing her on the cheek. Cammie tensed up at the act. Strangely enough, she didn't want Lauryn's affection right now. She shrugged out of her hold and kept her gaze trained on her locker. Maybe if she kept her distance, the ridicule would stop.

"What's wrong?" Lauryn asked softly. Although she shouldn't have been, she was kind of offended by what her girlfriend had just done.

"Nothing. My stomach hurts," Cammie excused herself quietly. Lauryn stepped back and gave her an odd look, waiting for her to admit to the real reason.

"Cammie, what's wrong?" Lauryn frowned.

"Nothing. I just said my-" Cammie began to repeat herself, but Lauryn cut her off.

"You're shit at lying, Camz. What's wrong with you?" Lauryn tried again.

"Nothing..." Cammie insisted. Her frustration increased significantly. Why was she so adamant about finding out? And why'd she have to do it here? She could feel her classmates' gazes nearly burning into the back of her head. She wanted to disappear.

"Why are you acting like that?" Lauryn questioned warily.

"I'm not acting like anything," Cammie countered irritably. If she was being honest with herself, she truly didn't know. And Lauryn was the last person that should've been treated that way. Everything from the day was weighing down on her, and she was taking it all out on Lauryn.

"Okay," Lauryn rolled her eyes. "Whatever," she mumbled as she backed up from Cammie. She trudged over to her own locker solemnly. Right as she got there, she looked over her shoulder to see if Cammie would follow, but she was already on her way down the hall.

Lauryn sighed and leaned against her locker. What the hell was her problem? Was it her? Had she done something wrong? She looked back in Cammie's direction one last time and saw her girlfriend pushing through the exit. She went to her locker and walked down the hallway, heading towards the bus.

On her way there, she tried to figure out what made Cammie push her away this time. All she could come up with was what Cara said. Maybe it was still affecting her. Maybe she'd completely disregarded everything Lauryn said to reassure her. It was probably plaguing her thoughts again and now she was acting on it. She was almost certain they'd gotten over that, but apparently not. It would just take some more convincing. And Lauryn was determined to do it.

As soon as she got on the bus, she scanned the seats for her girlfriend. She found her soon enough, curled into a little ball near the middle. Her headphones were in, which probably meant she didn't want any company, but Lauryn didn't care. She got Cammie's attention before gesturing to the seat, signaling for her to scoot over. Cammie looked up at Lauryn hesitantly. God, she was beautiful. Her eyes were a stunning shade of green today, and as Cammie looked her directly in the eye, she knew she couldn't deny her. She slid over quietly and just kind of looked out of the window, hoping she wouldn't say anything. That lasted all of two seconds.

"Cammie..." Lauryn called as she rested her hand on Cammie's thigh.

"Yes?" Cammie answered. She tried her best not to look at Lauryn, because if she did, she'd be induced under her spell. And she'd never be able to avoid her. It would literally be impossible. It kind of already was now, because she was being so persistent.

"When are you going to tell me what's bothering you?" Lauryn asked patiently.

"There's nothing bothering me," Cammie said as she looked out of the window again. There was nothing interesting out there, but it was keeping her from making eye contact.

"Okay," Lauryn relented. There was a certain tension between the two of them, but she had no idea why. Cammie was being so moody. It was hard to keep up. She didn't want to annoy her by being overbearing, so she just sat there in silence.

Maybe she was coming on too strong. Cammie had probably gotten tired of her. She assumed that they were drifting out of the honeymoon phase. Because while she'd usually be all over Lauryn, she was barely even looking at her. Lauryn couldn't help but feel like she'd done something wrong. She looked at Cammie, who was still looking out of the window and frowned. She retracted her hand and placed it back in her lap. Finally beginning to understand Cammie's desires, she got up and moved. She sat across from Naomi and Diana and put her own headphones in, opting to avoid conversation as well.

Naomi and Diana exchanged a look. They were both wondering the same thing. The status of their friends was unknown to the both of them. Things seemed to change in the blink of an eye.

"What the hell is going on with them?" Diana said to Naomi as she turned back around.

"Who knows," Naomi shrugged.

"I don't even think *they* know," Diana laughed. She didn't know how right she actually was.

"Do you know anything about it?" Naomi asked.

"Not really," Diana shook her head. "Cam is so into Lauryn, I only see her at lunch and stuff."

"Lauryn's mom said she couldn't see Cammie anymore or something," Naomi shared, careful to keep her misconception to herself.

"What? For real?" Diana questioned as she faced her.

"Yeah. She walked in on them kissing. I guess it was pretty bad," Naomi nodded. She had so few details, but she was willing to share them with Diana. The only person she would tell would probably be Allie. And Allie wouldn't tell a soul. Mostly because no one outside of their friend circle would care much.

"Dang," Diana said under her breath.

"Yeah. That's why Cam has been so quiet and sad and stuff. It's getting to her," Naomi reasoned.

She only had limited knowledge of their ordeal. The other girls hadn't really talked to Cammie and Lauryn much lately. They never really had time. Cammie and Lauryn were always off in their little world. Naomi, Diana, and Allie had grown closer with their absence.

The two started talking about something different, because their conversations were always ever-changing. Cammie got off of the bus unnoticed by everyone except for Lauryn. She watched her exit sadly. She didn't even say goodbye. Lauryn watched her walk towards her house longingly, hoping for a better tomorrow.

Cammie was completely oblivious to the inner turmoil she was causing Lauryn. In her mind, Lauryn was unbothered by her behavior. She seemed to get over things quickly. But little did she know, Lauryn was just skilled at acting. She'd learned not to wear her heart out on her sleeve. For the most part, Lauryn kept everything inside. Usually, no one ever cared enough to crack her tough exterior. This was true now as well. So although she was upset, she just retreated further into the corner of her seat and used social media to distract her.

»»»

By the time Cammie got home, she was exhausted. Without a word of greeting to her family, she quickly went up to her room. She closed and locked her door just before falling onto her bed. In one swift movement, she was under the covers and clutching her pillow. She hadn't even bothered to take her shoes off. With her gaze trained on the headboard of her bed, she reflected on the day.

She'd never been bullied before. The extent of her ridicule went as far as playful comments about how lame or nerdy she was. Only rarely did her feelings actually get hurt, but what she heard in the hallway was starting to get under her skin. That was dismissible, but the boy that showed her that picture was a direct attack. Her mind drifted back to Bri's judgmental look while she was talking to Lauryn in class. And it hurt her feelings. A lot. She was quite sensitive, but it was never enough to drive her to tears in the past. She felt dumb for crying over these petty things now.

It all seemed to pile on. This had undoubtedly been one of the worst and longest days of her life. So much had happened. School today was like a battlefield. If their words were weapons, she was going in completely unarmed now. They made her feel so inferior. Why should her sexuality matter to them? Her sexuality was a mystery to herself, yet all those people were labeling her and saying rude things about it. They knew nothing.

Shakily, she wiped her face with the back of her hand and walked over to her desk. She flipped open her journal and began scrawling long rants about the idiots she went to school with. She wrote until her hand cramped. Her script was more illegible than usual. It wasn't her fault, though. Blindly writing through blurry tears wasn't exactly the formula for good penmanship. As she repeatedly wiped her face, she skimmed over her work. Reading over it combined with her exhaustion from crying coaxed her to sleep. She succumbed to it as she doubled over the desk, resting her head on her arms.

»»»

While Lauryn was on her way home, all she could think about was Cammie. She mentally kicked herself for getting so carried away in her room that day. Maybe if she hadn't acted on her desires, they wouldn't be in this position right now. Lauryn couldn't shake the feeling that this was all her fault. If she wasn't so careless, they would probably be cuddling or something now.

Ever since they'd been in a relationship, Lauryn had little regard for the repercussions that would threaten them. Cammie used to resent the way they were confined to the stairwell, but Lauryn knew the deeper meaning behind it. Along with her initial discomfort with dating a girl, her motives stemmed from the reaction she knew they'd get eventually. She'd been hiding it as a way to protect themselves.

Even though her own insecurity fed into it, it was mainly because she did want to have to deal with everyone else's shit about it.

As soon as they'd gone public with their affection, she saw that it didn't bother Cammie in the slightest. While Lauryn noticed every subtle glare they received, Cammie happily walked beside her without a care. Cammie's resilience rubbed off on her. It was almost as if the two of them had switched positions. Now Lauryn was the one perfectly fine with their conditions, but it seemed like Cammie was agitated.

Desperate to talk to her again, Lauryn rummaged through her bag for her phone. Her fingers touched the case and she pulled it out, already in the process of unlocking it. When she was met with her home screen, it brought a smile to her face. It was a picture of Cammie sleeping on her chest. Her face was a bit squished, because she was deep in sleep. There was even a bit of drool hanging from her open mouth, but Lauryn was completely smitten. It was one of her favorite pictures of the brown-eyed girl. And Cammie had begged her numerous times before to change it, but she never did. She didn't plan on it either.

Lauryn chuckled at the picture and opened her text messages, preparing to send one to her. She typed out a quick hello, followed by a brief message asking how she was feeling. There was little hope that she would respond, seeing how she hadn't texted her back in four days. Regardless of if she got a response, Lauryn wanted to make sure Cammie knew she was on her mind. She cared about her so much. She always wanted to remind her.

By the time she reached her house, there was a goofy smile etched onto her face. Thoughts of Cammie always left her like this. It usually faded after a while, but when she walked through the door and saw Cara walking by, her smile vanished immediately. The tension in the air was so thick. Lauryn had a bit of a staring contest with her mother before diverting her eyes and heading up the stairs. That was how most of their encounters went ever since she'd barged in on them so rudely four days prior. Lauryn was great at keeping grudges. And she planned on it until Cara came to her fucking senses and welcomed Cammie back into their house. Surprisingly, Lauryn found that she wasn't missing out on much by not speaking with Cara. She hoped her silence spoke volumes.

"Why don't you just sort it all out? Both of you are being childish," Miguel scoffed. He'd seen them from his position on the couch. He was getting annoyed by both of them. The unnecessary hostility was giving him a headache, and he wasn't even involved.

"She doesn't want to speak to me," Cara shrugged.

"Then make her. This is getting ridiculous," Miguel demanded. He refused to see his family crumble over something that could simply be discussed.

"Fine," Cara groaned. She looked up in the direction Lauryn went and sighed. As she ascended up the stairs, she swallowed her pride. She knocked on the door timidly, *actually* deciding to knock this time around.

"What?" Lauryn called. She was sprawled out on her bed. She figured it would be Tori or Christian, since they were the only ones who seemed to respect a closed door.

Cara turned the doorknob slowly, regretfully opening it. The look Lauryn shot her when she made herself visible instantly put her on edge. Her daughter had never been so blatantly disrespectful. Her simple presence didn't warrant that level of hostility. At least not in her opinion.

"What?" Lauryn said again, her tone much colder than before.

181

"We need to talk," Cara sighed.

Those words always made Lauryn's pulse quicken. As Cara entered her room and closed the door behind her, Lauryn just stared at her. She didn't know why she wanted to talk now, but she was instantly defensive.

"Okay..." Lauryn trailed, motioning for her to start talking.

"About you and the girl..." Cara started, but Lauryn interrupted her already.

"Cammie," Lauryn corrected her as she rolled her eyes. This was bullshit. She couldn't even say her name. There was no way she'd come to terms with or was anywhere close to accepting it. They didn't need to talk.

"Right," Cara acknowledged before taking in a deep breath. "I just-" she started again, but Lauryn cut her off.

"You know what... Actually, just don't. Save it. Whatever you're about to say, I know you don't mean it," Lauryn groaned. "And I have to go, anyway..." she informed her mother as she got up and grabbed her bag.

"Lauryn," Cara admonished her as she approached the door.

"No, I have somewhere I need to be," Lauryn insisted as she opened the door and exited. She didn't let her mom say another word. She knew she'd probably be in more trouble when she got back, but she didn't care. She also knew that she was digging a deeper hole for herself, but she didn't care about that either. Her mother's calls were easily tuned out as she made her way down the stairs. Even Lauryn was stunned by her audacity. There would definitely be a punishment waiting for her when she got back. And she didn't even know where she was going.

She checked her phone for a message from Cammie, and wasn't surprised to find no such thing. Even on good days, Cammie wasn't much of a texter. The best way to get in touch with her girlfriend was by making a phone call. She did so often. Whenever they didn't sleep over, they talked on the phone until the early hours of the morning. Lauryn's favorite thing was slowly hearing Cammie's voice change as she grew sleepier. The raspy voice was almost always followed by deep, slow breathing. Falling asleep on the phone was inevitable and adorable. They never hung up.

Lauryn found herself lost in her thoughts. When she looked up, she was in front of Cammie's house. What the hell? Had her subconscious really brought her here? Maybe it was a sign. She knocked on the door tentatively, then got impatient and rang the doorbell. Within a few seconds, Sonya appeared at the door, greeting her with a smile. She unlocked it and held it open for Lauryn. With outstretched arms, she coaxed Lauryn into a hug. Lauryn fell into it graciously, and Sonya rubbed her back soothingly. Her maternal instincts immediately told her that something was wrong. She loved Lauryn like one of her own and could read her like an open book. She knew when she needed a hug.

"What brings you here?" Sonya questioned.

"I've got some stuff going on," she answered, waving it off with her hand. "Is Cammie here?"

"Yes, but I think she's sleeping," Sonya nodded.

"Can I go see her?" Lauryn asked tentatively.

"Of course," Sonya smiled and stepped aside, gesturing for Lauryn to go upstairs herself.

Lauryn sauntered up the familiar stairs and smiled to herself. Lately, this was feeling more like home than her actual house. She rounded the corner and strode towards Cammie's room. Her door was closed and Lauryn stood outside of it awkwardly. What was she even doing here? Cammie didn't want to see her. She'd

182

been painfully ignoring her for most of the day. Lauryn contemplated just turning around and going back home, but sticking it out with Cammie seemed like a much better idea than facing her mother again.

"Cammie?" Lauryn called softly as she rapped against the door. She got no response and called again, then she remembered that Sonya said she was sleeping.

In her mind, it seemed like a good idea to fix things with Cammie here. There was no one around. Hopefully, she wouldn't feel cornered. All Lauryn wanted to do was work everything out. She had no idea when her life had gotten so messy. But she retrieved her phone again to call Cammie in hopes of waking her up.

Lauryn heard Cammie's phone buzzing through the door, so it was probably on her desk or bedside table. Her dresser was far too cluttered for it to be making that kind of noise. The call went to voicemail and Lauryn groaned before calling again. Surely if she heard it through the door, Cammie heard it too. And she did. But she'd been trying to block it out. The vibrating was so annoying, she blindly reached to answer the phone just to make it stop.

"Hello..." Cammie answered with a scowl, yet to open her eyes. She grimaced at whoever was on the line for disturbing her nap, but the voice that carried through the line put a smile on her face.

"Hi," Lauryn responded softly.

"Hi," Cammie returned sweetly. Lauryn's voice just made her heart melt, and she'd only said one word.

"Do you mind if I come over?" Lauryn smirked as she leaned against the wall outside of her door.

"Um... Sure," Cammie relented. She squinted to see the clock, but it was too far away. "When?"

"Now?" Lauryn suggested squeakily.

"Sure," Cammie agreed. If Lauryn left now, it should give her enough time to clean herself up. She didn't really feel like explaining herself. And it wasn't even a big deal. She was over it for the most part anyway.

"Well... Go down and unlock the front door," Lauryn hinted.

"I will," Cammie assured her.

"I mean now," Lauryn laughed.

"I *will*," Cammie repeated with a groan.

Lauryn chuckled to herself and patiently waited for the door to open. Cammie lifted her head from the desk and looked around. She was looking for a mirror or something, but she didn't see any around. She hoped that she'd slept off her bad day and that she could start over with Lauryn. Maybe Lauryn would turn her day around.

"Camz..." Lauryn prompted as she trailed her finger along the wall.

"I'm going to do it. Don't rush me, woman," Cammie laughed lightly. "You're not even here yet."

"Okay. Yeah, you're right," Lauryn giggled in spite of herself.

"Yeah. So can it," Cammie warned her playfully. Cammie stretched and got up, finally heading towards the door. She turned the doorknob and heard the lock come undone. With her head down, she headed out of the door on her way downstairs. Lauryn nearly scared the living daylights out of her when she emerged from the corner. Cammie's hand flew to her chest in surprise and she stopped herself from yelling out.

"Fuck, you scared me..." Cammie pushed Lauryn in the shoulder.

"I'm sorry," Lauryn giggled. She placed her arm loosely around Cammie and burst into laughter again. "Sorry."

"I hate you," Cammie smirked. "I didn't think you'd actually be here..."

"Well, surprise," Lauryn giggled again as she leaned in to kiss Cammie. She did it so mindlessly, she'd forgotten that there was tension. Her kiss lingered for a few seconds, then she pulled away awkwardly. "Sorry," she apologized, unsure of if it was alright to kiss her now.

"It's okay," Cammie smiled. She was elated for that kiss. As she was leaning in for another, Lauryn frowned.

"Wait, what's wrong?" Lauryn questioned. In that moment, she took in Cammie's expression. Her eyes were puffy and red, despite the smile on her face. As she looked at her closely, she could make out the faint remnants of dried tears.

"Nothing..." Cammie answered honestly, momentarily forgetting that there was evidence from earlier on her face.

"Why were you crying?" Lauryn continued as her eyes softened tremendously. She grasped Cammie's waist and looked at her intently.

"I wasn't... I'm fine," Cammie assured her, shifting her gaze down to the floor.

"Babe, your eyes are red..." Lauryn informed her, assuming Cammie knew about the obvious tear stains on her cheeks.

"I'm okay, really," Cammie stressed.

"Are you sure?" Lauryn pressed as she stared her down, looking for the slightest falter in her words or actions.

"Yes. I just had a moment earlier. I'm okay," Cammie reiterated just before pecking Lauryn's lips.

She really was okay by now. The snide comments she'd endured earlier were in the past. It was okay. She was fine. She just decided to take it with a grain of salt. Sleeping it off proved to be the best method. It wasn't bothering her so much anymore. Their words didn't linger in the back of her mind and nag at her anymore. And maybe they would again tomorrow, but for now, she was alright.

For a second, she wondered if she should share the rude things they'd said with Lauryn. But she decided against it. It didn't matter. Dwelling on the problem wouldn't solve anything. It would just provoke hostility between them and the kids at school, and Lauryn had enough on her plate at the moment. Cammie didn't feel like Lauryn should have to bear the weight of her petty problems. So she decided to let it go.

"Well, if you say so... Then okay," Lauryn sighed. "How are you feeling now?"

"I'm good," Cammie smiled. That was the truth. Her nap left her feeling fully revamped.

"Good," Lauryn smiled as well. "As long as you're better than you were earlier..." she trailed, recalling how mercurial she'd been.

"Sorry about that," Cammie apologized as she stepped closer to Lauryn, enveloping her in a hug. She held her tightly, hoping to make up for her lack of affection throughout the day. Lauryn's scent surrounded her. With a faint smile, she ran her fingers down her back, threading through her hair on their way down.

"It's okay," Lauryn shrugged as her arms settled around Cammie's waist. "I just missed you."

"I missed you too," Cammie seconded.

"Which is weird... Because we've just seen each other at school. But I did," Lauryn smiled to herself as her fingers trailed along Cammie's back.

"Sorry for being distant. I was just upset," Cammie mumbled against her shoulder. "It wasn't you, though."

"It's okay, Camz. I'm just glad you're over whatever it was. I hate being ignored," Lauryn admitted. They'd yet to break their hug. They were just resting against each other, thriving in the warmth the other girl provided.

"I didn't mean to," Cammie frowned. In her defense, it hadn't even crossed her mind that her actions would make Lauryn upset. Based on her reactions, she didn't seem to care much. Maybe Cammie's intuition was a little off today.

"It's okay," Lauryn said again, and she felt annoyed that she had to keep saying it. "Can we go cuddle?"

"We are cuddling," Cammie quipped as she wrapped her arms tighter around the taller girl.

"In bed," Lauryn clarified.

"Okay," Cammie laughed. She began to tear herself away, but Lauryn clutched onto her. "What? I thought you wanted to go to my room?"

"I do. But don't let go," she negotiated dorkily. Her tone made Cammie's heart flutter. It was times like this that reality caught up to her. And now she was smiling like an idiot, simply because Lauryn was her girlfriend.

"I won't," Cammie promised. She then began backing up slowly, with Lauryn still attached to her. Their steps fell into sync, and Lauryn walked Cammie backwards into her room. The two of them toppled onto the bed together rather clumsily.

Right as her back hit the mattress, Lauryn pulled Cammie on top of her. She gently leaned up to capture her lips, then sunk back into the bed as Cammie settled her weight on her forearms. One strong arm kept Cammie in place, with her hand settling on the small of her back. Their kiss was chaste and slow. Lauryn found that the feeling of Cammie's lips against her own was second to nothing. It was her favorite thing on the planet.

Cammie twirled strands of Lauryn's hair around her finger while they kissed. Everything was so soft and slow. She leaned back a little and held her gaze. Lauryn was staring back at her so fondly, and Cammie was sure she mirrored her expression. When Lauryn broke out into a smile, Cammie mirrored that too. "I love you," they both said simultaneously. The unison caught them off guard for a second, but they laughed.

"I love you too," they said again, laughing a little harder when they said that at the same time too.

"Stop copying me," Cammie scolded her playfully. The smirk she wore was making her cheeks hurt.

"Stop copying me," Lauryn quipped.

"Don't do that," Cammie said seriously, although she couldn't get her facial muscles to stop smiling.

"Don't do that," Lauryn tested her.

"Lauryn..." Cammie trailed.

"Lauryn..." she continued, matching her tone and everything.

"You're so annoying," Cammie rolled her eyes as she lifted herself from on top of her. She positioned herself in front of Lauryn with her legs crossed.

"You're so annoying," Lauryn repeated as she sat up as well, copying Cammie's stance.

185

Cammie only narrowed her eyes at her. Lauryn was copying every little thing she did, all the way down to the way she sat. It didn't look like she would be stopping any time soon, so Cammie decided to have some fun with it. "I'm a big fat idiot," Cammie smirked.

"I know you are," Lauryn grinned.

Cammie laughed. She should've known Lauryn would do something like that. Her girlfriend was equivalent to a five year old when she wanted to be. And Cammie herself was just as immature. Perhaps that was why they worked so well together. They complimented each other nicely and reflected their qualities within themselves.

Lauryn reached out to take Cammie's hands into her own. Their fingers laced automatically. The act had become so natural, they did it without even thinking about it. Cammie leaned in, and Lauryn closed her eyes as she waited for the kiss. But all she felt was Cammie's nose rubbing softly against hers.

"I thought you were going to kiss me," Lauryn said. There was a hint of disappointment in her voice that made Cammie laugh.

"I did," Cammie giggled.

"What?"

"That was an Eskimo kiss," Cammie told her, giving her an odd look. "You've never heard of that?"

"No," Lauryn chuckled.

"It's like this," Cammie grinned as she did it again. Lauryn's nose was warm. But her whole body was always that way. "That's it."

"That's so cute. It tickled," Lauryn smiled as she wiped her nose with her hand. "But give me a real kiss, Camz."

Cammie obliged quickly, going in for another kiss almost instantly. They both smiled into it initially, and Cammie relaxed. Lauryn's hand was still tightly in her hold. Her other hand snuck up to hold Cammie's and she intertwined their fingers. Their lips were simply pressed together, moving sensually. For now, they didn't want anything more. Neither girl made a move to deepen it. Their pace was comfortable.

Lauryn, who craved more intimacy as usual, parted her lips. She took Cammie's bottom lip between hers and tugged on it playfully. Cammie smiled and relented, slipping her tongue into Lauryn's mouth. So far, her motives weren't driven by sexual desires. She just wanted to be closer. She pulled on Cammie's hands to pull her closer, because her neck was starting to hurt from the awkward angle. When they were closer, their kiss depended. It was inevitable, but they'd been prolonging it.

While they were engaged in their kiss, Cammie felt someone else's presence. Hesitantly, she pulled away from Lauryn, turning sheepishly in the direction of her door. It was wide open. Their luck had officially run out. The figure in the doorway wasn't Sophia, it was none other than Sonya. And she was standing there with an unreadable expression. Did they really forget to close the fucking door? God. They both had a sudden sense of déjà vu. Both girls braced themselves for her response. Lauryn closed her eyes, wishing she was anywhere else but there.

After a few beats of silence, she got up the courage to look at her. When she opened her eyes, Sonya was smiling at them. Why was she smiling? What the hell? Lauryn looked over at Cammie, who looked just as confused as she probably did. The couple waited for Sonya to say something. Anything. But she didn't. They just kind of had a staring contest.

"I told you things would work themselves out," Sonya said after a few more seconds, then she went on her way. She had no intentions of stopping in the doorway or watching their display, but she was on her way downstairs and happened to see them in passing. The sheer happiness Cammie seemed to exhibit brought a smile to her face, regardless of if she was kissing Lauryn or not. She liked Lauryn. Lauryn was good for her, in Sonya's eyes.

"What the hell..." Lauryn exhaled. The fact that she'd been holding her breath hadn't really registered. But the burning in her lungs let her know.

"I don't know..." Cammie mumbled, kind of skeptical about that situation. A faint smile was present on her face, only now understanding her mother's reference.

"Do you think she's mad?" Lauryn asked worriedly. The hand that was still holding Cammie's clutched hers a little tighter, for fear that Cammie would recoil again. She wasn't ready to lose her again when she'd just gotten her back the way she wanted her.

"No... Well, I don't know. She was smiling....." Cammie said tentatively, looking back in the direction her mother went.

"Well, she didn't kick me out. So that's a good sign, isn't it?" Lauryn joked.

"I guess so," Cammie laughed awkwardly.

"She seemed... Okay with it," Lauryn acknowledged slowly, unsure of if that was the right terminology. That much was true, from what she could tell. Sonya didn't blatantly disapprove. And if she did, she was keeping her comments to herself.

"Yeah. Ever since the girls found out, I kind of forgot what that felt like," Cammie reflected bitterly. "Approval, I mean," she clarified.

"What do you mean?" Lauryn asked, sensing that was a segue to something deeper that was on her mind.

"Nothing," Cammie dismissed it quickly. She began playing with Lauryn's fingers in hopes of distracting her. Her finger traced the outline of Lauryn's free hand on the bed. Lauryn's gaze was demanding her attention, but she wasn't going to look up.

"You're so secretive sometimes, babe," Lauryn sighed, but decided not to interrogate her. Annoyingly, she felt like she'd been pestering Cammie a lot lately.

"It's not a secret. It's just not a big deal," Cammie said sagely.

"Well, okay," the older girl relented. Lauryn wanted to ask what, but saved her questions for another time. Instead, she focused on Cammie's manipulation. The way she was grazing over the shape of her hand was placating.

"I love you, though," Lauryn smiled.

"I love you too," Cammie reciprocated, leaning in to steal yet another kiss from her girlfriend.

"I think I should probably go," Lauryn hinted as she caught the time on her phone.

Cammie pouted. "But you just got here..."

"I just wanted to see you," Lauryn laughed. "And I missed you. So I came. And I'd like to spend the rest of the night with you and sleep over, but I'd probably get in more trouble than I'm already in," she rolled her eyes.

"You haven't talked to your mom yet?" Cammie frowned. She didn't want Lauryn to sacrifice her relationship with her mother for the sake of their own. Knowing how family oriented she was, she couldn't really fathom that she'd kept

187

this up for so long. Even Cammie had to admit that Lauryn was being stubborn and immature.

"No," Lauryn scoffed. "She tried. But it was bullshit."

"Why?"

"She tried talking to me about you, but she wouldn't even say your name," Lauryn shared. For a second, she was scared that it would hurt Cammie's feelings again and make her withdraw from her. She watched her warily until she responded.

"It takes time, Laur. In her defense, you can't expect her to just go along with it..." Cammie mumbled. Cara found them in a compromising position. Things were just about to escalate, but then she barged in. Cammie shuddered. Cara probably thought she was some type of slut or something.

"*Your* mom did," Lauryn countered.

"I think you should go talk to her," Cammie suggested quietly. She ignored Lauryn's valid point and focused on her own thoughts. She didn't want Lauryn to reject her idea, because it was necessary.

"I don't want to," Lauryn shook her head.

"Okay," Cammie accepted her answer. "I just think you should..."

"What if it doesn't even fix anything?" Lauryn voiced her doubts out loud. He position she was in with her mother made her feel vulnerable.

"You'll never know," Cammie offered.

"I'll talk to her," Lauryn made up her mind.

Chapter 22

By the time Lauryn actually left Cammie's house last night, it was about nine o'clock. She settled on the idea that she would go home and talk to her mother, but Cammie reeled her back in and they ended up kissing and cuddling in her room for three more hours. Lauryn didn't know how that happened. They always managed to do that, but she wasn't complaining. In fact, she was grateful for it. Everything they did was helping to further stall the dreaded conversation with her mom.

When she returned home, no one was downstairs. She had the liberty of escaping to her room without a word. Cammie had the same treatment. When she went down to eat a late dinner, she joined her parents on the couch. Sonya didn't even give her a second glance. Nothing had changed. The atmosphere was normal and comfortable. It was a breath of fresh air to Cammie.

On Tuesday morning, she found that she was winded again. As soon as she set foot on the bus, the looks returned. Even in the relative darkness, she could see them. She had half a mind to just ask them what the hell they were looking at, but she couldn't get up the nerve. There was a reason they were staring, and she was pretty sure she knew, but why they cared so much was beyond her.

Instead of clambering towards her usual seat in the middle, she plopped down in the first seat and immediately laid down. Her book bag served as a pillow and she slumped over to rest on top of it pathetically. Cammie wasn't typically one to get so upset over such things, but it was getting under her skin. She thought she'd reacted so heavily to it yesterday because she was just having a bad day, but it was happening again. And she'd had a great morning. She woke up to an adorable good morning text from Lauryn, followed by a surprise breakfast, and the bus wasn't even late today. The day was off to a great start. And everything was just erased by those goddamn idiots.

The bus pulled off and Cammie's mood steadily declined. The closer they got to school, the more the foreboding feeling in her stomach worsened. When the bus came to Lauryn's stop, she could sense her presence. It dawned on her that she'd literally undone everything they worked to fix yesterday, in only a matter of minutes. Part of her wanted to tell her just to get it off of her chest. Lauryn always knew what to say to make her feel better about certain things. Cammie knew she would have some words of wisdom regarding her newfound issue.

As soon as Lauryn passed her, she lifted up to see her. Her girlfriend looked around for Cammie, then she accidentally made eye contact. Shit. Cammie laid back down quickly, but Lauryn was already on her way over.

"Why are you sitting up here?" Lauryn asked as she sat across from her.

"Someone was in my seat," Cammie shrugged.

"There was nobody over there when I came..." Lauryn said mindlessly.

Damn it. "Oh, well I guess they moved then," Cammie trailed. Maybe she should've checked before she went with that story. It suddenly dawned on her that she'd been lying to Lauryn quite often. Well, only little white lies, petty ones that didn't really matter much. She didn't want to make a habit of it, though.

"Yeah, probably. But good morning," Lauryn grinned. "You look beautiful today."

Cammie smiled. A genuine smile. Lauryn had that effect on her. And that was another reason why her day was going so well before she got on the bus. When she passed the mirror, she found that she was actually pleased with her reflection for once. "Thank you. You're beautiful every day," she responded cheekily.

"Eh, I'm alright," Lauryn brushed her off.

"Yeah. You're alright," Cammie teased with a smirk. Then she sat up and looked over at Lauryn.

"Mhm," Lauryn laughed.

"Did you talk to your mom?" Cammie questioned wantonly. It was kind of out of the blue, but she was wondering.

Lauryn bristled at the mention of it. "No..."

"Why not? I thought you said you were going to?" Cammie reminded her.

"Well, I got home late. A certain someone kept distracting me," Lauryn laughed.

"How rude," Cammie scoffed. "How did that certain someone manage to do that?"

"Well..." Lauryn mumbled as she moved Cammie's things over to sit beside her. "They kept holding my hand and kissing my face. I don't know if I remember correctly, but I think you were there?"

"Hmm, maybe. I think it slipped my memory. What exactly happened?" Cammie played coy.

"If I'm not mistaken... I think... I think it was *you*, actually. You kept doing this," Lauryn informed her as she guided her to her lips. One of her hands dropped down to pick up Cammie's hand and she held it tightly.

"Maybe you should show me again. I don't really think I understand how that's distracting..." Cammie feigned confusion as her free hand rested on Lauryn's thigh.

"Really? Well in that case, I guess I could show you one more time," Lauryn complied eagerly. She leaned in again, laughing as she went. Lauryn trapped Cammie's bottom lip between hers and sucked on it a little. When Cammie opened her mouth, Lauryn slipped her tongue in smoothly. Their heads bobbed in the same rhythm they'd grown accustomed to over time. Much to Cammie's dismay, she found Lauryn drawing back slowly.

"It was something like that," Lauryn smirked.

"Oh, well I can see how that might distract you a little," Cammie said happily.

"That's why I didn't get to talk to her," she concluded.

"Then I guess I can't blame you," Cammie sighed. "You'll talk to her soon?"

"Yes. Soon," Lauryn nodded. Not today, and preferably not tomorrow. But soon. Soon indeed.

"Good. I love you," Cammie grinned over at her.

"I love you too," Lauryn smiled back, matching her expression.

They fell into a comfortable silence. With the rumbling of the old bus and the murmuring of people behind her, she was once again conscious of their presence. For a few minutes, she had some relief. It was like Lauryn provided her with blinders. The judgmental stares didn't feel like they were burning into the back of her skull. No such thing bothered her. She'd completely forgotten. And maybe she should just forget that way more often. Allow Lauryn to distract her the same way she did. Cammie's brow creased in thought and Lauryn noticed.

"Are you okay?" Lauryn asked, then she frowned. Why had she been asking that so much lately?

"Yeah, why?" Cammie nodded.

"You look upset," she noted.

"I'm fine," Cammie shook her head.

There was a problem, but she wasn't comfortable talking about it. A big part of her felt like she was overreacting or that she was being oversensitive or something. She could've even been being vain. Maybe those people didn't even give a hoot about her and she was just so self-absorbed, she thought she was the center of their attention. That was probably the case.

"Okay. You'd tell me if you weren't though, right?" Lauryn clarified, because lately she'd been asking the same question and getting the same answer. Maybe she was just too attentive.

"Yes," Cammie lied again. She winced at how easily it came out. Maybe she wouldn't need lessons from Diana after all.

"I believe you," Lauryn smiled, and Cammie kind of felt a little bad. Even though it wasn't a total lie. If something significant happened, she would definitely vent about it to her.

"I'm glad you do," Cammie smiled falsely as the bus pulled up in front of their school. "But come on, Laur."

Lauryn quickly collected her stuff and got out of the seat. Cammie followed clumsily right behind her. With a wave of bravery, she grasped Lauryn's hand. Because of her new mindset, she convinced herself that no one was looking at her. But they were. When they entered the school, she felt it. That same feeling when she was walking down the hall alone resonated with her. But they weren't looking. They weren't. And the further she walked down the hall in hand with Lauryn, the less she started to believe it. She was just trying to be optimistic and give Lauryn nothing to catch on to.

"Lauryn," Cammie prompted as she scanned the crowd forming in the hallway. She didn't want to face them with Lauryn by her side. Not anymore. Nerves got the best of her and she was about to act on her damn impulses again.

"Hm?" Lauryn hummed lightheartedly from beside her.

"I have to go to um, the counselor's office. I never- uh..." she stalled, trying to come up with something believable. They got progress reports recently, didn't they? Maybe that could be it. "I forgot to get my progress report and my teacher said they'd have it up there," she added.

"Oh, okay," Lauryn nodded. She didn't notice anything peculiar about her statement or demeanor.

"I'll see you later," she bid her goodbye as she pecked her cheek quickly. "I love you," she offered a smile, just to seem genuine.

"I love you too," Lauryn reciprocated for the second time this morning. Cammie's hand fell from her hold and she smiled back at her as she was walking away. Lauryn watched her go with unbridled adoration. She thought that everything was finally resolved and over with, and that they were back on track. Wishful thinking was a terrible thing.

»»»

Aiden. That was it. He could be the solution to this problem. She never got weird looks from anyone when she was dating *him*. Because they were a *straight* couple. Girls being seen with boys was a normal thing. Maybe that was all she had to do to get this all to blow over. If she could prove to everyone that she retained the straight part of her sexuality, they would stop. Cammie was slowly getting fed up with everyone looking at her so much. It was only day two. Without the courage to confront them, she just had to accept it. But she didn't. She could just fend it off. And Aiden was the key to that - or so she thought.

She'd gone through five class changes and endured all types of glares and unnecessary comments. The cause of all of this was unknown to her, but she assumed it was because word had gotten out that she was dating Lauryn. Secrecy wasn't important to her and she didn't care much about people knowing, but she just wished they'd stop acting like she was some sort of criminal. Ignoring it wasn't as easy as she thought it would be. So while trying to disregard everyone, she'd been thinking of a resolution. Asking them wasn't an option. She just had to get around the problem.

Instead of meeting Lauryn at their usual meet up spot, she headed towards Aiden's locker. During the small amount of time they were dating, she'd gotten to know his schedule. For the most part, she knew where to find him at any given time of day. When she turned the corner of the specific hall, her suspicions were confirmed. Aiden was there putting in his combination. Cammie drew in a deep breath and approached him.

"Hi," she greeted him.

"Oh, hey," he said uninterestedly as he continued opening his locker.

"How are you?" she attempted to make conversation.

"Fine," he grunted. He had no intentions of making small talk with her. She could go make small talk with fucking Lauryn, for all he cared. His pride was slightly damaged by her. It was embarrassing for Cammie to go gay after dating him. He still felt like all of the nasty things he'd said about her out of anger rang true. Even though they weren't.

"Good. What class are you going to?" she questioned. Ever so casually, she looked around to make sure people saw her with him. And they did. So her plan was working so far.

"Math," Aiden said monotonously.

"Nice. I like math," she responded idiotically.

"Cool," he shrugged. Why was she still here? "Did you want something?"

"No. I just wanted to talk to you," Cammie countered sweetly.

"Oh," he mumbled as he finished switching out his binders.

192

"Yeah. So how are your grades?" she continued, then she realized she probably shouldn't have asked. His grades weren't doing so hot last time.

"Good," he lied. He was so annoyed. He started heading towards class, hoping she would buzz off in a different direction.

"Are you still playing basketball?" she chimed as she fell into step beside him.

"Yes," Aiden groaned. He was vaguely hoping that his one-word answers would let her know that he wasn't up for conversation, but that clearly wasn't the case.

"What position were you again?" Cammie wondered.

"Point guard," he said curtly. His walking pace sped up a little and he approached his classroom. He faced Cammie just before walking inside. "Don't you have a class to get to?"

"Yeah. I'll see you later," Cammie waved with a smile.

There. That should do it. She walked and talked with a boy for like, a whole four minutes. That ought to show those stupid nosy people that she wasn't anything worth speculating over. She was just a normal girl. And surprisingly, her tactic worked.

As the week went on, it dwindled. Slowly but surely. In the time she forced him to spend with her, Aiden slowly began warming up to Cammie all over again. Despite what he'd said about her looks, he realized that they weren't true at all. She was gorgeous. And as far as the bitch comments went, that was a stretch as well. She was so damn nice, and she was kind of funny. She was a little weird at times, but it was cute. His hostility decreased each time she came up to him. Meeting between classes had kind of become *their* thing instead of her thing with Lauryn.

That information didn't sit well with the green-eyed girl. She hadn't seen much of Cammie on Tuesday after the morning. Maybe she had things to do. She was so cute. She was probably trying to finish the last few problems on an assignment and turn it in early. She did that sometimes. And on Wednesday, she barely saw her at all. Lauryn didn't worry about it though, because that would be obsessive. Cammie didn't have to spend *every* moment with her, although that was typically what they did. She missed her on Thursday too. And on Friday, she assumed she didn't come to school. She progressively saw her less and less. Although it saddened her a little, she wasn't going to freak out about it.

»»»»

That was last week. Lauryn had been letting it happen without getting angry at first, but it was like Cammie went missing every fucking day. Was she back to avoiding her? Surely they'd gotten over that obstacle. Her mother's views were the only thing Lauryn could come up with as to why Cammie wasn't seeing her. Last week, at least she saw her at lunch. But now she was missing from there as well. Lauryn was being patient, hoping that maybe the next day, Cammie would show up and explain why she'd been gone. But she never fucking did.

She got her tray and trudged over to the table. Her expression was blunt, and everyone knew why. The way things had been going recently just annoyed her. It kind of made her mad. And underneath it all, she was saddened. All of this happening without any explanations hurt her feelings a little bit. But she masked it with prevailing anger.

193

"So I guess she's not coming today, either," Naomi assumed when she saw Lauryn walking up to them alone.

"I guess not..." Allie shrugged and waited for Lauryn to join the group.

"Where the hell is she?" Diana groaned when Lauryn reached the table.

"Like I would know," Lauryn scoffed as she set down her tray. She pulled out the seat and sat next to the empty one solemnly.

"Did you check the stairs?" Allie suggested, knowing that was usually her method of escape.

"Yep," Lauryn mumbled as she picked at her food.

"What about the roof? Didn't y'all go up there once?" Naomi suggested.

"She's not on the roof, Naomi," Lauryn rolled her eyes. "And even if she was, I'm not going to her. I'm tired of always being the one to go to her. I'm always asking her what's wrong and she never tells me. She just disappears. So whatever," she shrugged bitterly.

"Have any of you guys seen her?" Allie asked everyone.

"I see her in class... But not really anywhere else," Diana answered.

"Same," Naomi nodded.

"You see her in class because she has to be there. If she didn't, you wouldn't," Lauryn remarked quietly.

Diana and Naomi offered a new topic, and Allie fed into it. They tried to change the subject to get Lauryn's mind off of it, but they couldn't aid what was going on in her head. She was so bothered. In the one class they did have, Lauryn tried coming to her. Cammie started being the last to get there and first to leave, giving Lauryn no option to speak to her at all. It was so uncharacteristic. With each offense, the thought that Lauryn had unintentionally done something wrong was further etched into her brain. Why else would she be treating her this way?

"Camz and I only have one class together. We don't sit together and I can't talk to her in there even if we did," Lauryn interrupted randomly. Naomi had been speaking, but she stopped when Lauryn interrupted. "Sorry, ignore me..." she mumbled to herself.

"Cam isn't going to come to you about it, obviously," Diana stated. "So unless *you're* going to talk to her about it-"

"What is there to talk about when she keeps telling me there's nothing wrong?" Lauryn interrupted again. That was a rhetorical question. There wasn't an answer to it, as far as Lauryn could tell. She heaved a great sigh then she pushed her tray away and slouched over the table, resting her head on her arms.

"I don't know," Diana shrugged.

"Me neither. But what I was saying was..." Naomi picked up the previous conversation. Lauryn tuned all of them out. Her mind was too cluttered to listen to whatever it was that they were talking about.

Even if Lauryn *had* done something wrong, Cammie shouldn't have been too immature to tell her about it. Usually when she got offended by a joke made in poor taste or something of the sort, she'd let Lauryn know. Or if she did something out of line that made her mad, she'd call her out on it. Contrary to popular belief, Cammie had a mouth on her at times. She just needed to be pushed. She was very capable of articulating her thoughts and problems, so why wasn't she?

As she struggled to understand what had provoked this behavior, she proposed that maybe there wasn't a problem at all. Maybe Cammie was just too busy or something. Could it be that Lauryn was just getting too attached? Probably so. In the past, she'd never really seen Cammie much - and it wasn't a problem to her. But that was before they were dating. With them being so close and spending every waking moment with each other, it became routine for Lauryn. Maybe without Cammie by her side, she was just being picky.

"Am I just being too clingy?" Lauryn asked quickly, accidentally cutting off Diana this time.

"No. There's definitely something going on with her," Allie said resolutely.

"It's probably not you," Naomi offered.

"Yeah," Diana agreed, although she was annoyed that her statement had been interrupted. Now she'd forgotten what she was even talking about.

"I feel like I am," Lauryn whined and sighed deeply. Maybe it was just her, but whenever she saw her now, it was like Cammie was eager to get away. It was as if she didn't even want to be near Lauryn.

On the past Monday, she came up behind her and placed light kisses on her neck, but she felt the way Cammie tensed up. She was antsy. And on Tuesday, when Lauryn reached for her hand, Cammie conveniently shoved it in her pocket. Wednesday, Lauryn tried to kiss her and Cammie actually fucking turned her head. But it wasn't playfully like that day in her room. It was entirely different, like she didn't *want* to kiss her. Lauryn brushed it off, but these things were adding up. The first few days could be excused, but it had been a week and a half.

The dismissal bell rung and everyone started moving out of the cafeteria. Lauryn got up lethargically. Everything was just off. Lauryn was pretty good at forgetting about her problems or just getting over them, but this was sticking with her. Probably because it was a recurring issue.

»»»

Three more days passed. By now, Lauryn figured that Cammie must've been teleporting or something. She hadn't run into her in the halls now for over a week. In the middle of class change, she wondered if she should go to their spot. She did, because she couldn't bear to miss her if (for once) she actually showed up. Lauryn patiently waited for Cammie at the end of the hallway. The likelihood of her showing up was slim. And she was right. The bell sounded and he girlfriend was nowhere to be seen. Now she was late.

She briskly walked to class, jaded now that Cammie had stood her up again. Most of the time, she was willing to brave the risk of being late because at least she'd gotten to see Cammie. But she didn't enjoy that perk anymore. Because Cammie never fucking came. She walked into an administrator, who made her go get a late pass - making her later than she would've been. It pissed her off tremendously. When she finally got to class, she slammed her things on her desk loudly and dropped into her seat.

"Lauryn, what's wrong with you?" Allie questioned timidly. Her entire body seemed stiff and tense. And now her face was red. Was her fist shaking too? Jesus.

"Cammie," Lauryn answered shortly. Her frustration really couldn't be taken out on Allie.

"You still haven't seen her?" Allie asked incredulously. Lauryn vented to her about it on the phone about three nights ago. She figured that within three days, they would've found the time to work it all out.

"No!" Lauryn whined. "Has she talked to you? Is she mad at me or something?"

195

"No, I haven't seen her either," Allie said sadly. "Wait, actually I did. On my way here. I think I saw her with Aiden," she recalled.

Lauryn immediately turned at the mention of his name. Anger coursed through her system. Her jaw was set. She didn't even have a response. Fuck. Her fist clenched her pen so tightly, she thought she might've actually broken it if she didn't set it down. Of all people, Cammie was ignoring her for *him*? Fuck that.

"I don't know if it was her though..." Allie revised her answer when she saw how instantly furious she'd gotten. It was a teensy tiny little lie. It was definitely Cammie. That ass was unmistakable.

"It better not have been..." Lauryn grumbled. Aiden needed to stay far away from Cammie, because she was *hers*.

"Now that I think about it... I don't think it was. It was probably Becky. You know they're supposedly talking?" Allie tried to change the subject.

"Oh," Lauryn responded. She didn't give a single fuck about who Aiden was talking to. As long as he wasn't talking to Cammie.

"Yeah. I actually think they'd be cute together," Allie nodded.

"Yup," Lauryn said. Her mind was elsewhere. She tried to dismiss what Allie said. But it was there in the back of her mind for a good portion of the day.

»»»»

On Friday, Lauryn was determined to scope her out somehow. At the end of the day, she waited for her at her locker. She was using their system as an excuse. The way they made a trade-off with Cammie's journal every Friday seemed like a good enough reason to track her down, despite the fact that she didn't want to be the one that was always making an effort. When she saw her coming down the hallway, she grinned.

"Hi Laur," Cammie smiled brightly.

"Hey," Lauryn mirrored her expression. It was hard to keep up a grim expression while Cammie was smiling that way.

"How are you?" Cammie wondered as she gestured for Lauryn to step aside a bit, in order for her to access her locker.

"Good," Lauryn shrugged. If she didn't count the way she'd been ignoring her, Lauryn actually was doing pretty well.

"Good," Cammie chimed, clearly unable to detect the falter in her girlfriend's response.

"Yeah. Where's your journal?" Lauryn brought up, getting right to the point. She preferably would've liked to obtain it before Cammie made a bullshit excuse to get away from her.

"Here," Cammie fished it out of her book bag and handed it over without a second thought.

"Thanks," Lauryn said appreciatively. The atmosphere between them wasn't up to par. Through all of her failed attempts of affection, she figured that Cammie didn't want any. While she would usually express her thanks through a hug or a kiss, she'd actually had to express it *verbally*. Now she was just standing there awkwardly.

"You're welcome," Cammie offered a small smile. She did notice something different about their aura together, but she didn't put any thought into it.

"Well, I've still gotta go to my own locker... So..." Lauryn trailed as she waved the journal in the referenced direction. Cammie's back was to her, so she just left - unannounced. The urge to kiss her goodbye was so strong, but she suppressed it.

"Okay, well wait a second, I'll go with you," Cammie said after a few seconds, but she was speaking to no one.

When she registered that Lauryn had already walked away, she pouted. Even though they would get those dumb looks for being together, she wanted to allow herself a little time with her. She missed it. But she distinguished her figure amongst the crowd. Her suspicions were further confirmed when she saw the dark-haired girl clutching her journal. It brought a smile to her face, but it also made something click.

If Lauryn had her journal, she would see everything she'd written about what'd been going on. It wasn't like she felt the need to *hide* it from her, it was just that she didn't think it needed to be shared. And she didn't feel like explaining any of it. Knowing Lauryn, she would feel obligated to protect and defend her, which was admirable, but it would provoke unnecessary confrontations. Cammie wasn't a very big fan of confrontations. She was willing to let everything slide, but she knew Lauryn wouldn't be as passive.

"Wait, Lauryn," Cammie called down the hallway just as the older girl was about to walk away.

"Yes, Camz?" she answered hopefully, elated to be called back.

"I need my journal back," Cammie disclosed. The way Lauryn's happy expression faded into a frown made her sad, but it needed to be done. Things would get a lot worse if she knew.

"Why?" Lauryn asked sadly as she looked down at it, then back up at Cammie.

"Well, I haven't written anything else since the last time you saw it," Cammie conjured up on the spot.

"That's okay. I like to reread old things. I do that a lot," Lauryn admitted as she held onto her journal a little tighter.

Cammie's features softened upon hearing that fact. That was adorable. She could just imagine the way Lauryn did it - rereading old ramblings with her chin in the palm of her hand. Her girlfriend was the cutest. But she still needed it back.

"Well, I want to write something new for you to read and I'll give it to you on Monday," Cammie offered, careful not to seem too desperate for it. She figured that between now and Monday, she should have enough time to either cross through those rants or just rip them out entirely. She was allowing herself time to scrawl out something that would make up for it.

"Okay..." Lauryn relented dubiously. The way she looked at Cammie made the shorter girl feel a bit guilty for taking it back.

"Thanks," Cammie said quietly. "I promise I'll write something really good to make up for it," she assured her as she shyly looked up at her.

"Yeah," Lauryn muttered. She was disheartened by it, but convinced herself that when she got it on Monday, it would be worth the wait. Or she at least she hoped so. Parts of her were starting to doubt Cammie's feelings for her. When Cammie got on the bus and sat away from her, she wasn't surprised. To Lauryn, it just deepened the wedge further between them. She was getting used to it though.

»»»»

197

Based on the events of Friday, Lauryn once again thought things were on the way to getting better. An encounter surely must've been a move in the right direction. But after a Cammie-less weekend and no interactions whatsoever on Monday morning, she knew otherwise.

She felt like they would have good days and bad days, just like every other couple, but now this was getting ridiculous. Cammie was blatantly ignoring her, no matter how many attempts she made. And by now, Lauryn was seriously contemplating just ending it. It had only been, what? Like a month and a half? And they were already having problems. She didn't need the extra level of stress Cammie inflicted on her.

Cammie was really under the impression that Lauryn was indifferent to it all. She didn't seem to care about or mind her absence much. Cammie was planning on being seen with Aiden during the day and actually being with Lauryn all of the other times. But she hadn't seen her. The few times she did come into contact with her girlfriend, she seemed fine. They talked a little bit on the bus in the mornings and in the first few minutes before school started. Past that, she thought Lauryn wasn't really making an effort to see her. Initially, she felt a little guilty about spending time with Aiden. But if Lauryn was okay with it, that was great. It was like killing two birds with one stone. Even though she didn't necessarily know what the second bird was.

By the following week, Cammie had been getting adjusted to her new routes to class. Instead of going the way she frequently met Lauryn, she was going the way to cross paths with Aiden. As long as Lauryn wasn't bothered by it, it should've been alright. After walking and talking a little with Aiden, she rounded the corner to go her separate way. She was more than surprised when she made out Lauryn's figure resting against the wall, right next to her class.

"Hey," Cammie offered a smile when she came up to Lauryn. She was leaning against the wall with her arms crossed over her chest. But she stood up straight when Cammie came to a stop in front of her.

"Hey..." Lauryn responded.

"How are you? Why are you here? Did you get your class switched?" Cammie wondered as she looked at her in confusion.

"No, I didn't get my class switched..." Lauryn scoffed. "I came here because we need to talk."

"Oh," Cammie mumbled, shifting her weight slightly. That didn't sound good. She looked at Lauryn intently, trying to determine what the nature of this conversation would be. She seemed mad. Her body language was giving off all of the signs. "Okay... Talk about what?"

"Are you mad at me for something? What did I do to you? Just tell me. Don't sugar-coat anything," Lauryn sighed.

"What? No... I'm not mad at you...?" Cammie trailed. Where did she get *that* from?

"Then why are you acting like that?" Lauryn groaned. She looked up at the clock and saw that she only had a few minutes left. Slowly, she started heading for her class. Cammie fell into step with her automatically.

"Acting like what..." Cammie mumbled. Her eyebrow furrowed in confusion. What was she talking about? Simultaneously, she looked past Lauryn at the people behind her. They were looking at the two of them rather harshly. But Cammie swore their gaze was focused on *her*, not Lauryn. Damn. She'd just gotten it to stop, but it was back.

"You've been avoiding me..." Lauryn trailed. She paused for a second. Wait. What if she hadn't been? Cammie seemed really confused. And it wasn't like she was *acting* like she didn't know what she was talking about. It was like she *really* didn't. Lauryn desperately hoped she wasn't misinterpreting the situation.

Cammie avoided her eyes. She kept her head down as they walked together. She was going with the kindergarten logic of if she couldn't see them, they couldn't see her. Her gaze was trained on their feet below. Lauryn had on really nice shoes today.

"Okay, Cammie. What is it?" Lauryn challenged as she waved her hand in front of her face. When she got no confirmation or denial of her statement, she was mad all over again. To her, no answer always meant yes.

"Nothing..." Cammie shook her head.

"Babe..." Lauryn said softly as she tried to hold her hand. Cammie held it for a split second, then she flinched away. Lauryn threw her hands up in exasperation. "What the hell is going on with you?"

"What do you mean?" Cammie asked as she kept her head down. Quickly, she peered up at her. Then she looked behind her and shifted her eyes back down. People were still staring.

"Are you fucking kidding?" Lauryn asked as she came to an abrupt stop, clutching Cammie's arm to stop her as well. "This. What you're doing right now. You've been doing this shit slowly, and I'm sick of it. What the fuck? You've stopped kissing me, then you stopped hugging me, now you refuse to hold my hand, you've stopped going to our usual meetup spots, and now you won't even fucking look at me?" she emphasized as she counted Cammie's offenses on her fingers.

"I..." Cammie started, but words failed her. Since when was she mad about that? For the longest time, she thought she simply didn't care. She would've stopped a long time ago if she'd known it upset her.

"You're being such a coward," Lauryn rolled her eyes.

"What?" Cammie frowned. That was a little offensive.

"You think I don't know why? Cammie, she's *not* here. She *can't* fucking see us," Lauryn emphasized.

"Who can't see us?" Cammie questioned. Wait. So was Lauryn getting those looks too?

"My mom," Lauryn answered.

"Oh," Cammie responded. Her shoulders slumped. "You're right," she nodded. If Lauryn wasn't getting the same treatment as she was, then she wasn't about to tell her about it.

"Yeah... And it's really not fair to me that you're doing this. I have to deal with it too, more than you do, but you don't see me over here giving you the cold shoulder," Lauryn pointed out.

Cammie opened her mouth to speak, but stopped herself. The words she was about to say would've been a bold faced lie. "I didn't mean to" wouldn't be the truth. But it kind of would be. In truth, she didn't mean to do it when Lauryn put it *that* way. Cammie wouldn't say she was ignoring her or giving her the cold shoulder or anything of that sort. She'd just been avoiding her. In public, that's all. But it dawned on her that it was basically all the same thing. For once, she decided to hear Lauryn's side. She never really did. Miscommunication had been their problem from the start, and it never really got better.

"I'm sorry. Tell me how you feel. I promise I'll listen. I haven't been doing that lately," Cammie promised.

"*You* tell me how you feel. That's our whole problem..." Lauryn grumbled.

"I will... But how are you? What's wrong with you?" Cammie countered.

Lauryn ran her hand through her hair and sighed. She didn't feel like having a fucking heart to heart right now. Especially not in the middle of the hallway. She just wanted to get to the root of the problem. "Well, I'm kind of annoyed with you. You do things without telling me why and when you don't tell me, it makes me feel like I'm doing something wrong..." she expressed.

"You're not, I promise. Everything you do is perfect... It's not because of you," Cammie clarified immediately. She had no idea Lauryn had been harboring these feelings towards her.

"You hide almost everything. I never know what's going on in your head," Lauryn continued.

"That's just because some things aren't important enough to share. I don't like talking about my problems that often, you know that," Cammie frowned as she hugged her books to her chest. "Venting makes me sound like I'm looking for attention or compliments or something..."

"And you don't even come to lunch anymore," Lauryn added, disregarding her confession.

"That's because I just started going to the library," Cammie mumbled.

She hoped Lauryn wouldn't ask why. Everything she'd been doing for the past two weeks stemmed from the same problem. Walking down the aisles of the cafeteria made her feel insecure enough on a regular basis, but with everything else, she wanted to get out of that environment entirely. The bullying thing was spiraling out of control. Was that even what it was? They hadn't really said anything to her. The things she overheard were just dumb comments whenever she passed by someone. Who's to say that those words were even directed at her? This was all just a big mess.

"Well that's something I would like to know, Camz," Lauryn sighed as she ran her hand through her hair again.

"I'd tell you if you would've asked..." Cammie responded. Lauryn was guilty of not effectively discussing her opinions as well. Everything coming out now was news to Cammie.

"Maybe I would ask if you'd show up instead of evading me every chance you get," Lauryn remarked contemptuously.

"Stop blaming all of this on me," she requested softly.

Lauryn ignored her request. "And on top of that, I hear that you've been with Aiden lately? What the hell is that all about?" Lauryn remembered suddenly. They were almost to her classroom, but she was getting way too heated to think about dealing with class in that moment.

"I've seen him in the hallway..." Cammie admitted. Lying wouldn't get her anywhere. Part of her knew that Lauryn would get mad at that if word got back to her. She'd just convinced herself otherwise. The guilt returned almost instantly.

"But you won't come to me? Okay, Cammie," Lauryn rolled her eyes. That confirmation hurt. Allie was right. It *was* Cammie.

"It's only in the hallways. I walk with him on the way to class..." Cammie defended herself.

"You used to walk with me," Lauryn said bitterly. There was a vague sense of being replaced. If she was being replaced by fucking Aiden, of all people, there was obviously something she was missing.

"No, it's not like that," she assured her. The late bell rang above them, but they paid no attention to it. Around them, a bunch of students that did ran into their classrooms. But Cammie and Lauryn just kept on walking. Neither of them knew of their destination by this point.

"Okay," she responded distantly. Her pace sped up a little. She wanted to rid herself of Cammie's presence at the moment. Originally, she'd been planning to talk it through with her and drop her back off at class with a hug and a kiss, but *Aiden* could do that shit now.

"Lauryn..." Cammie prompted nervously. She couldn't seriously be getting jealous of Aiden, could she? She quickly extended her hand to stop Lauryn from moving away from her so fast.

"What?" Lauryn muttered. Her cheeks were flushed as she ignored Cammie's pleading gaze.

"Why are you leaving?" Cammie frowned. It wasn't like the bell had just rung or anything. The hallway thinned out as the people started to disperse, giving Cammie a little more confidence in talking with Lauryn.

The smaller girl tentatively slid her hand into Lauryn's, desperate to maintain some form of contact. Lauryn's eyes fell to their interlocked hands and laughed to herself sorely. "Now you want to hold my hand?"

"Don't do that," Cammie admonished her softly. She pulled Lauryn up to her a little, careful not to do anything to push her away.

"I'm not doing anything... But I have to go to class," Lauryn mumbled as she turned away. It was funny, because she held little to no regard for her class right now. She just wanted to leave. Maybe they could try again tomorrow. Or in two weeks. Whatever. Whenever Cammie decided to come back to her. She made a move to flee again, but Cammie's grip on her tightened.

"*Lauryn*," she said again, this time more sternly. Her tone commanded Lauryn to meet her eyes. When she did, Cammie saw a flash of Lauryn's true emotions. Those favorite eyes of hers were grey, meaning she was probably going to cry. Or snap. Whichever happened first. Cammie wanted to ward those negative reactions off.

"What?" Lauryn said for the second time.

Cammie didn't know what to say. Words seemed to fail her, although she never usually had that challenge. As she instinctively cupped Lauryn's face, she decided to let her lips do the talking. While they shared a painstakingly slow kiss, she found what she needed to say.

"Stop. I don't like him. Like, at all. I'm just using him for something... You really don't have anything to worry about, babe," Cammie stated clearly.

"All I have to go by is my own assumptions. You never fucking tell me anything. So what am I supposed to think when you start disappearing and then people say they saw you with Aiden?" Lauryn snapped. She could tell she was about to get an earful.

Cammie felt overwhelmed. She hated being yelled at, and now Lauryn was raising her voice and drawing attention to them. They'd successfully captured the attention of the few stragglers that still lingered in the hall. The glares that never seemed to stop was obviously focused on them now. *Both* of them. And wait, was Lauryn trying to accuse her of cheating or something? God. She didn't want to have this conversation here. Her eyes unintentionally filled with tears, and Lauryn scoffed when she saw it happening.

"No. You don't get to cry over this now," Lauryn rolled her eyes. She was being kind of harsh, but in that moment, she didn't care. She was fed up with everything, and this was her boiling point. Lauryn didn't know exactly what it was that triggered this explosion, but she was finally about to get everything out.

"I'm sorry... You're making me feel bad..." Cammie excused herself as the first tear fell. She wiped it quickly and kept her stare on the ground.

"How do you think *I* feel?" Lauryn countered. "You've been making me feel like shit all week. Ignoring me makes *me* feel bad too," Lauryn tried to express more rationally.

"I'm sorry..." Cammie said again.

"Stop apologizing and just talk to me," she instructed.

"I can't..." Cammie said. Her lip was trembling, and she tried to get herself to stop crying, but she couldn't.

"Tell me what's wrong," Lauryn phrased herself bluntly.

"Nothing, I just... I have to go to class, okay?" Cammie said as she wiped at her eyes with the back of her hand. She tried to get away, but Lauryn just pulled her back. Her anger decreased a little as she scanned over Cammie's face. Making her cry was not her goal. All she wanted to do was figure out everything, but that started to seem less likely the more Cammie's tears fell.

"Cammie..." Lauryn said softly. The turn of events was giving her whiplash. Just moments ago, she was the one on the brink of tears and ready to leave. Now she had to convince Cammie to stay.

"It's not a big deal. It doesn't matter," Cammie insisted. That evasive response pushed Lauryn again. It was like she was on a seesaw of emotions. Either she was enraged or on the verge of tears. Now she was enraged again.

"Fine. But you know what? No one has ever looked at me the way my own mother did, that day. You didn't hear the way she said those words to me. All you know was what I told you. You don't know the half of what happened, because I didn't want to fucking worry you. I didn't want you to be upset. And you have the right to be, but so do I. And I *am* upset. But I'm dealing with it! I thought we would fucking deal with this shit together, but every time I try, you push me away. So I'm done. Do what you want," Lauryn ranted as she wiped her face.

The look on Cammie's face almost made her instantly regret everything she'd just shouted. But for the most part, she didn't regret it. Those things needed to be said. She realized that she'd accidentally shed some light on some things she'd been keeping to herself. That whole speech was wild from beginning to end. Maybe if she hadn't been so emotional, she could've articulated her feelings in a friendlier manner, but she was.

"It's not about that!" Cammie nearly yelled.

She was sick of Lauryn thinking that was the *only* problem she could've possibly had. It wasn't about her fucking mother. She was over that the weekend it happened. That was *not* the issue. Before Lauryn had a chance to respond, interrogate, or accuse her of any more, she ripped her hand from her grasp and went off to class.

202

Chapter 23

Well then what the hell was it about? Lauryn just stood there, dumbfounded as Cammie's figure became tinier the further she went. She disappeared completely after a while and Lauryn just willed herself to go on to class. She made a pit stop at the bathroom to make herself look presentable and not as visibly upset as she was.

When she walked into the bathroom, she grimaced at the way she looked. She stared at her reflection until she felt well enough to go ahead to class. She was terribly late now. Not too eager to be tested or yelled at, her destination was the attendance office. When she finally obtained the stupid pass, she strolled into class determined to have a decent rest of the day. Yes, there was a problem at hand, but it didn't necessarily mean she had to sulk over it.

"How nice of you to join us," Mr. Bryant quipped when she handed him the pass.

Lauryn just went to her seat. His statement didn't require a response. He was lucky she decided to come at all. As she sat there, she tried to tune in and catch on to what he was lecturing about, to no avail. Her thoughts were still clouded. What the hell could Cammie possibly be talking about? And why couldn't she just tell her?

The entire time, Lauryn had been subconsciously playing with her charm bracelet. It hadn't been removed since her girlfriend put it there. When she registered what she was doing, a faint smile spread across her lips. She stroked it and smiled. Happy thoughts of Cammie were infinitely better than brooding about her. Why the fuck had she been thinking about breaking up with her earlier? Clearly, she wasn't in the correct mindset. She suddenly felt disappointed in herself. Their first problem, and she was just about ready to call it quits. Cammie was worth sticking it out. She loved her.

Although her mind momentarily filled with cute, lighthearted things she adored about the younger girl, she couldn't help but wonder what she'd been hinting at. Apparently, she couldn't tell her anything about it. Was it really that serious? What if it was family issues? Well, Lauryn had her fair share of that. If that was it, then the two of them could definitely share that burden. Lauryn couldn't figure out anything else that would make her withdraw from her. If it wasn't her, and it most likely wasn't family, what was it?

Cammie went through the same thought process as she sat in her own class. Both of them reflected on it and wondered. What was supposed to fill in the gaps? Lauryn was wondering what on earth could've provoked all of this. Cammie was worried about what was going on in Lauryn's household. They both had a bad habit of bottling things up. Only this time, someone had shaken it. Their minds were like soda bottles.

Cammie was sick of hiding things. All of Lauryn's accusations were true. Even though she'd yelled them in the heat of the moment, Cammie knew she meant them. While Lauryn was steadily trying to boost her mood, Cammie was wallowing in self-pity. She felt like everything was going wrong all at once. It could all be reversed if she just talked to someone about it. The whole idea of not wanting to burden other people with her problems wasn't working anymore. It was damaging her inside, holding everything in the way she always did. Everything was being blown out of proportion all because she just wouldn't express herself.

She'd come to her decision right as they bell rung. Telling Lauryn wouldn't be a big deal, but she needed to know exactly what to say. In hopes of figuring it out, she set out to find the cause of everything that'd been happening. The rumors had to start somewhere. She racked her brain to think of who would've started them all. Maybe it was Bri. Or Brandon. Or Aiden. The thought of it being Aiden seemed a little far-fetched. The way they'd been interacting lately kind of put him off in her mind. She figured it probably wasn't him.

Brandon's whereabouts were completely unknown to her. In terms of looking for him, she didn't know where to start. His schedule wasn't any of her concern. She recalled the day Lauryn confronted him about her journal. Apparently, he had the lunch right after theirs. Maybe she could interrogate him then. As she walked down the hall trying to figure out where he could be going now, she bumped shoulders with someone.

"Sorry," she apologized immediately and kept going.

"It's okay," a male voice said.

Cammie turned around quickly. There was only one person in the school with that accent. Or maybe not. There could've been others. She didn't know that many people. But she knew Brandon's stupid accent when she heard it. And she couldn't believe her luck.

"Brandon," she called out to him before he disappeared into the crowd.

"Yes?" Brandon paused.

"I need to talk to you..."

"Is it about Lauryn? Did she say something about me?" he asked hopefully.

Cammie rolled her eyes. "No. She didn't say anything about you and she isn't going to. Stop obsessing over her. It's weird," she scoffed. He was delusional. He genuinely still believed he had a chance. Delusional or not, it was the perfect segue into what she needed to ask. "It's actually about what *you've* been saying about *me*."

"Me?" he asked incredulously.

Cammie's confidence started to waver. Could she really do this? She wasn't used to being straightforward. She twiddled her thumbs nervously and glanced at him. "Yeah."

"What have I said?" Brandon questioned. He thought back to everything he'd said about the small girl in front of him. All he could think back to was that he called her the carpet muncher that took Lauryn away from him. Was that was she was going on about?

"You know what you said... So tell me," she tried to say as authoritatively as possible. She looked at him expectantly, wondering what on earth he could've said to make everyone suddenly hate her so much.

"I'm lost," he shook his head.

"You've been spreading things about me and I want to know what you said..." Cammie groaned.

"I haven't," Brandon denied that claim. He'd had his fair share in it, but he wasn't the source.

"Then who has? I'm sure you've heard everything..." she frowned.

"Everything about you cheating on Aiden with Lauryn? Yeah, but it didn't come from me," he said honestly.

Whoa. What? "What did you say?"

"Everyone knows about you cheating on him for her..." Brandon rephrased himself. "Your secret is out."

"Where did you get *that* from?" Cammie demanded.

"Aiden," he shared. "I was kind of offended, because that would've meant she was getting around on me too," he shrugged.

"*Aiden* told you that?"

"Well, yeah," he nodded.

Cammie felt like her head was spinning. If *that's* what was being told, suddenly all of the harsh looks were justifiable. That was probably the worst case scenario. Everyone must've deemed her the class slut. Cheating was unforgivable in most people's books. It was in Cammie's as well, and she couldn't fathom why someone would jump to that conclusion.

"Look, I've got to go," Brandon said as he casually looked up at the clock, leaving Cammie no time to protest as he walked away.

Well, that ruled Bri out. She stood there in shock. The urge to cry again was becoming so strong, but she'd done that enough for the day. It made her feel weak and stupid. As soon as they threatened, she blinked them back. Crying on her way to class wouldn't get her anywhere.

»»»

Cammie sat there with her face in her hands, too tortured by her thoughts to focus. Who was she becoming? In the past, she was never one to let her strife interfere with school. But she really couldn't get herself to pay attention. Linear inequalities were of little concern when everyone had formed these terrible opinions about her. How could she change their minds? If she denied it, no one would believe her. She would seem even more pathetic than she was already perceived.

Overcome with worry, she just slouched over the desk to hide her face. She wished she could turn back time before any of this happened. But if she did that, she'd still be fawning over Lauryn instead of actually getting to be with her. And even though Lauryn was currently mad at her, she wouldn't trade it for the world.

Diana was watching her curiously from behind. From what she could see, she was able to gather that her best friend was upset. But as usual, she had no earthly idea why. She was so annoyed that she was so scarcely informed on what had been going on with her recently. Not just with her and Lauryn, but Cammie in general. It made her feel helpless over there watching her being sad and she couldn't do anything to make her feel better.

Diana made up her mind then and there to take matters into her own hands. She needed to. The fact that Cammie was introverted was a well-known fact, but she was even starting to recoil from Diana. The taller girl felt that as a friend, she herself had been slacking. And as a friend group, all five of them had been. Sure, they offered words of advice to their relationship concerns, but they hadn't really there for the girls individually.

This was one of the few classes Diana didn't allow herself to talk in. Partly because she needed to pay attention, but mostly because the teacher was hard on them. Diana wasn't particularly fond of being called out in front of the entire class, so she kept her mouth shut most of the time. But as soon as they were let out, she barreled over to Cammie.

"Okay, spill. What's wrong with you, and tell me now because we only have a few minutes," Diana instructed her.

The way Diana came at her didn't intimidate her in the slightest. Contrary to her conditioned response of "nothing", she immediately divulged her difficulties. Her words moved faster than she could speak, but Diana understood her babbling. By the time she was finished, Diana was looking at her with the same solemn expression she had.

"Are you serious?" she frowned.

"Yes..." Cammie nodded sullenly.

"Damn. And here I was thinking you dropped your banana or something," Diana joked, trying to make light of the situation at hand. Her little joke earned a small smile from Cammie.

"Shut up..." Cammie nudged her weakly. "But you haven't heard what they've been saying about me?"

"No. And honestly, I think it's all in your head, Cam. *Everyone* isn't doing all of that. If anyone, it's just a couple of the same people. I've never seen anyone give you a dirty look. I haven't heard anything either," she responded.

"That's not in my head. I swear I can *feel* them staring at me before I actually see them," Cammie mumbled.

"I didn't say they weren't at all, I just said I don't think it's *everyone* like you think it is. If you ask me, I think the people you're talking about are just a bunch of Aiden's side-chicks. They're upset over whatever he told them. I think they're jealous of you," Diana shared her theories as the two of them made their way down the hall.

"They're not jealous of me..." Cammie shook her head. "They hate me. And he lied to everyone so it's not like I can just say it's not true..."

"Make him say it then," Diana suggested simply.

"He's not going to..." Cammie groaned.

"Shit, I'll make him then," Diana rolled her eyes.

"No... It doesn't matter anymore. It's already been done," Cammie countered quietly.

"It does matter. You can act like you don't care about all of this but I know you do. Everyone can tell. Me, Allie, Naomi, and Lauryn *for sure*," Diana informed her. "By the way, she thinks you're doing all of this because of her."

"Oh, I know," she frowned. "We kind of just had a fight. And she yelled at me."

"Well..." Diana raised her eyebrows. "All of this is happening because you won't just talk to people. Everything is always a misunderstanding and you never work to fix it."

"It's just not easy to 'just talk to people'," Cammie said with air quotations. "My problems are *my* problems... They don't concern other people, Diana. Nobody else cares and-" she began to explain, but Diana raised a hand and cut her off.

"That's where you're wrong," Diana countered. "People do care. Especially when it blows up like it is."

"Oh," Cammie said under her breath.

"And *I* care. If you think no one else does... I do. And I kind of miss you, loser," Diana smirked. She felt that the conversation was getting too sappy. So she flicked her in the side of the head for good measure.

"Ouch," Cammie grimaced and rubbed the now sore area. "But aww... I love you," she grinned as she enveloped Diana in a hug. She completely wrapped her limbs around the taller girl, who didn't move an inch to hug her back.

"Ew," Diana laughed.

"Love me," Cammie demanded as she hugged her even tighter. She brought her leg up to wrap around her as well.

"Gross," Diana giggled as she pushed against Cammie's head.

"Fine," Cammie huffed and let go, only because Diana would probably break her neck if she kept pushing against her that way.

"I love you too," Diana returned as she hugged her back. Finally. "Now get off of me."

"I knew you'd come around," Cammie smirked. "Thank you though," Cammie said seriously.

Diana's point of view shed some light on a wider perspective. Cammie finally grasped what it seemed like from the outside looking in, and she understood why Lauryn was so upset. Everything made sense. She wished she would've discussed this earlier.

"You're welcome," Diana responded genuinely.

The two of them parted when their separate classes came into view. Diana wrangled Cammie into another hug just before leaving, then disappeared into her classroom. Cammie entered her own class with a clear mind. Being upset and overwhelmed wouldn't bring her to any conclusions. She calmed herself down and took a seat, preparing to think of a rational approach.

As she went through the timeline of unfortunate events, it all led back to Aiden. Maybe Brandon was right. Things did start going wrong after she admitted to dating Lauryn. The fact that she was probably hurt his fragile ego. But she didn't understand. *He* was the one that broke up with her, so he had no reason to be so upset. During the time she was deciphering everything, her anger towards the boy increased exponentially.

The class passed quickly. It felt that way because she was so deep in thought for a large portion of the time. When she actually started to engage in the lesson, it was nearly time to go. Just out of habit, Cammie found herself going the route to see Aiden - preferably for the last time. Although Lauryn voiced her opinion about missing Cammie and wanting to see her in the hallways instead, she didn't really want to. Not now, anyway. This would probably be the last time she went this way. If all went well, she'd revert back to her usual path to meet Lauryn tomorrow.

Aiden's face lit up as soon as he saw her coming toward him. "Hey Cammie," he greeted her as he pulled her into a hug. She shrugged out of it immediately. "What's wrong?"

"I can't even believe you," she scoffed. How was he so affectionate after spreading that terrible rumor about her? Why was he just acting like nothing happened at all?

"What happened? What did I do?" Aiden asked worriedly.

"You told everyone I cheated on you with *Lauryn*?" Cammie reminded him pointedly. "Why would you say something like that?"

Aiden was surprised by her outburst, to say the least. It took him a second to figure out what she was talking about. The fact that he'd said it at all kind of slipped his mind. He'd said that weeks ago. He admittedly felt a little bad for lying on her, but he couldn't do anything about it now.

"Sorry?" he offered.

"Why would you say that?" she challenged again. She wasn't looking for an apology. She was looking for an answer. The apology would've been a nice touch, if it was genuine.

"I was mad at you," he said simply.

"For what? I didn't do anything to you..." Cammie's voice faltered. She tried to keep up her demeanor, but she was losing ground quickly. The thought of what he said threatened to choke her up, but she wanted to go for intimidating. It probably wasn't working, but she was willing to try.

"You were dating her. You don't know how much shit I got from my friends when they found out you dated a *girl* after being with me," he shared. "Do you know how bad that makes me look?"

Aiden was actually playing the victim. That was pathetic. In Cammie's eyes, that petty problem was irrelevant. It didn't call for what he said about her. Cammie was so annoyed, she didn't even know what to say.

"Do you know how bad *that* makes *me* look?" Cammie countered as she turned his words back on him.

"No. No one even cares about what I said," he waved her off. This bitch was crazy. She was really overreacting.

"Yes they do! For the past two weeks, people have been staring at me and talking about me - all because of what you fucking said," Cammie raised her voice, losing her temper as well.

"Chill," Aiden said as he attempted to place a placating hand on her side.

"No... You - You did all of this for no reason and you need to take it all back and tell everyone the truth..." Cammie warned him angrily. She was stuttering, but she hoped he could grasp how serious she was.

That gave him an idea. "Okay, I will," he nodded.

Cammie paused. She was expecting more of a fight than that. "You will?"

"Sure. If you take me back," he negotiated with a smile.

"What? No..." Cammie scoffed. She would never. Especially not under these circumstances.

"Come on, I miss you. I was getting over you, but then you started coming around again and I remembered how much I liked you before," Aiden crooned as he took a step towards her.

"What are you talking about..." Cammie mumbled as she backed up a little. She didn't want Aiden to make any advances on her. She was hoping that after this, he wouldn't want anything to do with her. And as far as "getting over her" went, she was tempted to call his bluff. Aiden "missing" her was really apparent whenever she saw him sucking some other girl's face off in the hallways.

"We looked so good together..." Aiden smirked as he circled his finger along her hip bone.

"Stop," Cammie said, backing up a little bit more.

"Come on, you used to love that," Aiden recalled.

"Not really..." she trailed as she pushed his hand away again.

"Cammie, come on. If you don't want me back, then why have you been chilling with me again?" he challenged.

Cammie considered telling him the real reason, just so he would leave her alone. But that was mean. It made her feel like a manipulative asshole, which, in a way, wasn't that far off. Because she didn't want her public standing to diminish any more than it had by his rumors, she kept it to herself.

"Because....." she dragged out uneasily.

"And I miss you," he softly reiterated, caressing her cheek. Cammie felt so uncomfortable. She'd been politely shrugging him off, but he couldn't take a hint, could he?

"I don't," Cammie said firmly. Her heart started beating a little faster. A bad omen loomed over her head. She felt an ominous feeling increase with each step she took back.

"If you go back out with me, I'll tell them I was just kidding," he explained with a smile that was slowly making Cammie sick. His concept of personal space was clearly lacking as he closed the distance between them again. Cammie was nearly backed up against the locker. She didn't really have another method of escape.

"Aiden..." Cammie trailed.

Why was she playing hard to get? The line between flirting and actually making her uncomfortable was blurred for him. He couldn't tell by her demeanor that she was nearly about to cry. And she couldn't tell that he was totally in a different mindset. Cammie yelling at him was kind of hot. And as she completely backed against the locker, she feared that Aiden was going to kiss her. He was leaning in. That's exactly what he was planning on doing until someone yelled out from down the hall.

"*Back the fuck up*," Lauryn's voice was heard over the casual murmuring of the hallway. Cammie looked in her direction hopefully, praying it was who she thought it was. When she saw Lauryn storming over to them, a wave of relief flooded her system.

Lauryn shoved him to the side and he narrowed his eyes at her, but decided not to push it. Lauryn's fingers closed over Cammie's wrist and she almost yanked her from the wall of lockers. Cammie thought she was still mad at her, so she prepared herself for the backlash part two. While she was being led down the hall by Lauryn, she acknowledged what that scene probably looked like. She was in for something else.

"Do you want this to be over? If you do, just fucking tell me," Lauryn challenged as soon as she pulled her aside. Outrage, indignity, and confusion were just a few emotions threatening to surface. She was trying her hardest to contain herself and not completely lose her shit.

"No! That's not what-" Cammie started to defend herself, but Lauryn cut her off swiftly.

"Actually, forget it. Fuck this," Lauryn gave up and dropped her arms by her side, realizing she was in no state to hear her excuses. Cammie reached for her hand to hold, and Lauryn just stared at her.

"Lauryn, wait. Let me tell you what-" Cammie tried again, but Lauryn was having none of it.

"You don't need to tell me *anything* now," Lauryn scoffed and shook her hand free of Cammie's grip.

"Laur, please just listen to me..." Cammie pleaded, more desperate now than she had been before. She was so frustrated by the fact that she couldn't seem to get a word out.

"I can't do this shit right now," Lauryn shook her head. Part of her wanted to hear her out, but most of her was absolutely livid at how she'd just found her. She'd literally *just* told her how she felt about her being with Aiden, yet here she was again. Was she about to fucking kiss him? And on top of that, she had the opportunity to explain her motives before, but she'd just run off like a fucking little girl.

"You can't do what?" Cammie asked nervously.

"This," she gestured vaguely as she motioned between the two of them. "What's going on right now. Right now, I just can't deal with you. This is too much," Lauryn groaned.

"I just want to-" Cammie attempted to explain again, but was silenced by Lauryn's hand. Cammie was determined to get her disposition cleared, though. When she started speaking again, Lauryn's strained voice drowned her out.

"*Stop*," Lauryn requested loudly, stopping Cammie dead in her tracks. "I don't care," she said, which was a lie, but she'd said it in hopes of getting Cammie to shut up.

Cammie was resilient, vowing to make herself heard one way or another. "All I need to say..." Cammie said tentatively as she took a few small steps towards her. She placed her hand on Lauryn's arm and prepared to blurt everything out at once, not caring if she wanted to hear it or not. "Is that-" she got out quickly, but her words hung in the air at the next thing Lauryn said.

"Don't touch me. Just... Leave me alone," Lauryn said as she pushed against her arm rather rudely. She'd told her nicely that she needed some space at first, but apparently bluntness was the only way Cammie could get it through her thick skull.

Cammie nodded and swallowed rather harshly. She could see that it just wasn't going to work. Not now, anyway. Lauryn eyed her for a split second, then turned on her heel to rid herself of the younger girl. As she walked away, Lauryn's fingertips rubbed at her temples. Headaches. That was all Cammie seemed to be giving her lately. She needed distance.

Cammie's world was crumbling. She was sure of it when she saw Lauryn bolting away from her. She wanted to follow her, but she knew it was in the best interest of their relationship and her own wellbeing to just let her go. Lauryn's perfect figure became blurry as Cammie watched her descend down the hall. By the time the dark-haired girl rounded the corner, tears had already began making their way down Cammie's face. In search of Aiden, who this all ultimately led back to, she whipped around to yell at him some more. He was gone as well. Cammie stood there with her face streaked in hot tears as multiple students brushed past her without a care.

When it rained, it truly did pour. Every single time. Everything was always the worst-case scenario. Misunderstandings turned into altercations that soon turned into one big explosion. That was definitely the situation at hand. Everything reached its peak, and now this was what she had to deal with. It was almost as if every positive aspect of her life was now in shambles. And it was all her fault.

»»»»

Why did she do that? As Lauryn sat in her room, gazing at all of the pieces of Cammie's writing, she wondered why the fuck she'd put it up there. But she knew. It was beautiful. It made her think of Cammie. And before, that used to be a wonderful thing. But it was just bringing her back to a bad place. While she was in this mood, she didn't want any reminders of the brown-eyed girl at all.

Driven by impulse, Lauryn reached up and snatched down the one piece of writing she'd taped above her headboard. She didn't ball it up, but she threw it to the ground. The catharsis was so gripping, she repeated the gesture with the page that was taped a little higher up on the wall. One after another, Lauryn began ripping everything of Cammie's she put up off of the wall. The papers fluttered into a pile on the floor.

With a scowl, Lauryn looked around her newly trashed room. She should've stayed at fucking school. If she were there, she wouldn't have had the chance to ruin everything she'd worked so hard to decorate. Skipping didn't help anything. It just left her alone with her thoughts. And she thought that was what she wanted, but not to that degree. Lauryn wouldn't dare trash the actual sheets. It was still sentimental to her. She still treasured it. She just didn't want any reminders of Cammie at the moment. But of course, she couldn't escape her for long.

»»»»

Meanwhile, the school day was coming to an end. Impatient students bustled out of their classrooms, eager to get home. Cammie was only eager to get to one place, Lauryn's locker. She darted over there immediately after class, ready to attack the problem head on. It really was getting out of hand. Hopefully Lauryn had cooled off by now, so Cammie could say what she needed to say. She just needed to put it out there.

She kept her eyes trained on the end of the hall she knew Lauryn would be coming from. The minutes ticked on, but still no sign of Lauryn. Cammie nervously looked up at the clock. Missing the bus was a threat now, but talking to Lauryn about everything was more important. She waited for a few more minutes, then decided she wasn't coming. Was Lauryn avoiding *her* now? If this was a game they were playing, Cammie wasn't very good at it. And she wasn't very fond of it.

Wearing a scowl, Cammie trudged over to her own locker. She grabbed her books and shoved them in her book bag. Then she slammed her locker closed and made her way towards the exit. Upon getting outside, she found that the bus lanes were empty. Fantastic. But maybe walking home today wouldn't be so bad. It would give her time to think, as well as giving her time to come up with a plan to fix everything.

While Cammie was walking, she felt a raindrop fall onto her cheek. Conveniently, she looked up to see grey skies. She thought it was fitting. Today was the gift that kept on giving, a series of unfortunate events. Depression was the theme, and the factors of the day were tying into it nicely. The drizzle turned into rain, which ultimately evolved into a downpour - and she wasn't even halfway home yet.

Long walks home in the pouring rain gave her ample amount of time to figure things out. If she couldn't locate Lauryn at school, she would go to the one place she knew her girlfriend would end up eventually. One foot after another, Cammie made her way on over to Lauryn's house. She hoped she would accept her presence, despite how they left things earlier. With shaking hands, she knocked firmly on the door. She tried to shield her face from the rain, which was accompanied by a full-on storm. Her entire body was drenched anyway, so even if it were to help, it wouldn't have done much.

The door opened swiftly, revealing Lauryn's dad. He looked confused, to say the least. He quickly pushed the door open wider and urged Cammie to come inside. "What are you doing walking out there in the rain?" Miguel asked, knowing Cammie couldn't drive yet.

Cammie remained where she was standing, ignoring Miguel's gestures to welcome her inside. Lauryn heard the knocking and commotion for upstairs, so she peered downstairs to see what the disturbance was about. When she saw her dad's expression and Cammie standing just outside, she quickly hid behind the wall. What the hell was she doing here? She just couldn't get a break, could she? No, she could not.

Miguel turned around to look at Lauryn, silently questioning if she knew about her plans to show up. Lauryn immediately shook her head no and moved her arms to accentuate her answer. "Tell her I'm not here," Lauryn called down as quietly as she could.

Her voice was loud enough for Cammie to hear, which made her slump her shoulders involuntarily. Her entire expression fell. Miguel looked between the two of them curiously. When he saw Cammie making a move to leave, he grasped her shoulders to stop her.

"You're not going back out in that weather," Miguel said pointedly, directing Cammie to come inside. Lauryn rolled her eyes and retreated back to her room, closing the door loudly. Cammie obliged hesitantly, not wanting to impose against Lauryn's wishes, but also not wanting to offend Miguel by insisting on going home.

The Miami heat made the rain bearable. She was only wet. But Lauryn's house made her feel like she was freezing. It didn't help that the air conditioner was on, blowing on Cammie and actually making her shiver a bit. Miguel noticed and cautiously guided her towards the stairs, motioning for her to go up.

"Go get a towel and tell Lauryn to give you some dry clothes," he instructed her, using his fatherly tone - as if she was one of his own.

"It's okay, Papa J... Really," Cammie assured him as she tried to head back towards the door.

"You are soaking wet. You'll be sick. Go," he said more authoritatively.

"Okay..." Cammie sighed as she ascended up the stairs sluggishly.

Great. How was she supposed to get out of this one? She didn't want to have to burden Lauryn for dry clothes. Although it was well known that she loved wearing her girlfriend's clothes, the circumstances were different. The two of them were in different places.

With her gaze on the floor below, she dragged over to Lauryn's door. She raised a soggy arm to knock on the door, then dropped it by her side. Lauryn didn't want her here. And she probably wouldn't even give her any clothes. This whole trip here had been made in vain. She hadn't cooled off at all.

Eager to prolong the question for a few more seconds, Cammie went down the hall. She came to the closet and opened the small door, picking out a towel amongst the colorful ones. She chose the periwinkle one. It reminded her of cotton candy and happiness, something she needed to cheer herself up a bit. She unfolded it and wrapped it around herself, immediately surrounded with the scent of clean linen and Lauryn. Two of her favorite smells were bundled into one. A small smile played on her lips as she dried her hair off a bit and tried to stop herself from dripping.

Lauryn opened the door to see if Cammie was still downstairs, but saw her at the end of the hall. She was drying her hair and was just resuming the towel's position around her shoulders when they locked eyes. Lauryn's heart ached at the sight. Cammie was so beautiful, even when she was drenched from head to toe with ruffled hair. But she was highly upset with her, so how cute she looked in the moment didn't matter much to Lauryn at all.

The few seconds Cammie held Lauryn's gaze was awkward. Neither of them knew what to say. But Lauryn motioned for Cammie to come over. An involuntary smile creeped onto Cammie's face as she walked over. She was going to give her a hug, but Lauryn turned away and went back into her room. Cammie's face fell. But she went with the logic of because she was wet, Lauryn didn't want to hug her. Not because she didn't want to. She knew that probably wasn't true, but it was going to get her to move forward.

"You need clothes, don't you?" Lauryn mumbled without looking at her. She was already in the process of getting her some by the time Cammie uttered a small confirmation. She pulled out a sweatshirt and some shorts and tossed them over to Cammie, who didn't catch either of them.

"Thanks..." Cammie sighed as she crouched down to pick them up. After changing with her back to her, Cammie notified Lauryn that she was finished.

"Okay," Lauryn shrugged without turning to her.

Cammie expected Lauryn to face her, but she didn't. Cammie stood there in her new outfit and frowned. She took the opportunity to look around her room, noticing something different about it. It seemed bare. She couldn't place why though. While trying to figure it out, she quietly inched towards Lauryn. Something crumpled under her foot, and she quickly stepped back to see what she'd ruined. It was a piece of paper. Several pieces of paper, now that she was looking down at it. And she recognized it. The size of the paper and the familiar handwriting let her know immediately that it was from her journal. She put two and two together and figured out why her room looked so empty. She'd taken it all down. And it was here before her.

If she thought she was crushed before, she had no idea. Things clearly wouldn't be going in the preferred direction now. Lauryn fucking snatched everything from the walls, leaving them almost completely barren. "Why did you... Why'd you take them down?" Cammie frowned.

"I was mad at you," Lauryn said, and Cammie thought back to Aiden. He'd said those exact same words to her a few hours ago. This was a proper expression of anger. Spreading rumors was not.

"Um..." Cammie trailed uneasily. "About the whole Aiden thing... I-" she started off, but Lauryn cut her off again.

"Don't," Lauryn shook her head, still not looking at her. Her stare was settled on the headboard in front of her.

"Lauryn, let me just tell you. Please," Cammie pursed her lips as she stared at the back of Lauryn's head.

"I don't want to hear about it," she denied her. If she would offer another topic of conversation, Lauryn would probably be more accepting.

"But-"

"Cammie, I really don't even want you to be here right now," Lauryn shared. She was being brutally honest at this point, not trying to spare her feelings anymore.

Well, okay. Ouch. "Well your dad won't let me walk in the rain, so... I have to stay here. And it doesn't make sense to *not* talk to you when we're both confined to the same space..." Cammie pointed out.

"I know, Cammie. But I can't deal with you right now. I don't feel like talking about this shit," Lauryn mumbled as she laid back across the bed.

"Why?" Cammie frowned. She figured now was the best time to overcome everything. When else would they be ensured privacy like this?

'Why'. That was a good question. Why had Cammie been ignoring Lauryn for the past two weeks? Why was she being so distant? Why was Lauryn never offered an explanation when she asked? Why was she only trying to explain now, when things were threatening their relationship? Why did it have to go that far before Cammie was willing to talk? 'Why' was a very good question to be asking.

Lauryn felt Cammie's burning stare on her, but she didn't turn around. She was so angry with her. It wasn't just from today, like Cammie probably assumed it was. It was from the buildup of multiple things. Things like defiance, the way Cammie still insisted on being with Aiden after Lauryn expressed herself to her. Things like lies, the way Cammie constantly had been. Things like misplaced blame, how Cammie tried to turn everything back on her. How could she get angry with Lauryn for being in the dark? Why was Lauryn even in the dark? A decent relationship didn't harbor those components. Maybe they should have some time apart.

"Laur?" Cammie prompted when she didn't answer her question.

"I think..." Lauryn's voice tapered off. She actually questioned if she had the strength to say those next words. She knew she wouldn't mean it, but maybe it was for the best. "I think maybe we should take a break for a little while."

Science had an explanation for everything. But what was their reasoning for the actual pain she felt in her chest, just from Lauryn's words alone? How would they explain the sudden shortness of breath she suffered from when the impact of what she said actually hit her? Which series of explanations would cover why her heart felt heavy, just from hearing something like that?

"What?" Cammie's voice cracked. That was out of the blue, what had she done now? Surely she must've misheard her.

"It-It'll give you some time to figure out some things and for me to figure out some things of my own..." Lauryn continued. She still couldn't look at Cammie.

214

Cammie felt like the world was closing in on her. She was frozen. She couldn't cry, she couldn't move, and she couldn't speak. All she could do then was hurt. And she did. Cammie felt as if her heart had just been ripped out of her chest. Lauryn got up the courage to turn around and look at her. But when she did, she wished she hadn't. Cammie's face made her heart completely plummet in her chest. She was visibly shaking.

"Are you sure...?" Cammie asked when she got the power to speak. Her throat was tight. It was hard to swallow.

"Yes," Lauryn nodded and shifted her gaze to the sheets below.

"Okay," Cammie's voice shook. Her breathing shortened even more and she really tried to catch her breath. Each attempt of composing herself was futile. She was about to break, and Lauryn knew it.

"Cammie... Don't cry..." Lauryn said tentatively as she looked back up at her. Cammie was standing in place with her eyes focused on nothing in particular. Her mind was clearly elsewhere, but she looked horrified. Internally, Cammie's thoughts were going a mile a minute. Her state of shock was too intense for her to externally function. Lauryn assessed her face and instantly regretted what she'd told her. She didn't mean it anyway.

"Camz..." Lauryn reiterated more softly as she slowly got up from the bed.

When Cammie registered Lauryn walking towards her, everything came out at once. Her strong demeanor completely crumbled. A sob left her lips, which was painful for Lauryn to hear. Cammie probably would've fallen to the floor if Lauryn's strong arms weren't wrapped around her now. She held her tightly, keeping her upright. Cammie just stood there. She didn't cling to her like she normally would. Why was Lauryn hugging her anyway when she'd just broken up with her?

Cammie wanted to ask, but she could barely breathe. She was crying heavily. Her nose was running and everything. In Lauryn's defense, she had no way of knowing her words would immediately affect her the way they were. And she was unintentionally making it worse on Cammie by showing affection. It seemed like she was desperately trying to keep her together. It was to no avail, because Cammie was expressing her remorse for this and everything leading up to it. Lauryn's fingertips trailed up and down her arm soothingly, trying anything to calm her down. It really wasn't working.

"Camz..." Lauryn said, nearly on the verge of tears herself. She couldn't think of anything to say besides that, knowing how placating the nickname usually seemed to be.

"I'm sorry..." Cammie wretchedly apologized against her shoulder. She finally hugged her back. At first, she was almost scared to.

"It's okay..." Lauryn assured her, still stroking her fingers along her arm. "I didn't mean it."

"Yes you did," Cammie countered. Within reason, she understood what provoked it. But it didn't stop it from hurting. It didn't stop her tears from flowing.

"I did... But I didn't. I can't," Lauryn struggled to explain, with her own tears spilling now as well. "I love you, but this is all just... I don't know. It's a lot to handle, Cammie."

Cammie embraced her fully, completely pulling Lauryn into her. The thought that she wouldn't get to hug her like this for a while prompted her to clutch her tighter. There was virtually no space between them. She leaned back a little to hold her gaze, but her features were blurred due to her tears. She wanted to fend it off somehow. She wanted to fix it. Breaking up this soon just was not an option. It couldn't be.

"I'm sorry... We can talk about it. We don't really have to break up..." Cammie offered shakily. Her words were slurred and as they ran together, she hoped Lauryn could comprehend what she was trying to say.

"I think we need it for now," Lauryn disagreed subtly. That contradicted what she'd just said, but she wasn't in her right mind right now.

"No..." Cammie sobbed. "We don't have to... W-We... We can... We can just..." she struggled to come up with any alternatives. Her voice was shaking horribly, and she barely understood herself. She cursed herself for not being able to form a coherent sentence.

"Don't make it harder than it has to be..." Lauryn requested softly. "Please."

That response caused another round of sobs to rack Cammie's body. It meant she was serious. She really did want to break up. Maybe it wasn't official and it wouldn't be for long, but it tore her apart anyway. There was no difference between 'taking a break' and 'breaking up'. They both felt the same way, although one term was meant to be less brutal than the other. If it was even possible, she seemed to start crying harder than before. At this point, Lauryn figured she was just completely inconsolable. Her chest was heaving. She was so distraught, she hardly knew what to do with herself.

Lauryn was used to being the strong one. Of course she was upset as well, but Cammie was entirely different. Lauryn kept herself together long enough to be there for Cammie. She was often the shoulder to cry on, and now was no different. With strong arms, she hugged Cammie tightly to her chest. Cammie's tears were soaking through the thin fabric of her shirt, but Lauryn didn't mind much.

Cammie tried to take advantage of their position. The terrible feeling that Lauryn wouldn't approach her in the following days refused to let up. It was almost inevitable. With that in mind, Cammie instinctively dipped forward. Lauryn allowed their lips to touch for a brief second, then she turned away from it. It just didn't feel right. Everything was fucked up now.

"I think you should go..." Lauryn said as she loosened her hold on her.

That hit Cammie harder than anything else. That was it. It was over. That was the end of it. Taking one last good look at her, she stared at her face for a minute or two. Lauryn's cheeks were flushed, indicating how upset she was herself. Her lips were pressed together as she looked at the floor beneath them desolately. Her dark hair nearly covered her face, but Cammie was still able to make out her features. Even when she was crying, she was painstakingly beautiful. But she wasn't hers anymore.

Lauryn felt her gaze settled on her, but she resisted the urge to look back at her. Cammie was obviously taking it harder than Lauryn was, but then again, it probably hadn't hit her full force yet. Seeing Cammie break down in front of her was steadily chipping away at the wall Lauryn was desperately trying to maintain. The older girl wanted nothing more than to wipe her tears and kiss away her sadness, but oddly enough, she couldn't. It felt strange. The conflicting feelings she felt towards her were foreign. Her decision was a good notion. Their balance was off, and they needed to restore it. Maybe in a few days or weeks, they could give it another shot.

Cammie drew in a deep breath slowly. Her eyes were still trained on Lauryn, who was still refusing to meet her gaze. More tears spilled involuntarily, but she'd given up on trying to stop them. She lifted her hand to wipe them away for now and prepared to say one last thing before leaving.

"I love you," she nearly whispered. It was almost inaudible, but Lauryn heard her and it prompted a steady stream to cascade down her face.

"I love you too," Lauryn reciprocated. Right when she said it, Cammie picked up her hand and tentatively brought it to her lips. She kissed her knuckles and gently let go of it. The action nearly destroyed her. She wanted to kiss her lips, but felt like she would overstep her boundaries if she did. So, that would just have to suffice.

The gesture threatened to choke Lauryn up. She was in tears, but she wasn't bawling like the shorter girl was. Not yet, at least. She was on the borderline of a breakdown similar to Cammie's. Lauryn loved her so much, and there was so much love between the two of them. She couldn't really let her go that way, but she knew it was necessary. The instinct to reciprocate was overwhelming, so Lauryn stepped forward and pressed a kiss to Cammie's forehead. Her lips lingered against the space right between her eyebrows, but she moved away when she heard Cammie whimper quietly.

With red and puffy eyes, Cammie was finally allowed eye contact with Lauryn. She blinked away as soon as their eyes met. When she did, Cammie looked completely defeated. Cammie knew her time had officially run out. No more words were said. No more looks were exchanged. Nothing else happened between them at all. She turned away from Lauryn and walked out. As soon as she made it downstairs, she grabbed her still-drenched book bag and fled her house. She didn't care what Miguel said. Lately, it seemed like running away was the only way she'd been leaving their residence. She hadn't been there since the encounter with Cara. And now, she knew she wouldn't be going back for a while.

Lauryn felt lost. Whenever she'd broken up with people in the past, Cammie was the one who usually helped her get back on her feet. Of course she had Naomi, Diana, and Allie to turn to, but she liked Cammie's intuition and advice the most. But she couldn't talk to her. *She* was the one Lauryn had ended things with. Knowing that only caused more tears. Her pillow was sporting a nicely sized wet spot, but she couldn't stop. The reality of what she'd done hit her. Now Cammie was gone, and she'd never felt more alone.

»»»

Lauryn got on the bus quietly the next day. She kept her eyes straight ahead, careful not to let them stray over to Cammie's general area. While she used all of her self-control to just get to her seat, she was completely crestfallen. Tori jokingly told her that she looked like a lost puppy last night at dinner. Her expression probably hadn't changed much between then and now. Her outfit seemed to match her mood. Dressed in all black, she boarded the bus and immediately laid down.

Determined not to look in Cammie's direction, she decided to listen to music and look out of the window or *something* to keep her distracted. She used the flashlight on her phone to locate her headphones in her bag, then groaned when she realized she'd left them on the desk. She resumed her position laying down on the seat, just opting to try and go to sleep.

It was almost working, but the rumbling of the bus combined with the conversations heard all around her made it hard to find peace. She closed her eyes and tried to block everyone out. One conversation in particular made her perk up. "Cammie ... Aiden," was all she heard. She'd caught the tail end of whatever the person had said and decided to tune in.

"Yeah, I heard they were back together or something," she heard someone say. It kind of sounded like Drew.

"But isn't she gay now? I thought she was with that Laura girl or whatever her name is," another person countered. That sounded like Marielle.

"I thought so too, but I've seen her being all over him again," Drew recalled.

"Do they still have a thing?" Marielle questioned.

"I don't know. She probably has a thing with both of them. She's a slut," Drew laughed.

Lauryn's face burned with anger. Why the fuck were they saying those things about her girlfriend? She paused for a second to mentally correct herself. Cammie wasn't her girlfriend anymore. But that didn't mean she just had to sit around and let people slander her in her absence. Cammie was her friend before she was her girlfriend, and Lauryn would've defended any of them.

"*She is not*," Lauryn said pointedly as she sat up, turning around to face them. Her assumptions were correct. Marielle and Drew both looked at her like a deer in headlights. Fucking idiots.

"What?" Drew asked, looking at Marielle in confusion.

"Cammie isn't a slut, shut the fuck up," Lauryn snapped and turned back around, resuming her position laying down. She didn't get to stay there long. The bus pulled up in front of the school and Lauryn shot up, eager to separate herself from everyone else.

What the fuck was that all about? People degrading their peers and spreading rumors was a common factor in high school, and Lauryn was used to overhearing stupid comments. But Cammie had never been their topic. Lauryn wondered what provoked her to be theirs as she filed into the building.

Chapter 24

This had to have been one of the worst days *ever* for Lauryn. Because she'd spent nearly all of her previous evening crying her little heart out, she hadn't completed any of her homework assignments. She hadn't studied either, so she was pretty sure she bombed the pop quiz in her history class. And of all days, everyone seemed to choose *this* one to speak to her. Even people she didn't talk to on a regular basis seemed to want to make conversation with her. She had to try really hard not to be such an asshole to undeserving people. It was tedious.

"Dang, Lo. You look like you got hit by a bus," Diana teased when she saw Lauryn trudging into their anatomy class. She hadn't seen her all day. She was missing at lunch time. But unbeknownst to Diana and the rest of their group, Lauryn opted to eat lunch with her other classmates today - just to steer clear of Cammie.

"Thanks, Diana," Lauryn said curtly as she took her seat beside her. She slouched over the desk immediately in hopes of discouraging any attempts of conversation.

"Can I call you Regina George?" Diana continued.

"Diana," Lauryn groaned. "I'm really not in the fucking mood," she said simply. She knew Diana was only joking around, but it was pissing her off at the moment.

"What's wrong with you?" she questioned sadly. For a second, she thought it was because what she'd said had offended her. "You don't really look that bad. I was kidding."

Lauryn knew it was the truth, though. The bags under her eyes were a clear indication of her lack of sleep. She laid awake nearly all night, tortured by reliving everything about their painful breakup. She didn't bother doing her makeup or putting together a nice outfit. So her less-than-perfect skin was sporting all of its flaws, and she'd dressed herself in sweats at the last minute. Her mood wasn't very nice either. She'd been irritable and quiet all day. She probably did look like she'd been hit by a bus. She felt like it too.

"Nothing," Lauryn muttered.

"Cam is rubbing off on you," Diana rolled her eyes. She was used to hearing that bullshit response from the brown-eyed girl.

"Can we not talk about her right now?" Lauryn sighed as she buried her face into her hands.

That let Diana know there was seriously something wrong. Under most circumstances, Lauryn would jump at any opportunity to talk about Cammie. She would usually spend most of the period rambling dumb stuff about her to Diana.

"What the hell happened?" Diana demanded.

"Nothing," Lauryn said again, really not in the spirit to bring it up. It was still fresh. It was an open wound that she'd been trying to avoid all day.

"Girl," Diana deadpanned, wishing she would just come out with it at once.

"We broke up," Lauryn shared.

"What?! No!" Diana cried out, making everyone turn back to look at them.

"Yup," Lauryn nodded in a daze. "So how was your day?"

"Why?" Diana whined. "Who did it? You or her? What the hell, why?"

"I really don't want to talk about it, Diana..." Lauryn complained as she ran her hand through her hair in exasperation.

"It was you, wasn't it? What the hell?" Diana assumed as she stared at the side of Lauryn's head.

"Yes, okay. Now can you just drop it?" Lauryn requested flatly.

"Did she tell you?" Diana questioned.

"Tell me what?" Lauryn sighed.

"About everything all those people were saying?" Diana informed her. "Because if she told you and you broke up with her anyway then-"

"What people?" Lauryn frowned. She thought back to what she'd overheard on the bus. Wasn't that just a one-time thing?

"So she didn't tell you," Diana realized and rolled her eyes. She contemplated just telling Lauryn herself, although it wasn't her place. It was Cammie's job and she had the right to say it, but maybe if Diana did, it could salvage their relationship.

"Tell me what?" Lauryn grumbled, growing irritated at the fact that everyone seemed to know something about her girlfriend that she didn't. No - Her *friend*. Just Cammie. She really had to stop letting the G word slip. She wasn't anymore.

"She's kind of been getting a few looks and side-comments," Diana started out quietly, refraining from catching their teacher's attention.

"For what?" Lauryn probed.

"Well... People think she's been getting around with you while she's with Aiden," Diana shared tentatively.

"Why the fuck would they think that?" she scoffed.

"That's what he told everyone," Diana shrugged.

"So they think she's cheating on me with him?" Lauryn tried to understand.

"Well, no. That asshole told people she was fucking around with *you* while they were together. He made her seem like a hoe," Diana shrugged.

"But they broke up a long time ago..." Lauryn said flatly.

"Exactly. So it's all bullshit," Diana concluded.

"Well, that's fucked up. Why would he say that?" Lauryn asked angrily. Everything was just pissing her off more than usual today.

"I don't know," Diana shrugged.

The last thing Diana knew about Cammie's plans was that she was going to talk to Aiden. What happened between then and now was completely unknown to her. She had trouble filling in the blanks to figure out what caused their relationship's demise.

"I'm lost. What does that have anything to do with why we broke up?" Lauryn brought up, struggling to relate it to the two topics.

"She didn't tell you because she thought she could handle it herself or something. Cam thought she couldn't tell you," Diana offered. "So she just didn't talk to you at all."

"She's not stupid enough to think she can't talk to me about something like that, Diana. I think you're wrong about that. I would've fucking helped her. She knows that," Lauryn scoffed.

Trust was a major component of their relationship. Lauryn prided herself on how open and honest they usually were with each other. They always talked things through. It was one of the main reasons Lauryn and Cammie worked so well together. They had trust. If Cammie ever thought for a second that she couldn't share something with Lauryn, they weren't as well off as she was thinking.

"Okay," Diana relented. She knew she was correct. Cammie told Diana herself. That came straight from the source. But Cammie was obviously going through some mental lapses, so Diana decided to just let her fend for herself. If she ended up ruining everything in the process, so be it. Diana kept the rest of her explanation to herself. She could clearly see then that it was a lost cause.

Their conversation ended with that. Lauryn's mind was reeling. There was absolutely no way Cammie ever thought she couldn't talk to her. They talked about everything. Heavy subjects and lighthearted topics came and went like clockwork.

But maybe Diana was right. There was no doubt that the bullying thing was probably true, she had evidence from this morning. Lauryn just had trouble coming up with a reason why Cammie wouldn't tell her about it. She told her everything, or at least she *thought* she did. Lauryn was staring to second-guess a lot about their relationship.

Cammie was just wondering how it all got to this point. It was undoubtedly her fault, but why had she done all of that? She should've just told her. Who knows, maybe Lauryn could've solved everything from the beginning and they'd still be going strong right now. But she didn't. She kept everything concealed and waited until it all blew up in her face. By the time she was ready to share her perspective, Lauryn was done with her. She never wanted her to be done with her. They'd just gotten started, and she was done already. She'd ruined everything.

Cammie doubled over and buried her face in her arms. She thought that by now, she would've cried herself dry. But tears were incessant. They never stopped, they were just on hold. She pulled herself together long enough to complete her assignments, then she started thinking again and the waterworks started back up with it. It was a cycle. She was a mess today.

And on top of that, she hadn't seen Lauryn at all. The tables had truly turned. Now, it was Lauryn skipping lunch periods and missing out on going to their meet up spots. It was Cammie going to their stops with a glint of hope, and it was Cammie that kept getting crushed when she didn't show up. It was Cammie sending out ignored texts to Lauryn and getting sent to voicemail when she called. It was Cammie that couldn't seem to come in contact with her, no matter how hard she tried.

221

There was a small reminder that Lauryn loved her, though. She thought back to the actual break up. It wasn't vicious. It wasn't brutal. It might've felt that way in the moment, but it wasn't. Lauryn was so gentle with her. She held her while she cried and kissed her face before she left. There was no yelling or storming out. It was relatively stable.

But Cammie wished Lauryn would've cursed her out or something, so she could blame the breakup on impulse. She wished there had been yelling and screaming, so she could say they'd gotten caught up in the moment. All she wanted was an excuse for Lauryn, so Cammie could say that she didn't mean what she said. She wished it went any other way than the way it did, because with the way it actually happened, it let her know how much Lauryn had made up her mind. Lauryn *actually* wanted it. Her calm demeanor was a testament to that. And that information hurt Cammie more than anything.

Despite the fact that she understood Lauryn's logic and somewhat agreed with it, Cammie really wished they had an alternative. Breaking up probably wouldn't solve anything. It would just hurt. Lauryn let her down so softly, then left her to crash and burn alone. Cammie wasn't a fan of exaggerations, but she really did think that she was suffering from a broken heart. Breaking up with Aiden did not feel this way. It was completely painless, and kind of a relief. But when Lauryn did it, everything hurt. There was a constant dull aching in her chest. She wore a permanent frown. Her movements were slow and she had no drive to do anything. Maybe she was depressed. Cammie usually hated when people self-diagnosed themselves with those things, but that was probably the only option for this state.

Lauryn was a perfect copy. She was better at holding everything in. For Lauryn, her room was the only place she allowed herself to break down. Her pillow held all of her tears, which was disgusting, but it did. Neither one of them found a solace in anything. Lauryn was contemplating just getting back together with her to make the pain go away. The sole purpose of breaking up was to sort their shit out individually, but all they had been doing was having separate pity parties.

The party continued as soon as she got home. Lauryn could barely get into her house good before the tears threatened to spill. She tripped going up the stairs because her blurry vision made her miscalculate where the actual step was. When she fell, she just stayed there, feeling like there was no reason to rise again. So she just hunched over, hugging her knees to her chest in the middle of the stairs. Her arms folded on the stair above her and she just cried that way. It felt like hours. Everything was falling apart. It was only day one of their breakup, but Lauryn had already cried more than she had in the past six months. She wasn't typically much of a crier.

She stayed bowed over the stairs until she felt a hand on her shoulder. "Lauryn..." Cara called to her softly, her voice laced with concern and sympathy.

Lauryn lifted up for a second to see her mother, then she ducked back into her arms. Unexpectedly, Lauryn felt Cara rubbing her back in slow, soothing motions. The older woman took a seat beside her and rubbed her back until Lauryn's whimpers were less consecutive.

"What happened?" Cara asked when Lauryn got particularly quiet.

"Wouldn't you like to know," Lauryn said bitterly. Despite the fact that she was consoling her, she couldn't find any compassion towards her mother.

"Don't be that way," Cara warned as her hand slowed.

"Sorry..." Lauryn mumbled, acknowledging how rude that was. "I'm just..." she trailed, feeling awkward disclosing her problems to her mother. She never really had before.

"You can tell me," Cara encouraged her with a soft smile.

"It's Cammie..." Lauryn hinted, figuring Cara would get up and leave right then and there.

"What about her?" Cara asked encouragingly.

"We... We broke up," Lauryn admitted hesitantly. While she was expecting her mom to jump with joy, she stayed still. She remained silent.

"I'm sorry," Cara frowned, actually a little disheartened by the fact.

"Yeah..." Lauryn shrugged.

"You know, for the longest time... I was just hoping you'd snap out of this phase and find yourself a nice boy to associate yourself with..." Cara shared the obvious, and Lauryn scoffed. She didn't need this shit now.

"Don't... Can you please just-" Lauryn requested, but Cara interrupted her.

"Let me finish," she pleaded. She was finally trying to take Miguel's advice to mend things with her daughter, if only she would let her.

"Okay?" Lauryn relented.

"When I first saw you two together..." Cara started, gauging Lauryn's reaction to this new direction. She didn't brazenly discourage it, so she continued. "I was upset. I was mad, even. I guess I always knew... But it was hard to get used to. When I saw what I saw that day... It made it all real. It was too much. I was being childish... And I'm sorry," Cara apologized.

Lauryn didn't know what to say. Was she actually apologizing? Was it sincere or was it just spurred on by guilt from seeing her cry? She didn't have the answer. And she didn't say anything. She just looked at her mother, waiting for her to continue. And she did without any promotion.

"That girl- Uh - *Cammie* came along and completely swept you off of your feet. It's obvious now. I'd never seen you so happy. And I've never seen you like this," Cara pointed out as she gestured to Lauryn's current state. "It's clear how much you care about her-"

"I love her," Lauryn interrupted. She said it mostly to herself, but to Cara as well.

"Yes... And I can tell that she thinks she does, too-" Cara attempted to continue, but Lauryn cut her off again.

"I love her so much," Lauryn choked out as another round of tears started up.

"Do you?" Cara asked, knowing just how real a first love could seem. She was genuinely under the impression that Lauryn was simply infatuated with Cammie. Miguel told her all about the way they ended up being together - with the journal and all. But it only drove Cara to believe that Lauryn was reciprocating those feelings based on obligation. She didn't really love her.

"*Yes*," Lauryn cried. She resumed her position with her face buried in her arms as she just completely allowed herself to feel it all. Expressing grief this way was foreign, but talking about it only made it worse.

Cara watched her fall apart and wisely chose not to bring up what she was thinking. In hopes that Lauryn would come to her senses and figure it out soon enough, she dropped it. Their fragile mother-daughter relationship was on its last leg, but she offered some words to appease it.

223

"I can see now how much she means to you. If it all works out... Well, then, I guess I'll just have to be alright with that. I was ignoring it, but anyone can see how happy she makes you. And she's a good girl. What's meant to be will be, mija. There's always a rainbow after the rain," Cara expressed in conclusion.

"No, there's a sunset," Lauryn muttered. The very mention of it made her sob again. Cammie was involved in everything.

"What?" Cara questioned, not catching on to Lauryn's reference. It was *their* thing. Of course she wouldn't know.

"It was something Cammie always used to- Never mind," Lauryn shook her head. She didn't want to share. That was their thing. Even if it was over now, sunsets would forever carry Cammie's essence.

"Well... Alright," Cara brushed it off. "Why don't you get up now?"

Lauryn surprised herself and her mother when she wrapped her arms around her. She enveloped Cara into a surprisingly tight hug, which caught both of them off guard. Neither of them could remember the last time they'd hugged - *really* hugged. It was always a quick side-hug that didn't really mean anything. They hadn't hugged this way in forever. It was nice.

When she pulled away, Cara kissed her forehead. She grasped her shoulder gently and hugged her again before urging her to go upstairs and clean herself up. Lauryn followed her advice and found herself in the bathroom. She looked at her reflection and thought back on the conversation with her mom. 'What's meant to be, will be' lingered in the back of her mind.

In regards to how fast and hard she'd fallen for Cammie in such a short period of time, Lauryn was willing to bet that they *were* meant to be. This all stemmed from a communication issue. All they needed to do was to sit down and actually fucking talk to one another. They needed to do it without Lauryn being immature and storming out. They needed to do it without Cammie getting overwhelmed and not being able to speak her mind. They needed to do it without any hostility. They needed to have an open mind and a clear heart. Perhaps that was what Lauryn meant when she'd broken up with her. Only now, it was definitive.

»»»

Awkward. No matter how much Lauryn wanted to approach Cammie to have that much-needed conversation, she couldn't. Everything was awkward. The first time she tried to come to her, Cammie just smiled and excused herself. Her motives weren't the same as before. She was just too nervous to make conversation, and Lauryn picked up on that. The second attempt was less direct. Lauryn waved at her to get her attention during class. She got it for a split second, then Cammie got called to answer a question, foiling Lauryn's plan.

She couldn't help staring at Cammie, though. The depth of Cammie's words always left her content. The articulate manner in which she delivered her answer to the teacher's question only made Lauryn want her even more. That should be her girlfriend. She should be able to call her that again. But it just wasn't time yet.

Forced to accept the fact that Cammie wasn't ready to talk, Lauryn had to resort to just stealing glances. While Lauryn was usually met with tender eyes that oozed affection when she turned around, all she saw now was the side of Cammie's head. Whenever Cammie looked over at Lauryn, all she saw was the hair that shielded her face from view. Each time one looked, the other looked away. But their connection was felt without locking eyes. They just knew when the other was looking at them. It drew their attention unlike anything else. They were just kind of ignoring it for now.

»»»

Both girls were presented with the chance to speak the next day. They accidentally crossed paths in the hallway. Lauryn hadn't directly heard her favorite voice in over two days. Eager to have some type of interaction with her other than the not-so-subtle staring, she spoke to her.

"Hey," Lauryn waved slightly, trying to determine what this encounter would entail.

"Hi," Cammie responded, almost eagerly.

"How are you?" Lauryn asked casually, hugging her books to her chest.

"I'm okay... You?" Cammie asked, going for as natural as possible.

"I've been better," Lauryn answered honestly, not bothering to sugar-coat anything. She'd been feeling terrible, much like the girl in front of her.

"Oh, yeah. Same," Cammie nodded.

"I miss you," Lauryn blurted out before she got the chance to change her mind.

"I miss you too," Cammie agreed quickly, as if she was getting that off of her chest.

"That makes me feel a little better," Lauryn shared as her lips formed a ghost of a smile.

"I'm glad," Cammie offered a smile as well. "It makes me feel better too-"

The warning bell blared through the intercom, scaring both girls and interrupting Cammie. Neither of them made a move to leave, though. It was funny to think of how pretentious Cammie used to be when it came to being tardy. Now, what time she got to class was of none of her concern. The shift was alarming, but she didn't care much about that either.

"I'll see you around," Lauryn bid her goodbye politely and pulled her into a friendly side-hug.

Cammie wanted to say more, just to be in her presence. But she didn't. The small conversation they shared was enough for her. A wide smile spread across her face when she saw Lauryn walking away from her. It was like she was back to her crushing days, when she'd obsess over minuscule things like that and gush about it in her journal later on. But of course, she wouldn't. Back then compared to now, this was nothing worth obsessing over. In fact, it was kind of sad that they were back to this point. But on the bright side, at least they were talking now. Sort of.

»»»

Three days passed since their last encounter. Cammie hadn't seen much of Lauryn and vice versa. Neither girls were making an attempt to make amends. They were letting the breakup run its course. Things weren't nearly as hostile anymore. They were just being cordial to each other. Cammie had just started getting used to the emptiness she constantly felt. It was like before they dated, but worse. Nothing filled the void Lauryn left. Writing, singing, playing guitar, nor sleeping provided a solace. She was constantly sad. Days passed with a few jokes cracked and a couple of smiles, but nothing was genuine. Lauryn was really the only thing that made her

225

happy, but she didn't have her anymore. She was just getting by and going with the flow.

Lauryn was going through the same sense of withdrawals. Everything she used to enjoy doing with Cammie didn't feel right anymore. She never went into the stairwell, because what was once hers had become theirs. She hadn't eaten her mother's pancakes, because it provoked memories of Cammie as well. She wouldn't even look towards a window around nightfall due to the fact that Cammie nearly owned everything relating to the phenomenon. Each aspect of her life she once enjoyed became tainted with Cammie's essence, and despite her endeavors, she couldn't get away from her.

The breakup put Naomi, Diana, and Allie in very awkward positions. Naomi warned them in private that Cammie and Lauryn dating would ultimately have some repercussions, but she had no idea how right she was. To them, it felt like they had to choose sides. They empathized with both ends of the problem, yet understood why they couldn't meet in the middle. Sick of all of the feuding, Naomi strove to be a catalyst.

"We have to do something," Naomi sighed as she witnessed Cammie entering the cafeteria sullenly.

"I know... I was just thinking that," Allie nodded. While Naomi was vouching for team Lauryn and Diana was leaning more towards team Cammie, Allie had trouble distinguishing between the two. Relatively, they both were in the wrong. Allie couldn't justify one side any more than the other.

"My poor heart is breaking," Diana frowned as she animatedly wiped a fake tear.

"Lauryn won't even eat with us," Naomi pointed out. She literally pointed, because Lauryn was in the process of sitting down at a table halfway across the cafeteria.

"We're all being replaced," Diana joked.

"Kind of..." Allie mumbled. "So we need a plan."

"What are we gonna do?" Naomi frowned.

"We can lock them in the same room and force them to talk," Diana suggested.

"What?" Allie laughed. That was probably out of the question. Knowing them and how stubborn they were, they'd probably just stay in their respective corners until someone let them out.

"Well, that's how animals mate," Diana shrugged. "They've gotta get all that frustration and tension out somehow..."

"I don't really think that's how that works, Diana... But okay," Naomi giggled. She kept the fact that they'd already gotten a little busy to herself. Cammie was right. If Diana knew, she'd never let them hear the end of it. She was already bad and she didn't even know.

"Dang, she's already coming. We'll talk about it later though," Allie informed them as she caught sight of a desolate Cammie striding over to them with her journal in hand.

"Yeah. Later," Diana nodded.

"Hey," Cammie greeted them all unenthusiastically.

"Feeling any better?" Allie asked as she placed a hand on her shoulder.

"I guess. Have you ever dealt with this?" Cammie sighed.

"Dealt with what?" Diana questioned.

226

"It's like, nothing helps. Everything reminds you of them. And you're sad all the time because they're never there the way they used to be..." she elaborated.

"Kind of. When I broke up with Aaron sophomore year, I thought it was the end of the world," Naomi nodded, able to identify with Cammie. "Do you even remember him?"

"Yeah. You were so cute," Allie nodded.

"Well, I don't even think about him anymore. I never thought I'd be able to say that, considering how close we used to be and how much I cared about him. It's weird looking back on it," Naomi reflected out loud.

"You get over people," Diana acknowledged, thinking back on her similar experiences.

"Yeah. So Cam," Naomi turned to Cammie specifically. "It'll get better. It may take a while, but you get over people... Like Diana said."

Cammie listened and nodded, letting their words resonate with her. For about two seconds. Then she pushed it away. Cammie didn't want to get over it. All she wanted was to take Lauryn into her arms, kiss her face, and tell her how much she loved her. She didn't view things as though they were some obstacle to get over and eventually forget about. She wanted to fix it and move on, making things better than they were before. *That's* what she wanted. So Naomi's advice didn't help anything.

"Yeah... Thanks," Cammie tried to smile, but it just didn't work out. She wasn't happy. Things weren't looking up either.

"Are you okay?" Naomi asked worriedly.

"You look like you're about to cry again," Diana said sympathetically.

"I'm okay," Cammie brushed off their concern.

"Here," Allie said knowingly, handing out a few paper towels. The tears would spill soon. She knew they would, based on the way Cammie kept blinking and swallowing.

"Are you sure?" Naomi frowned.

"Yeah. I'm just gonna go get some fresh air," Cammie excused herself, already on her way out.

She pushed through the doors, then found herself outside. Her skin was immediately bathed in the sunlight. She squinted from the brightness and brought her hand up to shield her eyes. Skipping crossed her mind, but there was nowhere she could go and be completely isolated - until she thought of the one place she knew that she probably would be.

Her feet led her off of school grounds before she had the chance to stop herself. Who was she nowadays? As she stealthily escaped the school campus, she took into account what she was actually doing. Three months ago, she would've never done this. She was in changing in ways that didn't contribute to her character. The reputation she'd worked so hard to maintain over the years was surely diminishing. No one saw her as the quiet, smart, funny girl anymore. Well, no one ever really thought she was funny except for Lauryn. But because of Aiden, they all thought she was promiscuous and shady. Her friends probably thought she was a Manipulative little liar. Those words had never been associated with her before.

And now she was skipping and not doing her assignments. Undoubtedly, her grades were dropping. The last time she'd actually gone home and completed each of her homework assignments was too long ago to recall. Studying was rare, unless she was studying Lauryn's features. Freaking Lauryn. In Cammie's mind, she was the greatest factor in her life. But was it possible that she was a negative element? Things were going just swell before she started really getting involved with her. Cammie looked back on it all.

Since Lauryn, there had been ruptured relationships, distance between the relationships she salvaged, dropping grades, less respect, and a hazy logic. Maybe Lauryn wasn't as good for her as Cammie had initially been thinking. With time away, she realized how badly she was turning out. Nothing was severe or threatening, but it was happening. She was glad she took notice of it before something really bad happened. Maybe she needed to just reel things in and screw her head on straight. Was that what Lauryn meant by they both had some things to figure out? Possibly.

Cammie tuned into her surroundings when she approached the park. She tried to recall the way Lauryn pulled her along, but couldn't. During the time they were walking, Cammie was lost in her thoughts. It was like she just blinked, and there they were. A little bit lost, Cammie found herself wandering around the outskirts of the park. There was some other entrance, she knew that much. But where was it?

For a few more minutes, she searched for it. She'd nearly circled the fence when she saw a small opening. It was only big enough for animals to get through, so clearly that wasn't her destination. With a groan, she resumed walking. She desperately tried to recall where the hell Lauryn had gotten in at. It was true that she stared at her entirely too much. She remembered the way she watched her that night. Why was she even going here? Obviously she wanted to be alone, but why did she come *here*? This spot held one of her most cherished memories with the green-eyed girl. Their first time was here, as strange as it was.

The entrance was relatively close. This terrain was familiar to her. She remembered walking up the hill. It was all coming back to her now. She remembered the way she couldn't avert her eyes when Lauryn's muscles flexed as she moved the branch out of the way. It sufficiently hid this secret entrance. Cammie hoped that this was it. She grasped the branch, which didn't budge at first. It took all of her strength to hold it back long enough to slip by it. God, was she weak.

Cammie exhaled in relief when she recognized the spot, finally. Lauryn's little book bag was lodged in the bush, just like it was the last time. Cammie clambered over to retrieve it, then she took out the blanket. That blanket was special and all, but they should probably wash it. There was no telling what was on it.

Just for good measure, Cammie flipped it onto the other side. Once it was evenly spread out, she took a seat on it. Through the outlook, she gazed at the passing wayfarers, the athletic jogger that seemed to be fitting exercise into everyone's undoubtedly busy schedule, the mother pushing the stroller, gawking down at the little person exploring the new world around them, the man taking his dog for a walk, seemingly having no fret or concern for the time of day. All of those people crossed paths leisurely.

Cammie watched all of them, wondering what was going on in their life to make them so at ease. They had no obvious shortcomings or problems bothering them. No clear mental strife was present in their demeanors. For a second, she was envious. She wished she could revert back to her usual happy and lighthearted ways, but she couldn't bring herself to that point just yet.

As a form of healthy and more level-headed reflection, she took out her pen and began writing everything she'd come to terms with earlier in her journal. Her stance on the situation seemed to shift. From this point of view, she could see things for how they were and how they would most likely turn out. It wasn't a totally bad connotation, but it could easily end up for the worst. Cammie scrawled away in her journal, the way she'd gotten back into the habit of doing. It wasn't necessarily a happy moment, but she was content as she was scribbling all of her jumbled thoughts. The nice, quiet environment of Lauryn's secret spot made her feel relaxed.

Opening her journal and flipping it back a few pages, she started to skim over her writing. Boy, was she a cynical being. The stuff in there recently was brutal. If it wasn't her that wrote it, she would've been a little alarmed at the amount of pessimism. It wasn't rocket science, anyone could see just how hard she was taking it all - but it was still surprising to know that all of those harsh words and perspectives came from her.

The serenity the secluded area offered was disturbed by a sudden movement from her peripheral vision. Cammie heard rustling in the bushes and her scalp prickled in fear. What if it was a huge mutt, ready to maul her? Or a bear? What if it could sense her fear? Or what if it was some type of pedophile? Would her screams of peril be heard from all the way over here? She watched the entrance warily, ready to run if it was something threatening. The figure that emerged from the scrubs wasn't threatening at all. It was none other than the girl that had been causing all of her inner turmoil. The two of them locked eyes and Lauryn froze. There was a bit of an awkward silence before Cammie decided to say something.

"Lauryn?"

Chapter 25

"Cammie?" Lauryn squeaked in response, just as surprised to see her as Cammie was.

Destiny had a funny way of working out in the universe. She'd come here to be alone, only to find the very cause of her inner turmoil sitting right there. It was like their time had run out, forcing the two to be together by some miraculous twist of fate. And what were the odds? Cammie skipped school just like Lauryn had. Neither had seriously done it before, and the one time they did, they ended up in the same place. It was serendipitous.

"Hi..." Cammie greeted her, already feeling awkward. She closed her journal timidly and made a move to stand up, suddenly hit with the sense that she was intruding.

"Uh, what's up?" Lauryn said cautiously, slowly making her way over to Cammie. Her confusion was ill-disguised. Although she was ecstatic to see Cammie here, her face betrayed her emotions. Cammie gathered that she was upset with her for being here, but it was quite the contrary.

"Nothing. I just came here to... I don't know, actually. I guess I just kind of ended up here... But I'll go," Cammie excused herself quickly. The awkwardness between them was killing her.

Lauryn watched her scramble to get up in amusement. She was so cute when she was nervous. Lauryn looked on as Cammie dropped her journal in the process of standing up. When she bent over to pick it up, her phone slipped out of her pocket. While picking up her phone and the journal, she refused to look up at Lauryn. The older girl just decided to let her finish before saying anything.

"Camz, you don't have to go anywhere," Lauryn said softly. A small laugh escaped her lips at Cammie's flustered antics.

"No, this is your spot. I'm not even supposed to - I don't even know why I'm here," Cammie shook her head and insisted on leaving. If she would've taken the time to look at Lauryn, just once, she would've seen the tender expression she wore. It would've been easy to tell that she didn't want her to leave at all.

Lauryn crossed her arms and leaned against the tree branch, waiting for Cammie to face her. Cammie was too busy looking for an alternate escape route, seeing how Lauryn was blocking the only one she knew of. Crawling out through the little outlook in the bushes crossed her mind, but that would just make her look stupid. Taking her clumsiness into consideration, she'd probably fall. She could always ask her to move, but that would probably be rude. Why wasn't teleportation a thing yet?

"Sorry," Cammie said meekly, moving towards the exit and just hoping she'd move on her own.

"What are you sorry for?" Lauryn questioned. "If I remember correctly, this is *our* spot now. Just like the staircase," she pointed out.

"Oh," Cammie mumbled. She looked up at Lauryn, but was unable to read her as well as she hoped.

"You have the right to be here just as much as I do," Lauryn smiled. The smile calmed Cammie's nerves a little bit. Maybe this wouldn't go so badly after all.

"I guess," Cammie shrugged, despite the fact that she didn't really agree much.

"Can you come here?" Lauryn requested evasively. Disregarding the conflicted way she felt about her now, she wanted her affection. She craved it. She opened her arms wide and looked at her expectantly.

Cammie didn't argue, but instead found herself moving towards Lauryn without hesitation. Lauryn's grin only widened when she saw Cammie coming.

Cammie immediately closed the space between them. Small arms instinctively wrapped around Lauryn's body and their bodies fit perfectly together. Cammie nuzzled her face into her neck and inhaled the scent she'd been missing so much. Lauryn did the same, really taking the time to appreciate this hug. Thin fingers stroked Cammie's back slowly and she tried to recall the last time the two of them had been this close. The tension and awkwardness between the two girls faded with every second spent in the other's arms. Being in Lauryn's arms felt like home, and she was definitely homesick.

"God, I've missed you," Lauryn said against Cammie's hair. The confession wasn't like last time, blurted out just for the sake of saying something. This time, it was genuine. She really wanted Cammie to know it.

"I missed you too," Cammie seconded almost instantly. Her words were spoken against Lauryn's skin, and she saw goosebumps appear from it.

"I missed you so much," Lauryn sighed happily, just before kissing her cheek. The threat of overstepping boundaries was nonexistent. She missed her and she deemed it the appropriate time express it. Her hand circled Cammie's back in slow motions, reveling in the feeling of it like she used to.

It lasted for a long time, but it wasn't awkward. The girls felt a sense of rejuvenation during their hug and could've kept it going for a little bit longer, but Cammie was the first to pull away. She pulled back and looked at the taller girl, smiling subconsciously as she stared. Cammie wasn't naïve enough to think that everything was fixed now based on a simple hug, but it sure felt like things were infinitely better already.

"I did too," Cammie shared truthfully. In her mind, Lauryn would never be able to comprehend just how much she did. It was somewhat like torture having to be without her. Relying and depending on people had never been Cammie's goal, but there was no doubt that Lauryn was her crutch.

"Let's sit down?" Lauryn offered as she gestured over to the blanket. Cammie nodded and took the few steps over there. When she sat down, she sat with her legs crossed. Lauryn crouched down next to her and sat with her legs outstretched.

"How are you?" Cammie asked quietly.

"I'm okay," Lauryn shrugged. There had definitely been happier times, but things weren't just *terrible* anymore. "You?"

"I'm alright..." Cammie trailed off, and Lauryn instantly knew she was holding her tongue about something. She saw straight through her demeanor. All of Cammie's facades were easily distinguishable.

"Are you really?" she asked intuitively.

"Yeah," Cammie answered a little too quickly for Lauryn's taste.

"You know, you can tell me if you aren't..." Lauryn hinted, brushing her leg softly with her fingertips. "You can still talk to me."

Cammie bit her lip and hesitantly looked up at her. Could she really tell her? She feared that if she divulged her feelings too soon, Lauryn would get awkward and distant again. On the other hand, she was nervous about finally telling Lauryn and having her resent her for keeping it from her all this time. But isn't that what caused all of this to happen? One way or another, she had to find out. Holding it inside was making her go crazy. She had to get it off of her chest. If she stayed cautious about everything, she'd never find her answers. With that in mind, Cammie suddenly wasn't so scared of the unknown. Albeit, it seemed to be a lose-lose situation.

"Okay," Cammie exhaled. "Brace yourself... It's a lot."

"That's okay," Lauryn encouraged her. Her hand rested on Cammie's knee, then it started caressing her thigh slowly. Her motives weren't sexual, it was an attempt to calm and comfort Cammie. It was working.

"No, really... It's a long story," Cammie laughed lightly, already feeling more at ease.

"Take a look at where we are right now. We've got nothing but time, baby," Lauryn countered gently.

Cammie ignored the way her heart skipped a beat at the name. Lauryn called her baby so effortlessly. The name fell from her lips without a care, and it gave Cammie heart troubles. Whatever, though. It was probably just a little slip up. Cammie shook her head and mentally told herself not to look too deep into it, to avoid setting herself up again. If she took another fall, there was no guarantee she'd get up the next time.

"I've been sad," Cammie stated the obvious. She was going to say heartbroken, but didn't feel like being dramatic.

"Yeah, me too," Lauryn agreed.

"No, like... Really sad. I don't think I've cried this much in my entire life," Cammie admitted.

Lauryn felt a little bit disheartened at that fact, although she exhibited the same behavior. It hurt to know that she was the cause of the beautiful girl's tears, but they both had their fair share in it. "Me neither."

"But I mean even before you..." she trailed off, unwilling to say it. She felt like if she said the words 'broke up', it would make it more real. "You know. It was bad. It didn't really get better. I just kind of gloss over it and don't think about it as much. That's probably why I'm not crying right now," Cammie shared.

"Was it that bad for you too?" Lauryn questioned, regrettably able to identify with everything she was saying. She wasn't catching on to what Cammie was trying to allude to.

Cammie nodded subtly. "Yeah. Whenever I thought about it, my chest *actually* hurt."

"Why was it?" Lauryn frowned.

"You broke up with me..." Cammie deadpanned.

"I know that..." Lauryn huffed. "But I mean why was it affecting you so much? To the point that you felt it physically?" she elaborated.

"Because it was kind of like you didn't let me get a word in. I wanted to tell you everything but you just kept shutting me out. I feel like if you would've just listened to me, we could've avoided it. It made me feel like crap knowing that I couldn't get through to you," Cammie trailed off quietly, feeling a little awkward about sharing her point of view.

"I know," Lauryn acknowledged. "And I'm sorry... But you can tell me now? If you want?" she proposed. After coming to terms and finding a relatively easy solution, Lauryn was ready to get the full story. Miscommunication would no longer be an issue. They were going to talk things out right here, right now. Fate had put them in the same place, at the same time, completely alone, just for that reason.

"Are you sure? Do you even care?" Cammie asked. She winced at the way it came out. It was a little bit harsher than intended.

"Um... Yeah?" Lauryn scoffed.

"I just meant... You wouldn't let me tell you last time. You *said* you didn't care," Cammie remembered desolately, the memory still fresh. Still painful.

"I was mad. I didn't really mean that. Of course I cared, Camz," Lauryn mumbled, feeling a little guilty about what she'd said.

"It didn't seem like it," Cammie shrugged. As many times as she relived their breakup, every word exchanged between them was almost etched into her memory. She could easily recall every emotion felt in the moment. Lauryn hadn't said she didn't care flippantly. It was like she really wanted Cammie to leave her the fuck alone. Despite the way she may deny it, Cammie knew she most likely meant it at the time.

"Well, I promise you that I care now. Please tell me," Lauryn said seriously. In an attempt to make Cammie grasp her seriousness, she placed her hand on top of hers.

Her touch sent a chill down Cammie's spine. Their eyes met, and the energy between them shifted. Lauryn's gaze settled on Cammie's lips, and hers were parted as she stared at Lauryn's. They both had the same thought, but Cammie couldn't succumb to it. Not this soon. She cleared her throat and sheepishly removed her hand. Kissing would distract her from trying to tell Lauryn everything.

"So... If you're okay with it... I want to tell you now," Cammie said.

"I'm all ears," Lauryn smiled, regardless of that awkward moment. The pull she felt towards her was ridiculous. It was hard to sit still while Cammie was in such close proximity. But she was actually willing to listen to her this time, *really* listen to her. Her anger had gotten the best of her both times before, so she'd cut her off and walked out. And the last time, her impulses led her to break up with her. So now, completely reigning in all self-control and temperamental issues, she sat there patiently and waited for Cammie to begin.

"People have been saying things. And looking. It doesn't sound like a big deal, but it is to me because I don't know how to deal with it. I thought it was because we were dating and I thought that if I wasn't around you as much, they would leave me alone. I'll admit, I was being stupid and inconsiderate, but I honestly thought you didn't care. So I started being around Aiden a lot more in the halls because I wanted people to see me with him instead of with you... I thought it would work, but it didn't really... But I kept doing it because it kept getting a little better. And it was all for no reason, because the real reason everyone was being so mean wasn't because of you - well, it kind of was... But not really," Cammie rambled without looking up at her, but she slowly met her eyes.

Lauryn's expression was unreadable. Her defensive stance had clearly resolved, but as Cammie looked at her, she couldn't tell what she was thinking at all. She couldn't perceive anything currently. She twiddled her thumbs nervously. Lauryn was actually giving her a chance to speak, so she took the opportunity to continue.

"I didn't know why everyone was treating me that way and I talked to Brandon because I thought it all started with him, but it wasn't. He told me it was Aiden... He spread something really stupid about how I apparently cheated on him with you or something... Which actually explains a lot... And what you saw that day was me coming to him about it because I was so sick of everything," Cammie rushed, then she took a deep breath. She'd never said that many words in so little time in her life.

"Why didn't you tell me?" Lauryn frowned. Mentally, she was going over the things Diana tried to tell her. Diana was right.

"Because I thought I could deal with it by myself. I didn't want you to worry about what was going on with me because you have your own problems to deal with," Cammie expressed.

"We could've sorted it out together..." Lauryn offered sadly. It pained her to just now hear of everything Cammie was going through. Suddenly, everything that'd been going on with them was justifiable. She wasn't nearly as mad or annoyed with her as before.

"I wanted to ignore it," Cammie admitted. "But I couldn't."

"You really shouldn't let their bullshit affect you, babe-" Lauryn began, but Cammie shook her head.

"And I knew you'd say something like that. I just wanted to keep it to myself. I didn't feel like it mattered. At first, it really wasn't that big of a deal. I kind of went home and cried about it and I thought it would just blow over... But then it all spiraled out of control. I'm sorry," Cammie concluded her explanation with a big sigh.

"It's okay," Lauryn said immediately. Everything was a huge misunderstanding. It wasn't about Cara at all, thankfully. "I missed you a lot," she admitted for the third time.

"I missed you too," Cammie seconded. That much was true. She hated the way she spent so much time with someone who didn't even deserve a second glance. Time that should've been spent with Lauryn, at that. "And I'm sorry."

"Stop apologizing," Lauryn admonished her softly.

"But I was being so stupid," Cammie rolled her eyes at herself. Where was her mind? How could she have thought that plan would've possibly worked out in her favor?

"I agree," Lauryn laughed. "But if you're sorry, then I'm sorry."

"What would you have to be sorry for? You literally didn't do anything at all," Cammie looked at her sideways.

"No," Lauryn shook her head. "I didn't listen to you. All of this could've been avoided if I just pulled my head out of my ass for a second and heard what you had to say. But I didn't. Now that I think about it, I was really being a bitch. So for that, I'm sorry."

"You weren't being a bitch. You were entitled to all of that," Cammie countered.

"No I wasn't. It was fucked up. Don't make excuses for me," Lauryn disagreed.

"Okay," Cammie relented. Her mindset and opinion about it didn't change, but she wasn't going to argue. She was never mad at Lauryn. She just wished she would listen to her. But it was okay that she didn't. She didn't deserve to be listened to after what she did.

"Cammie," Lauryn called to her softly.

"Hm?" she hummed in response.

"I love you," Lauryn reminded her, just because she hadn't said it in a while.

Cammie faced her with an expression Lauryn would never forget. It was like she was overjoyed to hear that, even though it wasn't for the first time. Her eyes widened a bit and her lips formed a smile. It was a genuine expression Lauryn hadn't seen in about two weeks. All of her other smiles were forced, but this adorable one was real indeed. A few seconds passed, and you would've thought Lauryn had told Cammie she'd won the lottery or something.

"I love you, too," she declared giddily.

"Why are you smiling so hard?" Lauryn asked with a smile of her own.

"Because I thought you didn't anymore," Cammie shrugged. "Hearing you say it again just... I don't know. I'm happy."

"What?" Lauryn remarked incredulously. "No... I could never - Why would you think that? I love you a lot... I even told my mom," she mumbled.

"You told her what?" Cammie asked as she looked at her.

"I told her that I loved you," Lauryn said clearly.

"*You did*?" Cammie gasped.

"Yeah. We had a talk... Everything's okay now," Lauryn shrugged, not too eager to divulge anything more about it.

"What did she say?" Cammie probed. She'd been telling Lauryn to talk to her mother for a while now, and she finally had.

"She said she knew already... And she reiterated everything *I* already knew about how she felt about it initially," Lauryn paused, and Cammie thought she was finished.

"Oh," Cammie frowned. That wasn't much progress at all. The goal was to fix everything, not open old wounds.

"No, but then she kind of told me how she came to terms with everything... I was kind of in the middle of a breakdown during it, so I guess *that* told her how much I cared about you. She recognized my feelings... And your feelings... And she didn't seem too eager or happy about it... But she did say she would be okay with it," Lauryn explained in full.

"She's okay with it...?" Cammie repeated, hesitant to believe it. Lauryn only nodded. "Really?"

"Yeah. It's not like we can make out in front of her or anything," Lauryn laughed. "But she's not completely against it anymore. I think it's more of a mutual ignoring than acceptance..."

"That's a little progress," Cammie shrugged.

"Yeah. But I think it'll get better, Camz," Lauryn nodded.

"It already has," Cammie said as she cracked a smile. Then she yawned.

"Yeah," Lauryn grinned widely. The older girl wrapped her arm around Cammie's waist and pulled her into her.

Cammie's head rested on her shoulder and her hand wandered around to clasp over Lauryn's. Lauryn pressed a sweet kiss to her forehead and leaned into her slightly.

"I missed this so much," Cammie admitted. "Eight days is too long."

"Tell me about it," Lauryn agreed. She smiled subconsciously at the fact that Cammie had been counting. It made her feel less weird about doing it herself.

Cammie leaned back enough to hold Lauryn's gaze. Her eyes fell to her lips, which she had been longing to kiss for a while now. It had been days since she'd felt those heavenly lips against her own. "I really want to kiss you now," Cammie confessed quietly.

"Well, no one is stopping you," Lauryn challenged with a smirk. She was feeling the same pull, all the while.

They both leaned in at once, connecting their lips in a chaste kiss. Lauryn let out a content breath at the sensation. Her lips moved slowly against Cammie's, just reveling in the feeling for a few seconds. The two kissed slowly, just familiarizing themselves with the gesture all over again. Their vibe had been disrupted, but it was quickly returning to normal.

Craving intimacy and general closeness, Lauryn's hands started wandering down Cammie's back. Their lips were still attached, but Cammie soon opened her mouth in an attempt to amplify it. Lauryn easily allowed her access. As soon as her tongue invaded Cammie's mouth, she gripped her a little tighter. Both of them soon became consumed in the familiar frenzy of lips, teeth, and tongue. Cammie tried to suppress her smile, reveling in the fact that she still knew her way around Lauryn's mouth. Kissing her now, it was like they'd never missed a beat.

Taking their location into consideration, being in broad daylight and all, they mutually decided to settle down. Cammie sat back down on the blanket and giggled from sheer happiness. Lauryn had been stealing glances at her and plaguing her with butterflies the whole time. Cammie wanted to say something so she could catch her breath.

"How'd you even find this spot? Because I was looking for it for like ten minutes and I couldn't find it at all..." Cammie broached with a gentle laugh.

"I found it on accident, actually. That hole wasn't there. Christian, Tori, and I did that a few years ago. He kicked a giant ball through there and I found it when we were looking for our ball. It took us a while to find out how to get in here too, since none of us could fit through the hole initially," Lauryn shared.

"Oh," Cammie raised her eyebrows.

"But then I just kind of pushed the branch out of the way and found this little area. They forgot about it. So I guess it's all mine. Well, ours now," Lauryn grinned as she laced her fingers with Cammie's.

"I like the idea of something being ours," Cammie smiled down at their intertwined hands.

"Me too," Lauryn said cheekily.

"How'd you end up here?" Lauryn asked curiously. She knew why she was here, but why was Cammie?

"Overwhelmed," Cammie answered evasively. "At lunch, they were telling me all about how I could get over you and stuff and I was just like I don't *want* to. Then I went in circles with myself and came to the conclusion that I had to leave before I started crying again."

"You don't want to get over me?" Lauryn smiled, purposely ignoring everything else she said.

"No. Never," Cammie shook her head. "I want to be with you... That's all."

"I'm glad we're on the same page then," Lauryn seconded.

Cammie was catching on to all of Lauryn's subtle responses. She just didn't know how to react to them. They made her happy and further confirmed the thought that Lauryn wanted the same things, but she didn't know how to articulate it. So she just redirected the conversation again.

"How did you end up here?" she asked the same question Lauryn asked her, followed by an adorable yawn.

"A little bit of the same reason. I needed to escape my own thoughts, which is impossible, but I thought coming here would be distracting. I was pleasantly surprised," she answered.

"Escape your thoughts for what? What were you thinking?" Cammie asked.

"I don't know. A bunch of shit," Lauryn waved it off.

"Oh. Me too, I guess," Cammie mumbled.

Instead of being a hypocrite and expecting Cammie to open up to her while she kept things to herself, Lauryn decided to divulge a bit more. "I was thinking about you. It's always about you. We were in a bad spot and it was messing with me. Even when I didn't see you or talk to you, I was thinking about you, Camz. And it fucked me up because like, things between us were complicated. I kept second-guessing my decision to break up with you and then being stubborn about it and kind of refused to talk to you. I was at war with myself a lot of the time. Today, it just got to be too much," Lauryn shared openly, making herself vulnerable and susceptible to rejection. But she didn't think she'd be rejected. It seemed like Cammie was in the same boat as her.

"I had no idea," Cammie admitted. "I thought you were just done with me and just didn't care anymore."

"Not at all," Lauryn groaned. "I wish it were that easy," she laughed. But she saw how Cammie's expression fell a little bit. "No, like... It was hard on me, but it was worth it. It brought us back together in the end," Lauryn reasoned.

"We're together again?" Cammie inferred hopefully.

"If you want to be," Lauryn nodded.

"Do *you*? You were the one that ended it and I don't want to get back together if you don't think we're ready," Cammie stated logically.

"Ready for what? We were both clearly miserable without each other..." Lauryn pointed out.

"I don't know. You're right," Cammie disregarded what she'd just said.

"So... Are we? Because I want this with you," Lauryn expressed. For once, she decided to wear her heart out on her sleeve. Being passive and quiet about her feelings wouldn't work to her advantage. The new perspective shift on how to make their relationship work was based on communication and openness. Lauryn wanted to implement it, starting now.

"I do too," Cammie nodded resolutely, a goofy smile already spreading across her lips.

"I missed calling you my girlfriend. I still did it in my head anyway. I had to keep correcting myself, which was annoying," Lauryn confessed. "I'm glad you are."

"I'm glad you are too," Cammie replied dumbly, not really having the words to properly verbalize her immense happiness.

"I love how we never ask. It's always just kind of implied," Lauryn smiled.

"Well, you did ask," Cammie deadpanned.

"Not really," Lauryn disagreed.

"Yes you did. You said '*are we*?'" Cammie reminded her, trying to mock her voice.

"Okay, smartass. I meant I've never said the words 'Cammie, will you be my girlfriend?' or 'Camz, will you go out with me?' I never asked," Lauryn elaborated.

"You did just now," Cammie said cheekily. "And my answer is yes. I would love to be your girlfriend."

"You're so dumb," Lauryn shook her head. Cammie's smirk was visible from her peripheral vision. Lauryn whirled around quickly to peck her lips. The shorter girl interrupted their kiss with her laughter, making Lauryn completely enamored with her. "Why are you laughing?"

"I'm so happy," Cammie answered as her eyes fell to the grass below, where she was plucking strands of grass.

"You're so cute, Camzi," Lauryn praised softly, looking at the girl fondly.

"Thanks," Cammie grinned bashfully.

"I love you," Lauryn said just before kissing her cheek. If they couldn't go any further due to their location, she wanted to take advantage of all of the chaste and loving gestures she could get away with.

"I love you, too," Cammie reciprocated instantly as she mirrored what Lauryn did.

"What were you writing before I came?" Lauryn asked as she gestured to the idle journal laying by their feet.

"I wasn't writing anything. I was reading," Cammie responded.

"I haven't read anything of yours in a long time..." Lauryn hinted. She thought back to when Cammie asked for her journal back that day, then never brought it back to her.

"I'm not even sure you want to read this..." Cammie warned her.

"I always do. Why wouldn't I?" she questioned with a tilt of her head.

"I don't know... It's just kind of dark, I guess," Cammie shrugged.

"I want to see. I love the way you write down exactly what you're thinking in the moment. It's real. I want to see how you felt during all of it," Lauryn pleaded.

"Okay... But can you not read *all* of it? I was looking over it and I'm kind of embarrassed by how negative I was being. I don't want you to see that side of me," she requested.

"Sure. Just... Show me whatever you want me to see," Lauryn agreed to her conditions without a second thought.

Cammie nodded and flipped open her journal and skimmed past a few cynical pages. She regretted how blunt she was. But in her defense, she didn't think Lauryn would be coming back to her or that the stupid journal would even be a factor for them anymore. She'd never been happier to be proved wrong in her life.

"This one is kind of a weird poem... Thing... Whatever it is. I wrote it when I missed you," Cammie said as she pointed to it.

I wanna lay my head on your breast
And listen to the melodies going on in your chest.
But instead, I'm stuck in my own bed.

"I like that," Lauryn approved. Rhyming things always got extra points with her.

"It's alright," Cammie brushed it off modestly.

"It's wonderful," Lauryn said pointedly, giving Cammie a look for not taking her compliment.

"Thank you," Cammie revised her response meekly.

"You're welcome," Lauryn brushed it off, then looked at her expectantly.

Cammie understood the notion immediately and sighed, skimming over more entries. A therapist would probably be contacted if someone stumbled upon this stuff. She spilled her heart out on these pages, and her heart was so bitter in that time. Everything was so blunt and harsh. She was a realist, a pessimist, a cynic. The world was so monotonous and grey without Lauryn, and it was all reflected on these pages.

"Actually... I don't care if you read it. Just read it later. I don't want to be here when you do," Cammie said as she closed it, unable to pick out anything else that was okay to share out loud.

"Okay," Lauryn agreed as she took it from her. "I won't read it here. I'll read it later."

"Okay," Cammie offered a smile, then she yawned. Again.

"Why are you so tired?" Lauryn giggled.

"I don't know. I write at night and then I just kinda pass out whenever. I don't really sleep much," she admitted.

"Are you sleepy now?" Lauryn questioned, although it was pretty obvious.

"A little," Cammie nodded.

"Then go to sleep, Camz," Lauryn instructed her as she smoothed back her hair.

"I want to talk to you," Cammie shook her head.

"You're literally about to fall asleep anyway," Lauryn laughed quietly and motioned for Cammie to get off of her. Lauryn stood up and helped Cammie up too, then she picked up the blanket.

"Are we going home?" Cammie inferred. She thought Lauryn was packing up.

Lauryn shook her head no and continued doing what she was doing. She walked over to the tree shielding them from view and placed the blanket in front of it. Then she crouched down to spread it out evenly. Lauryn took a seat there with her back against the tree at a comfortable angle. She opened her arms wide, signifying that she wanted Cammie to come to her. With a goofy grin, Cammie clambered over to her and was immediately wrapped up in her embrace. Her favorite place in the world was back. She sighed happily and tried to cuddle Lauryn as best as she could, given their position. Cammie's head rested on Lauryn's chest and Lauryn cradled her body in a way that made her feel safe.

"I love you so much," Cammie mumbled against her skin.

"I love you more. Go to sleep," Lauryn smiled as she kissed the top of her head.

"That doesn't exist here. It's not 50/50, or 60/40, or 70/30... It's 100/100. We're in love and that's all there is to it, babe," Cammie countered and turned on her side.

"I guess that's a better way to look at it," Lauryn laughed.

"Yeah," Cammie giggled raspily, becoming sleepier by the second. It was a battle she was losing rather quickly.

"Alright, good night," Lauryn laughed fondly, peering down at the girl she'd undoubtedly fallen in love with. She was content with that in itself.

"It's just a little nap," Cammie replied softly, steadily losing her battle to sleep. Her eyes fluttered open to see why Lauryn hadn't said anything back yet, but she was met with a soft expression. The look radiated love and Cammie had never felt more important in her life. *She* was the person Lauryn was looking at that way. Wow. Whatever she did to deserve being the recipient of her love, she was grateful for it.

Lauryn reached out with a smile and gently closed Cammie's eyelids herself. By now, Cammie was succumbing to sleep too quickly to fight it anymore. Lauryn coaxed the younger girl to sleep in her arms. The steady rise and fall of her chest calmed Lauryn in a way that made her want to sleep as well. Lauryn leaned her head back against the tree and drifted off herself.

»»»

Lauryn was the first to wake. Surprisingly, she had little concern for the time of day. But she could take a wild guess and assume that it was probably around seven or eight. The colors and hues in the sky gave it all away. She thought it was a bit symbolic. Here she was, outside watching the sun set with the girl of her dreams. The same girl that found a solace and metaphor in the very phenomenon. Part of Lauryn wanted to wake Cammie up so she could enjoy it with her, but she also wanted to let her sleep.

Opting to let her sleeping beauty rest for a few more minutes, Lauryn took the time to admire it by herself. Instead of just a pretty orange, this sunset was remarkable. The sky was a kaleidoscope. Various blues and yellows and purples and oranges decorated the sky. It was a maze of color with strokes that just fit perfectly amongst the others. Lauryn didn't want to be selfish and let Cammie miss it, so she nudged her softly until she began to stir. When Lauryn thought she would open her eyes, Cammie only cuddled further into her side. She reminded Lauryn of a baby. And she was. She was her baby. But she needed to see this.

"Camz," Lauryn prompted quietly, tickling Cammie just under her ribcage. Cammie flailed and opened her eyes reluctantly, glaring at Lauryn for waking her up that way.

"What time is it?" Cammie asked adorably as she began to rub her eyes.

"I don't know, but look," Lauryn hinted as she pointed up at the sky.

Cammie looked overhead and Lauryn watched as her groggy expression turned to one of fascination. As much as Lauryn knew Cammie would appreciate it, she found herself appreciating it just as much. It meant something to her. It meant a lot to the both of them.

"My mom said there was always a rainbow after the rain," Lauryn said suddenly. "And I said no, there's a sunset. She was so confused."

"That's cute," Cammie smiled.

"I'm so grateful this is our thing. No one else understands," she continued. "Well, I mean... The girls might... But for the most part, it's just us."

"Yeah," Cammie nodded against her. Speech wasn't really an option at the moment. She was still in the process of coming to.

"It really is a perfect metaphor for bad things. The sunsets leading up to this one haven't been nearly as beautiful," Lauryn reasoned.

"Thanks. And I know, right? I'm actually kind of proud of it," Cammie smiled as she sat up. If she stayed laying down on Lauryn, she would probably fall back asleep. She sat between Lauryn's legs and leaned back against her body. Her girlfriend's arms held her close and clasped over her stomach.

"You should be," Lauryn praised her quietly. The intimacy she craved was insatiable. She buried her face into the crook of Cammie's neck and started placing chaste kisses along the length of it.

"This is nice," Cammie said in reference to everything about that moment.

"No, this is perfect," Lauryn corrected her. One hand moved from around her waist to point up at the sky. "This is our sunset," she said symbolically.

"It is," Cammie nodded. That was clear. She understood the full extent of Lauryn's implication. For the most part, everything was straightened out. Their sunset as a couple had finally come. And even further, the sunset above was an accurate representation of the beauty of it all. It was more beautiful than usual, quasi to this moment. Being in Lauryn's arms now felt ten times as good to Cammie.

"This is the one I've been waiting for," Lauryn admitted.

"Me too," Cammie agreed. "And so are you."

»»»

The next day, Cammie and Lauryn were inseparable. They made up for all of their time apart by literally never letting each other out of their sight. They were together before and after school and between every class change, no matter how far apart their classes were. They saw each other more than they did before the break up. Holding hands, hugging, kissing, and general contact never diminished. Cammie found that people were still giving them looks, but it didn't bother her anymore. She was happy. Lauryn's was the only opinion she cared about. It was the only one she would take to heart.

It shouldn't have taken her that long to acknowledge the fact that those people were irrelevant. In some ways, it was like the break up was good for them. Their relationship was thriving now, strengthened by all of the hardship. The intimacy they shared was unwavering. When they were together, they never broke contact. It was nauseating and comforting to their friends all at once. The trio saw the girlfriends approaching them at lunch, walking with their hands tightly intertwined.

"I am so happy," Diana gushed when she caught sight of the two of them.

"Why?" Allie asked as she looked back in the direction Diana was smiling dumbly at. She kind of squealed when she saw them too.

"What?" Naomi asked just before turning around as well. "Oh my God!!!"

Cammie smiled shyly at her friends' reactions and buried her face into Lauryn's shoulder a bit. It was only Naomi, Diana, and Allie. Why was she feeling bashful in front of them now?

"Hey guys," Lauryn laughed as she tried to pry Cammie from her side long enough to sit down.

"We were just about to have an intervention for y'all," Allie informed them with a small laugh.

"She's not kidding," Cammie told Lauryn seriously, who was taking it as a joke.

"No, like we were literally about to devise a plan and stuff," Naomi smiled, shaking her head in the direction of the youngest girl.

"Desperate times call for desperate measures," Diana shrugged.

"I don't think you guys could've done anything. It had to be on our own, and it was," Lauryn smiled at Cammie, who was currently shoving pizza into her mouth.

"What ended up happening? I swear, I never know what's going on with y'all anymore," Naomi said as she began picking and prodding at the various foods on her plate.

"Yeah, Cam. You went to 'go get some fresh air'" Diana said with mocking air quotations. "and then you never came back. And when you do come back, you come back with Lauryn attached to your hip. What the hell did we miss?"

"A lot," Cammie mumbled through a mouthful.

"Are you gonna explain or..." Allie prompted, eager to hear their story just as much as the other two girls.

Cammie swallowed her food slowly and looked to Lauryn, waiting for her to answer. She always took the lead in these kinds of discussions. Lauryn just gazed at her passively, waiting for Cammie to divulge everything. *She* was the one that had been asked, after all.

"Well, I went to the park. Lauryn ended up there somehow too and we talked. I told her everything. We fixed most of it but I'm pretty sure we still have some more to discuss..." Cammie trailed, looking at Lauryn for confirmation. When she nodded, Cammie continued. "Yeah. And we said sorry and stuff and hugged and had the best kiss ever," she giggled and turned to Lauryn to confirm that too - which she did eagerly. "And... Then we cuddled and watched the sun set together. It was nice. The perfect ending to our storm," she concluded.

"You watched the sunset? I saw it too. It was so pretty last night. I took a picture," Allie grinned, thinking back on it herself.

"Yeah. It was beautiful. But I don't need a picture to remember that one," Lauryn grinned. That special moment would be forever etched into her memory. Everything about that day would.

"Lame," Diana teased as she watched the sappy interaction.

"You make Lauryn a big ol' softie," Allie noted with a smile.

That much was true. Cammie brought out a side of Lauryn the four of them had rarely seen her exhibit before. Maternal urges seemed to manifest in Cammie's presence, making her infinitely more gentle and caring than she usually was. Her cool demeanor melted into nothing short of a puppy. Cammie made her bashful. She

242

made her wholesome. She made her glow. Cammie had a power over Lauryn that Allie was sure she wasn't even aware of.

"I do?" Cammie laughed.

"She's different with you," Naomi agreed.

"Yeah. Instead of looking like she's about to kill someone, she looks like she could explode into rainbows and butterflies at any second," Diana pitched in.

That last description offended Lauryn a tad, but she ignored it. Diana had a funny way with words. Their accusations were true. She had a major soft spot for the girl perched next to her and manipulating her fingers under the table. That soft spot was more commonly referred to as love. Because she loved Cammie, she was a different version of herself when with her. A better version.

"You turn Cam over here into a lovesick fool too," Diana added.

"Puppy love," Cammie smiled.

In Lauryn's mind, she didn't like that term in reference to their relationship. It was a state; A temporary one at that. The way she loved Cammie wasn't temporary, or at least she hoped it wouldn't end up that way.

"I think it's a little more than that, babe..." Lauryn commented quietly, closing her fingers over Cammie's and bringing their hands into a tight hold.

"Oh, well... True love, then? Is that better?" Cammie suggested.

"That's cliché," Naomi disagreed.

"Maybe... But I think it fits. We've got an intellectual, physical, and emotional connection... And true love encompasses that as a whole," Lauryn concluded as she used her hands to emphasize exactly what she meant.

"Mhm," Cammie nodded. "And it's unconditional. There are no parameters. There's no one reason, it's everything about you. It's inspiring and devastating all at once. This love is all of that."

"It's stealing glances at you when you're not looking or watching you sleep and feeling like you haven't noticed everything yet - like you haven't admired them for long enough yet," Lauryn brought up, recalling the way she had done just that yesterday.

"It's being completely obsessed with you but feeling like you haven't paid enough attention," Cammie nodded, able to identify with what Lauryn was explaining.

It was like she and Lauryn were the only people in the room; in the world. She was completely enamored with the girl sitting beside her. Every fiber of her being loved her. The connection she felt with her was unmatched. It couldn't be compared to anything else they'd shared in the past.

"It's being kept awake every night because I'm so in love with you, I can't stop thinking about you long enough to go to sleep. You're so hypnotizing," Cammie continued, filling Lauryn's stomach with infinite butterflies.

"So are you, Camz. The way I feel about you now has left me completely powerless. I'm helpless. I'm weak. You've got me wrapped around your little finger and I don't even think you know the extent of how much I mean that. Even before, what we had was special... But I'm exposed to it now. Once I let you in the way I didn't know I needed you to be, it blossomed into this thing that I can't control anymore. This love just kind of sprouted and embedded itself deep inside of my heart and I'm just defenseless against it all. It's like, I love you so much, I can't be me without you anymore. You are a part of me. You're like the other half of-" Lauryn started rambling, but Diana's interruption cut her off.

"I'm gonna throw up," Diana exaggerated as she watched the two speaking to one another. Had they actually forgotten that the rest of them were there?

"I'm sure they weren't even finished yet - am I right?" Allie smirked.

"You may be a little right," Lauryn nodded, a bit embarrassed. Fingertips brushed at the back of her neck while she blushed. She was fucking *blushing* right now. Her friends were right. She was definitely different when it came to Cammie.

"I know," Allie said proudly.

"You okay?" Diana laughed as she waved a hand in front of Cammie's face, breaking her from her trance.

Cammie was gaping at Lauryn. Her eyes were glued to her side profile, although she wasn't the center of Lauryn's attention. How the hell could she be feeling that way about her? Cammie didn't feel worthy of being on the receiving end of those words, of that magnitude of love. Maybe, just maybe, Lauryn was actually falling for Cammie the way Cammie had so many months ago. Years ago. Things weren't so unrequited anymore. She couldn't even believe it. Happiness filled her to the core. It threatened to make her cry, but she reeled it in just in time. They couldn't spill here, not in front of her friends. They'd never let her hear the end of it. She already got teased for how sappy she was on a regular basis.

"Yeah. I'm fine," Cammie nodded, shifting her gaze to her lap to maintain her calm composure.

"You guys are everything I want my boyfriend and I to be," Naomi sighed, wishing some guy would show her the same attention. Mason was okay, but they definitely didn't have what Cammie and Lauryn had just portrayed.

Cammie hoped they could find someone that could offer them a fraction of what she shared with Lauryn. Cammie genuinely wanted Naomi and Diana to find someone that swept them off of their feet the way Lauryn had. Diana more so than Naomi, because she was still with Mason. And Allie had Trevor. They'd been going strong for about two years now, if she wasn't mistaken.

"You'll find someone. I found her on accident," Lauryn smiled, nudging Cammie in the side.

"Yeah. It was the best accident that's ever happened to me," Cammie agreed as she faced Lauryn. She pecked her lips quickly and just grinned to herself.

"Your sunset is coming. Just keep that in mind," Lauryn said to the rest of them cheesily, pulling Cammie back into her side and kissing the top of her head softly.

Chapter 26

"I *love* my dress for prom," Diana emphasized loudly on her way to the bus. It was merely another one of her schemes to convince Cammie to tag along. The small brunette voiced her opinion on prom and all of its festivities and announced her distaste in doing so. It dampened Lauryn's spirit, having wanted to do something special for her. The other three girls promised to help persuade her, and Diana was back at it again.

"I thought you didn't have a date?" Cammie recalled as she caught up to her.

"I don't need one, thank you," Diana flipped her hair playfully. "I'm taking myself."

"Of course you are..." Cammie laughed, knowing how independent the taller girl was. If there was a person that didn't need a date to attend a party, it was Diana.

"I mean, I kind of wish you'd go so I wouldn't have to be *all* by myself," Diana pouted a little. Her lip jutted out as she looked down at Cammie, trying to play the guilt card.

"You won't be by yourself. Allie and Naomi are going, remember?" Cammie brought up as she fell into step with her.

"Yeah, no. I'd rather not be the fifth wheel to those two," Diana gagged for dramatic effect. Her teasing was always in good nature. The mentioned girls and their boyfriends always made an effort to include her in their conversations and strove not to make her feel awkward. It almost always worked. Besides that, Diana was pretty sure she could rock that party all by herself.

"Oh, yeah," Cammie nodded, considering how awkward it would probably be for Diana when they would be enthralled with each other. Speaking of the said girl, Cammie spotted her a few feet away, coming towards them. "Hi Naomi," Cammie greeted her by name when she fell into step with them.

"Hey guys," Naomi waved as she brushed past a few people going in the opposite direction. "What were y'all talking about?"

"Prom," Diana answered, raising her eyebrow subtly. She exchanged a knowing look with the darker girl and silently prompted her into action.

"Oh, cute. When Mason asked me, I almost cried. He was so sweet," Naomi shared, adding to the conversation.

"Oh my god, aww!" Diana grinned widely. "How'd he do it?"

"He got the football team to do it on the field. They all held up little signs with letters on them. It spelled out Naomi, prom, and a whole bunch of hearts. I was surprised he went out of his way to do it," Naomi gushed happily, smiling to herself as she relived it.

"That's adorable, Naomi," Cammie commented genuinely. She did, however, wonder about Lauryn's prom-posal to her or vice versa. If she were to go, that is.

"Yeah. I wonder how Lo would do yours," Naomi hinted. "Or... How you would do it for her..."

"I don't know. We haven't talked about prom, so I'm pretty sure she doesn't plan on going either," Cammie assumed.

"Oh. Well, I'll see you guys later," Naomi dismissed herself as they came to a stop in front of their bus. She'd finally gotten her car keys back, regaining her freedom of travel.

Diana and Cammie both mumbled their goodbyes and gave her hugs. As they were boarding the bus, another crowd had gathered in the middle of the street. Apparently there was yet another prom-posal going on. Cammie, as well as everyone else on the bus, clambered towards the windows to get a better view. Cammie stood on her knees in the seat, earning herself a reprimand from the bus driver. As she stood up straight, she squinted to see the commotion in the brightness of the day.

Jacob had decorated his car windshield quite creatively to ask Bea to prom. The pair had been rooted for by quite a few people, so the crowd that knew them were ecstatic to see their one true pairing going to prom together. A bunch of people were gathering around and the mixed reactions were quite noticeable. Either they were smiling broadly at the pair or scowling at them, their jealousy overpowering any congratulatory feelings.

Cammie sighed and sank back down into her seat. Part of her wanted to retract her statement about not wanting to go to prom. The dance itself didn't appeal to her, but the hype of it made it seem like fun. The whole idea of a big elaborate prom-posal was adorable. If it happened to her, she would probably melt. Things like that didn't usually happen to her. But now Lauryn was in her life, opening a whole new window of possibility.

Speaking of Lauryn, she was the last to get on the bus - as usual. Cammie didn't know why she was running late today, but she'd learned not to question it. Lauryn was never punctual when it came to the bus. Ever. So when she plopped down next to Cammie, the younger girl just laughed and slid over.

"Hey, baby," Cammie greeted her with a tender kiss on her temple.

Lauryn smiled softly and leaned in to kiss her lips, breaking away after a few seconds. "Hi," she responded simply, since her heart was still racing and she was still out of breath.

"Did you see Jacob asking Bea to prom?" Cammie asked as she looked back out of the window at the crowd that was now dissipating.

"Nope. I was too busy running to get here," Lauryn shook her head. Then she leaned back to take a deep breath, throwing an arm around her girlfriend as she exhaled. Just like in those cheesy movies.

Cammie grinned dorkily at her and reached up to brush over her fingers. "I'm not surprised," she giggled. "But I saw it. It was really cute. He wrote on his windshield with one of those cool chalk markers."

"That's cute," Lauryn nodded as she briefly looked out of the window.

"Were you going?" Cammie asked tentatively.

"You weren't, so I guess I wasn't," Lauryn answered hesitantly. She almost blew her cover.

"Do you want to go?" Cammie rephrased herself. If Lauryn originally wanted to go, but changed her plans because of her, she would most definitely accompany her.

"A little bit... Yeah," Lauryn affirmed quietly. Her eyes flashed towards Cammie's, trying to see what was going on in her mind. She kind of had trouble detecting her exact thoughts from her expression alone.

"Oh, okay," Cammie grinned. "Me too, then."

"Yeah?" Lauryn smiled broadly, linking their hands together.

"Yeah," Cammie nodded resolutely, one hundred percent confident in her decision. Who knows? Maybe prom could end up being a little fun.

"Perfect," Lauryn said under her breath. And with that, Lauryn's plan was officially in motion.

»»»

"Switch balloons with Diana," Lauryn instructed Naomi, who was holding the wrong letter balloon. As she stood back, the display said "PORM?" instead of "PROM?", like it was supposed to.

Diana and Naomi switched the wrong balloons again, spelling out "PMRO" now. The only person that was correctly in place was Allie, who was holding the balloon with the question mark on it. A little bit frustrated, Lauryn just walked over and situated the balloons herself as Naomi, Diana, and Allie burst into laughter.

A few days after Cammie confirmed that she'd attend, all of the girls were attempting to help Lauryn pull off her prom-posal. They'd all gotten passes to aid her, skipping the last fifteen minutes of their last class of the day. It was now Friday. Prom was in a week and a half and this was Lauryn's final step for the preparation.

"Okay, now could you just move a little to the left, Naomi?" Lauryn directed the girl that was still giggling profusely at their spelling mishap. It really wasn't that fucking funny. "Naomi!"

"What?" she laughed, only attentive now because her name was called. "Sorry, what?"

"The letters are being hidden because the balloons keep floating in front of each other. Can you move over to the left so there's enough space?" Lauryn repeated herself calmly. Her calm demeanor turned into irritation when Diana whispered something into Naomi's ear, causing her to laugh again instead of following instructions.

"Can you guys take this seriously for a minute or should I just get someone else to do it?" Lauryn scoffed when they ignored her directions for the second time.

"I don't know why you're stressing so hard about this. Chill out. Cam wouldn't care that much, so I don't think you should," Diana sighed once her laughter faded. Why the hell was she so pressed?

"I just want to make it special for her. She'll be here at any minute and you guys aren't ready," Lauryn answered in a whiny tone that made Naomi roll her eyes. But in Lauryn's defense, the other prom-posals she'd witnessed only inspired her to make hers bigger and better for Cammie.

"What else do we have to do except for stand here and hold these?" Naomi questioned, a little annoyed at Lauryn's bossy demeanor.

"Nothing. Just make sure it spells prom correctly," Lauryn snapped. The frustrated girl flipped her hair off of her shoulder and raked her fingers through it as she looked up at the clock.

"Calm down..." Allie said softly, noticing how close Naomi and Diana were to being done with her. They didn't *have* to do this. Lauryn wasn't exactly being pleasant company.

"I'm sorry," Lauryn apologized, looking back at her three best friends. "I just really want this to go the right way. Especially because this'll probably draw a crowd. I don't want to look like a fucking idiot trying to do this. I'm not trying to be a bitch, I just want it to be perfect," she excused herself as she ran her hand through her hair again. The obsessiveness of the gesture only further indicated how stressed she was.

"Cam would've thought it was perfect if you just asked her by text, Lauryn. It's really not that big of a deal," Diana deadpanned. She wholeheartedly believed it too. Cammie was a simple soul. But it was cute that Lauryn cared so much about the presentation. Her dedication to Cammie was the only reason she'd let her rude ass slide. This time.

"Probably," Naomi nodded in agreement.

She should be coming down at any time now. The dismissal bell would ring in just a minute or two. When it did and a torrent of eager students poured out of their classes, her eyes were in search of a familiar brunette. She scanned the crowd for the short, timid girl that was most likely hugging her books to her chest. When she found her in the crowd, Lauryn's heart rate spiked in anticipation. Holy shit. It was happening. Why was she so nervous?

"Fuck," Lauryn muttered under her breath as she scurried to get her poster. She held it in front of her and waited for Cammie to weave through the crowd and see it.

People started gathering around and they pretty much formed a circle around Lauryn's presentation. Tori escorted Cammie through the crowd and led her to Lauryn. The way Cammie's face lit up at the sight suddenly made putting up with Lauryn's dictation worth it in her friends' eyes. Cammie brought trembling hands to cover her mouth, which was hanging wide open. Her eyes darted from the balloons, to the candy, to the poster, then to Lauryn's shining face.

"Lauryn..." Cammie trailed off in amazement. As she took in everything presented to her now, she was rendered speechless. The balloons were a nice touch, but the poster was what really captured her attention. It was a beautiful painting of a sunset that she was pretty sure Lauryn painted herself, which she did. The specific one she had in mind was the one they watched together, the day they got back together. Surprisingly enough, Cammie recognized it.

"If you say yes, these are all yours," Lauryn smirked, waving the box of candy in her direction.

"Of course I'm saying yes..." Cammie laughed and closed the distance between them. She had no regard for the group of onlookers they'd accumulated.

She pulled back from their hug and slowly connected their lips, placing a hand on Lauryn's cheek as she kissed her. "I love you. Thank you."

"You're welcome," Lauryn responded happily. Knowing that it was all over made her feel incredibly redeemed.

"You even got the girls to help," Cammie noticed as she unwrapped herself from her girlfriend.

"Yeah. Thanks, by the way," Lauryn addressed the girls that were still clutching the balloons.

"I think you owe me five dollars now," Diana hinted as she held her hand out.

"You're paying them five dollars to help...?" Cammie laughed up at Lauryn.

"No... Diana, what the hell?" Lauryn made a face.

"Interest fee," Diana said instantly, motioning for Lauryn to place to money in her hand.

"I am not giving you five dollars," Lauryn laughed and rolled her eyes at the taller girl.

"It was worth a shot," Diana shrugged as she dropped her hand.

"I guess you won't be the fifth wheel after all," Cammie teased. "You'll be the *seventh* wheel now."

"Um, no? You know that dude Alfred?" Diana asked as the crowd started to dwindle. The people had witnessed Lauryn's invitation and now they no longer had anything to look at.

"Yeah? The older guy that's obsessed with you?" Naomi laughed.

"I agreed to go with him," Diana shrugged.

"Diana..... Why..." Lauryn trailed, not bothering to hide her disapproval. "You should've gone with Donnie."

"He's going with someone though. And I don't know. I guess I just got tired of avoiding him," Diana laughed.

"That's so cute. At least you're giving him a chance. Who knows, sparks could fly," Allie smirked and wiggled her eyebrows suggestively. "Oh my goodness. Now that we're all going, we should plan some stuff to do before and after."

"I think that's a great idea," Lauryn smiled as she hooked an arm around Cammie's waist.

"We can do each other's makeup and hair and maybe we can even meet at Waffle House afterwards!" Allie excited herself as she planned aloud.

"Why not before?" Cammie asked, knowing that she'd probably die of starvation if she had to wait until *after* prom.

"Why Waffle House?" Naomi added as she scrunched her face up, laughing at the suggestion.

"We can't eat before because knowing you, you'd spill something on your dress," Lauryn answered Cammie. "And Waffle House just because she's Allie," she turned to answer Naomi.

"You don't even get waffles when you go," Diana pointed out from experience.

"Everything else is so good..." Allie excused herself quietly.

"Well, okay. So, Waffle House afterwards... But before? What are we doing before?" Cammie asked as she tightened her grip on the poster, because it was steadily slipping between her fingers.

"We could help each other get ready. We can meet at my house or something," Naomi proposed. "I'll do everyone's hair and we can just take turns with the makeup and stuff."

"Okay, nice," Lauryn agreed to that game plan. "But what about transportation? How are we gonna get there? Who's taking us?"

"Me, obviously," Cammie raised her hand.

"So who's taking us?" Lauryn laughed, dismissing her girlfriend's claim.

"Probably me or Allie," Naomi assumed. "Me, most likely. Since we'll be at my house."

"You're right," Diana affirmed, mentally laying out their prom schedule.

"Yeah. What time should we try to meet?" Naomi questioned.

"I don't know, but we can figure out the details when the date is closer. Isn't it in like two weeks?" Lauryn recalled as she started to play with the hem of Cammie's shirt.

"Yeah, I think," Diana nodded as she looked up at the time. "Shit, we need to go," she said in reference to the bus that would pull off in a few minutes.

"I'll see you guys later," Allie waved as she pulled Naomi away as well.

"Bye," Cammie bid her goodbye before turning to Diana and Lauryn. "And then there were three."

"Two," Diana corrected her as she gestured in the direction of her locker.

"And then there were two," Cammie revised her statement as she turned into Lauryn, wrapping her arms around her waist. She pecked her lips one time and simply smiled up at her.

"Why are you so fucking cute?" Lauryn smiled back and rested her forehead against Cammie's.

"Why are you so beautiful?" Cammie countered, looking directly into her eyes.

"Why did I know you'd say that?" Lauryn wondered aloud in amusement.

"I'm predictable," Cammie shrugged, tightening her hold on her waist. "Lauryn... I just realized something."

"What?" Lauryn asked.

"They stole our balloons," Cammie informed her with a pout.

"I don't know why I take you seriously sometimes," Lauryn shook her head, beginning to head towards their bus.

"This is serious! I had plans for those, man," Cammie sighed as she trudged alongside her girlfriend.

"Then I'll get you some more," Lauryn promised as she kissed her face in the midst of trying to catch the bus. When she pushed through the doors, she sped up to a jog when she saw them preparing to depart.

"God, you're rubbing off on me," Cammie groaned as she began running to keep up with Lauryn's pace. The two girls made a beeline for the bus and made it there right as the bus driver began to inch forward. He glared at them, but opened the door to let them on.

"But did you miss it?" Lauryn quipped as she took her seat.

"Almost!" Cammie emphasized as she filed in beside her, plopping into her seat.

"Almost, but we made it. So shut up," Lauryn said sweetly, clasping her hands together in her lap.

"Fuck," Lauryn groaned as she scanned over the calendar. Her eyes nervously darted from the column to the dates underneath, praying that she'd read it wrong.

"What?" Cammie asked, hearing what she'd muttered under her breath.

They were lying on Lauryn's bed, silently completing their homework assignments. Surprisingly, they worked well together. The atmosphere was quiet and focused as they worked. They were both in comfortable positions on their stomachs. Lauryn had taken a break, opting to check out her softball schedule. What she saw there had the potential to ruin everything.

"What date is prom again? The twenty-fifth?" Lauryn clarified as she looked over the schedule again.

"Yeah... Why?" Cammie frowned.

"You've got to be fucking kidding me," Lauryn grumbled before burying her face into her arms.

"What, babe? What's wrong?" Cammie urge as she placed a hand on her lower back.

"I have a fucking softball game on the same day as prom," Lauryn shared, finally informing her girlfriend.

"Really?" Cammie asked desolately, suddenly fearing that she wouldn't be able to go. Wait. When did she start wanting to go so badly anyway?

"Yeah... Fuck that," she scoffed as she pushed the paper off of the bed. "I'm not going."

"No, wait... You have to go. Won't you get in trouble?" Cammie presumed, nervously trailing her fingers along her spine.

"Probably. But I'm not going to a game I have every week instead of going to prom, which only comes once a year," Lauryn reasoned defiantly, already finalizing her decision in her head.

"You can't just do that," Cammie warned. "What, are they at the same time or something?"

"No, probably not..." Lauryn acknowledged hesitantly. "But what about the whole glam process? I want to look pretty, not all sweaty and gross like I just came off of the field..."

"Well if the times aren't interfering, why don't you just go to both? We can set aside some time for all of that," Cammie proposed, looking at Lauryn's side profile. "And you're pretty even when you're sweaty and gross," she grinned.

"Thanks," Lauryn laughed. "And because I'll be sore and tired, Camz. I'm always a little sore after games. I already know I won't exactly feel like dancing..." she shared, already well aware of her tendencies.

"Then I'll give you a massage right after your game," Cammie promised as she ran her hands over Lauryn's toned shoulder blades for example.

"Will you?" Lauryn asked in amusement as Cammie kept doing the firm gesture.

"Mhm," Cammie hummed softly as she leaned over to kiss her. She moved Lauryn's long and flowing hair to the side and placed a gentle kiss on the nape of her neck.

"Well then I guess I'll have something to look forward to," Lauryn smirked. Her voice was low and sultry, the same tone that had grown familiar to Cammie during spring break.

"You could say that," Cammie laughed as she stilled her movements, instead laying on top of Lauryn's back.

"Or... Maybe I don't have to look forward to it. You know, I've been feeling a little tense lately..." Lauryn trailed, hoping Cammie would take her hint. She longed for the feel of her soft hands along her body.

"Really? You don't feel that tense," Cammie disagreed as she dragged her hand down her back.

"I totally am," Lauryn insisted as she turned around to look at her. Cammie was biting her lip as she slid her hands further down, now groping her ass. Lauryn could tell just by her girlfriend's body language that she wasn't at all turned on. Cammie was being playful, that's all.

"Then you should be nice and ready for that massage on the night of prom," Cammie teased as she lifted off of her, resuming her position next to her.

"You suck," Lauryn sighed when she realized that was as far as Cammie was planning on going.

"You love me," Cammie stuck her tongue out at her. She picked up her pen and adjusted her notebook back in front of her so she could finish her last few questions.

"Yeah. You're lucky that I do," Lauryn scoffed blithely as she sat up.

"I know," Cammie admitted quite seriously. That wasn't a part of their banter. She honestly felt lucky for being on the receiving end of Lauryn's love and affection. Just because she was, she draped her arm over her girlfriend and leaned into her shoulder.

"Don't get all cute on me now," Lauryn pushed her away gently.

"Why? What did I do?" Cammie giggled, looking up at her.

"You're a fucking tease and you know it," Lauryn mumbled as she gripped her pencil, trying to think of which homework assignments she had left, if any.

"I do no such thing," Cammie disagreed as she placed her head back onto her girlfriend's shoulder.

"You always do shit to me and then just stop," Lauryn laughed and finally allowed her to use her as a pillow.

"It's fun. I know the effect I have on you," Cammie shrugged. "You make it way too easy."

"That may be true... But you always start something you have zero intentions of finishing," Lauryn teased her back.

"I'll definitely finish it... It's just a matter of when," Cammie quipped. "You might never see it coming. You think I'm starting something new... When I'm actually just continuing something from earlier..."

"Yeah, whatever babe," Lauryn shook her head, ignoring the tantalizing way her fingers brushed over her skin.

"So, look forward to it on game slash prom day," Cammie smirked as she stopped touching her altogether.

"Mhm, because I really expect you to want to do anything with me after a game, when I am both tired, sweaty, and most likely smelly," Lauryn laughed, knowing the likelihood of that was slim.

"I will. It'll be fun. And I'll finally get to come see you play," Cammie grinned, changing the topic smoothly.

"I'm probably gonna suck, knowing you're there. You'll make me nervous," Lauryn predicted, going into thought about seeing her girlfriend in the crowd.

"You won't suck. I'm sure you'll be great, baby," Cammie assured her with a smile. The two girls made eye contact and Lauryn offered a small smile of her own.

"I don't know, I'm a little rusty. I'll probably miss everything that comes my way," Lauryn assumed, thinking about her performance at practice.

"No you won't. Just focus and you'll be fine," Cammie promised. She'd seen Lauryn play countless times before. In her previous season, Cammie attended every single game. Lauryn played flawlessly back then, so she should still be great now.

"I can't focus on the game when I know you're there. I'll keep looking at you instead," Lauryn laughed. "You're a major distraction, Camz."

"I am not," Cammie disagreed in the midst of tracing patterns into Lauryn's hands. "I used to go to your games all the time. You were perfect every time."

"That was before everything. Everything was so different," Lauryn said in a daze as she looked back on it. Seeing Cammie in the bleachers was something she could remember clearly. There was never once a time where emerald eyes scanned the crowd and didn't land on Cammie's chubby little face. The signs were all there, she was just so oblivious to it. Cammie could've been her girlfriend so long ago, but she'd just never opened her eyes.

"Yeah, I know," Cammie acknowledged. She reflected on it for a minute, then pushed the thought away. "It's different now, but I'm still the same me."

"Except I see you as so much more than I used to," Lauryn countered. Her perception of her compared from then to now was like night and day. Nothing could be prepared her for the way she'd eventually end up feeling about her.

"Really?" Cammie questioned.

"Yes," Lauryn confirmed happily.

"How do you see me now?" Cammie asked curiously.

"The love of my life," Lauryn answered easily. There was no need for anything else to be said. That title alone encompassed every golden thing about the beauty next to her. Her kind heart, her gentle ways, her terrible jokes, her impeccable body, her kisses and her touch, her beautiful mind and soul; Everything.

Lauryn was vaguely aware of the way Cammie's innocent trailing had stopped. When she glanced at her face, she could see her girlfriend frozen in a way. Those favorite lips of hers were parted slightly and her eyes were crystal clear. Cammie's emotions could always be detected through her eyes. Right now, she was surprised. Maybe even shocked. Lauryn assumed she'd be used to hearing things like that by now, but that surely was not the case; Especially when her words were spoken with so much conviction and passion.

"Camz?" Lauryn called out as she waved a hand in front of her face.

"What the hell," Cammie breathed when she finally got over the initial shock of it. She was so touched by the older girl's words, she just needed a moment.

"What?" Lauryn asked with an amused smirk as she waited for her answer.

"The love of *my* life just told me *I* was the love of *her* life. Forgive me for taking a moment to process it," Cammie teased as she buried her face into the comforter. The last of her words were muffled, but Lauryn still understood.

"I'm the love of your life?" Lauryn reiterated. It was touching to hear, although it wasn't new information.

"In the flesh," Cammie nodded. "But you already knew that."

"I mean, I guess so... But that still doesn't mean I'm used to hearing things like that. You know?" Lauryn shared as she moved back against the headboard.

"If *you're* not, then you know *I'm* not. It just means so much more when it's coming from you," Cammie expressed as she laid her head against Lauryn's chest. She was perched on her lap listening to her heartbeat. This was hands down her favorite position to cuddle. Spooning was a close second.

"I'm sorry it took so long for me to see that it was you," Lauryn frowned as she caressed Cammie's body.

"What? To see that what was me?" Cammie questioned, not following her apology.

"The one," Lauryn clarified. "I know how cliché it sounds, but I really think you are."

"Aww, Lauryn..." Cammie cooed as she wrapped her arms around her gently, burying her face into her skin. "And cliché is cute."

"Cliché is lame," Lauryn countered as she sat up, pulling Cammie against her chest.

"We've only been in a relationship for like two or three months... But like, I know that I am in love with you. There's always been a love between us... Something special. But I'm the biggest dumb ass in the world for not realizing it sooner. I wonder where we'd be if I hadn't been afraid of my feelings when I first started to think I liked you," Lauryn mused out loud.

"I don't know. Probably a lot less problematic. But in a way, I'm glad things happened the way they did. No matter the pace, I'm just glad we finally ended up together," Cammie shrugged. Any turn of events would be fine with her, as long as they could revert back to this very position at the end of the day.

"I am, too," Lauryn agreed, despite her guilt. If she was the one that had to stand on the sidelines while Cammie went through her share of unworthy boys, she would probably have just given up. But Cammie didn't. She stuck it out for her until a miracle happened. "I love you."

"I love you too," Cammie reciprocated, then she felt Lauryn's lips against her cheek.

"And I can't wait to take you to prom," Lauryn whispered against her skin.

"I'm so excited, Laur," Cammie shared as the corners of her lips turned upwards into an adorable smile.

"A few days ago, you didn't even want to go at all," Lauryn laughed, recalling the way that same girl had to literally be forced into going.

"That was before everyone started talking about it and before all of these people started being cute with their prom-posals... And before a little cutie decided to do one for me," Cammie responded as she pinched Lauryn's cheeks.

"I had to get the girls to convince you," Lauryn admitted as she swatted Cammie's hands away.

"Why didn't you just ask me?" Cammie raised an eyebrow.

"I wanted you to be surprised. And it worked out perfectly," Lauryn grinned. "I'm surprised you didn't cry."

"I'm not a cry baby," Cammie defended herself like a child.

"You cried on Valentine's Day," Lauryn argued back with a smirk.

"That was different," Cammie dismissed her evidence. "How long have you had that planned?"

"A while. I've been working on your poster for about three weeks, I think," Lauryn estimated, looking up at the ceiling as she tried to recall. It was well before yesterday, she knew that much.

"You're perfect. And amazing. And thoughtful. And sweet," Cammie said as she grasped her cheeks, kissing her between every praise. When she was finished complimenting her, her thumb brushed over her bottom lip. "And you're freaking talented."

"Thank you, Camz," she giggled after Cammie's shower of compliments. She brushed it off modestly and they fell silent until Lauryn promised something that had been on her mind. "I'm gonna make prom so special for you. You're gonna have the time of your life."

»»»»

The softball atmosphere was great. The dust, the bugs, the heat and sweat... It was just how Cammie wanted to spend her day. All sarcasm aside, it was - in a way. Despite prom being in a few hours, there was no place she'd rather be than supporting her girlfriend at her game.

Admittedly, Lauryn was in the dugout for most of the game due to her year taking off. It didn't leave Cammie with much to look at on the field and she was a little bored. To make up for her boredom, whenever she made eye contact with Lauryn, she'd make a silly face. Lauryn would do one back and the both of them would giggle profusely. It annoyed the hell out of the people surrounding them, but it made the time pass easier.

To Lauryn, it meant the world to see Cammie in the stands. In the past, she was always there, but the circumstances were different now. Every other time, it was just her best friend supporting her at her game. But now, it was her *girlfriend* supporting her at her game. And this game was on the same day as their prom. Instead of going to get her hair and nails done, she was sitting there patiently, getting all sweaty. The thought of it made her heart swell. Cammie was a keeper for sure.

When it was finally Lauryn's turn to bat, she and Cammie were caught off guard. "Get your head out of the clouds, Lauryn. Get your ass on over there to bat," Coach Cowell grimaced as he gestured to the field.

Lauryn nodded and jogged out to bat, her nerves catching up with her a little bit. She looked up at the source of all of her inner turmoil and found a solace within that same smiling face. Cammie screamed and gave her a thumbs up from her position in the stands. Lauryn smiled to herself, then blocked her out. If she was going to try and make her proud, she had to get her mind off of her for a second. She gripped the bat tightly and stared at the pitcher fiercely.

That ball came in way faster than she was expecting. She didn't swing. Instead, she ducked back and out of the way. She took a moment to clear her head as she walked around the plate. She'd never done anything like that before. That wasn't a ball either, it was a strike. She hit the bat on the ground a few times before resuming her stance.

"It's okay, Laur! You've got the next one!" Cammie shouted at the top of her lungs, making Lauryn grin back at her. Right when she turned back around, the ball whizzed past her.

Strike two.

255

"Sorry!" Cammie called back out, making a face when she realized that strike was her fault. She vowed to hold her tongue, just so she wouldn't distract her again.

"Shit," Lauryn muttered under her breath as she shook off her strike. She mimicked swinging twice before retaking her position. She refused to strike again. Her sole focus in the moment was that ball. On the next pitch, she swung as hard as she could and was rewarded with a satisfying crack that resounded through the field.

Upon hearing that, she was off. Lauryn ran as fast as her legs would take her. The brunette zipped past first base and was onto the second. She hit it and was about to try for third, but saw the ball moving from her peripheral vision and retreated back to second. She'd only gotten a double, but it felt good to get anything. At least she didn't strike out.

As she leaned over to catch her breath, Cammie's yelling was suddenly perceptible.

"*Go Lauryn!!! That's my girlfriend! Woo! Go baby*!!!" Cammie screamed and jumped and hooted and hollered all at once, a sight that made Lauryn laugh. When they made eye contact and she saw Cammie's face squished against the fence, it brought the biggest smile to her face.

Lauryn blew a kiss at her and Cammie made a goofy move to catch it, shoving it in her pocket. The green-eyed girl laughed again, earning a few glares from the other players on the field. It was then that she remembered where she was. There was a damn softball game going on around her, but all she could see was Cammie.

The final score showed six to two, ending in a tragic loss for Lauryn's team. Nevertheless, Cammie bolted out of the crowd and met Lauryn near the dugout. The widest smile was on her face as she ran towards Lauryn, regretting the decision as she caught up to her and was out of breath. Although her lungs were on fire from that small amount of exertion, she threw her arms around a sweaty Lauryn and hugged her tightly.

"Camz," Lauryn laughed as she hugged back her rambunctious girlfriend. "We didn't win..."

"So? I can still hug you whenever I want," Cammie countered as she resumed her strong hold.

"Okay," Lauryn squeaked as she buried her face into Cammie's neck.

"And I'm proud of you, babe," Cammie shared as she pulled back enough to meet her eyes.

"Does that mean I can have a kiss now?" Lauryn assumed, not bothering to suppress her growing smile. A solitary finger tapped Cammie's lips as she awaited the inevitable.

"Mhm," Cammie granted as she eagerly pressed their lips together. Her arms hung loosely around Lauryn's neck as Lauryn's arms settled around her waist.

"I love you," Cammie proclaimed as Lauryn's quick breaths hit her lips. She leaned in again and as she did, her hands fell to grab her ass. The subtle smirk Cammie felt forming against her lips made it hard to continue kissing her, so she broke away.

"Feeling a little bold, aren't we?" Lauryn laughed as she grasped her forearms, gently pushing her hands away.

"Maybe a little," Cammie bit her lip as she dropped her hands by her side. "Are you tense?"

"Not really," Lauryn answered truthfully, forgetting all about Cammie's little promise for after her game. When she remembered, she changed her answer. "Actually, yeah... Kind of..."

"Later, then..." Cammie hinted as she stepped back from her. "Come on. My mom is taking us back to your house. I think your parents have to go somewhere."

»»»

"Camz," Lauryn called once they stumbled into her room.

"Yes?" Cammie responded as she trailed in behind her, exhaling loudly as she stretched.

"Is it later yet?" Lauryn whined. Throughout the entire car ride, she'd had to endure Cammie's teasing in the back seat. Her hand was innocently on her thigh, then kept inching upwards. The older girl actually had to trap her hand between her thighs in order to prevent her from continuing, which she assumed she probably would've. Cammie's little game had left her hot and bothered ever since.

"I don't know, is it?" Cammie quipped with a smirk as she retired to Lauryn's bed, sprawling out and taking up as much space as possible.

"Yes," Lauryn decided as she crossed over to Cammie, jumping on top of her. Cammie made an inhuman garbling noise as Lauryn landed on top of her that made the softball player laugh.

"Get off of me," Cammie grumbled as she pushed against her shoulders halfheartedly. In all honesty, she loved it when Lauryn straddled her the way she was. The brutal pouncing was the only part she wasn't necessarily fond of.

"Why don't you love me?" Lauryn pouted as she stayed put.

"I do love you," Cammie responded meagerly, pouting at the fact that Lauryn would even say she didn't.

"Then give me that massage you promised," Lauryn challenged with a wide grin.

"You'd have to get off for me to do that, Laur," Cammie said smartly and gave Lauryn a look, indicating that she should get off. Lauryn followed suit and clambered off of her, opting to sit cross legged against the headboard.

"Well, I'm off. Still no massage," Lauryn pointed out as she began shaking her legs impatiently.

"Quiet," Cammie ordered in a thick Russian accent. "Lay down."

Lauryn giggled at her voice and obeyed her instructions, crawling towards the middle and plopping down on her stomach in a heap. She rested her chin on her arms and looked at Cammie expectantly.

"Good. Now close eyes," Cammie directed her, still keeping up her accent. The turn the situation had taken was tickling Lauryn so much, she barely even heard what she'd said.

"You're so dumb, babe," Lauryn giggled into her arm and laid down with a goofy smile.

"Do you want massage or not?" Cammie growled, looking down at Lauryn with her best menacing glare. An amused smile took over her cover, but she quickly resumed character.

"Yes," Lauryn laughed, nodding and finally complying. She bit her lip to suppress her laughter and closed her eyes once more. "But, wait... I should probably go shower really quick..."

257

All Cammie heard after that was the sound of Lauryn's footsteps disappearing into the bathroom. Their atmosphere was now wholly playful. Lauryn could see that if Cammie was going to actually give her a massage, that's all it would turn out to be. Nevertheless, she was taking a quick shower indeed. After a few minutes or so, Lauryn came back into the room wearing a devilish grin and the clothes she'd just taken off. Cammie was confused as to why she didn't change, but didn't ask any questions. Once Lauryn locked the bedroom door, she made her way over to the bed. Lauryn was about to receive the best massage of her life.

"Ready?" Cammie questioned as she came towards Lauryn, putting her knees on either side of her hips. She lowered herself to sit on the squishy flesh of her butt, which was unsurprisingly a comfortable seat.

"Yes," Lauryn mumbled her assent.

As soon as the words were out of her mouth, Cammie's hands were on her back. Contrary to her own knowledge, she actually *was* a little bit sore. Cammie's touch was soft as the heels of her hands worked on her upper back. Her thumbs were rubbing circles into her shoulder blades, which added to the relief. Lauryn buried her face into her comforter as Cammie relaxed her.

"Feel good?" Cammie asked with her very thick and very fake accent.

"Mhm," Lauryn's muffled response came from below, which brought a smile to Cammie's face. Her head was ducked into her arms and her hair was still in a ponytail from her game. The beautiful dragonfly tattoo on the nape of her neck was visible and Cammie leaned down to give it a kiss. After that, she tugged on the band and freed Lauryn's hair from her ponytail before continuing.

"Good," she laughed and switched to a new tactic. Her hands glided over the entirety of her back, then back up. The feeling of her toned muscles beneath her made her smirk. Then she gently began the chopping motions along her back. She made sure not to do it too hard for fear of hurting her. Lauryn hummed in satisfaction from below and it sounded like a vibration to Cammie. It made her laugh.

As she made her way down, she couldn't help tickling her. Her fingers dug into her ribcage, making her flail underneath her. "Cammie..." Lauryn groaned as she made a move to get up.

"No, don't. I'm sorry," Cammie chuckled as she leaned down to wrap her arms around her, kissing her cheek sloppily.

"You better not tickle me, Camz," Lauryn threatened as she relaxed and settled back down in her previous position.

"I won't," Cammie promised. Instead of tickling her, she had a better idea. Other plans. She slid down and was now sitting on the backs of Lauryn's thighs. For a second or two, she took the chance to admire the way her ass looked in those pants. Softball pants were a blessing. Especially in Lauryn's case.

A cheeky smile took over Cammie's features as she squeezed Lauryn's ass a few times, making her turn around to look at her. Lauryn was wearing the same smirk she had.

"Glutes were very tense muscle," Cammie excused herself, her accent making its miraculous return.

"I'm sure," Lauryn laughed. Cammie was definitely taking advantage of the opportunity to grope and feel her up, but she wasn't complaining.

Without getting distracted, she reverted her attention back to the massage she was supposed to be giving. She'd run out of ways to massage her, kneading and chopping being the only two methods familiar to her. So instead, she opted to just caress her flawless figure until she felt the need to stop. Small hands just kept skimming over the fabric covering her back. Frustratingly, there was too much of a barrier between her and Lauryn.

Deciding to test her limits, Cammie began inching up Lauryn's shirt a little bit. Lauryn knew it was inevitable, but the act still excited her. Her torso lifted off of the bed long enough for Cammie to discard her shirt, then she laid back down. Cammie's warm hands came into contact with her bare skin and Lauryn smirked, despite herself.

"Removing shirt helps get deeper tissue," Cammie grunted in her terrible accent as her hands continued to work.

"Of course," Lauryn agreed jokingly, but refusing to stop her.

"This is in the way," Cammie announced as her fingers grazed along the clasp of her bra.

"I think you're right," Lauryn mumbled an agreement against her arm. Within seconds, her bra was off and tossed onto the floor. Those favorite soft hands of hers were gliding across her back and the maximized contact elicited a sigh of pleasure from Lauryn.

Cammie soon tired of doing the same repetitive motion and wanted to "massage" another part of her body. It suddenly dawned on her that giving massages was just an excuse to touch all over her girlfriend. In that moment, she decided that they'd have to participate in this more often. "Turn over," she instructed her as she got off of her.

A giddy smile spread across Cammie's lips as her eyes landed on Lauryn's exposed chest. It made Lauryn laugh, because her boobs seemed to make Cammie so happy. All Lauryn did was watch Cammie's expression in satisfaction, knowing she was the cause of her beautiful smile. Soon enough, Cammie was perched on top of her, caressing the taut muscles of her stomach. She was taking her time with it, simply refamiliarizing herself with her impeccable body. God, she was perfect.

Her gropey little hands made their way up to Lauryn's breasts, cupping and kneading them in a way that made her breathing deepen. Cammie bit her lip as she continued, watching Lauryn's reactions carefully. Lauryn's mindset wasn't so innocent anymore. She started to think that Cammie's massage was more like a new form of foreplay for the two of them. A breathy moan fell from her lips and she reached around to place her hands on Cammie's hips.

"Mhm, very tense muscle," Cammie laughed as she continued kneading at her breasts, using her excuse from before as to why she was doing it.

"Camz, I don't even think my boobs *are* muscles..." Lauryn half laughed-half moaned.

"Shh, *I* am expert," Cammie countered as she pressed a finger against Lauryn's lips to silence her.

"Oh, definitely. You're right. My bad," Lauryn giggled again before shutting her mouth and just letting Cammie do her thing. Her hands slid down her torso to give it some attention. Cammie noticed the way Lauryn's abdomen tightened as she skimmed over it with her fingertips. Somehow, she was able to guess that the reason for it wasn't due to her softball game. With a smirk, she leaned down to place a gentle kiss on her stomach, watching as the muscles contracted again and her breathing deepened.

"Kisses soothe the tension," Cammie mumbled against her abdomen, conveniently losing the accent. Lauryn felt like her words rang true, all while building the tension elsewhere.

"Are you sure about that?" Lauryn responded under her breath, only to have Cammie lean down and kiss her lips. Her hand soothed the skin along her side as her kiss lingered for a few seconds.

"Positive," Cammie grinned when she pulled back. Lauryn's lap was particularly comfortable, but Cammie moved off of it anyway. She settled herself between her legs, still trailing up and down her body. The younger girl littered kisses all over Lauryn's stomach, marking the new territory. She sucked on the area between her belly button and the waistline of her pants, smirking when she left a mark there.

"Did you just give me a hickey on my stomach...?" Lauryn asked from her position laying down. She leaned up to see the damage and laughed. Typical.

"Maybe," Cammie taunted with a small shrug as she gripped her hips suggestively.

"Is this still part of the massage?" Lauryn quipped as she watched Cammie's lips grazing around the fazed skin.

"No," she said simply.

"I figured," Lauryn laughed. "What is it then?"

"This is part of me making love to you," Cammie corrected her, pausing her kissing adventure to make sure it was alright with her. In truth, when she proposed giving her a massage, she didn't intend for it to end sexually. But she'd really underestimated the way the act would leave her feeling.

Lauryn's breath hitched in her throat upon hearing her claim. Well, shit. Wasn't sex supposed to happen after prom? But at the same time, they'd never been the advocates of normalcy. Lauryn's lips curled into a bashful smile, all while growing immensely turned on. The reactions Cammie elicited within her were always contradictory. She made her feel shy yet confident, a beautiful contrast.

When Cammie saw that Lauryn wasn't going to argue about it, she took it upon herself to continue. Although she wasn't used to taking the lead in their sexual escapades, she was willing to go by trial and error. Taking off her own shirt seemed like a good step. Trying her best not to be clumsy and embarrass herself, she peeled the article off and set it down beside her. When she was shirtless, Lauryn reached up to run her hands over her smooth skin. As she was about to get up to switch positions, Cammie stopped her.

"It's your turn. You did me last time," Cammie said as she grabbed Lauryn's hands, interlacing their fingers as she stared down at her.

"Okay," Lauryn relented with her eyebrows raised. She was enjoying the dominance shift. Her back rested against her bed once more as she waited to see what Cammie had in store for her.

"I kind of want to take my time and make it special, but we really should be getting ready to meet the girls soon..." Cammie expressed.

"Camz, every time is special to me," Lauryn laughed. "Like, you're literally giving me parts of you that only *I've* had before. That's pretty fucking special. Each time, all I'm thinking is that *I'm* the lucky person that gets to have and love and cherish all of you. Only me. It's special. No matter how long it lasts or how quickly we get finished," Lauryn concluded, grasping Cammie's chin and pulling her into a sweet kiss.

"I love you. So much," Cammie emphasized, speaking against her lips because she didn't want to lose the contact.

"I love you too, babe," Lauryn reciprocated genuinely, rubbing her thumb over her knuckles.

260

"I love all of you," Cammie leaned up to kiss the space between her eyebrows. "I love your mind. You're so smart and insightful and thoughtful," she started. She kissed her lips once and smiled. "I love your mouth. It says sweet, funny, and intelligent things... And it's not too bad at the whole kissing thing either..." she smirked. "And I love your cute little nose," she continued as she tapped it lightly, making her girlfriend giggle. "The nose piercing is a nice touch, too," she added.

Lauryn looked up at the girl she was completely enamored with and sighed happily. She was about to devise a response, but Cammie wasn't finished yet.

Cammie continued down her jawline, then she trailed her lips along her neck. The small girl sucked on Lauryn's pulse point, causing her to draw in a sharp breath. "I love your reaction when I do that... To that spot right there..." she said seductively.

Cammie continued her journey downwards and trailed light kisses down her chest. The kneading returned as Cammie failed to resist the urge to do so. Finding her tiny bit of self-restraint, she stopped and planted a deliberate kiss just above her heart in the midst of it. "I love your heart. You're so selfless and compassionate and loving... You have a really big heart, Laur... Which people don't give you enough credit for. But I see it. And I love it. And I love the way you love me," she smiled appreciatively down at her, making her eyes soften.

Lauryn thought she would spontaneously combust, simply from the overpowering love she had for Cammie. Her girlfriend was making her demonstration so heartfelt, yet so sensual, Lauryn didn't know which side to succumb to. Each gentle touch was driving her insane while every word made her heart feel full. She could've been driven to tears by what Cammie was saying, but she also could've been writhing and moaning from the way she was touching her alone. Cammie was causing her a lot of inner turmoil. So she just laid there helplessly, gazing at Cammie in adoration.

"And I love your body," Cammie shared when she finished with that part of her. Once again, she found her lips ghosting over the tight muscles of her stomach. "You are perfect to me, with every birthmark and stretchmark and whatever else anyone might see as a flaw. I don't see them as flaws at all. I see them as a part of my Lauryn. My beautiful girlfriend," Cammie praised her as her fingers blindly wandered to the imperfections mentioned. Then, they drifted further down, brushing past her pants to tease her center.

The sensation of her lips on her there and her hands roaming her body finally made Lauryn moan. Sure, Cammie's words were powerful, but touch was an entirely different factor. She was finally giving her center some much-needed attention. Cammie's nimble fingers started to undo her pants and pull them down without any instruction. Lauryn smirked in anticipation as she saw Cammie lift up to take off her own pants. Her girlfriend was now sporting her underwear whereas Lauryn was nearly completely uncovered.

Cammie discarded her own pants and threw them to the foot of the bed, coming back over Lauryn when she was finished. Her fingers hooked under Lauryn's remaining garment in preparation to pull it off as well, but she paused. Instead, she rubbed her center through her underwear with a smirk, carefully watching Lauryn's facial expressions as she did. Lauryn moaned again and closed her eyes tightly as Cammie's finger moved against her at a tantalizingly slow rate.

"Camz, please," Lauryn whined. The cute vibe Cammie had going on was overshadowed by her lust in the moment.

Cammie smirked, hearing the desperation in Lauryn's voice. Her tone was so hot. Her thoughts drifted back to what Lauryn had done to her and she wanted to give her the same treatment, but didn't exactly know if she should just dive into that first off. So she started with the one thing she knew how to do well. After fully exposing her, she positioned a finger at her entrance. Only deciding to tease it without satisfying her needs, she kept her eyes trained on her face. Her finger kept dipping inside her core without really going the true depth of what Lauryn wanted. It was evident in her face. Her eyebrows kept furrowing in frustration and her mouth was slack, letting soft moans escape, only to be replaced by groans of impatience.

"Are you ready?" Cammie asked sweetly as she grinned at her, enjoying the eagerness she exhibited.

"Obviously," Lauryn scoffed as she glared down at her.

"Really? Couldn't tell," Cammie laughed at Lauryn's helpless state. Her finger continued to stroke at her core, applying more pressure but refusing to slip it in.

"Cammie, I swear-" Lauryn's words got cut off when Cammie's finger disappeared inside of her. Her sentence was replaced by a particularly loud moan. She thought she was ready. But she wasn't.

Having done this a few times now, Cammie knew exactly what she was doing. She knew just what to do to make her hips lift off of the mattress, how to elicit those high-pitched moans, and how to make her girl fall apart by her touch. She knew Lauryn's body better than her own. Lauryn was completely at her mercy. Cammie was dragging this out purposefully. She didn't want to make her come just yet, she had one more thing she wanted to please her with. It was about time now.

Lauryn had the habit of keeping her eyes closed as she focused on finding her release. Needless to say, when she felt Cammie's mouth on her, it came as a surprise. Her back arched and profane language filled the room. Cammie's name was moaned several times, which was music to her ears. Using her tongue to pleasure her girlfriend quickly became Cammie's favorite way. Licking, sucking, and kissing the most intimate part of her girlfriend was an enjoyable, yet laborious task. Actually doing it was wonderful, and she was rewarded for it by Lauryn's incessant sighs of contentment.

She soon felt Lauryn's hand tangling in her hair, even pulling at it when she did something particularly satisfying. It was easy to tell when she was close. Her hips bucked with every other stroke of her tongue, and Cammie wanted to make her feel as good as *she* made *her* feel. To intensify the sensation, Cammie added her finger while she continued to push her towards her climax. Lauryn soon came undone, louder than ever before. Lauryn didn't last long enough for Cammie's taste, but she definitely wasn't complaining about it. The sight spurred on Cammie's own release, although she hadn't even been touched.

Cammie rested her head on Lauryn's thigh, just like she'd done to her. If Lauryn's deep breathing was any indication, Cammie assumed that she'd fulfilled her wish. She mirrored the way Lauryn made love to her and surely did not disappoint. Lauryn's body laid still and idle as she tried to recuperate from that intense high. Slightly shaky fingers raked through her hair and her eyes fell to meet Cammie's, offering her a lopsided smile. Cammie laughed at how sated she looked.

"Are you good now?" Cammie asked after a few moments more of just enjoying each other's company.

"Perfect," Lauryn nodded, cupping Cammie's face affectionately as she smiled down at her.

"Great," Cammie awarded her a quick kiss and got off of her completely. "Now we're really pressing for time. We *have* to get ready."

»»»»

"We'll open the door on the count of three," Allie announced with her hand on the bathroom door handle.

Diana was helping and styling Lauryn. Both were situated in Naomi's room. Cammie was being glammed up by Naomi and Allie. All three were situated in the bathroom. The girls decided Cammie would need the most assistance, because she was awfully fidgety and was unable to sit still. It would've taken twice as long without Allie's help. For the last hour and a half, they'd been doing their hair, nails, and makeup. It was nice being pampered the way they were, although they knew they couldn't get used to it. This was definitely a one-time thing.

"Wait, I'm almost finished with Ralph," Diana called back as she rushed to fluff Lauryn's hair so that it fell down her back in the right way. The part in her hair was just being uncooperative. She tossed it to the side and accepted the way it looked, figuring it was good enough. "Okay, open."

"One... Two... Three," Allie counted down as she theatrically opened the bathroom door, gesturing to Cammie like a showgirl.

"Oh my god," Lauryn gasped when she saw her. Like, she actually gasped. Her girlfriend looked *gorgeous*. That was the most flattering word but even *that* seemed like an understatement.

Naomi had taken the reins with choosing Cammie's look. Naomi was the one that hung out with Lauryn the most, so she knew which styles she liked best on her. Allie was also pretty perceptive to Lauryn's preferences when it came to style, so she was able to aid Naomi's endeavors to find Cammie the perfect dress in Lauryn's eyes. They bickered a lot about their choices. Naomi was too far on Lauryn's edgy side and Cammie was too stubborn about her own conservative taste. Allie was the peacemaker between them and provided a way for them to meet in the middle. The dress all three of them settled on was a mixture of all of their touches.

"Holy shit," Lauryn exhaled as she scanned over Cammie's body appreciatively, taking in every delicate curve.

They knew her well. The white dress made Cammie look adorable. It was hugging Cammie's perfect curves in a way that gave Lauryn the need to catch her breath. It exemplified her tiny waist in contrast to her huge ass, the ratio being uncanny. Her stomach was exposed, displaying her abs and tanned skin beneath a strap. The dress itself wasn't fancy at all, but it worked for her. The piece covering her torso was silky and it connected to a floral skirt, which was very soft and comfortable. Cammie couldn't have picked a better dress herself.

Thanks to Allie, Cammie's hair was styled into a half up-half down do. It was loosely curled, making it look wavy instead of actually curly. Her nails were done, Allie decided to go with the simple French tips look. Knowing Cammie wouldn't want to go too heavy on the makeup, she did what Cammie always did. She gave her a cat eye and applied some mascara and eye shadow to compliment the dress. They'd done well. When Cammie saw herself in the mirror it brought a smile to her face. She actually felt as beautiful as she looked.

263

"Wow..." Cammie breathed as she looked at her reflection then down at herself.

"Aww... My little Cam is growing up," Diana playfully wiped her fake tears. Cammie smiled bashfully and picked at the bottom of her dress, simply because she needed something to do with her hands.

"You are so beautiful," Lauryn praised her quietly.

"Look who's talking... Laur, you're absolutely gorgeous," Cammie returned her compliment. "All of you are, really."

"Thanks, Cam," Naomi flashed a smile and twirled around to show herself off.

"So are we not gonna talk about how they totally had sex before they got here?" Diana ruined the moment in her typical fashion, smirking at the two girls who now resembled deer in headlights.

"Diana!" Allie squealed, throwing her head back in laughter.

"We said we weren't gonna say anything..." Naomi reminded her as she shook her head, laughing as well.

"We didn't..." Lauryn denied their claims as Cammie said "We weren't..." with flushed cheeks.

"Girl," Diana attempted to stifle a laugh. "You don't know how hard it was trying to wrangle Lo's sex hair into something presentable," she said knowingly.

"I had a *softball* game..." Lauryn mumbled an excuse.

"Mhm," Naomi laughed. "That explains why y'all were an hour late... The game was over four hours ago."

"I hate you guys," Lauryn gave up trying to convince them otherwise.

"It's about time though," Diana mentioned. "Even though most people do all that *after* prom..."

"Will somebody please kill me right now?" Lauryn groaned as she hid her face in her hands.

"No, because then there couldn't be a next time," Cammie teased as she pried Lauryn's hands down.

"Gotta go," Diana said as she held a hand up, stopping her from going any further. It was only fun when Diana did it.

"Stop it, babe. I want to see your beautiful face," Cammie pouted as she used more force to take her hands down. When she'd moved her hands away, she pecked her lips quickly.

"Camz, I... Wow," Lauryn tried to express once, more but failed. Her speech was actually gone. With Cammie right in front of her, she saw that she was the most beautiful person in the room. And there were a *lot* of beautiful girls in the room.

Naomi was donned in her white dress, with her newly dyed hair and flawless makeup. She was absolutely stunning. Diana's dress was periwinkle. It was short and sweet, making her look as beautiful as ever. Allie was the only one wearing a gown. Hers was white as well, extending all the way to the floor. She had to gather some of it up to walk, especially since she was so short. She wanted to take it seriously because this was her last prom, being the only senior of the group.

"You girls look amazing. You're all so so so so so beautiful," Allie complimented all of them genuinely as her eyes went from one girl to another.

"Thanks, Smalls," Diana grinned as she pulled Allie into a hug, making her stumble into her hold.

"You're welcome!" Allie smiled when she regained her bearings, giving Diana an all-consuming bear hug.

Cammie was rendered speechless when Lauryn was presented to her. She was wearing fucking red, which should've been illegal within itself. The color contrast only made her look more intense, with her black hair, pale skin, and red dress. Diana hadn't done anything to her hair but curl it a bit to make her natural waves more prominent. Her eye makeup reminded her of what Lauryn fixed herself up with in Venice. The cut of the dress was pretty low, but it was covered by a sheer fabric that was transparent. The push-up bra made her look even better. Cammie knew she'd be stealing glances at her chest all night. Lauryn's dress was relatively simple, but it was made beautiful because it was Lauryn who was wearing it.

"And I thought you were beautiful before..." Cammie started off but was cut off by the girl on her right.

"Let's save the sappy stuff for later. We need to go. I don't even know where it is and y'all know I always get lost downtown..." Naomi interrupted as she picked up her purse, gesturing towards the door.

"Yeah. Even if we leave now, we'll probably still be late," Lauryn assumed, well aware of how unpunctual each of them were - with the exception of Allie.

"Fashionably late," Diana corrected her as she bent over to retrieve her own purse. The rest of them soon followed suit and put the finishing touches on their appearances. Then they all shuffled downstairs to take a few pictures and selfies before filing into Naomi's car.

》》》》

"How long do we have to stay here?" Cammie asked in Lauryn's ear when she finally ventured over to the refreshments table.

"Why? Do you want to leave?" Lauryn inferred in the midst of helping herself to a few crackers.

"Kind of..." Cammie admitted as she leaned against the wall. She was being a professional wallflower, watching Naomi, Diana, and Lauryn dancing. Allie had been off with Trevor for about an hour or two now. Cammie just made that spot against the wall her home for the past hour or so.

"You're not having fun?" Lauryn frowned, looking a bit disheartened by it. It wasn't that she was surprised, Cammie hadn't wanted to come in the first place. It was just that Cammie allowed herself to let loose a little while ago, but now she was being reclusive again.

"I was at first... But it got kind of boring. And now my feet hurt," Cammie grimaced as she bent over to rub her feet symbolically.

"You didn't bring a pair to change into?" Lauryn asked incredulously, gesturing to below. Like always, she was wearing her grandmother's white Sketchers.

"Wow... Okay, I can't be seen with you," Cammie announced as she dramatically made a move to step away from her. Lauryn grabbed her wrist and pulled her flush against her own body.

"Meanwhile, I'm comfortable and you're all sore," Lauryn shrugged and smiled condescendingly.

"You are wearing Sketchers at prom. I refuse to be associated with you in any way," Cammie laughed, playfully turning away from her girlfriend once more.

265

"Camz....." Lauryn pouted as she resorted to a different tactic. Her arms wrapped around Cammie's waist and she rested her chin on her shoulder, kissing her neck softly.

"Do you think this place has roof access?" Cammie questioned randomly, placing her hands over Lauryn's arms.

"There's a balcony somewhere I think," Lauryn offered instead.

"Yeah, but like... A roof?" Cammie reiterated.

"There's obviously a roof, Camz," Lauryn giggled as she looked up at her.

Cammie rolled her eyes. "Can we go to the roof?"

"We don't know anything about this place, babe. This isn't the school. I think we could actually get arrested for trespassing or something," Lauryn hesitated, thinking logically.

"We wouldn't get caught..." Cammie mumbled.

"I wouldn't risk it," Lauryn declined, not wanting to ruin this so far perfect prom night by going to jail.

"Fine. Then let's go to the balcony," Cammie proposed a safer plan, brushing along Lauryn's arm with her fingernails.

"What is with you and escape?" Lauryn laughed at her persistence.

"I just don't want to be here. I've been here for too long. There's way too many people and everyone stinks. The ones drinking smell like alcohol and the ones that aren't smell like sweat. The music is too loud and people keep bumping into me. It's not a pleasant environment. I don't like it. Can we please go somewhere else, baby?" Cammie ranted about the inconveniences of prom as she turned around in Lauryn's arms to give her a convincing pout.

"I can't say no to that," Lauryn sighed, knowing fairly well that any further resisting would've been in vain. Cammie, being the cute little shit that she was, wouldn't let her get away with denying her.

"I know you can't," she smiled victoriously and pressed her lips against her very whipped girlfriend's.

"Where are we going?" Lauryn sighed and unwrapped herself from Cammie.

"On an adventure," Cammie responded mysteriously.

"Oh God," Lauryn laughed and wondered just what Cammie was getting up to.

"One question," Cammie asked as they began walking, their location still unknown.

"What would that be, baby girl?" Lauryn responded, brushing her fingertips over her cheekbone.

"Can I have a piggy back ride to wherever we're going?" Cammie asked, resembling a small child. Her eyes were wide as she looked at Lauryn pleadingly.

"The things I do for you..." Lauryn playfully rolled her eyes, but hunched over anyway. "Only because you didn't bring another pair of shoes."

"Yay!" Cammie squealed as she placed her hand on Lauryn's shoulders to steady herself before the leap. After a few unsuccessful attempts to get on, she made it. Once she was up there, she gave Lauryn a sloppy wet kiss on her cheek to express her gratification.

"Ew," Lauryn grimaced as she wiped off the saliva Cammie left. "You're so disgusting..."

"You love me," Cammie retorted as she tightened her grasp around Lauryn's torso.

266

"So much," Lauryn affirmed as she set off to go wherever Cammie would lead her.

»»»

Cammie eventually learned to let Lauryn do all of the talking. When she mastered this skill, things worked out in their favor. After letting Lauryn convince one of the employees to grant them access up there, the couple found themselves up on the balcony. Cammie was in awe of how the hell they ended up here, but knew it was all credited to the green-eyed girl.

Cammie envisioned the balcony to be some small, open, secluded area. It was anything but. This balcony was pretty large, extending from one end of the building to the other. It had a nice view of the city, even though it wasn't very high up. It was spacious enough to have a few pieces of furniture situated in the middle. It was nice. Along with Lauryn, she was pleased with the quiet serenity.

The younger girl was leaning over the railing, looking up at the night sky in stupefied wonder. Once again, there were little to no stars out, due to them being in the heart of Miami now. Nevertheless, she was fascinated. The sky was just as beautiful while it was wallowing in darkness as when the colors were changing during the sunset. Thoughts of what could've been beyond what her eyes could see were plaguing her mind.

"Laur?" Cammie called as she kept her gaze focused on the oblivion above.

"Hm?" Lauryn responded, spending the moment of silence between them the same way Cammie was. Downstairs, she'd helped herself to a friend's drink, but she only had enough to get a buzz. In her faintly intoxicated state, she was just staring blankly up at the sky. Nothing philosophical was going on up there.

"Up there is crazy," Cammie said ominously, silently contemplating her significance on earth.

"What do you mean?" Lauryn asked as she glanced at Cammie's flawless side profile.

"There's so much out there that we don't even know about. I mean, NASA researches it and all of that, but I'm betting that they don't know the half of it. They've found those nine planets - yes, I'm still including baby Pluto - but I guarantee you that there is just a whole 'nother world we've got no idea about. Earth is so confined, you know? Like, with gravity and everything... We've just got all of these limits. Beyond all of the forces and all of the atmospheric layers, what else is there? I refuse to believe that as much as our brains can conjure up, the only things that exist are the things that have been proven. That's all anyone wants you to believe. If you explore the possibilities, even a little bit, you're written off as crazy. I don't think it's crazy. I think they're our future. We owe everything we know now to the person that got a little curious. I don't know. I'm off my rocker a little bit. I just think that there's more to it than just what meets the eye," Cammie concluded her rambling with a great sigh as she slumped over the railing.

"Damn, I'm in love with you. Your mind is something else. You're over there thinking all that, and I'm just thinking about you," Lauryn admitted by her side. Cammie made valid points, but she was too buzzed to contribute to the profound topic she'd just brought up. She was nowhere near drunk, but she just wasn't in the mood to talk about anything that deep.

"I'm usually thinking about you," Cammie confessed with a small giggle. "But it's just fascinating. Most people look up, and they see blue. I look at the sky and my mind just goes a mile a minute about all the possibilities. So much keeps us from finding out just what oblivion itself is. What if there are just some aliens on some other planet a gazillion light years away, trying to find out about *us*? In the big scheme of things... We're probably just a bunch of specks," Cammie babbled some more, keeping her eyes trained on what was above.

She wasn't conscious of the enamored way Lauryn was looking at her. While she went on and on, she had no idea that Lauryn was falling even harder for her. Watching her speak about something as passionately as she was about the unknown was so fulfilling to Lauryn. It was captivating, really, just watching her talk. Although she'd been listening, the visual Cammie offered was just entrancing to her. And she agreed. She just had other plans in mind instead of moving the conversation along.

"Well, guess what," Lauryn posed with a dopey smile.

"What?" she raised an eyebrow, facing Lauryn once again.

"Of all of the specks in the world, you'd have to be my favorite," Lauryn shared fondly as she reached out to cup her face, bringing her toward her lips.

"You've been spending way too much time with me. That's something I would say. Stop stealing my lines," she responded through laughter. She was laughing as they kissed.

"Sorry," Lauryn mumbled an insincere apology as she kept up her broad smile.

"Sure you are," Cammie nudged her shoulder. "What do you think?"

"What do I think?" Lauryn repeated her question. The music from below was still faintly perceptible. It gave her an idea.

"Yeah," Cammie nodded once, assuming she would hear Lauryn's opinion about space.

"I think..." Lauryn tapered off as she pushed away from the railing and stalked over to the center of the balcony. Cautiously, she bent over to drag the coffee table to the left side, clearing the space in the middle.

"What are you doing?" Cammie questioned as she turned around at the commotion.

"Moving this stuff," Lauryn grunted as she used all of her strength to get that heavy lounge chair from the center of the space to the side. She continued rearranging furniture until there was a relatively wide area cleared.

"Why?" Cammie asked curiously, amused by Lauryn's strange antics. Slender arms folded over her chest as she watched her girlfriend's strange behavior.

"Because, here's what I think," Lauryn grinned. "*I* think... We are but two of seven *billion* people, you and I. Our planet earth is just one of probably about a million other planets or galaxies or whatever, but we're both here at the same time. Cammie, you and I are in the exact same location on the same day, enjoying each other's presence. Now, there are twenty four hours in a day and several thousands of seconds... But that day will go on and another will begin. Try as we might, but we'll never have *this* moment ever again. So with this moment, I want to spending it dancing with the most beautiful girl I've ever laid eyes on," Lauryn articulated her thoughts, extending her hand towards Cammie as she stood in the middle of the area she'd cleared. "That's what I think."

"Was that your intricate way of asking me to dance with you?" Cammie giggled. "You think we should dance?"

"Perhaps. Depends on if I can have this dance or not..." Lauryn smirked, still holding out her hand for Cammie to take.

"Of course you can," Cammie laughed as she closed the distance between them.

"Well, in that case... Yes. That was my intricate way of asking you to dance with me," Lauryn confirmed her statement dorkily, pulling Cammie closer to her.

Lauryn kissed her yet again, which she didn't seem to mind. Her hand settled on Cammie's lower back and her nails grazed the skin there. The shorter girl felt her smile against her lips, and she brought her even closer. Rarely had there been a time where Cammie was happier than she was in this moment. Calmly, she leaned her head onto Lauryn's shoulder and reached around to hold her. She inhaled her heavenly scent as Lauryn's hands found their way to her lower back. The two of them began swaying slightly, a gesture of romance. This was Lauryn's attempt at slow dancing, but it soon got boring.

Taking Cammie by surprise, Lauryn took her hand and twirled herself around. She started humming along to a song Cammie didn't know, and she just watched her in amusement. Cammie wasn't even conscious of anything going on beneath her in the actual prom atmosphere. All she was concerned with was the girl right in front of her. Cammie retreated to the chair Lauryn had moved across the room. She planned on just watching her move.

Or she was going to, at least, before Lauryn tugged on her hand with enough force to pull her from the seat. Cammie was once again pressed up against her. Then Lauryn started dancing. Not dorkily or even sensually - she was dancing as if they were in the ballroom.

The older girl grasped her hand again and then they were off. The couple sauntered from one side of the balcony to the other. Surprisingly, Cammie was light on her feet. She was simply following Lauryn's lead, although she knew neither one of them had any clue what they were doing. The balcony and sky faded from her focus as her eyes settled on the beautiful girl guiding her.

There was a twinkle in her eye and a treble in her laugh that made Cammie fall deeper in love with her than she already had been. The way her hair fell over her shoulders and framed her face made Cammie's heart flutter. Her lightheartedness and simple joy elicited the biggest smile she could muster. Her surprising grace and touch released a torrent of butterflies in Cammie's stomach she didn't know could be so powerful.

Lauryn laughed. Nothing was funny, she was just impossibly happy. Cammie mirrored her. The melodic sound of their laughter drowned out the music - which they were probably off beat to anyway. But then the song ended all too soon. Cammie let go and stepped back, trying to catch her breath. They made eye contact and burst into laughter all over again.

"I am so in love with you," Cammie told her between ragged breaths. Her attempts to compose herself were pointless. This type of joy couldn't be contained.

"As I am with you," Lauryn said eloquently, still giggling.

"You're such a dork," Cammie laughed as she took her hand into hers again. After their spur of the moment dancing, she longed to feel her touch. She brought her hand to her lips and kissed it softly. Cammie's thumb ran across her knuckles afterwards, and they were having a staring contest.

The way Lauryn looked at her made her feel whole. It was the way she used to look at her, way before things were even close to being reciprocated. It was as if she was her sun, her moon, and all of her stars. They were the only words she could think of to express the magnitude of that look. Lauryn would never have to say she loved her ever again. If she looked at Cammie the way she was right now, she would know forever.

Chapter 27

February 7, 2018

Here we are. Can you believe we've made it this far? I know we've always made false promises about how we'd be infinite, and I know we've had countless bouts of drama that threatened it, but we're still going strong. You and I started dating on February 11, 2014. (Yeah, I remember. I have to, because a certain someone always forgets our date and our anniversaries. But I'm not saying any names.) (It was you.) Throughout three horrendous break ups, two other exes, and broken friendships, we managed to make it. And now I'm writing this to you a few days before our four year anniversary (not counting the times we were broken up).

It's almost that time again, Lau. I've said those three words a variation of times, for hundreds of different reasons, using several methods. I've spelled it out on your skin, whispered sweet nothings in your ear in the middle of the night, written you things that flaunt my exemplary vocabulary, sang you heartfelt songs with lyrics that were unoriginal - but still held the same sentiment, and a bunch of other things I don't feel like writing. So, I don't have to say it. I'm going to attempt to get through this without saying it, but I'll probably lose my own challenge.

Four years down the road, I find it funny how far we've come. I remember the way you used to say it before you truly meant it. I was so cautious and I felt so bad because I was already deeply in love with you then, but you still loved me in a friendly, platonic way. Now, I don't hesitate to say it back. I know you do. You've proved it to me time and time again. You say it without words. As the cliché as the saying goes, actions certainly do speak louder than words. You say it loud and clear every time. Together, we slowly figured out that expressing love can be in different forms.

We've stopped wearing the jewelry. I used to pretty much regard taking off my necklace as a sin, but I've come to learn that our commitment isn't measured by material things. You were so worked up the day I came home to your dorm and it wasn't around my neck, but when I told you what I thought, you took off your charm bracelet. I don't know, I saw that as another sunset for us. Years later, and I'm still freakishly obsessed with sunsets.

We don't touch each other as much now, but it's because we don't need to. You radiate as much love when you're alone on one end of the couch while I'm perched on the other as you do when I'm in your arms and vice versa. You don't have to keep your arm around my waist or your hand in mine when we go out anymore, because people can automatically sense that there's something between us. I think we used to feel like we had to use touch to convey the way we felt, but we don't. We don't have to make a show of it. That's another sunset.

It's funny, though. Do you remember how scared we used to be? You used to be terrified to admit to dating me. I used to take it personally, but I understand now. I can't really hold it against you because of that whole fiasco I did that caused us to break up the first time. We both have our moments. We're idiots. But I'm glad you're my idiot and that you chose me to be yours, amongst everyone else.

You never cease to amaze me. You're still equally as beautiful now as the first time I laid eyes on you. I don't know how you manage to do it, but you seem to get more attractive every day. You've still got the same galaxies in your eyes that made my heart implode all of those years ago. Nothing has changed about your gorgeous smile or those mesmerizing lips of yours. Your body still works wonders for me too. I really think you could let yourself go in every aspect and still be the most beautiful woman I've ever been blessed enough to –

272

"Camz!" Lauryn called from across their dorms, interrupting Cammie's flow.

And now you're calling me. Always nagging aren't you?

"Yeah?" Cammie yelled back. Their neighbors probably hated them. They were always shouting at one another if they were in their respective rooms, because who had time to actually get up and walk there?

"Come here, babe! I have something to show you!" Lauryn hollered back to her girlfriend and smiled dumbly down at what she'd found. Her fingertips grazed over the cover as her anticipation grew.

Cammie laid her pen down slowly and pushed away from her desk. Her swivel chair made her turn, and she just sat there for a minute as she spun around and around. She kept herself going and picked up momentum when she propelled herself even faster from the side of her desk. The room was just a blur of colors as she continued to twirl in her chair.

"Cammie!" Lauryn yelled for her again, and Cammie begrudgingly lowered her feet until she slowed to a stop. It was probably a good thing. She was getting considerably dizzy. The room was still spinning.

"I'm coming!" Cammie assured her as she gripped the armrests of her chair. God, she should really stop doing that. It always took a few moments for her to stop being so disoriented. At twenty one, she was still as childish as she was when she was ten.

As she opened her door and walked next door to Lauryn's room, Cammie had to keep a hand on the walls to make sure she didn't topple over any moving boxes as she inched towards her girlfriend's dorm. She hoped their roommates wouldn't mind the clutter. At least it was a sign of moving out. Seconds later, she found herself in Lauryn's cluttered study area.

"What did you find?" Cammie asked as she pressed the heel of her hand to her temple.

"Were you in the middle of writing a bestseller?" Lauryn inferred before she turned around to see her girlfriend. When she actually took in the sight of her, she narrowed her eyes. "Or were you spinning in your chair again?" she sighed as her eyes scanned over her groggy girlfriend.

"No," Cammie said incredulously. What on earth could've given her that impression? She was definitely in the middle of writing something, but it was a bit too personal to be published.

"Of course you weren't," Lauryn laughed and rolled her eyes fondly.

"Enough about me, what did you want to show me?" Cammie changed the subject and waved her off.

"I was clearing out my bookshelf and putting things into separate boxes... You know, the donations and the keepsakes... And so I was looking through all of these books I haven't read in a while, and I came across this instead," Lauryn beamed as she encouraged Cammie to come closer. When she stood by her side, Lauryn grinned and pointed down at the journal she'd found. "Look, babe."

Cammie leaned down to scrutinize the book, but it wasn't at all familiar. "What is that?"

"You don't remember?" Lauryn's expression faltered a little bit.

"No, I don't think you've showed this to me before," Cammie said, bemused.

"Oh yeah..." Lauryn said in remembrance. It always was just kind of a personal thing she did by herself. There was no motive to hide it from Cammie. She just never got around to it. "I kept a journal too. When we started dating."

"And why am I just hearing about this now?" Cammie slapped her shoulder lightly, making a face at her.

"I don't know. I just found it. I could've sworn I've shown this to you before, though..." Lauryn trailed off, scratching the side of her head in confusion.

"Well, you didn't," Cammie narrowed her eyes at her and flipped open the cover.

"I'm showing it to you now?" Lauryn offered with a nervous smile, hoping it would make up for keeping it to herself.

"Now," Cammie mocked her playfully and slid the journal closer to her. She took a seat in Lauryn's office chair and placed it in her lap. The smaller girl had to reposition herself, though, when Lauryn lowered herself into her lap as well. Cammie giggled and pulled Lauryn up on her comfortably before reaching around her body to sift through the newfound journal.

While Cammie's journal was chock full of sappy observations, pretty words, and intricate metaphors and comparisons, Lauryn's was not. The green-eyed girl's was a lot less dense. Hers were full of pictures. It started out as a scrapbook, with only pictures of the two of them. Whether it was a Polaroid or an iPhone picture that got printed out, she didn't care. She stuffed all of them into that journal, regardless. As their relationship progressed, Lauryn morphed it into a better idea. It was a timeline dedicated to herself and to Cammie - to them. It was a compilation of their cute texts, receipts of gifts, pictures, copies of some of Cammie's writing, significant items... But mostly pictures.

"There are no captions?" Cammie noted as she flipped through the first few pages. The few pictures she did include in her journal had detailed descriptions underneath, but Lauryn's did not.

There were so many things in here from their first year of dating. Cammie remembered all of it. It was then that she understood why Lauryn hadn't put any captions on them. They were engraved into her memory. It was easy to recall the details of every single picture she gazed at.

"Laur, look at this one. Isn't that from our graduation?" Cammie inferred as she tapped one of the pictures. In it, Cammie had a face-eating grin as she clung onto Lauryn's back. It was after the graduation ceremony and they'd taken off their caps and gowns. They had on nice white dresses, since they'd stripped off their hot gowns. The picture was taken as Cammie and Lauryn ran through the now-empty football field. Everything from the graduation was over. All that was there was the two of them.

"Yeah. Diana took that. I remember it like it was yesterday," Lauryn affirmed fondly, a smile gracing her features at the thought of it. "We were talking about your journal and how weird it was that we were out of high school and stuff... We were running on the field afterwards and Diana took the picture."

Following the summer of their junior year in high school, Cammie had filled up her journal completely. From cover to cover, her writing was scrawled onto every page. The difference lied in the pages. There were specific sections that Lauryn could distinguish easily. It was quite clear that there was a before and an after. It was a beautiful story Lauryn always found joy in unfolding. Cammie's feelings and reality only continued to blossom, the further you delved into it. It was so raw and unedited. It was probably Lauryn's favorite possession.

Lauryn remembered bending over, motioning for Cammie to hop on her back. Cammie happily obliged and jumped on board, and then they were off. Lauryn ran like she was an airplane, with her arms out wide. Because she wasn't supporting her weight, Cammie was simply holding on for dear life. Despite the strain on her muscles from Cammie's weight, Lauryn was laughing giddily. The realization of being out of high school gave her an overwhelming high that day.

Diana had been waiting on them to take pictures together. She continuously called them from the entrance to the field, but Lauryn and Cammie were disassociated. In her hands, she held an expensive camera. Diana, determined to get her pictures one way or another, snapped the picture that would later become one of their favorites.

"I remember when Diana showed it to us. Both of us were like *what the hell...*" Cammie remembered with a light laugh.

"I love candids of us," Lauryn turned and nuzzled her face into Cammie's neck.

"Like this one?" Cammie pointed out another picture, shying away from her girlfriend's affection. It always tickled when she did that.

"Do you remember this?" Lauryn asked when she cast her eyes down to where Cammie was pointing. Her expression softened as she looked at the two of them.

"How could I forget my first concert with you?" Cammie responded instantly, feigning offense. "It was one of the first things I ever bought with my own money..."

"I still think you robbed a bank," Lauryn shook her head fondly. "But, yeah. I remember the concert. They were great."

276

"Yeah, it was a fun night," Cammie nodded and thought back on that time. "Those pictures you took of me looked so cool. I love concerts so much," she commented as she turned the page, looking at all of the candid pictures Lauryn had taken. She looked so in her element.

"You're my favorite muse," Lauryn shared fondly, kissing Cammie's cheek tenderly. "I can't even begin to tell you how many pictures I've taken of you that you probably don't even know about," she giggled.

"I like pictures of us *together* more," Cammie changed the subject, feeling awkward about having so many pictures taken of her. Off-guards were never particularly her favorites. Something was always out of place. She was always the forced smile or the tense hand on hip. She was the deer in headlights and the awkward pose. She was the one that blinked and the blurry figure. With Lauryn by her side, she felt a lot more tolerable. She had never been more photogenic. "You know, we're better together."

"Can't argue with that," Lauryn agreed as she scanned over all of the pictures they'd taken together in Venice. It was spring break of their junior year of high school.

They flipped through Lauryn's journal for a while in relative silence. It was a nostalgic journey. Cammie liked the way Lauryn never included captions. She enjoyed trying to remember the specific details that each photo entailed. It was a trip down memory lane for sure.

"Oh my god, you have it!" Cammie squealed when she saw her all-time favorite picture.

"Which one, this?" Lauryn burst into laughter when she saw one of her most cherished pictures of Cammie. It was the day they'd gotten their matching sun and moon tattoos, and it was such blackmail material. Cammie's face was red and scrunched up with tears streaming down her face. She was laying on her stomach, still in the extended process of getting her tattoo done. She cried a lot that day, but it never failed to make Lauryn laugh. She was such a wimp.

"*No.* Burn that picture," Cammie groaned and made a move to take it out, but her actions were far too slow for Lauryn's. Lauryn swiped the book from out of Cammie's hands and pushed it away from her.

"But it's so cute," Lauryn disagreed and pouted at it in adoration.

"I look disgusting," Cammie sighed. She hated that picture, and she hated Christian for taking it. Lauryn looked godly there, as she usually did. The sun emanating from the window bathed her skin, giving her an illustrious glow. Her head was thrown back in laughter as she taunted Cammie's misery. Meanwhile, Cammie was laying there in the other chair, looking like a monster. Sometimes, she hated taking pictures with Lauryn because she always paled in comparison.

"That was one of the funniest days of my life. You were so cute," Lauryn caressed her cheek as she focused on the picture once more.

"I just remember the pain. That was the worst thing I've ever willingly put myself through," Cammie sighed and subconsciously let her fingers graze over where it lied on her shoulder blade.

"I think it wasn't so bad for me because I kept letting him distract me. He was talking to me about college and shit. When he tried asking you the same questions, you cried and told him to shut up," Lauryn added, failing to suppress her laughter that time. She was so tickled by the situation and how they'd reacted completely different to the same processes.

"Ha-ha, very funny," Cammie rolled her eyes. That was not fun at all. She resented Lauryn so much that day, but she'd never regret it. Their sun and moon tattoos had a place in her heart that was tantamount to sunsets. "But I'm not talking about that one."

"You *did* look cute," she insisted with an airy giggle. "Which one, then?" Lauryn looked down at the book once more. All of them were her favorite.

"This. I think Naomi took it. It was a few weeks after we got our tattoos. We went to the beach, remember?" Cammie attempted to describe the details since the memories weren't coming back to her from the scenery alone.

"Oh, that?" Lauryn grinned when she recognized it. "Yeah that was your lock screen for a few months," she was able to recollect the details now. It was a very nice picture. The two of them were just silhouettes against the budding sunset. Their figures were united in a kiss. It was beautiful.

"Yeah, I know! But I didn't know you had it in actual picture form... You took it on your phone," Cammie added excitedly.

"Actually, Naomi took that picture. I don't even know when she took it. I remember when I discovered it, I was like what the hell. I couldn't even tell that it was us," Lauryn nodded as it all came back to her slowly.

"This is my favorite picture of us, I think," Cammie declared and lifted the journal to scrutinize the picture further.

"You say that about basically every picture you see," Lauryn noted.

"Well," Cammie paused, knowing she couldn't discredit Lauryn's point. Every picture *was* her favorite. Any picture taken of her and the girl she was madly in love with could be considered her favorite. Except for the ones where she looked ugly. Not those. But most of them, yes. "So what? I love pictures with you."

"Oh really? I hadn't noticed," Lauryn nudged her shoulder playfully.

"I love the pictures. But with this one, I love the *story* behind it - making it a legit favorite," Cammie reasoned, sliding her fingers over the glossy film.

"Tell me the story, baby," Lauryn requested and turned around slowly. It twisted her back awkwardly, so she simply repositioned herself. Smoothly, she transitioned to the straddling position in Cammie's lap.

"No problem. Gather round, children," Cammie announced loudly to no one. Lauryn was the only other person present in their tiny dorm room. They liked it that way.

Cammie delved right into the story, and as she recapped it to her, it felt a lot like a flashback to Lauryn.

Why Cammie always suggested going out at the most inconvenient times, Lauryn didn't know. But she'd kind of gotten used to it. Cammie just loved to drag Lauryn outside on what seemed to be the hottest days of the year. It never failed. After an exhausting car ride, they'd found themselves at Tampa Beach. Thankfully, Cammie's old backseat driver tendencies faded away. But she still had her moments. The nearly four hour drive was due to Cammie's claim that every beach was different, although Lauryn found a solace anywhere that had sand and water as far as you could see. She would've been fine with going to the beach they always went to back home, but she'd given in to Cammie's wishes. They made the trip with Naomi, because they hadn't hung out in a while. Extensive car rides pretty much ensured at least a little bit of bonding.

279

They'd rented a cheap room in a motel not too far away from the beach itself. The girls truly got what they paid for. Next time, Lauryn promised to dedicate more time to looking for quality hotels. Due to the bugs and broken air conditioner, they tried to spend as little time there as possible. They made it a reality in their three-day trip. Each day was spent on the beach or shopping. Being in the room at all just made them all feel dirty.

On their final day, there was a party of some sort going on. Obviously, they weren't invited. But they had no shame in crashing the strangers' party. They made themselves scarce around anyone that remotely looked like the hostess and just milled around for an hour or so. Cammie tired easily, and Lauryn didn't see the point in staying if her girlfriend was no longer participating.

Alone, the two girls ventured way out to the far end of the beach. They were secluded here. The beach wasn't heavily populated this evening. Following at least twenty minutes of endless walking, Lauryn's calves began to protest at the strain. "Babe, I think this is far enough. I'm tired," she complained as she grabbed Cammie's shoulder.

"I wasn't trying to get away. I thought we were going on a walk," Cammie laughed and came to a stop. "Want to sit down?"

"Please," Lauryn nodded and already started to crouch down.

"It's nice here," Cammie said after a few seconds of silence. The two girls were sitting side by side, but not touching. They didn't have to be intimate *all* the time, and they'd been realizing that recently. Lauryn's simple presence was enough for Cammie and vice versa.

"Yeah," Lauryn agreed. It would be nightfall soon. The scenery here was amazing, although any beach scenery was automatically considered amazing in her eyes. The water was a nice, clear blue instead of a murky brown or green. The palm trees they found shade under were a nice touch as well. The beach was clean, with no trash left in the sand. Above, the colors were beginning to change. It was almost Cammie's favorite time.

"Being in a group of drunk people isn't exactly my idea of fun. I'm glad you came with me," Cammie offered a smile, happy for Lauryn's compromise.

"What would I have done if I'd stayed?" Lauryn countered, and Cammie just shrugged.

The two of them were sitting on a sand dune. The slight elevation gave them a clear view of the water and a serene environment to take in. Below, the waves gently lapped over the shore. There were no people down on this end of the beach. That was a perk in Cammie's eyes. She loved being alone with Lauryn. It was an invitation for spontaneity without an audience. It was a chance to give into temptation, no matter what the temptation was. They could dance, sing, or simply run around in circles because it was just the two of them and they were so at ease with each other.

"I love being alone together," Cammie sighed contentedly as she dug her hands into the sand. The tiny grains went between the spaces in her hands and they felt cool and refreshing. The sun was starting to set, making most of the heat dissipate.

"That's quite the oxymoron," Lauryn pointed out. "But, me too."

"It's perfect. We can do anything we want and nobody is here to stop us," Cammie beamed, elated to have some alone time. "It's me and you against the world."

"Always," Lauryn nodded happily, resisting the urge to correct her grammar.

"Who even ventures this far out? I don't think the parking lot even comes out to here," Cammie assumed, twisting around to look behind her. All she found was more sand and some plants. She was correct.

"Losers that enjoy going on random walks, leaving their poor girlfriend behind to catch up with them," Lauryn teased her with a light giggle.

"*There* y'all go," Naomi huffed from a distance, out of breath as she jogged over to where her two best friends were sitting.

"I guess we spoke too soon," Cammie sighed as she straightened up to address Naomi.

"What are you doing all the way down here?" the tired girl questioned, making a face at the distance she had to go to find them.

"I was just following her," Lauryn shrugged, wondering what explanation Cammie had for Naomi.

"I wanted to go on an adventure," Cammie smiled dopily up at Naomi, who was now standing before them.

"Of course you did," Naomi chuckled and shook her head. "But can y'all do me a favor?"

"Depends on what it is," Lauryn said, looking up at Naomi wearily.

"I need to borrow your phone," she pleaded, clasping her hands together.

"For what?" Lauryn scrunched up her face at her odd request.

"This guy back there has been talking to me all night. We're really hitting it off. He asked for my number and I was gonna get his, but my phone is dead. I just need to get his number and you can have your phone back, I promise," Naomi explained quickly, looking over her shoulder in the direction of the said boy.

"You kids and your smartphones," Lauryn mimicked an elderly person as she begrudgingly retrieved her phone. Sullenly, she handed it over. Naomi smiled widely when it was in her possession. "You easily could've said it out loud or wrote it down or-" she began, but Naomi was already sprinting back to where she came from.

"That didn't last very long," Cammie giggled at the exchange. "The moon is out already," she broached, now that it had caught her eye. She noticed the faint shape peeking out amongst the clouds.

"I love when you can see the moon during the daytime. It's cryptic, huh?" Lauryn said wistfully, looking up at the sky with her knees to her chest.

"Definitely," Cammie agreed, nodding her head subtly.

In silence, both girls took their own time to make their own observations. Lauryn laid back with her knees still up. Cammie stayed seated the way she was. Inside both of their minds, they were contemplating the same things. They were wondering about oblivion once more. Cammie was having inner ramblings similar to the ones she'd said aloud to Lauryn on the night of prom. Her insistent belief in aliens abroad was unreal. Lauryn was simply looking at the spread of colors in the sky, admiring the sun and the moon at the same time. It was low enough to where she could look at it for a little bit without hurting her eyes. This was pure bliss to her.

"Baby?" Lauryn prompted randomly, sitting up a bit to gaze at her girlfriend.

"I love it when you call me baby," Cammie gushed as she smiled down at the sand, her cheeks taking on a rosy tint. "But what?"

"Tell me the story about how the sun loved the moon so much he died every night just to let her breathe," Lauryn requested cheesily, knowing Cammie had seen various pictures with that caption ample times online.

"I've got nothing," Cammie shrugged.

"I want to hear one of your stories, Camz," Lauryn pleaded. Amidst her poems and ramblings about Lauryn, Cammie wrote short stories in her journal in the past. Since then, Lauryn randomly enjoyed hearing something off of the top of her head from time to time. The words that would come out of her mouth could never really be predicted, but that was what Lauryn enjoyed the most.

"Okay... Once upon a time, the sun and moon were alive and well. Their relationship flourished until the sun's tragic and unfortunate demise. I trust that you know the story about how he loved her so much, he died every night to let her breathe, right?" Cammie began in her extra raspy storytelling voice, instantly grabbing the green-eyed girl's attention.

"Yes, I believe so," Lauryn played along and sat up, now sitting cross-legged in front of Cammie.

"Ah, yes of course. But do you know the reason why?" Cammie questioned, like she had the wisdom about it all. In reality, she was winging all of this. Her mind was moving rapidly to find a way to connect it all to make sense.

"No, tell me. Tell me!" Lauryn said excitedly, and Cammie laughed because her eyes shone like a child's.

"Well, before the sun died, he picked two humans on this here earth to symbolize his love for the moon. He wanted someone that wouldn't have to go through a life or death compromise. Someone who was brave, honest, and beautiful - who was capable of receiving and giving love to their fullest potential. Do you know who he chose?" Cammie questioned, ready to reveal her answer. She bit her lip in anticipation as she waited for Lauryn's response.

"No, who? Who?!" Lauryn shook Cammie's shoulder violently, legitimately acting like a five year old. Cammie brushed her off and laughed at her for a few seconds before regaining her composure and getting back into character.

"He chose *us*. You and I were the only ones chosen by the sun and moon *themselves* to love each other until death truly do us part. For I am the sun. I love you to pieces. He's instilled the same love and affection he has for the moon in me, and that's why I give it to you," Cammie said, proud of herself for coming up with that on the spot. "It just goes to show why I'm the one obsessed with sunsets and you're the one always wearing dark colors," she added with a small giggle.

"Whoa," Lauryn exhaled as she gazed up at Cammie, who couldn't stop seeing images of little Lauryn doing the same thing.

"You, my love, are the moon," Cammie persevered, grasping Lauryn's chin gently to ensure eye contact. "That is why you're able to return all things I give to the same magnitude. That is why you love me unconditionally, even when you can't explain or understand why. That is why we are together. The universe worked hard for us to be together, you know?"

"Camz..." Lauryn tapered off, getting slightly misty-eyed as Cammie kept going. She wasn't expecting to hear about a story featuring the two of them. In truth, she thought she was in store for a silly story regarding aliens or something insane.

"Not finished," Cammie held a hand up, smiling at the effect seemed to have on her. "The sun has instilled all of his love into me, and the moon instilled all of her love into you because she couldn't live in a universe where she had to watch the love of her life die every night *for* her. It made her feel terribly guilty. That's why she also gave you compassion, selflessness, and generosity. She wished she had the same qualities her beloved sun had. So she gave them to you," Cammie continued as she touched just where Lauryn's heart was in her chest.

"Cammie, I-" Lauryn began to praise her, but was silenced by her finger against her lips.

"I'm almost done," Cammie gave her a small smile, keeping her fingers pressed to her lips. "We are their symbols. Their undying love for each other lives

284

on through you and I. Because of their compromise, our love can be infinite. The end."

Before the final words were even out of Cammie's mouth properly, Lauryn rushed forward eagerly to capture Cammie's lips in a meaningful kiss. She took her face into both hands as she kissed her deeply. She was speechless, simple as that. She'd always had a gift for conveying her thoughts without words, and Cammie definitely understood her gratitude for the story. Lauryn wasn't necessarily kissing her lustfully, more so like she was trying to express everything she wanted to say through her kiss, but she couldn't speak fast enough. It was rushed, but Cammie easily matched her pace. Soon, it slowed. They were lazily bumping mouths with no concept of time.

Meanwhile, Naomi finally made her trek back towards where Cammie and Lauryn were sitting. It was a bit darker now, so it took a little longer. Admittedly, she'd spent a little more time down with her prospective crush. He was wonderful and things were going just swell until she realized she still had Lauryn's phone.

The dark-skinned girl stumbled upon the two of them engaged in a seemingly passionate kiss. Against the slew of colors and hues in the sky and the oceanic view in the background, all she could see was their silhouettes. Their features weren't visible due to the nightfall. What she could see was the silhouettes of two figures that were radiating love. From their embrace alone, she knew they were sharing a moment. Perhaps they'd like to preserve it. Stealthily, Naomi opened the camera app on Lauryn's phone and snapped a picture of the two of them, leaving it for Lauryn to discover later. Then she hit the power button and strode on over there to make her return noticed.

"Oh shit, yeah... I do remember that," Lauryn realized after Cammie finished retelling the story.

"It's by far one of my favorite memories," Cammie nodded, elated that Lauryn remembered as well as she did.

"I think about that story you told me all the time. You're amazing, Camz," Lauryn complimented her and dipped forward to grace her lips with a quick kiss.

"It just came to me, I don't know," Cammie responded bashfully. "It's my favorite because it was one of the few times I was talking to you and it just brought tears to your eyes. You're not very emotional, so making you cry at all is an accomplishment... Well, happy tears, I mean. For whatever reason, it made you cry. I loved that."

"I cried because I was overwhelmed. I remember it perfectly now. I was just sitting there waiting for you to tell me some dumb story about silly things, but you related the story back to us. It caught me off guard, to say the least. I was just fucking speechless. You do that to me a lot," Lauryn laughed, pressing her forehead against Cammie's, looking at her intently.

"You make me speechless just by looking at me. You don't even have to say anything and there I am, dumbfounded," Cammie returned genuinely. It was kind of happening just by having Lauryn in her lap and looking at her that way. She was so intense, it was easy to be overwhelmed.

"What color are my eyes today?" she asked as she slowly draped her arms around Cammie's neck.

"Beautiful," Cammie beamed, giddily placing her hands on Lauryn's soft curves.

"Beautiful isn't a color, Casanova," Lauryn corrected her.

"They're... Grey. Kind of. There's a little blue in there... They look shimmery? I guess? I don't know, they're dark today," Cammie attempted to explain, but Lauryn's eyes were a mystery. Giving them one simple color barely did them any justice. They always had some cool undertones going on or speckles of something. They were never just simply green or blue or grey.

"Cool," Lauryn raised her eyebrows.

"What color are *my* eyes today?" Cammie asked theatrically, batting her eyelashes and showing herself off.

"Still that shade of brown I fell in love with all those years ago," Lauryn shared smoothly, not even skipping a beat.

"Good one," Cammie nodded her approval.

"I learned from the best," Lauryn grinned. She was so eager to lean forward and just connect their lips, but she was restraining herself.

"Aww," Cammie crooned, biting her lip. "Thank y-"

"I'm talking about Allie," Lauryn interrupted her.

286

"Alright, get off," Cammie said immediately as she released her hold and pushed against the older girl's thighs.

"No, I'm sorry," Lauryn apologized as she clung onto Cammie's body. She buried her face into her neck and secured her arms around her back. It would be pretty much impossible to pry her off in this position.

"Seriously, Laur. We need to go ahead and finish putting things in boxes. The movers are gonna be here in a few days and we haven't even really started yet," Cammie took initiative and tried to ease her koala of a girlfriend off of her.

"You are no fun," Lauryn sighed in defeat and unwrapped herself from her.

"I've just spent an hour looking at pictures with you!" Cammie exclaimed in offense. "Was that not fun?"

"I know, but now you're making me do work again and I don't want to," Lauryn pouted and crossed her arms, looking way too adorable for Cammie to just stand there idly.

"I don't want to either, but we have to," Cammie tried to pacify her with a kiss, but Lauryn kept up her little act for a few more seconds before she dropped it.

"Fine," she sighed and shrugged her shoulders, abruptly turning from Cammie and heading back to the bookshelf.

"I'll be right back," Cammie excused herself as she kissed her cheek and escaped back to her dorm next door. Once inside, she sauntered back over to her desk, where she'd previously been writing Lauryn another anniversary letter.

When she made it over there, she quickly glanced behind to make sure Lauryn hadn't followed. Her girlfriend was presumably still focused on her books, not on Cammie at the moment. So she quietly folded up the letter and stashed it somewhere deep inside her current journal. She didn't want Lauryn to find it early like she had in years prior. Each year, she foiled her own surprise by just leaving it out in the open for Lauryn to see it. This milestone would be a surprise and she wanted to make sure of it.

As she looked around, her dorm room was full of boxes. Lauryn's looked the same. The school year was coming to a close and they had big plans of officially moving out on the last day. There were big boxes and small boxes all the same. They'd found a small apartment whose price wasn't too ridiculous. Their last year of

287

college would be spent in their own home after staying in a dorm for three years. They didn't even share dorms, so this would be the first time they got to experience living together. Both of them were ecstatic about all of the possibilities.

Cammie smiled at the thought of it and closed her journal, making her way back to Lauryn. A few light rays were peeking through the window when she re-entered. It drew Cammie's attention, so she looked out of it for a few seconds. It dawned on her just how much time they'd wasted looking through Lauryn's journal, but she wouldn't have wanted to spend it otherwise. The sun was setting on another day, and another chapter of her life. In a few short days, she'd be moving into an apartment that she'd share with her girlfriend. That realization sparked her next comment.

"Looks like our newest sunset is on the horizon, babe," Cammie said hopefully as she looked at Lauryn, who had gone back to her task of organizing the bookshelf into respective boxes. When Lauryn only smiled at her, Cammie mirrored her expression and bent down to help her.

40726192R00179

Made in the USA
San Bernardino, CA
27 October 2016